THE MASTER OF CLOUDS

*For Dad,
Hayley,
Alex, Lana
and Em.*

Published Short Stories by the same author

Think With The Wise But Talk With The Vulgar (1995)
The Nostradamus Widow (1996)
Commemoration Day (1998)
Of Kith And Kin (2010)
Totem (2011)
The Colour Of The Wind Erodes The Shape Of Time (2013)
Dodge Sidestep's Dastardly Plan (2013)
Contractual Obligations (2014)
Dodge Sidestep's Second Dastardly Plan (2015)
Gliese And The Walking Man (2016) - Soundtrack to the Short Story (2016)
https://syngenic.bandcamp.com/album/gliese-and-the-walking-man
On Loan (2016)
Dodge Sidestep (and Martin's) Final Dastardly Plan (2016)
The Armageddon Coat (2017)

Published Essays

Writers' Workshops (1995)
Research (1995)
Boldly Queuing (1996) (With Neil Jones) Interzone Issue 104
Putting on the Style (1997)
A Brief History of Sci-Fi and Fantasy Film Scores (2008)
Artful Theakering (2015)
Drunk and In Charge of a Magazine (TQF) (2016)

THE MASTER OF CLOUDS

BY

HOWARD STEPHEN WATTS

This is a work of fiction. Names, characters, places and incidents either are a product of the author's imagination or are used fictitiously. Any resemblance to actual persons, living or dead, events, or locations is entirely coincidental.

First published in 2015 by Kindle Direct Publishing

This revised and extended edition published in 2022 by Kindle Direct Publishing

Copyright © Howard Stephen Watts, 2015, 2022

The moral right of the author has been asserted.

Cover art / layout and design by Howard Stephen Watts.
Cover photography by Howard and Emma Watts

Proofreading by Emma Watts

CONTENTS

Prologue

One ~ The Arrival of the Kaltesh

Two ~ The Trophy

Three ~ Family

Four ~ Yan

Five ~ Hulneb

Six ~ Inside

Seven ~ Outside

Eight ~ Decisions

Nine ~ The Holy Citadel

Ten ~ Heresy

Eleven ~ A Murderer's Memories

Twelve ~ Conversations with the Dead

Thirteen ~ Revelations Cast in Stone

Fourteen ~ A Funeral for the Faith

Fifteen ~ Judgement

Sixteen ~ Visitors

Seventeen ~ Parentage

Eighteen ~ The Dead

Nineteen ~ Sharing Wine

Twenty ~ Beneath

Twenty One ~ The Festival

Twenty Two ~ Ascension

Twenty Three ~ The Deepest Levels

Twenty Four ~ The Garden of Discontentment

Twenty Five ~ Victory for the Holy Church

Twenty Six ~ The Grand Event

Twenty Seven ~ The Salandorian

Twenty Eight ~ Destinations

Twenty Nine ~ Departures

Thirty ~ Sool Nalesh

PROLOGUE

As he slept in the darkness of his prayer tower, his father's book lay open on the floor by his side. Earlier that night he had started the tome for the fifteenth time, but he would not finish the book again in his short lifetime.

...and after a century of toil constructing the city wall, your family arrives at the great ravine, falling away a league and a half beneath them. There, the river Breede surges indifferently. The water is swift, and no animals venture to ford her; no man can combat her strength. You watch from your mother's papoose as the architects stand on the precipice and stare at the mountain opposite. Its jagged face hides in the clouds above, mocking their efforts at construction. They turn their backs on the contemptuous mass as the wind spirals around its coarse features, whistling a high-pitched cackle to sadden everyone.

The architects sit around their campfires in the cold desert night, devising a plan. After three cycles of planning your father, five brothers and two sisters stand, tools in hand, to join the other stonemasons. Together they turn their determined faces toward the mountain. Driven on by ambition, your father leads a team carving steps down into the ravine, to the river flowing violently below. There the architects divide everyone into six groups and instruct them in the assembly of wide, wooden bridges to span the raging waters. After many months of labour and death at the hands of the river, your father's team is the first to reach the opposite shore. He is congratulated by the architects and rewarded with raw gemstones and a hearty meal for his workers and their families.

Now you climb the mountain, assisting your frail mother with her tired limbs, higher and higher over the cycles, carving steps up into the rock. Your people build mining communities beside the treacherous footpaths, and many die excavating precious minerals and ore to smelt and fashion into tools. Then the morning finally comes when the first stonemason stands defiantly on the mountain's summit. You are there with him, clutching your chisel, hammer, and the memory of your parents, staring down to the foundations of the city and the Trophy far below, where Tal Salandor waits.

You teach your skills to your children and watch them join the thousands of others carving, sawing, pulling, pushing, hammering and tearing away at the mountain. They shape its hardened soul into giant blocks and haul them down into the ravine. Over the many periods of darkness the wall across the ravine grows, its smooth-polished face reaching up from the furious depths towards the unfinished wall waiting at the precipice. At last the two meet and you watch, exhausted, from your bed, frailty preventing you from being a part of this glorious achievement.

The wall stretches across the desert, embracing the Trophy like two broad, stone arms, but the architects are not content. They demolish the mountain, removing its soul until the wall stretches across the ravine and a dam waits behind the barricade wall to restrain and channel the waters. You listen in the silence of the day's end. The mocking cackle of the wind around the mountaintop is now nothing more than a soothing, respectful lament for the loss of its gigantic friend, and you wish your parents were alive to hear it.

The architects, still unsatisfied with their achievements, return to the wall, bringing it full circle until it spans the ravine and meets across the carcass that was once the mountain.

They remove the sediment from the desert floor until they reach the bare rock. They carve and shape the rock until it is smooth and level. They create a vast, shimmering plain inside the boundary wall with your idol, the Trophy, Oosah *(or* Agasanduku, *as the blaspheming barbarians call it), at the centre. They excavate sewers and basements, construct wide avenues and thoroughfares, parks, lakes, polished colonnades, courtyards, palisades, homes, schools for your grandchildren and stables for the animals. Hundreds of minarets, born from the dressed stone of the mountain, rise into the desert air and one becomes your home. Fortifications top the wall, and at every half-league around this perimeter, a giant telamon stands, over two hundred men high. A hammer and chisel folded across their chests, their stone eyes keeping watch over the barren desert sands for defilers and heretics.*

At the bottom of the ravine, the people carve huge, open-mouthed faces into the Western Wall, harnessing the wind gusting over the river Breede. Behind these mouths, they filter the air through a maze of gradually narrowing channels, until its strength is reduced to a gentle breeze to cool your home at the height of summer. The abundant supply of water, flowing from the snowy peaks of the Goraknath Mountains, far to the north, is filtered and channelled to every building in the city.

You watch and wave at the ceremonial parade of several thousand people as they journey to the abandoned towns and cities nestling on the green expanse by the southern ocean. They return months later with soil and plants to seed the city. Three seasons pass and the desert blossoms with colour. Trees line the wide thoroughfares; fruit-bearing orchards flourish. A great park meanders through the city, a green belt of grassy slopes and terraces, of waterfalls, streams, bridges and cool, damp corners where the children run and play.

Your city is immortal. Your ancestors have thwarted the desert and the mountain, tamed the river's brutality and moulded them all with their bare hands. And as the last building claims the last block you listen, from the comfort of your bed, to the celebrations that continue throughout the night. Then you drift into your final, long sleep, to begin your journey to the Garden of Contentment to join

Tal Salandor, waiting for you there with your forefathers.

**Excerpt from: *'A Stonemason's Life.'*
Chapter I of 'The First Sacred Book of Oosah:
The Construction of Abeona'
~ Abridged and translated by Ulu Varanack III. ~**

ONE

THE ARRIVAL OF THE KALTESH

He tried to stretch in the cramped darkness, curled into a foetal position, keeping his eyes closed as he struggled to capture the fading echoes of sleep inside his head. He was vaguely aware that an unfamiliar and unusually soothing tone had spoken to him, and as he lost the struggle and his mind wandered slowly away from nullibiety, he remembered a word the voice had said. He tried to question the invisible speaker in his dream, but as he opened his mouth to speak, his voice was at once foreign to him. He felt the comforting presence turn and depart, as if aware of the imminent return of his consciousness, of which it was unable to be a part. He reached out to pull the speaker back, his fingers thin wands of white clawing against the black inside his head, but he could not reach. He tried to follow, but paralysis gripped him as the presence hurried away. The word the stranger had spoken – vague, confusing, urgent and foreign – hid beneath his blanket of slumber to give him companionship, only to vanish as he fully awoke.

Sol Timmerman opened his eyes, slowly hoisting his tall, lean body into the darkness of his minaret. His mind ached from yesterday's arguments with his wife, Roanne, and their struggle to find common ground concerning the upbringing of their son, Opi. Her unrelenting desire for another child had entered the argument also, and at that he had retired to his private prayer tower to read. Staggering to the circular window, he swept back the thick drape, removing the darkness that always seemed to make the room much larger. The city of Abeona stretched beneath him. Beyond his high estate wall the tiny lights from thousands of torches illuminating the thoroughfares and alleyways flickered in the half-light, causing the ancient buildings to shimmer like molten rock. Lanterns glowed yellow behind the thick leaded windows of huddled cottages and towers. His eyes followed this glow as it wandered to the distant false horizon created by the city wall. This gargantuan edifice stood like a man-made mountain range, protecting the dwellings nestling far beneath it. His gaze continued above the wall into the sky and, as he stared, the few stars seemed to mirror the lights of his city. He frowned and scratched the back of his neck, suddenly aware of a single word, a remnant from his dream that had been left behind by the speaker as they hurried away.

Hathranelzra.

He tried to find a voice for the word, but only the inner tone of his own thoughts spoke, and the word became his. He concentrated on it, struggled to reference it, to understand its substance or meaning. It had neither a connotation nor relevance he understood, so he cast the word aside and watched the flickering stars and city lights surrender to the approaching daylight. The city gradually lost its fluidity, the molten buildings transforming into a hard, cold maze of archaic beauty. A chill set about his shoulders, so he dressed his lower half and picked up his remaining clothes and official adornments.

Pushing open the tall oak door, which had been left ajar, he trod a narrow balcony curving forward onto a high, open, stone bridge, leading to the family tower some four hundred paces distant. Looking below, he saw his team of gardeners tending his terraces of flowers and shrubs by lantern light. Some were weeding on their hands and knees amid the winding pathways intersecting the borders of adult plants, while a young girl with a little wooden cart carried away the invading waste to be burned later. Some of the younger gardeners drenched the dark brown earth from tin watering cans, necks shaped like swans, water trickling from open beaks. Others stood upon ladders, harvesting fruit and berries, while below them others pulled vegetables from the earth. As he continued along the bridge, the twisting terrace pathway below emerged from the greenery and straightened out to a gravelled trail, lined by narrow beds of small plants, soon to be bright with primary colours. This path led to the base of the family tower and surrounded it, allowing access to the four covered doorways placed around it at equal distances. To the left-hand side of this gravel lane lay paved avenues, columns of white marble lining the way to a circular fountain surrounded by an acre of dark green lawn. To the right of the path sat the single-storey buildings of the servants' quarters, stables and livestock pens. He turned to his right where several shallow breeding pools of fish, water-lilies and edible weed lay in a line, and he stopped for a moment as he heard shouted instructions, watching as four servants raised a rectangular section of nets from the bottom of the smallest pool. It carried a dozen or so silver-backed minips up into the early morning air, flapping, gaping and curling over each other in the stillness. Upon instruction from the eagerly pointing cook, a young lad seized the three largest fish, the remainder being lowered back into the water. Sol watched with amusement as the gangly cook placed the fish into a wooden bucket and ran toward the family tower, clutching the bucket to his chest. He appeared to Sol to resemble the fish he prized so much as he traversed the garden path, weaving awkwardly between the gardeners pruning beneath his feet.

Sol's estate was a spacious oasis of magnificence amid the cramped city. His every whim was catered for by his legion of staff, but he was not content; truth still eluded him. Disquieted by this thought, he turned his gaze back to the family tower. It was five times the diameter of his private minaret, its eastern face softened by crawling ivy, its surface bulging with guest accommodations, his library, study, the family room, and several other rooms he had not yet had the time or interest to explore. He looked up. Curling from a chimney came a black smoke, forced up from the kitchen deep within the bowels of the building. The break of night's fast was in preparation.

As he reached the balcony encircling the tower he could hear Opi playing in the family room with Ebe, his pet Gen'hib-Maun. He stood and listened as the little creature jabbered back to Opi as he chastised it, unaware of his father's presence. It was a game he had seen countless times before, but he, like Opi and Ebe, never grew tired of it. The little creature noticed him and looked up, and Sol placed a finger to his lips and shook his head, ordering Ebe to remain quiet. Behind them, Roanne looked up briefly from discussing the laundry arrangements with the housemaid, ensuring her favourite garments for the family and staff would be clean and ready for the upcoming festival, and that the guest accommodations would be suitably dressed if needed. Sol took a step back and continued along the balcony to the tower's opposite side, where it overlooked the city wall and the eastern desert beyond.

As he stood watching the first rays of morning sunshine lap across the desert, he braided his long black hair, carefully carrying out the morning dress code ritual of a Grade One Theorist. Instinctively and with considerable speed he wove thin strands of blue ribbon into his locks as a glint on the horizon caught his attention. He stopped and squinted out into the desert. The glint came again, and he quickly removed the lens cap from Roanne's telescope, crouching to focus the instrument into the deep desert.

There, a single figure marched purposefully across the dusty terrain, carrying a colourful banner which Sol instantly recognised. He turned and strode into the tower, hurrying down the wide corridors where his presence drew bows of respect from his staff.

Roanne dismissed the housemaid and spoke without looking up from folding Opi's clothes as Sol appeared in the doorway.

"Did you sleep well?" Her dark eyes shone with

curiosity as she lined up the folds of the thin fabric, brushing her long brown hair from her rounded face after placing the garment into the basket. She stood a head shorter than her husband, slightly taller than average for a female; her shapely figure the envy of many women, her skin bronzed by the sun, her eyebrows shaped neatly to sharp points and her full lips holding the shine of a deep red balm.

"Only for a short while, then the dream came again." His voice held a hint of apprehension,

his eyes disappointment. He returned the housemaid's bow as she hurried away with the basket of clothes.

Roanne sighed. "You must seek help over this, Sol," she said, glancing up as she realised that, for the first time, he had failed to argue her point, noticing his troubled expression with a little concern. "What's wrong now?"

He spoke quietly, "They're here, a full day early."

She ran past him out onto the balcony, but now there was no need to use the telescope. Two black rivers of caravans were advancing towards the city.

In the Watchtower, by far the highest point of the city, where its shadow touched twenty smaller towers surrounding it to measure the day, the Monitor's eyes widened as he too noticed the Kaltesh caravans. He turned sharply, tugging the keys from his sash. Fumbling, he unlocked the semi-circular glass cabinet that sat at one corner of the small hexagonal room, pulling on the rope hanging there. Beneath him, wood and metal creaked and groaned as he teased from the proclamation bell its dull tolling.

The bell's low notes went bouncing off pointed rooftops, coursing through the darkened alleyways until they had touched every dry and dusty hidden corner and every sleeping ear of the city like welcomed gossip. The sound swept across the west veranda of the Timmerman family tower, through the family room, forcing its way along the wood-lined passageways to touch Sol and Roanne standing on the balcony. Now nothing more than a dying echo with a suggestion of sadness to its timbre, the sound hung heavily in Sol's heart. He wrapped his arms around Roanne's waist, resting his chin on her shoulder as they listened to the bell. The giant red orb of the sun now blazed before them, and here and there, rocky outcroppings pointed long spindly fingers of jagged shadows towards the city, reminding Roanne of accusing arrows of which the marching lines took heed. The Kaltesh dulled the sand, until after a short while the horizon was black with hundreds of caravans.

Sol took a step back and turned his face from the scene.

Roanne had lived in the city for twelve cycles. Before taking permanent residency, she had been one minuscule part of the caravans she now watched. She had seen the ancient walls of the city she now inhabited, and understood how her people were currently feeling, how their emotions would leap forth along with their relief, how the prayer songs would have begun on first sight of the Abeonian towers reaching to the sky. How the young would dance through the sand until they reached the city gates, how the old would weep with relief, mothers waking their children, some to see the city of their idol, *Agasanduku,* for the first time.

Peering through the telescope she focused on the leading line.

As she watched, the junior celebrants unfurled the bright colours of the Jalinprabda banners and began to record the end of another successful chapter in Kaltesh history. Following this, the noble families unfurled their own banners, most of which had been repaired or newly woven during the journey to Abeona.

Sol slumped at the breakfast table as Roanne turned to face him, arms folded.

"What's wrong? My family will be here soon. We can

celebrate the festival together once again."

He glanced up at her and forced a brief smile. "I look forward to seeing them again, Roanne, you know that." Clasping his hands together he leant forward. "It's just that we have made considerable progress since the last festival. Your father will no doubt refute the findings of our church. That could create an uneasy atmosphere during the festivities. Besides, it's Opi's day today. I can't disappoint him again – I promised him a trip into the city centre, to visit the Square. He's of the age now to experience *Oosah* for the first time."

She sat opposite him and placed her small hands on his clenched fists, feeling his tension. "Mirrimas is not an unreasonable man, Sol. He will listen to you, and respect the church's conclusions – you know that. Take Opi out for the morning, you owe him that, considering the many times you've disappointed him. I'll make your apologies to my father, and we can all meet later."

"You know I have confidence in your father; it's your mother's influence upon him and the rest of the tribe which concerns me, and concerns the Twelve Grand Cardinals. She's too eager for conflict, and I'm worried she'll poison your brothers' minds with her obsessions. At best, your older brother, Hulneb's, behaviour is arrogant and unpredictable; she could tip the balance in her favour."

Roanne shook her head, then tilted it to one side as she spoke, letting her hair fall halfway across her forehead. She knew there was an element of truth to her husband's concerns, as Hulneb embraced the romantic obsessions of his Kaltesh forefathers on his mother's side of the family. "Oh please, Sol! My mother's position in the tribe is ineffective, as is the law. She may have my father's ear, but my father listens only to his heart over such matters – she knows this. As for Hulneb? You embarrassed him in front of everyone during the last festival tournament games, if you remember?"

He shrugged. "It was a wooden practice sword I threw

to him, in a Kaltesh *Ticandra* move he should have known. We lost the match because he dropped it."

"He didn't drop it, Sol, it caught him squarely in the back. It was embarrassing for him! Anyway, don't worry about Hulneb. Father will keep him in line."

She smiled, remembering her mischievous younger brother, pushing aside her husband's fears. "I can't wait to see Tulteth – he's nearly sixteen. He'll get on well with Opi – give him the companionship he needs, for a while at least."

Sol looked up at her and removed his hands from her grasp to continue braiding his hair. Her comment concerning his absence as a father went unanswered, as there was no point in continuing last night's heated arguments. He had made his position clear. The comfortable lifestyle she enjoyed so much, their social standing, the frequent Church functions, the college lectures and celebrity status came at a price, and that price would always be his time spent working and the comparatively small amount of time remaining to spend with his family in private. The majority of Grade One Theorists working in Abeona remained single, free of distractions which could possibly impede their search for truth.

"What was that noise?" said a voice behind them. "That wasn't the measure bell."

They turned to see Opi. The little boy stood barefoot, his long blond hair tangled from sleep, wearing a creased white cotton tunic, his light blue eyes looking with avid curiosity from one parent to the other. Ebe followed behind him to stand by his side.

"That was the Monitor's second bell," said Sol, turning. "You're right, not a measure. The bell you've just heard tells everyone visitors are on their way." He patted the seat beside him. "Come and sit down; breakfast will soon be ready."

Opi sat at the table as his father continued. "Then, after

we've eaten, we'll visit *Oosah,* as promised."

Opi's eyes filled with excitement. "I can't wait to see it, dad!"

Roanne shook her head and stood, pulling a sash set into the wall, ringing the servants' bell.

"Sol, after breakfast I'm going to ride out to meet my parents. They will expect it."

"Of course," he said, his eyes remaining on his son, nodding as a servant appeared in the doorway. He waved her forward, and she hurriedly set down three bowls of steaming fish, which Roanne began to dress with fruit from the platter at the centre of the table.

"We'll meet you at the tenth bell, at the main entrance to the Square," said Sol. "That will give you enough time to settle your parents in, and give Opi and me plenty of time together. We can all call upon your parents as a family after the first period of darkness, or invite them to stay here. There's plenty of room."

She nodded as Opi spoke. "Who are the visitors? What do they want?"

"You'll remember them – the Kaltesh," answered Sol, picking up a knife. "They are your mother's people. They have come to the city for the festival and to pray in the sight of *Oosah* alongside the Abeonians, to pay their respects to the dead and the freedom they gave us many thousands of cycles ago." He looked across the table to Roanne, but her eyes had fallen to the balcony overlooking the desert.

TWO

THE TROPHY

Sol held Opi's hand as they walked through the narrow, cobbled streets between the walls of the Cardinals' estates. The cool morning air carried a hint of bellkai oil from the blackened torches lining the way, colouring the morning with a sweet perfume. The city was slowly coming to life around them as they reached the last of these passageways, the inhabitants preparing for the upcoming festival. Parents stood upon ladders, tying colourful banners across their cottages, children shouting adjustments from below. The aromas of freshly baked bread, boiling meats, fruits and vegetables escaped from open kitchen windows and coursed through the alleyways.

The Cardinal held out his hand as a public cart approached, nodded his thanks to the driver and handed him a couple of tokens. "We'll ride halfway, then hire an animal," he said to Opi, as they sat.

A Cardinal taking public transport was unheard of, but Sol insisted upon showing Opi the city from every perspective, determined his privileged position would not mar the child at such an early age with a sense of social superiority. Several of the commuters looked surprised at these two well-manicured passengers with their expensive clothes, and Sol simply nodded and smiled to them as the cloth-covered cart crossed the Dedwen Bridge towards the centre of Abeona. This bridge was the largest of eight that traversed the wide, meandering moat, protecting the city centre and the Trophy several leagues distant. Opi leant out of the cart to look behind as it rumbled on. There, a handful of vessels were moored at jetties that jutted into the water haphazardly, as if fearful of the opposite shore. Beside them, tiny boats bobbed about in the early morning haze as the wake from a city worker's barge kissed their hulls, sending crisp crests of broken light along their cracked paintwork. He turned to face forward, enjoying the breeze that swept across his face. There, the sheer inner wall of the city centre rose high from the water, its defences of darkened arrow slits evenly placed like rows of squinting eyes. There were no moorings here, just the stains left behind by the water's seasonal rise and fall.

Once the Dedwen Bridge was traversed the cart rounded a corner into a large square with many tall-arched passageways leading from it. They disembarked, Sol placing his son upon his shoulders. Beyond the centre arch stood a herd of a hundred or so ganapti, grazing on bales of Farrengrass tops. Opi watched as several of the large quadrupeds raised their long heads and turned as they approached. The animals continued chewing instinctively, heavy eyelids blinking slowly with indifference. Then they lifted their heads and bellowed as father and son walked closer, the herd snorting a few times in reply before resuming their early morning feast.

A figure appeared from behind the animals and approached them.

Sol set Opi down and straightened his robes. "Good morning," he said, holding out a hand.

"Good morning, Cardinal," said the ganapti herdsman, as he noticed Sol's robes. He bowed, and hurried over to shake the offered hand.

"What can I do for you at such an early measure? After all, you're not here to theorise with me, are you?" he said, waving his herding staff at the younger man.

"I need a strong and obedient animal for the duration of the festival. Ours is sick and in need of rest. Besides, I cannot expect my son to walk all the way to the Square of Remembrance."

The herdsman stroked his beard once, then pinched his nose with his forefinger and thumb. His dark eyes narrowed as they fell upon the boy. "The Square. I see. Follow me," he said with a wink.

Sol perched Opi back onto his shoulders as the herdsman carved a path through the grazing animals with his staff. The docile creatures obeyed their master's demands and ambled aside, allowing the trio into their centre where the younger animals grazed with their parents.

"Here, this one should do," said the herdsman, patting the ganapti on its long slender neck.

Opi watched with interest as Sol examined the animal's hide. It was blemish-free, the short, coarse, off-white hair covering the creature shining in the morning sun a sign of health, contentment and selective breeding.

Opi's head was now level with the animal's. The young boy reached over slowly and stroked its large, leathery ears. They twitched and Opi giggled as it shook its head and bellowed. Then the animal slowly turned its head to look at him, and he felt its hot breath upon his face. Opi looked cautiously into its yellow eyes. They were clear and healthy, holding personality and a subtle hint of intelligence, he decided.

Sol crouched down, reaching up to place Opi at his side, much to the boy's disappointment.

"This is how to select a ride, Opi," said Sol, examining the ganapti's legs. They were strong and muscular, the hair conforming to every bulge and curve perfectly, without any sign of parasites or disease. The feet were clean, the grey nails smooth, with thin veins of white running laterally through them. He tapped the animal's ankle three times and it obediently lifted its foot, revealing a thick shoe of iron beneath each of the five toes.

The herdsman crouched next to Sol, speaking quickly. "I broke her in myself last season. She knows the rules of the streets well, and I recently fitted her with new shoes. As you can see, they're of the finest quality."

"Dismount," ordered Sol, glancing momentarily at the herdsman.

The animal responded by sitting with its hind legs tucked neatly under its body, folding its front legs to its right side.

Sol turned. "This animal will be fine. Price?"

The herdsman rubbed his chin and looked to the ground, pushing discarded Farrengrass buds around with the tip of his staff. He tilted his head to the side then spoke slowly to himself. "A Cardinal, but not just any Cardinal – I recognise you now. You're Sol Timmerman, aren't you?"

Sol nodded.

"Grade *One* Theoretical scientist?"

Sol lifted his head back a little, then looked down at Opi.

The herdsman leant on his staff. "I would think such a fine animal, fit for a Grade One Cardinal and his son, deserves a high price. Eighty tokens for the hire of this animal and a saddle – and you can keep her for the duration of the festival, for a favour."

"Which is?"

"Bless my family, my business and livestock on the first day of the festival."

The two men held each other's stares for a few moments. Finally Sol spoke. "A comfortable twin saddle to fit us both and you have an agreement."

The little man grinned and bowed. "I'll saddle her up for you right away."

Opi sat in the front saddle as Sol directed the ganapti out of the square and through the high-arched tunnel leading to a minor thoroughfare. The animal's iron shoes echoed around them as it ambled along, rocking both father and son gently from side to side.

"How far is it to the Square now, father?"

"Several leagues. We'll take my usual route though the Priests' Quarter."

The animal sniffed in the darkness, aware of the scent of others of its kind at the busy junction ahead.

"It won't take too long, Opi," he said, trying to reassure

his son. "Believe me, it's worth the wait."

Roanne approached the eastern gatehouse tower that stood to the right of the massive gates of iron and wood that separated the city from the desert. Extending above the gates were the ancient stone ramparts and battlements of the garrison buildings. Almost two thousand cycles ago they had housed several regiments of soldiers and their families. The garrison's sun-bleached pillars were decorated with pictograms and family crests, telling the story of its construction. Here and there, several of the carvings had eroded, leaving the observer with only a disjointed story to follow.

She tethered her ganapti then hurried up the steps that curled around the tower towards the gatehouse door. A slope connecting each step with the next had worn into them, the only clue left behind by the soldiers and their families of the tower's habitation so long ago. She stopped and listened, turning to face the tower above her. The building stood silent and restful, and she felt humble warmth from the blocks as if they were at ease with her presence. Leaning back against the wall, her eyes wandered over to the empty garrison accommodation above the gates.

Scoured by sandstorms and spring rain, the exterior projected a sorrowful face of neglect. Once hard and angular, its features had now softened into a pitiful smear against the bright morning sky. Nobody ever took the slightest interest in the building. It was a feature of the city only those very few who ventured into the eastern desert ever saw. Kaltesh traders lowered their heads in respect as they passed beneath it, for death had leapt from those once proud battlements during the conflict of long ago, cutting down their brethren as they fought for their beliefs. Neither the city's architects nor archaeologists gave the garrison favour. The architects were too busy designing and building other structures to work on the building, and it was decided it would be disrespectful to restore the garrison to its former glory, a glory remembered for so many deaths on both sides. The few city archaeologists ignored the building, as sandstorms quickly covered their finds, as if unwilling to allow any secrets it held to be fully unearthed.

As an amateur archaeologist, Roanne respected the structure. Along with the Holy Citadel of the Twelve Grand Cardinals, it was a place very few people knew much about, whereas the histories of many other buildings in the city had been well documented. Only when they needed to be rebuilt did the buildings of Abeona offer any information as to the archaic lifestyles of their builders and former inhabitants. This structure, however, would stand as long as the city itself. It was part of the sacred gate, a place of romantic speculation and unidentified truths. Sonnets had been written about it, children's nursery rhymes sang of it, mothers telling naughty children, *"the ghosts from the gate will come to haunt you if you don't behave"*, and myriad fables were recounted and altered every night in taverns and alehouses concerning it. These spurious anecdotes were not for her, for she preferred the cryptic songs told by the wind as it twisted through the weathered remains of the intricate galleries and terraces. She stopped and listened for these songs, but the wind had died now, so she allowed her eyes to roam the garrison. From nowhere a chill touched her, despite the warmth of the morning. The tension the people once living there must have felt seemed to linger in the blocks and reach out to her. She shivered, lowered her head and continued to climb, wrapping her robes tighter around her shoulders and forcing her hands beneath the folds. But the chill followed her up the slope and invaded her thoughts, and she imagined what life must have been like in the garrison all those hundreds of cycles ago.

She stood in the tiny, cold dwellings where the children had slept next to their parents, the huge, vaulted dining halls echoing with laughter and falsely jovial exchanges. Above her, the sentries trod the battlements, waiting, wishing they had never volunteered for duty at the gate. Her mind grew weary of the cramped conditions, the daily routine. She felt their tension; smelt the apprehension hanging in the air. The drunken laughter of the men became stale to her ears, along with the sounds of children's innocent play and their mothers' nervous chatter. All served simply to fill the empty space leading towards the inevitable day of the Kaltesh attack.

At once the battle raged inside her head. Arrows and spears creased the sky above the garrison. An endless torrent of crudely tempered hate fell in sparks against the cold stone floor on one side, and a growing sea of wood and metal sprouted from the dry sand, on the other. Inevitably, these splinters of detestation found their mark, cutting through the armour of the soldiers atop the battlements. Their bodies fell, some lifeless as they hit the flagstones, others realising their grasp on life and everything they hoped for their future would very soon ebb away.

Below, the Kaltesh pushed their wooden battle towers toward the gates. Their arrows and spears splintered the gate, and the brave foot soldiers attempted to climb the uneven ladders created by so many spears. A few of the Abeonians responded with valiant determination, taking even the bravest Kaltesh by surprise. They leapt over the battlements, swords in hand, colliding with the nomads climbing below. Weapons clashed, strangers' eyes met. Love for their families and religious beliefs gave strength to all as death covered the sand.

In the bunkers, the sound of the battle echoed through the passageways and the women clasped their hands over the delicate ears of their children. Many couldn't bear to listen and ran, but there was no escape from the garrison. The city's first line of defence was cut off from the tranquillity it served to protect, and the women found only locked and barred doors to pound against as the second line of defence waited silently on the other side for the first sight of a coward or a Kaltesh face.

She remembered the story her mother had told her many times before drifting off to sleep. *And then the Kaltesh breached the gate, cut down instantly only to be replaced by their brethren, trampling over the dying in single-minded determination to reach their goal. And reach it they did, commanded by your foremother of generations passed. Ritma, the Kaltesh warrior High Priestess. They surged through the city, unstoppable, merciless as the Abeonians fled. But they didn't give chase as expected, for the Citadel of the Senior Grand Cardinals was their only objective.*

The garrison protecting the bridge leading to the Citadel fell in less than a measure. Ritma stood upon the roof of a pavilion, halfway along the bridge. Soaked with sweat and the blood of hundreds slain, she held her sword high in the air, calling her warriors onwards to the Citadel's unprotected gates. She jumped down, watching them surge past her, hungry for the heads of Abeona's ruling Twelve, and as they battered the gates a low rumble filled the air. It grew and the bridge's substructure shook. As she watched, the way ahead crumbled into the depths below, her brave warriors falling to their deaths amid the rubble. She turned to retreat to the safety of the garrison, fearful of a possible assault of arrows from the Citadel, calling to her tribesmen to hurry. But as they turned, the way to the garrison crumbled also, leaving Ritma and her few generals stranded on an island of rock with only a narrow pavilion for shelter from the sun. And marooned there they starved to death, Abeona's cowardly sacrifice at the gate and garrison successfully removing her as the Kaltesh warrior leader.

Roanne took a deep breath and discarded the burden of these thoughts. The hopelessness of it all, the suffering and anguish of so many seemed to remain in the building above, as if a net of emotion had captured the events of long ago and the walls fed off them.

She hurried towards the main door of the tower that was set back into a defensible corridor, illuminated by torches lining the walls on either side. As she entered the corridor the tension left her, the newness of the door ahead blocking out impressions of the distant past and replacing them with the reality of the present.

"Roanne Timmerman, wife of Cardinal Sol Timmerman," she shouted, after knocking upon the door. After a short time the sound of bolts and catches unlocking gave way to the squeak of the door as it slowly opened. A tall, bony figure, bald, with sunken cheeks and eyes stood in the doorway, dressed in a thin, white canvas tunic. Peering from around his waist were several children identically dressed. He ushered them back into the darkness with a staccato voice and single wave of his hand. Roanne noticed his joints were disfigured by arthritis.

"What do you want, young woman?" he asked bluntly, squinting at her face, illuminated by the torch he held.

"The Kaltesh approach, Gatekeeper. I require admittance into the desert to greet them. They are my pe–"

"I have no time for such foolishness, young woman! My sight's not what it once was, but I too heard the bell. My children and I have many tasks, the cogs and wheels of the gate mechanism need to be cleaned and greased. Gears must be engaged to pull the inner walls aside. My wife must–"

She cut him off. "Have your eyes not detected this emblem?" She pointed to the crest above her right breast and the Gatekeeper took a step closer. "I am the wife of a Cardinal – you cannot deny me admittance into the desert."

The old man sighed, then gave a condescending grin. "So, *you're* Roanne Vela of the Kaltesh, wife of Theorist Timmerman?" He continued slowly, "I've heard talk of you, and your family." He bowed stiffly, forced a smile and held his back as he struggled to straighten up. "My sincerest apologies," he said sarcastically. "Make your way to the gates, Kaltesh."

Roanne nodded her thanks as the door slammed, then hurried down the winding steps. As she descended, she could hear the old man shouting instructions behind the walls, his children shouting back. She waited, facing a stone wall that reached up to the battlements. A grinding filled the air as, at last, the wall separated down its centre, dust, sand and tiny stone chippings creating a veil before the wooden gates. Then a low-pitched cry of tired metal filled the air, as a double doorway appeared at the bottom right-hand corner of the gates. Roanne mounted her ride and hurried through the opening onto the sand-covered roadway.

The ganapti picked up speed along the thoroughfare as Sol rubbed his heels over its ribcage, holding a steadying hand around Opi's waist as they overtook a merchant cart. The animal negotiated the seven lanes with ease.

The young boy laughed. "This is fantastic, father!" he shouted above the clatter of the metal shoes on the flagstones. "So much faster than old Ganu,"

"You're right, Ganu's old," answered Sol. "Perhaps we should consider buying this animal. I'll ask the herdsman when we return her. Hold tight now." Sol kicked the animal's ribs and reined her past another cart, weaving in and out of the others sharing the thoroughfare.

Opi screamed with excitement. He had never moved so fast and so high off the ground. The flagstones below became a blur as Sol pushed the animal to its limit for a few moments, then pulled her in behind an empty velocipede to travel at a respectable trot.

Opi noticed the shape looming through the haze above the tallest of the far-distant buildings. "There!" he shouted, "Over there...is that it, father?"

"The Trophy, *Oosah*," said Sol. "The only remnant

from a long, terrible and bloody war in which our whole world fought for freedom."

"A war, with the Kaltesh?"

"No. The war was fought *alongside* the Kaltesh, against the occupants of the Trophy, *Oosah*."

Opi stared at the gigantic object. "But how did we defeat them?"

"We're not entirely sure. That's one of the reasons the theoretical scientists study *Oosah*. We certainly outnumbered the invaders, but we need to discover as much about it as we possibly can, should the invaders return in an attempt to conquer us again. But so far, considering the many tens of hundreds of cycles we've spent attempting to unlock its secrets, we've learnt very little. Written records from those ancient times are few. You'll learn more concerning this part of the city's history during your next term at school."

Sol directed the animal onto a slip lane and brought her down to walking pace. Ahead, a queue leading to the public entrance to the Square of Remembrance had formed, where traders, merchants and pilgrims mingled.

He unbuckled the boy's harness and lifted him onto his shoulders. From his elevated position Opi was afforded a view over the boundary wall and into the Square of Remembrance. The view took his breath. The Square stretched as far as he could see. Here and there the early arrivals had set up camps and stalls, temporary makeshift dwellings of varying sizes and complexity. Far behind all this rose the immense shape of the Trophy, which seemed to grow from the stone floor itself. Now the sunlight broke through the cloud cover and danced across its surface, creating a shimmering haze on the horizon high above the people. Sol placed Opi back in the saddle and rode on toward the Cardinals' entrance, where four armed Deacons admitted them with a casual wave. Once inside the Square they dismounted and Sol tethered the ganapti to a cooling post next to a trough, handing a few coins to the animal keeper to watch over her. As soon as Sol's back was turned Opi started to wander off.

"Opi! Come here. Stay at my side. I don't want to lose you in the crowd," said Sol, sternly.

The boy turned and walked back to join his father, who patted the ganapti as it drank from the trough.

He looked up to his father, speechless, his head full of wonder.

"I'll answer all of your questions on the way," said Sol, taking his hand. "Come on, we'll take a velocipede."

They climbed aboard a one-man rickshaw, Opi sitting upon his father's lap. Once they were comfortable Sol signalled the driver and the small covered transport started on its way. The tents, stalls and temporary settlements created a maze of streets and alleyways which the driver passed through skilfully.

"So, are you enjoying the day so far, Opi?" asked Sol above the clatter of the wooden wheels across the flagstones. The boy nodded, his attention captivated by the activity unfolding around him.

Sooner than Opi had expected, the shops and stalls thinned out. The driver of the velocipede stopped, unbuckling his harness and turning to them. "That's as far as I'm allowed to take you, Cardinal. Your tariff's eighteen tokens."

Sol set Opi down, paid the driver and took his son's hand. As he led him across the dusty flagstones he regarded the visitors around the edge of the settlements. A knee-high wall marked the boundary between the settlement area where makeshift dwellings were allowed, and the sacred ground of the Trophy's hallowed domain, where they were not. Several worshippers sat upon the wall, staring with the expressions of wonder and inquisitiveness Sol had seen so many times before. Others had turned their backs to it, their eyes closed in prayer as they rocked back and forth.

Now the gargantuan shape was within walking distance, solid, not a lie or a distant, cloud-like apparition to be explained away as a natural phenomenon or ignored as inconsequential. As Sol and Opi approached it, the grey, green and yellow tones of the surrounding stonework seemed to be part of a dream, remote and altogether unwelcome against the colourful curving hulk of the object.

"Although we're almost a quarter of a league away, you can still appreciate *Oosah's* size from here," said Sol.

The hazy shape of the monolith defied the blocky, architectural shapes surrounding it, with sweeping curves and intricate projections. A few of the oldest buildings positioned at the edge of the Square made unsuccessful attempts to copy its style, resulting in ungainly ugliness. The buildings behind these old mimics stood larger and adopted the style of their Abeonian architects, as if pushing the other, smaller buildings forward for judgement. At once *Oosah* filled Opi's peripheral vision, the city's reality vanishing to be replaced by an object totally alien to him.

Sol felt the unusual inner warmth he had always felt when seeing the object. To him, the buildings, the Square, even the very people sharing their lives alongside his lost their importance. He turned for a moment to look at the city. Everything except Opi standing at his side dwindled to insignificance. Turning back to Opi he watched his son's eyes feed off the object. He took in every detail, every curve, shape, protrusion and colour. At once Sol knew he would have a mountain of questions to answer before the day was at an end, and this he relished. It had been many weeks since he had spent time alone with his son, as there was always so much work for him, so much research and study, and the boy was growing so quickly. Now he had seen his father's place of work, their time together would be much more rewarding.

As they wandered towards the object, they came to a lift gantry where a queue had formed.

"Look! Can we see it from above?" asked the boy, pointing up.

Sol smiled, "Of course."

They joined the queue and waited.

The gasps from the young people aboard the lift as it ascended told Sol they were all viewing the Trophy for the first time. From their elevated position, the object was revealed in all its glory. It stretched for a league and a half into the distance, resembling a colossal flat fish turned edge on, covered in bulges, protrusions and coloured panel markings that twisted over its surface like scales. These designs had faded here and there from constant exposure to the extremes of climate. In a few places the markings had vanished completely, revealing a bare skin of metal beneath. Thousands of black windows shaped like teardrops were set into its surface at varying levels, ideal nesting places for birds. At its centre, long scars of silver metal were apparent. Along its back, three graceful projections swept up and out from the surface, reaching high above the tallest steeple of the Square's cathedral.

For a few moments Sol forgot he had his son in the lift with him as his eyes wandered over the surface of the object, and it seemed a new detail became apparent every time he studied it.

The lift stopped and the group stepped out onto a rectangular observation platform that protruded over the hulk. Families, scholars and worshippers stood wide-eyed as the wind blew across the platform, ruffling Sol's cloak as if trying to distract him. No one spoke, not even Opi, who always seemed to have something to say, no matter what the occasion. After a few minutes Sol noticed his son's gaze was fixed upon the buildings surrounding the Square.

"Opi?"

"How was it moved into the Square, father?"

He crouched down. "Our ancestors were led to this site by Tal Salandor, our father and saviour, teacher and first son of our world, for only he knew where the invaders made camp. Our sheer numbers overthrew the foreigners, and their last survivor sealed *Oosah* as Tal Salandor fought with him inside, not only preventing the people from assisting Tal Salandor, but also from learning the secrets hidden within. Our ancestors deemed it easier to build a new city here, with our Trophy at the very centre, rather than alter the existing capital at the Tethes ocean shore to accommodate it. The records remaining from that time suggest it took approximately three hundred cycles to complete this city, but we are unsure about that. One day the son of the world will return, to answer all our questions concerning this life, and the next. We must all pray and give thanks to the first son, the giver of freedom in this life, our guide to the next, once the veil of death greets us." At once Sol was aware he was sermonising, as Roanne had often pointed during social occasions. *'You're preaching again, Sol,'* she would whisper to him. *'There's no need to bring work along with you everywhere we go.'* He looked up, noticing a few people had turned to listen to his story and had that same bewildered expression as his son.

Opi tugged at his father's robes. "Look, down there. There's another scaffold, leading to a bridge close up to its side!"

Sol nodded. "Yes, that's where I theorise."

"Can we get up close to *Oosah,* father?" asked the boy, excitedly.

Sol stood, looking down at his son. His request was unprecedented for a child of his age.

"No, I'm afraid we cannot," he replied, as firmly as his pride in his son would allow, "although that is where I spend a considerable amount of my working day." He looked over to the scaffold. "The gantry actually leads inside."

"Inside?" Opi repeated, incredulous. "But you said it was sealed! We could... and you could show me–"

"No arguments."

"We've plenty of time, *please,* dad!"

Sol looked down into his wide eyes, and was reminded of when he had asked his father's permission to enrol into the Church college to join him, and was turned down for no reason other than an emphatic, 'No.' He knew if he wanted Opi to follow in his rather uneven footsteps he couldn't decline his request. He crouched down once more and held Opi's hands. "Perhaps we could," he closed his eyes and lifted his head sharply as Opi opened his mouth to speak, and his son understood the silent instruction and remained quiet. "If so, then only for a short time. I have to visit Uncle Yan and hand him my final report before the end of the day, so we could ask him then." He winked at the boy. "He may allow us inside."

THREE

FAMILY

Roanne halted Ganu, wiping her brow with the back of her hand and squinting into the distance. The huge caravans, twelve men high and twenty men wide, sitting on their eight barrel-shaped wheels, crept across the sand like a herd of bizarre wooden buildings. Each vehicle was a three-tiered, multi-roomed home, added to and repaired over many cycles. She heard them creak as they swayed in the heat, watching figures sitting on shaded balconies, smoke from cooking fires reaching high into the dry air. Family banners fluttered in the breeze and occasionally a hunting bird swooped down to an outstretched arm, returning with a sand rat or gathran snake. Ten ganapti, grouped in pairs, pulled each vehicle, with a few hundred or so replacement animals bringing up the rear of the convoy. Old women ambled behind, collecting the animals' droppings and placing them into baskets upon their backs. Her nomadic people were still a long way off, and Roanne's eyes darted about, impatient to see her father riding proudly at the head of the cavalcade. She missed the old man greatly, and secretly his was the only companionship she regretted leaving behind. The tall man with his long grey hair, craggy face and dark, trenchant eyes was an image of pure nobility to her, and his expression could change in an instant. He commanded the tribe with an uncanny astuteness bordering on magic, some believed; his judgements fair, his punishments fitting the transgressions. There was always a story upon his lips, either fictitious or handed down through his family, and when he spoke, all listened. Some believed he could see the colours of the different winds as they coursed through the air and could walk the land following these shapes as easily as one would follow an Abeonian street map. Others believed he could read the signs preceding a weather change, in the shapes and speed of the clouds against the sky, just as easily as he could read a page from a book.

She shielded her eyes from the glare as she noticed a figure running towards her. The stranger stopped a hundred paces distant and studied her. She waved her hands above her head, frantically shouting.

"Hold! What is the heaviest baggage of the Kaltesh?"

The figure took a few paces forward, "An empty purse and heart. Is that you, Roanne?"

"Tulteth?" She dismounted, walking slowly forwards to greet her younger brother.

Then they ran to each other, kicking up the sand, and as their bodies met, they held each other in a long embrace.

"It's so good to see you, Tulteth," she breathed, squeezing him tightly, resting her chin on the top of his head, noticing the tension in his frame. She wondered why the younger son of the family was leading the tribe in the position of First Son. Had something happened to Hulneb, their older brother?

"I've missed you so much, Ro, and I've visited you and your city in my thoughts many times. It's so good to see you." They separated and held hands, regarding each other, his brightly-coloured clothes causing a frown to crease her face. She held the fabric of his sleeve and rubbed it between her fingers a few times before looking at him. "The finest silk?"

He explained in a whisper. "I'm now the eldest son." His head dropped as he bit his bottom lip. "I'm so sorry, Ro, but we didn't have time to visit and tell you. Times have been hard for us." He took a deep breath and looked up. "I now hold Hulneb's position as First Son, and he is now High Celebrant. Father died seven seasons ago."

FOUR

YAN

Yan Arramosa sat behind a curved, ebony desk, smoking a pipe of grey Farrengrass. The sweet aroma from the burning leaf filled his spacious classroom, along with its veil of green smoke, hanging motionless in the warm air. His eyes roamed around the room; his forty student priests were all working silently, illuminating their Books of Truth. Then his eyes fell back to the pile of Cardinals' reports sitting on his desk; all needed careful study and appraisal before their theories could be either discarded or passed on to the Senior Archbishop's tower for blessing. Only then could they enter the Holy Citadel and the hands of the Twelve Grand Cardinals. He drew deeply on the pipe and began to write a note as he exhaled.

A knock upon the door forced him to look up. Hurriedly finishing his writing, he placed the single sheet of paper into an envelope, fastening it with his official wax seal. Brushing down his blue and gold robes he addressed the envelope in front of him. The knock on the door came again.

"Enter."

Sol walked in, closing the heavy doors behind him, turning as a thin smile touched Yan Arramosa's grey lips. Several of the students glanced up, and a whisper slowly grew to a murmur as they recognised the tall figure standing at the door.

"Continue your work," said Yan, and the room fell silent again, save for the scratching of quills upon parchment.

"Well, Sol," said the Archbishop, standing with a little difficulty and waving him forward, "To what do I owe this visit?" He held out a plump hand. "Please, sit."

Sol bowed, walking forward to shake his mentor's hand

vigorously, smiling broadly at the older man now as they both sat. "This is an unofficial visit, Yan," said Sol quietly, as he arranged his robes, "apart from this." He handed over his latest theories in a sealed envelope. "It's Opi. I brought him to see *Oosah* this morning–"

Yan held up both hands, disturbing the blanket of smoke with the envelope. "You needn't say any more. I've been expecting this since the day he was born. Your father did exactly the same to me, oh, twenty or so cycles ago." He leant forward, dropping Sol's report on top of the pile without looking at it, then poured two goblets of water, handing one to his guest. "Here, share water with me." He glanced at the measureglass upon his desk then pointed to it. The sands had almost completely passed through. "If you could wait just a few moments?"

Sol nodded once and took a sip of water, replacing it upon the desk as Yan stood, walking to the front of the class. Upon the desk, an object caught Sol's eye, causing him to frown. It was an arrowhead, but unlike any he'd seen before. He picked it up, turning it over in his fingers. The shaft had been cut cleanly just below where the tang would hide, but the arrowhead's stem mated with the shaft perfectly. He ran his fingers over the join, but couldn't feel the transition. What was the most surprising, as he closed one eye and looked at its tip, was the fact that the blades, midribs and barbs were perfectly symmetrical and smooth, the metal a dull silver much like a marriage of pure silver and pewter. He replaced it as Yan spoke to the class.

"Replace your quills and return refreshed after your prayers."

The students hastily collected their study books and filed out of the room, several bowing to Sol as they passed, he returning their respect.

As the last student closed the door behind him, Yan walked back to his seat, placing his pipe in its holder while he drained his goblet, slamming the vessel down onto the desk. He refilled the pipe from a copper urn, turning his back on his guest to face the circular window dominating the wall behind his chair.

"Speaking of your father, the sweet flavour of his day has sadly long since passed," he said with glazed eyes, as he watched the square below. He raised his eyebrows and sighed. "Back then, regulations were much stiffer than they are today. There were forms and procedures, formalities, customs and rituals to be followed to the letter." Taking a spill of paper from a box upon his desk he held it to a candle flame, then lit his pipe, inhaling in long, slow movements of his chest. Coughing a cloud of smoke he turned to face Sol. "It was, without a doubt, a far more romantic era to play an active role in. Nowadays, my time is taken up by baby-sitting classes such as this, or cross-referencing the latest theories with those going back as far as the written records," he waved absently toward the wall on Sol's right, where ancient books and papers were neatly archived in twelve abecedarian aisles ten men deep and three men high, "or interviewing priests who believe the dreams following a night's heavy drinking and lying with a whore hold the key to *Oosah*, and their promotion to Cardinal." He glanced at the doors as he paced behind his chair. "Idiots!"

"Yan, I wondered–"

"*Never* wonder, *always* theorise! You've been told that a thousand times, by your father, myself and your instructors."

Sol nodded his apology and finished his water.

The old man closed his eyes. "I'm sorry, Sol. It's just that–" he stopped himself and turned, forcing a smile, slumping back into his chair to look down at the envelope upon the desk.

"Just what, Yan?"

"The Kaltesh are almost with us."

"I know. Roanne's riding out to meet her parents." Sol relaxed a little, arranging his flowing sleeves over the arms of the chair. "But surely that's not what's troubling you?"

Yan's expression remained impassive as he spoke quietly. "I'm sure this festival will be as peaceful as they've always been, even though our guests are somewhat early." Clasping his hands together, the older man leant forward. "Sol, there's not much time before the next class. Let me ask you, what *exactly* are you expecting to find in that... that, *thing* out there?" The words just reached across the table as he jabbed a thumb over his shoulder to the window behind him.

"Thing? You mean *Oosah*," said Sol, confirming with some surprise, rather than questioning the Archbishop's meaning.

Drawing deeply on his pipe and removing it from his mouth, Yan's unblinking eyes wandered up and down the slender stem, despite the smoke. "I'll make my point, but for your ears alone. Understand?"

Sol shifted in his seat, disturbing the neatness of his robes. "I understand."

"How many men have wasted their lives searching for answers inside? Thousands, perhaps even tens of thousands of Theorists have come and gone over the cycles, with their own unique ideas, searching, theorising, and presenting their evidence. What were they *really* looking for, Sol?"

"Truth and salvation, obviously. That's what all Theorists work for, you know that."

"Well, yes, but *what* truth exactly, and *whose* salvation? A truth for the greater good of Abeona and the church, or a truth for themselves? Salvation for the entire world, or a personal salvation fuelled by ambition and the lure of celebrity?"

Sol leant forward in his chair, glancing sideways, opening his mouth to speak, but Yan held up a hand for silence. "What if just one of those answers points unequivocally towards Kaltesh beliefs? Can you imagine the impact that would have on your personal philosophy, and for that matter, our entire culture?" Yan's tiny eyes, pinpoints amid his chubby face, hid beneath his heavy eyebrows. In spite of this, they gleamed mischievously, probing with intense curiosity.

But Sol held their intensity with his own confident stare, aware he was being baited, but unaware why. He relaxed, calming himself, determined not to lose his composure.

"These are ancient concerns, they have no place in this time. Countless Theorists have disproved them over thousands of cycles. Tal Salandor's Books of Truth confirm this. The books the Kaltesh once burnt at the city gates, starting the first holy war. He raised his voice slightly, "It is my duty to remind you: if your words were heard by a Deacon, you would– "

The door opened behind them and Sol fell silent, watching as a line of priests filed in and took to their desks.

Yan looked over to his students, giving them instructions as Sol thought about his mentor's attitude. Obviously something was not right with the old man, and Sol noticed anger etched into his face as he leant over the table towards him while the priests settled into their seats.

"Yes, yes," he whispered, quickly turning the measureglass over before easing both hands, palm down, towards the tabletop, urging Sol to lower his voice, "I know all about that. You're avoiding answering my question, Sol." He took the pipe from his mouth, jabbing the damp stem accusingly towards him as he spoke. "Listen, this is not part of an official evaluation of your work. It's no secret amongst the members of the Church you have theorised correctly with an accuracy of eighty-nine percent all through your priesthood, and eighty-two percent since your elevation to Cardinal. I'm sure you're aware just how very few Church members have matched these figures since we began recording them. You have an uncanny talent. In time, your elevation to Grand Cardinal is inevitable, allowing you to share their truths and work with them to unlock the ultimate truths." He leant a little closer. "Let me be blunt. I believe you've spent too much time looking for Church answers rather than your own. Your father's greatest asset as a Theorist was his ability to shift his perspectives, to remove himself from his 'title'. Simply put, when others looked to the left, he looked right. When they stared upward, he looked down. This gave him unique insights no other Theorist had ever entertained. *You* can learn from his methodology. You must simply ask yourself, what truth are you longing to reveal? Then perhaps you'll realise you can find that truth elsewhere."

Sol looked over to the priests to see if any of them was watching, his eyes remaining on them as he spoke. "My father was said to be a drunken womaniser. Convicted of murdering his cleric and book carrier, bringing shame to the Timmerman name. Thankfully his death in the collapse of the old Ravine Quarter tenements saved our family's honour." Sol's eyes wandered to the window behind Yan, his voice trailing off. "A divine execution – the city itself crumbling upon him to silence his heresy, the day before the executioner's sword was scheduled to fall upon his neck, on the last day of that festival, before the eyes of the Kaltesh."

Yan looked down at his desk, hiding the fact he knew otherwise, his thoughts in turmoil. At last he let out a deep breath before speaking. "Your father told me, *'If you find yourself standing beneath a solid canopy of lies, the light of truth will illuminate you.'* Now! Answer my question!"

"TRUTH! What else is there?" shouted Sol, slamming his palms on the table. "Whatever that truth is, I want it, want it for the greater understanding of this city and myself. I'm not interested in my father's ramblings. Tal Salandor's words – *'Whoever discovers me will stand at my side for all eternity,'* – that's what I know I'll find!"

Sol turned back to see the young scholars staring at him. Every pair of eyes condemned his lack of control. Yan looked over to his students, their curious eyes falling back to their books once they had met his.

"Truth? A hundred lies are potentially more valuable than a single truth." Yan sat back in his chair, enjoying the creak it gave. He smiled weakly, speaking slowly as Sol shook his head, glancing at the students that had now become an audience to their exchange. "No, let them hear," continued Yan, "for a single truth leads down a single path, whereas a hundred lies weave multiple avenues of possibilities, ultimately unearthing truths aplenty along their way."

"Is that what you're teaching your students now, Yan?"

"No, that's what your father told me, what I'm *forbidden* to teach. It's up to you to decide if it's a truth or a lie." He gestured towards his students. "Not teaching such certainly limits their exploration of possibilities," he held his arm out to them shakily, "gelding the poor, hapless souls like ganapti, blinkering them in the midst of their most passionate, wide-eyed desire for answers!"

He stood and walked to the window behind his desk once more.

The figure was still there in the street below, he was sure of it. Watching his every move, measure by measure. He scanned the crowds strolling by. A few beggars held out bowls for food or money, couples stopped to pass the time of day with friends. But he couldn't see his 'silhouette' as he had called it, that unknown soma that had stayed with him for the past sixty days, following his every move.

Sol stood and looked around the classroom as the students hastily returned to their work. There, illuminated by candles, were certificates of Yan's academic qualifications. Painted likenesses, of the highest artistry, of Yan and his family, from many different stages of his life, lined the oak-panelled walls. To his left, upon a pedestal, entombed in a cabinet of glass, sat a large, carved stone model of the Trophy. The craftsmanship of the woodwork in the room was exquisite, the furniture hundreds of cycles old. Noticing the reports upon the desk, Sol wondered why the old man had become so talkative when he obviously had work to complete before the festival. Perhaps it was the pressure of the festival itself and the arrival of the Kaltesh, as it was one of his duties to ensure their stay was as comfortable and incident-free as possible. Then his eyes discovered the envelope upon the desk, and as he turned his head to read, he realised it was addressed to him. He stood, joining the Archbishop at the window. Yan glanced his way momentarily, as though he had forgotten Sol was there. Finally Yan spoke, his eyes still fixed on the thoroughfare below.

"Tell me. How would you feel if the Church decided to halt all Theoretical studies?"

"That would never happen," answered Sol with a start. "The Grand Cardinal's edict tells us *Oosah Agasanduku* will be studied until every secret behind each seal is discovered and Tal Salandor's remains are found – or the end of existence – whichever comes first. If the latter, then obviously theories would not be needed, as the truth would be ours in the Garden of Contentment. The Abeonians will know the truth of *Oosah*, either in life or death."

Yan nodded. "But what if studying *Oosah* brings about the end of time?"

Sol folded his arms and smiled. "It's an old fear, one I'll not entertain. Besides, we would still know the truth."

"At the cost of the lives of those who do not believe in Tal Salandor, individuals who are simply happy to live their lives within the city walls?"

"They will all be saved, taken to the Garden, given the lower terraces to tend, as Tal Salandor watches over them from the shade of the tree upon the hill."

"To nurture fruits and vegetables, to raise and slaughter livestock to feed the so-called true believers luxuriating upon the higher terraces above?"

"At least they will be saved, unlike in Kaltesh beliefs."

Yan looked down at the thick gold wedding bangle adorning Sol's right wrist and Sol noticed this. "Roanne's lack of conformity to our beliefs is not in question here – what would you have me do? Cease my vocation lest my actions bring about the wrath of the Almighty, causing my wife and myself to be parted in the next life? Is that what's worrying you, Yan?"

The Archbishop shrugged, raising his eyebrows, aware the conversation could run in circles for the remainder of the morning.

"I'm just asking you to consider all possibilities and alternatives, for your own well-being, that's all." He turned to face the class. "Look at them, Sol. You can almost smell their determination; I can see it in their eyes when I teach them, their hunger, their unrelenting focus toward the one goal. Don't you find that a little sad for such youngsters?"

"Noble, I'd say, not sad. Has it ever been any different?"

The older man looked grim as he remembered. "Yes. *Your* obsession was worse."

"Obsession? It was – it *is* – my calling, Yan. There is nothing as important."

Yan turned back to the window. "Nothing? But what of your son? Would you be happy with such a life for him?"

"Opi will eventually make his own way in the city. Roanne has made it all too clear to me she will see to that."

At last Yan seemed to fully relax, raising his voice so it carried across the classroom to the eager ears of the priests.

"Speaking of Opi, I theorise he wants to see inside *Oosah*?"

Sol nodded.

"And where is the lad now?"

"Waiting with your cleric in reception."

"You are aware of the regulations regarding minors and the memorial, aren't you, Cardinal?"

"Yes, there are no such written regulations."

Yan sat back in his chair, Sol sitting opposite. "Correct. Only Grade One Theoretical Scientists, Deacons of *Oosah*, positions above, and their assistants can be admitted. I suppose you're going to tell me you want a pass document appointing your son as your assistant for the day?"

Before Sol could answer, Yan prepared the document,

hastily scribbling instructions. As he imprinted his seal in wax at the bottom of the page, he spoke, this time lowering his voice for Sol's ears alone. "Many Bishops are saying Sol Timmerman will be the next Grand Cardinal. Others say he will follow in his father's footsteps and join him spreading ganapti droppings around fruit trees in the Garden of Contentment, long before his time."

Sol shrugged. "And what do you say, Yan?"

He placed the pass in an envelope, sealed it and handed it to his guest. As Sol reached forward and tried to take it, the old man's grip remained firm and their eyes met.

"I say an intelligent man should keep his options and his eyes open at all times. What do you say?"

Sol smiled, relaxing at last. "Above everything, I am a scientist and Theorist and cannot imagine being anything else. *Oosah* is my life."

Yan released his grip and Sol looked down at the envelope addressed to him upon the desk. "Is that for me also?" he asked, reaching for it.

The Archbishop shook his head, snatching it up. "This contains information I'm sure you will be eager to clarify for me. A *personal project* – something I have been working on to relieve the tedium that is teaching and lecturing." He held it out to Sol, who refused it with a shake of his head.

"I'll be only too pleased to assist you, Yan, upon the condition you deliver that letter to me in person, whilst visiting us one evening after the festival. We can relax in my grounds, eat, share water and talk some more. Roanne and Opi would love to see you. You haven't visited us in such a very long time, and it's clear there's much you'd like to discuss with me. Let us do so, once they have taken to their beds."

At last the older man managed a half-smile, closing his eyes as he spoke. "Agreed."

Sol stood, pausing for a moment, regarding his old mentor before waving the pass in the air as he headed toward the doors. "Thank you for this, Yan. I owe you a good deed."

Yan nodded, "Thank you, Sol, and goodbye," he answered, forcing a smile as the Cardinal closed the doors behind him. *'Perhaps, Sol, I'll collect that good deed sooner than you think,'* he thought, placing the envelope between the folds of his robe, silently sobbing for his complicity against the background of scratching quills.

FIVE

HULNEB

Roanne tethered her animal to the family caravan and ran up the wide wooden steps onto the rear deck to embrace her mother, Rillian. As they held each other, small finger-cymbals and chimes suspended from the canopy above sang tiny metal notes, washing through the spirals of incense burning in brass pots either side of the steps. Roanne closed her eyes and took a deep breath, savouring the powerful aroma, allowing it to conjure up images of the times she had spent with her family, and times she had missed. She held back the heaving of her chest as her sorrow struggled to escape, and as they parted, Rillian caressed her daughter's face, her dry hands relishing the smooth skin of her daughter's cheeks. The old woman took her by the hand and led her inside, where they sat amid many purple, citrine and burgundy silk cushions.

"You are healthy, Roanne; your husband has provided well for you," she said with a wrinkled smile. Her fingertips traced along Roanne's jaw. "I see you've let your hair grow, as you said you would. Somehow it suits the weight you have gained."

The younger woman could not hold back her tears. They gathered beneath her eyes, threatening to spill over onto her cheeks and she quickly wiped them away, running her fingers through her tangled locks, styling them as best she could. "I always regretted my day of ascension, father cutting my hair as short as a ganapti yearling's. But look at me – sand in my eyes, and my hair styled by the wind!"

"Obviously the wilderness has missed one of its most beautiful children, as I have, Ro. Thank you for meeting me – you have made me very happy."

Roanne stopped tidying her hair and clasped her hands in her lap, taking a deep breath. "Tulteth told me. What happened? How did Mirrimas die?"

Her mother bowed her head and spoke quietly. "It was during the season of water. Mirrimas ordered the tribe down through the canyons of Alviadlee to the Tethes Ocean. He planned to harvest there for a while, depending on the tides." She stopped briefly to adjust the cushions supporting her back and Roanne assisted her. "The journey through the canyons was without incident, and quite tranquil. Birds heading to the coast were our only company; they watched us tread the black sand beside the river as we followed their flight. It was voted we spend a day herding wild ganapti to increase our stock. Mirrimas seemed uneasy with this, he was impatient to continue with the schedule he'd compiled, insisting we be on time for this coming festival. Hulneb convinced him we would make up the time by travelling at night, for one period every other day, using the new animals we'd tamed. They argued much."

"Why was he so concerned with time? It had never been that important to him."

Rillian shrugged, looking down at her hands resting in her lap. "Oh, I don't know. Your father began to act oddly when he returned from his last solace upon Mount Goraknath. He summoned the family elders; they talked for days, argued a little – the usual."

"What do you mean when you say he acted oddly?"

"I don't know, Ro, perhaps it was just the imaginings of an old woman – no one else thought he was behaving differently when I asked. He just seemed distant, as though something concerned him deeply. He acted like this until we reached the meeting of the seven tributaries. He relaxed then, was more the old Mirrimas."

"Did you voice your concerns to him personally?"

"I didn't feel there was any need, Ro. As I said, whatever was troubling him vanished as soon as we reached the ocean. We let the animals graze upon the shrubland and we set camp. The following morning he woke early, saying he was going down to the delta to collect balias shells and ripened enillios weed for breakfast, leaving instructions for the families to lay out the nets later that morning, as he planned to harvest during first tide. I decided to collect firewood, so I went to wake Hulneb to help me, but he wasn't in his caravan." Rillian wiped a tear from her eye. The many silver bangles adorning her wrists – one for each year of her life – clinked together, adding discordant metallic notes to the chimes overhead. She waved her hands around in the air as if to conjure up the words from her mouth, to help her describe the images she found so difficult to recall. Her voice faltered. "Mirrimas seemed to be away for such a long time, so when Hulneb returned I told him to hurry down to the shore and find him." Her skin grew pale as she remembered. Her eyes spilled over with tears and the moisture trickled down her thin cheeks, finding many tributaries carved into her complexion. "When Hulneb returned I could tell by his face something was wrong. I heard him calling for Tulteth. I followed them on a ganapti and found them leaping across the tide pools towards the water's edge. Hulneb pointed, and jumped in. I hurried to the edge and saw them pull Mirrimas from the water. His skin was so pale, his body cold and bloated and a net tangled around him. There was a deep wound on the back of his head. He'd slipped on the rocks, knocked himself unconscious and drowned."

Roanne held her mother tightly and both women wept, rocking from side to side almost imperceptibly against the motion of the caravan.

"It's been so difficult for the family, but Hulneb has done well taking your father's place. Tulteth was at an age when he really needed his father, to help him find his place in the tribe. Hulneb has been very supportive, teaching him our adult ways and helping him with that difficult transition between child and man. Poor Tulteth, and this just after returning from his Alonetime."

"Death surprises us in the midst of our hopes, sister,"

said a deep, authoritarian voice from behind them. A tall, broad figure appeared at the drape at the opposite end of the caravan. "And every day death takes a step closer to us, as we take a step further away from our birth."

Roanne wiped the tears from her mother's eyes and then from her own before turning to face her elder brother. She took a few moments to calm herself before speaking, noticing how much he had aged during the three cycles since the last festival. He had shed a considerable amount of weight, replacing his body fat almost entirely with muscle. His face had lost its youthful glow, hidden beneath a patchy, dark red beard and moustache. His brown eyes stared hard and unforgiving; the pupils like black pearls, his general air one of calm, confident authority. Then she noticed her father's High Celebrant robes and jewellery, and as the silence between them lingered a slight smile touched his face.

At last she spoke. "What of the nets, Hulneb. Have you investigated?"

"Clean water and a full purse to you also, Roanne," he said, answering her deliberate failure to greet him in the traditional Kaltesh verse of goodwill.

"Well? Have you?"

"Life is for the living, not for the dead. And what nets do you speak of, Roanne? As I understand it, the people of your city catch fish by draining the water from the tanks they were bred in. Why would you need a net?" He took a step forward and she felt the floorboard beneath her shift under his weight. "Could it be your husband has at last discovered he has faster legs than you?"

She stood and walked over to him as two aides appeared from the curtain behind him, standing with their hands upon the pommels of their short-swords. With a casual wave of his hand his personal guards disappeared behind the drape.

"Enough! If your father could see your behaviour now, he'd have you both skinning and gutting Gen'hib-Maun for a season!" shouted Rillian in a croak. She shuffled between them, facing Hulneb and pointing a crooked finger at a heavy golden necklace sitting around his shoulders, constructed from five interlinking chains with hexagonal medallions of Kaltesh symbols. He stood two heads taller than his mother, and respected her by crouching as she spoke.

"Your position demands you will honour your family by listening to your sister. She is still a member of this tribe, and will not be slandered or mocked by you." She spoke with slow deliberation. "I will not hear mention of this during the festival, from *either* of you. You will settle this, now."

Hulneb kissed her on the cheek. "Mother."

Rillian turned without looking at Roanne and pulled a heavy drape aside to shuffle into the next compartment.

Hulneb's gaze fell upon his younger sister. "Guards. Send my water carrier."

He motioned for Roanne to sit, as behind the drape the sound of a door closing could be heard.

She spoke in a whisper, remaining on her feet. "I ask you again. What of the nets, Hulneb? Mother said Mirrimas told the tribe to wait until later in the morning before casting."

He shrugged, aware he had to speak of the conclusions he'd reached an age ago. "No doubt the nets were discarded from the previous season. It's obvious–"

"No doubt? Since when have we discarded the value of a net? It's obvious someone decided to harvest early, despite father's instructions. Either way, someone is responsible for our father's death, of *that* there is no doubt."

Hulneb shook his head. "It was an accident, Roanne, nothing more."

"But Mirrimas was an expert fisherman. Remember he told us how his father taught him to read the tides, taste the salt on the wind, to choose his path with care as he negotiated the rocks of the delta. He taught us both!"

"Mirrimas was an old man, Roanne. An old man whose heart was that of a child."

She took a step closer to him. "Did you examine the nets yourself? Each family weaves with a slight difference. Could you tell which family they belonged to?"

Hulneb sighed, shifting his weight to his left foot. "They were a standard weave. One Mirrimas had perfected for the previous harvest. They were strong and light, woven from the hair of a hundred female Gen'hib-Maun, cured and sealed in fat. Ideal for snaring throd fish and minips, his favourite, *if* you remember?"

"My life in Abeona hasn't stifled memories of my father!"

He nodded absently as the water carrier entered from the opposite side to Rillian's private compartment. She crouched beside Hulneb with a large glass bowl of clear water, yellow and white cactus petals floating on the surface. Hulneb took the bowl and motioned her to leave.

He took a sip and held it out. "Here sister, share water with me."

She resented his tone. It was more a command than a request. "I will not, Hulneb. Not until you fully investigate father's death. Someone is responsible. Our own edicts tell us, *'Liars and murderers are children of the same tribe, and liars ride upon debt's back.'* If someone of the tribe knows the truth, then they owe a debt of honesty to themselves, the tribe, and our family. Mirrimas would not have let such an incident pass without investigation. It's your honour-bound duty to uncover the truth."

"Listen to yourself, Roanne," he said, raising his voice. "You sound like your husband. 'Uncover the truth!' Our father suffered an accident, nothing more. You're creating fantasies to fill your boredom. No one has anything to gain by our father's death."

She glanced at the gold around his shoulders for a moment then walked to Rillian's drape. "Mother, will you spend the duration of the festival in our tower? I've had rooms prepared for you. I'd love you to spend time with Opi; he's grown to be a wonderful boy."

The drape parted, revealing the old woman's smile.

"That I'd like very much, Roanne."

She kissed her mother on the cheek. "I'll meet you when the caravans have settled and the formalities are complete." She turned, pushed past Hulneb, and went out onto the deck to untie her ride.

Hulneb watched his sister from his throne atop the lead caravan. He took several gulps of water then wiped tiny droplets from his wispy beard, tipping the remaining water onto the dry deck planks beside him. "This is for you, sister," he murmured, as the city gates crawled apart and she galloped into the city.

SIX

INSIDE

Exotic aromas greeted their nostrils as they walked through the crowd towards the Square of Remembrance. Visitors from the fringe settlements, along with city traders, were selling their specialities: clothes, footwear, fabrics, furs and skins, crude and inaccurate clay idols of the Trophy. Various sized barrels of aged ale, wine, spirits, and Bella-Pennu water from the northern settlements were stacked and labelled for sale in their various types. A Kaltesh trader fried cured strips of Gen'hib-Maun and Sol steered Opi away from the stall. Cured Farrengrass in all its different colours and varieties hung in large bunches waiting to be sampled, and jewellery of semi-precious stones tinkled together in the breeze and shone in the sunlight. Puppet shows held the attention of small groups of children, while mime artists, musicians and gaming tables of possibility competed for adult trade. Opi stopped as four Obnibian jugglers threw fire sticks high into the air and over to each other, before blowing orange flames from their mouths above the crowd of spectators.

"Opi? I thought you wanted to see inside." remarked Sol.

"Can we stay and watch for a while? There's so much to see!"

"This is just the first stage of the festival, Opi," answered Sol, shaking his head to the performer as one of the jugglers held out a scarred palm for a token of appreciation. He held his son's shoulders as they walked through the crowd. "These are the early arrivals, and the Square will be overcrowded within the next few days. You can join them when you've finished your holiday studies, with your mother and me."

Behind the crowd, Sol's eyes fell once again on the

Trophy. As the people danced and indulged excessively in its name, the giant object stood oblivious above them. Spiritual and moral lessons were for the schools, colleges and religious publications to teach, and as he watched the revellers it was obvious that for many festival attendees those lessons had either been forgotten, or purposely cast aside.

He helped Opi climb into the seat of the velocipede and glanced at the boy as he sat next to him. Opi would have the easiest time over the next two weeks, he decided. Yan had a pile of documents to process and priests to instruct, Roanne had her family to entertain, and he had his own private theoretical research and a speech to complete for the last day of festivities. He smiled and ruffled the boy's blond hair. All Opi had to do was enjoy the celebrations.

After a league, the velocipede stopped. Sol paid the driver, and they made their way through the edge of the crowd to a lift scaffold. There, two Church Deacons stood either side of the heavy metal gates. The Deacons were the militia of the city; it was their sworn duty to police and enforce commandments laid down by the city's governing body, the Twelve Grand Cardinals. Those learned men carefully selected Deacons from the many hundred hopefuls that enrolled into the Church colleges upon completion of their schooling. Scores of these purposeful individuals harboured ambitions high above their capability, and were plucked like unripe fruit early in their careers for training to become Deacons in the hands of the Bishops and their servitors. A Deaconship, although lowly in Church echelons, was nevertheless a highly coveted position, for the perquisites consisted of above average accommodation, respect from the community, and the self-esteem of knowing every aspect of the Holy written law.

Sol bowed slowly then stepped over the small boundary wall, the Deacons dutifully returning his respect.

Opi frowned. He had never seen Deacons dressed like this before. They wore a black tunic instead of the standard orange, and this was crossed with a green and gold sash, held at the shoulder with a large gilt-bronze brooch with the face of a bizarre, horned beast. But their highly decorated robes were not only for show, for beneath their apparel they carried formidable falchion swords and were highly trained in their use. Upon their backs, hidden by the long drop of their capes, sat small shields decorated with coloured cut diamonds, to reflect the sun and dazzle opponents. Sheathed in black ganapti hide round their waists was a collection of twelve various-sized throwing daggers, each carrying the crest of a Grand Cardinal upon the pommel. Red and silver helmets of tempered steel enclosed their heads, the faceplate remaining open at all times. These regalia were assigned exclusively to the Deacons of the Trophy, an order under the direct supervision of the Senior Grand Cardinal. They had sworn a solemn oath to lay down their lives protecting the Trophy from the people, and indeed, the people from the Trophy, if need be.

Sol placed a hand on Opi's shoulder as he spoke. "Cardinal Sol Timmerman and my assistant. We have a pass document from Archbishop Yan Arramosa." He tapped Opi on the shoulder.

The boy held out the envelope sheepishly. The taller of the two Deacons took it, produced a dagger from beneath his sash and slit the envelope open. He removed a black leather glove and tucked it under his belt, then pulled the document from the envelope to carefully check every detail.

"Everything is in order, Your Holiness. Please, step this way." The Deacon turned on his heels, nodding to his colleague who took a key from beneath his sash. He unlocked the gate and stood to one side as Sol and Opi followed the Deacon inside a small cage. The Deacon secured the gate and nodded to his colleague who pulled a lever set into the stone floor. Below the flagstones the lift gear system slowly lowered a paddled wheel into one of the many waterways coursing beneath the Square of Remembrance, causing the lift to jolt sharply upwards.

Opi held his father's cloak tightly as this sensation sent a shiver though him, and Sol placed his hands on the boy's shoulders to steady him as they sped upwards. The ground fell away quickly, revealing the Square and the mass of people diminishing beneath them. Beyond, the streets reached out to the walled horizon, like water trickling across a flagstone. The surface of the Trophy loomed closer, and Opi feared the lift would strike the object, but its curved surface receded as they traversed its centre and the lift jolted to a halt. The Deacon produced his own key, unlocked the gate and pushed it open, its hinges giving a high-pitched metal screech.

From here, level with the entrance, ten men wide and three men high, the object displayed a uniformity of design, and its true vastness was at once apparent to the boy as he gazed along its length, shielding his eyes from the glare. He tried to define it, to understand its sudden familiarity.

"Come on, son. This way."

Opi stumbled across the small gap onto the gantry, short of breath, and Sol turned to him. "Are you alright?"

As the gantry creaked in the silence, Opi looked up at his father, nodding apprehensively as he felt the slight sway of the framework beneath his feet. Everything seemed so very different to him from up here. The surrounding buildings lost their towering magnificence, and were now just a distant blur. Freed from the aromas of the city, the dry air caught in his throat as the wind swam through his long blond hair like invisible fingers, as if to hinder his sight. He looked down, pushing his hair from his eyes. The gantry floor was constructed of sun-bleached planks over a thin metal frame, knotholes in the tired timbers here and there revealing the great distance to the ground below.

"It's okay, son. Just keep walking straight ahead. We're quite safe."

They continued forward, the sharp curves of *Oosah*'s hull sweeping above and below, side-to-side, until it filled their field of vision.

Sol walked proudly up to the entrance, where the darkness of the interior caused Opi to hesitate, dragging on his father's robes. Sol turned to his son with concern. Many thousands before him, eager to see the interior, had ventured just this far, then fled to cower by the lift gate, shouting for the Deacons to take them back to the comfort of the ground below. However, as Sol watched, Opi's curiosity conquered his fear and his expression changed.

For a few moments the Deacon watched them. Sol thanked him, showing his own lift key, at which the Deacon returned to his guard duty below.

Opi noticed that up close, the surface of the object was covered by myriad markings. Symbols from its culture, other unknown features and contours Sol prayed he would one day understand.

"Father! It's beautiful!" exclaimed the young boy. He reached out between the gantry railings to touch the surface. He drew his hand back rapidly. "Father, look!" he shouted.

"What's wrong?"

"The Trophy! It's alive, father! I was reaching out and it... it touched me!"

Sol smiled. "It is not alive, Opi. Watch." He held a hand out over the gantry an arm's length from the surface. "Now, as I bring my hand quickly towards *Oosah*..." As he did so, the mirror image of his hand, reflected in the deep, multi-coloured sheen, suddenly reached out in a solid mass, meeting his hand halfway with a loud slap of the two palms. He drew his hand back from the impact and the extended hand from the Trophy instantly receded into the surface, vanishing as if it had never been there.

Opi stared wide-eyed between it and his father.

"Two hundred and eighteen cycles ago, a priest named Sur Orison theorised this as a defensive attribute. He concluded *Oosah* is coated with a substance that reflects an image like still water in a pool. However, the surface not only reflects the image, but also has the ability to push outwards with an exact contoured replica of any object that comes too close to it."

"Why?" asked Opi, reaching out to the surface once more.

Sol crouched down, pulled up his sleeves and extended his two forefingers horizontally so they pointed toward each other. "Imagine. Any object approaching at great speed, a projectile like an arrow or a spear," he brought the tips of his fingers together, "would be met with equal mass and force, cancelling any offensive assault."

Opi withdrew his hand and copied his father, much to Sol's delight.

"During the rainy season, the surface ripples as it sends thousands upon thousands of tiny spikes to meet the downpour. It's quite a sight."

"What happens to the water?"

"Some of it evaporates, the remainder trickles down the surface to be collected as holy water for the sick to bathe in." Sol stood. "Now listen very carefully, Opi. Please, do *everything* I tell you, and do *not*, under any circumstances, touch *anything* once we're inside, unless I say so. Do you understand?"

Opi nodded nervously.

"Walk by my side then," said Sol, smiling down at him.

Roanne watched the Kaltesh vehicles assembling and their inhabitants disembarking in the caravanserai. Rillian appeared from the crowd, flanked by four fully-armed Kaltesh warriors, with two handmaidens bringing up the rear with her belongings. "Our estate is not far, mother," said Roanne, taking her by the arm.

"Estate? Surely you share an accommodation tower near the ravine?"

"Sol's a Grade One Theorist now. We've moved up from the Ravine Quarter. We now have our own land, livestock, servants and gardens. There's plenty of room for you and your handmaidens to stay with us during the festival – Tulteth and Hulneb also, if they would like."

They began to walk as Rillian replied. "I see, but I still cannot understand why you haven't grown tired of waking in the same place every morning."

Roanne squeezed her mother's hand gently. "I do from time to time, but I'm happy knowing Sol and Opi are nearby." As Roanne led the group away, a preliminary welcoming party of Bishops accompanied by a squad of Deacons, met Hulneb and the tribe elders.

Opi shuffled forward to bring him within three short paces of his father.

"Now, son. This is the first seal, opened nearly two thousand cycles ago by the first successful Grand Cardinal, Ksa Ellendale. He theorised the designs surrounding this area proved it was an entrance, and for thirty-seven cycles he worked on it until it opened."

"It's beautiful! So smooth inside!"

"Come on then, follow me." Sol walked across the threshold onto the floor of the corridor. The wedge-shaped entrance was brighter than outside, the sunlight reflecting from its white interior walls. The entranceway had remained open for hundreds of cycles, nothing more than a gaping segment one ten-thousandth of the Trophy's overall area. He took a few paces into shadow, enjoying the coolness of the metal beneath his feet. Gradually, flickering light from above filled the corridor ahead, illuminating the enclosed area and the miniature dunes of sand where the floor and walls met. Sol turned to see his son still standing in the comforting warmth of the sun. "Opi, please. There's nothing to be afraid of. You wanted to see inside, remember?"

"I... I don't want to. I've seen enough. Can we go home now please?" He said, staring at the panels above Sol's head.

Sol looked up for a moment and chuckled. "Don't worry, there's nothing to be afraid of. Somehow the corridor knows I'm here and sends light from the ceiling to illuminate the way."

Opi took three steps closer, stopping at the threshold. His head filled with questions, unable to give any one priority or voice as he looked up at the glowing panels set flush into the ceiling. He looked to his father, mouth partially open, then suddenly ran to Sol with outstretched arms.

Sol crouched to meet him. "Well done. For many cycles after the first seal was opened, these lights were considered the work of evil spirits, ghosts of the dead who once travelled inside. We now know it is just a mechanism. Theoretically, the light is triggered by my body weight, detected by the floor beneath my feet, but we do not know how the light is channelled. Mirrors positioned upon the outside top surface could direct it, in much the same way our water and cool air is channelled through the city from the ravine. Or perhaps it is stored somewhere deep inside, to be recalled when needed, like water from a well."

Opi nodded slowly as he studied the corridor walls. "What is it made of?"

Sol strode to the wall on his right. "We do not know, entirely. The floor is a metal of some type, but the walls and ceiling are soft and lightweight, and can be cut easily with a sharp blade." He turned. "Although that practice was deemed sacrilegious shortly after the first seal was opened. Small samples taken by Ksa Ellendale are exhibited in the Church college museum, at the Ellendale shrine."

Opi turned from the wall. "Thank you, father, for bringing me here. Perhaps one day we could visit the museum?" He turned to leave.

"So you want to go home now, Opi?"

The boy stopped and Sol smiled broadly at him. "This is just a connecting corridor. I know you'll like what's beyond this next seal."

"You mean there's more?"

Sol held out his hand. "Much more."

"Your estate is truly wondrous, Roanne," remarked Rillian, as she looked out from the balcony across the city. "And Abeona, spires and towers, abundant as blades of grass; such a view of the city I've never seen."

Roanne joined her. "There seems to be a new tower built every season. Your rooms are ready, mother. I hope you'll find the evening temperature..." she stopped in mid-sentence, noticing a plume of black smoke curling in the distance. "I won't be a moment." Returning with her telescope, she focused it into the city. "I thought so," she said with a tremble to her voice, "There's a fire coming from the Square of Remembrance – near the Trophy."

"An over-zealous baker? Perhaps too much fat to fry the Gen'hib-Maun?" offered Rillian, squinting and shielding her eyes.

"No, the vendors' stalls are not allowed anywhere near the Trophy – hallowed ground, mother."

The old woman tutted. "Can I see?"

Roanne lowered the height of the instrument and Rillian looked out over the city, watching the smoke for a while. Then she directed the instrument away from the Square and her gaze fell upon an area of Gal Bapsi Park, with its elevated grassy terraces and clumps of trees where children ran and played. "There are a few things concerning your father I must tell you, Roanne, but before I do, you must promise to mention none of what I say to your husband, not yet."

Roanne kept her eyes on the smoke, her hands clasping her forearms at her waist. "Things? What things?"

The old woman watched as several children fought a

make-believe battle across a terrace, their wooden swords thrusting, cutting and parrying, juvenile mimics of pain, glory and death against invisible enemies.

"Things that could give him cause to fight for his beliefs. Sol, Hulneb, both good men, passionate for their religions, very much alike in that respect. Different sides of the same token, if you like?"

The children stood, brushing grass from their clothes, then ran off up a hill towards a statue and the shade it afforded, bowing to the forlorn stone figure as though it were their leader.

"What I am prepared to tell you could lead to a great conflict between our people. The Kaltesh cannot afford that."

'Conflict?' thought Roanne, her stomach churning.

"We're not ready, daughter," said the old woman, filling the silence between them.

"Ready?"

"We are unprepared, is perhaps a better word, An Abeonian phrase that has no Kaltesh equivalent."

"Ready for what?"

"Victory of course – divine retribution, avenging the Abeonian capture of *Agasanduku*, and the murder of your ancestor, Ritma."

"Mother, please, you *still* support such a fantasy, that the Kaltesh could conquer this city?"

"It is our right. Hulneb is weak, choosing to delegate rather than take a firm grip of the tribe. I've told him a hundred times, if he continues refusing a wife, then at least father as many children as he can with the company he keeps. They would be strong – future warriors. All men should do so, and we will eventually reach a time of readiness. But, if your husband were to ascend and take up residence in that citadel of fools, certainly after acting upon the information I have, it could lead to war."

Roanne realised instantly a tip in the balance, furthering proof in Abeonian belief would lead to conflict. "I understand," she said quietly.

The children held hands and ran around the statue of Grand Cardinal Gal Bapsi, her once-proud stance and defiant expression eroded into a stooping posture of disapproval. The children picked up their swords, running off to begin another conquest.

Rillian stood back from the telescope. "I am an old woman, Roanne. I have seen so much of this world. I have seen as many good things as bad. My beliefs have been questioned on many occasions, but it has only been my faith in those beliefs that has held them solidly in my heart. Now I am saying I am questioning my faith, to the point that I don't know what to believe. Mirrimas caused this just before he died, after his return from Mount Goraknath." She turned, faced her daughter and sighed. "Roanne, I don't believe either Sol or Hulneb has the self-control to keep to themselves the information I possess. They would both twist it to bolster their religions, to give them another tool to argue with – especially Sol. He is too eager to discover a truth that could so easily ruin him, and always has to take an argument that much further, never accepting anything on face value. Mirrimas used to say, *'He hunts during the night when his eyes cannot see,'* and told me he was concerned Sol's obsessions could lead to his downfall, and when he falls, both you and Opi must fall with him. I have no desire to see this. As for Hulneb, as we both know well, he has spent most of his life trying to prove himself. Now, he has the opportunity."

Roanne took a few paces forward and leant on the stone coping of the balcony. There, a small-leafed ivy had crawled up the outside wall and over the edge. She began to prune the new shoots with her fingers. "I cannot promise not to tell Sol, mother. If the information you have leads to the truth of *Oosah*, then it is my duty to inform him, as the wife of a Cardinal."

Rillian glared at her daughter. "What about your duty to the people of this city, and for that matter, the Kaltesh, Opi,

Tulteth, all of the children, be they Kaltesh or Abeonian? Do you not hold their lives in higher regard than the glory of your husband's truth?"

"Mother, the Holy Church needs any information concerning *Oosah*, however trivial or private. If the people that constructed it were to return and attempt to conquer us once more, Abeona would need to defend everyone, including the Kaltesh. The answers can only lie within. This city and its inhabitants are everyone's first line of defence."

Rillian detected the superior note in Roanne's voice and moved to her side.

"So, Sol's philosophy has infected you after all. The cycles spent in this city with these people have swayed your beliefs in favour of theirs, even to the point of you calling *Agasanduku Oosah*."

Roanne shook her head. "No, that's not true. I'm voicing a possibility, simply giving you my reasons for passing on the information you have. My beliefs are my own. If anything I'm the thin edge around the coin Sol and Hulneb are the faces of, in between and joined to both by the thinnest rim. I'm still part of the whole, but a separate part unto myself. Perhaps this possible conflict between Abeonian and Kaltesh is exactly what the invaders have planned. To either emerge and destroy the victorious, or side with the weaker against the stronger, then turn upon them once they are no more."

Rillian turned and nodded to her daughter. "Perhaps. That is why we must be ready." She shuffled into the cool shade of the family room to make herself comfortable. After a few moments, Roanne abandoned her pruning and joined her.

"For now I will choose to remain silent. You have to think upon this. Ask yourself if you can trust your husband to take the correct course of action. But," said Rillian, taking an object from a pouch inside one of her bags, "Mirrimas made this for you. He told me it was to be your wedding anniversary gift."

She held in her palm a long chain of beaded silver. The intricate workmanship Roanne recognised instantly as Kaltesh. The old woman slowly pulled the chain from her palm with her thumb and index finger, to reveal a small object dangling from it by a single hoop of silver. Roanne could see the pendant was a metal of some kind; part of it fused to a small piece of black rock that had been ground down and polished smooth. The object itself, partly embedded in the rock, was cold, elaborate in its design, reflecting the sunlight in myriad colours, and unlike any Kaltesh jewellery she had seen. The old woman placed it around Roanne's neck. Its coolness soothed the warmth in her chest, relieving the tension in her shoulders caused by their conversation. She found herself relaxing as she examined it, turning the pendant over in the palm of her hand to wonder at its complex detail.

"You remember how your father liked to tinker with his toys. Most of them still adorn our private chambers aboard the royal caravan, and, I imagine, his concealed cave in the Goraknath range. He always said working on such objects helped him think. I suspect he intended the pendant to be for one of your fine city artists to paint the likenesses of Opi and Sol on either side, to then be encased in glass."

"It's beautiful. Thank you," said Roanne, finally placing it beneath her tunic.

Rillian rearranged her cushions as Roanne poured two goblets of water and handed one to her mother. She took a sip and waited for Rillian to do the same, then said. "I've arranged to meet Sol and Opi in the Square of Remembrance at the tenth measure. Would you join me? There is just time for a prayer for father before we should leave."

"Yes. Mirrimas would have liked that. I trust you can still ride, Roanne?"

"Of course," she said, placing the goblet on the table.

"Then we'll take two of my animals after I lead the prayer and you complete it."

Sol stood at the end of the corridor. There, many tiny different shapes and shades of bare metal were inlaid against the wall. He pressed a combination of symbols and a low hum like the breath of a sleeping ganapti slowly filled the corridor.

Opi took a few steps back, hiding behind his father's cloak as the wall ahead slid up into the ceiling. The tiny dunes eroded as the wind blew them into the darkness and Sol walked ahead, greeted by a diffused light that came from white panels around the walls. Opi stumbled forward to join him, looking up at the room extending high above his head. He counted six seals, a pair on each of the three walls, far above the reach of his father. Beneath these, each wall held an alcove nearly the entire width of the wall.

"Father," said Opi pointing to the seals, "could the invaders fly?"

"We don't know, Opi," said Sol, glancing upward. "It has been theorised this is a garrison, and there are ladders behind these seals. Perhaps the invaders climbed down to assemble in this room before launching their attacks. The Church built scaffolding up to the seals and studied each one for eight hundred cycles, but there is not a control surface alongside any of them, like that on the exterior. Come on, this should interest you." He walked to the alcove on the far wall. "Three alcoves. The two either side reveal corridors leading up to unopened seals. The Church currently has seven Cardinals working on each. This seal, however, was unlocked just twelve cycles after the first, by Grand Cardinal Jan Marrandant."

As before, Sol pressed the raised emblems to the side of the seal and it slid apart. Beyond, a corridor continued for five hundred paces and Opi hurried along with his father.

"Are all these seals unopened?" asked the boy, pointing

to the alcoves set every ten paces into either side of the corridor.

"I'm afraid so. Any one of them could hold a thousand questions or a thousand answers. There's just so much work."

Finally they reached the end of the corridor.

"Now Opi, how do you think this seal is opened?"

"As before, a combination of those emblems?" enthused the boy, pointing.

"Correct. Would you like to try?"

Opi grinned and stood on tiptoe, stabbing at the emblems with an enthusiastic finger. Nothing happened. He turned to Sol and scowled.

"Patience. Try again."

He did so, then a third time with no response. "Father, please open it!"

Sol walked forward to stand directly in front of the seal. He pressed a combination of emblems and a slender tray appeared from beneath. Pulling back his sleeves he entered a second combination, the symbols illuminating his fingers with a yellow glow as they were depressed. The seal immediately slid upward into its frame.

As they entered, a red globe positioned high above them slowly cast light, filling a huge, spherical auditorium. They stood on a walkway that hugged the wall around the circumference, a low railing in front of them.

"Now, this could be dangerous, Opi. Stay close to me and remember, don't touch anything."

The young boy stared in awe. Silently a sphere appeared in front of them, revolving slowly on its axis. Wispy, off-white clouds were drawn across part of its yellow and green surface, hanging above mountains and waterways, meandering across a giant, white-poled continent, as other, smaller land masses appeared on the surface.

"The eye of Tal Salandor. Now. Watch, Opi," said Sol, placing his hands on the boy's shoulders.

Gradually, a shape emerged from the cloud cover upon

the sphere and revolved into view. The tiny object sat alongside a thin, winding line, reaching down from the white northern pole.

Sol crouched and pointed. "Do you see that line, leading to that rectangular area sitting at its right-hand side?"

"Yes," answered the boy quietly.

"Well, that line is the great river, Breede, and the rectangle is Abeona, our city. This entire sphere is our world, and this is the view Tal Salandor has from the celestial pathway, as he leads the departed of this life to the Garden of Contentment."

"But how does it work, father?"

He looked down at his son, squeezing his shoulders for reassurance. "We are seeing through Tal Salandor's eyes," he said quietly, "as he keeps watch over us."

As the minuscule image of the city drew level with them, Sol followed, keeping pace with it and taking Opi by the hand. "This way. As you can see, there are alcoves with seals all around this room. Exactly one hundred seals, and only twelve have been opened, one by each of the Grand Cardinals' families. They all lead to corridors with seals at their end, and I opened two of those seals a few Cycles ago."

The boy spoke quickly, "What did you find?"

"Empty rooms, each with another, smaller seal set into their corners. Those are my current assignments."

As they approached the first open seal, Opi noticed a huddled shape in an alcove ahead of them. He tightened his grip on his father's hand. "What's that, over there?" he asked, pointing.

"It's okay, it's only a Gen'hib-Maun skeleton. We found several in this chamber and one halfway back down the corridor. It has been theorised and subsequently concluded the invaders kept them as pets, just as we do. I theorise they were trapped as the seals were closed and locked during the final battle. They must have starved to death."

Opi let go of his father's hand and crouched to take a closer look at the bones. "Poor thing. I wonder what you were called?"

"Cardinal Timmerman!" a voice shouted from behind them. They turned to see the Deacon who had left them on the platform outside running towards them. He slid to a halt on the smooth floor and caught his breath while composing himself.

"Please, Cardinal, you must come outside, now. It's the..."

"Slow down. What's wrong?"

"Sir, it's better if you just come with me," the guard's pleading eyes quivered nervously as they darted towards Opi. He looked back to Sol and quickly shook his head. "The boy, sir, I wouldn't..."

Sol crouched down and held his son by the shoulders. "Opi, sit down and wait here for me, and remember, don't touch anything. I'll be back in a short while. Okay?"

The boy bit his lip, looking up to his father. As their eyes met he nodded slowly, speaking quietly, "Yes, okay, dad."

Sol kissed him on the forehead, and Opi watched his father run off. He looked down at the skeleton and sat beside it, cross-legged, sighing. "Well, I suppose it's just you and me for a while."

SEVEN

OUTSIDE

They ran along the gantry, their cloaks billowing behind them, and Sol heard the commotion from below over the clattering of the gantry boards. Glancing down to the Square, a plume of black smoke rose leisurely into the air. A sweet aroma filled his nostrils, an aroma he had never experienced in all his thirty-three cycles in the city. They entered the lift, the Deacon slamming the gates, shouting to his colleague below, "We're in, Jak! Now!" Slowly the lift descended. A few feet from the ground, Sol kicked the unlocked gate open, jumping down, the Deacon following close behind.

The people were running blindly around them. Women's faces were streaked with tears as they carried their children away, their delicate features blank with horror, scarred for life by a dreadful image. Several men scrambling past mumbled apologies to Sol and the Deacon as they fought their way to the cause of the commotion. A circle of morbid onlookers eight men deep had gathered around the scene. Sol pushed through to the front where the silent, awestruck faces opposite remained fixed, illuminated by licking flames as the crackling and popping of the fire filled their ears.

There, kneeling in an attitude of prayer, was Yan Arramosa, wreathed in flames. A flaming torch lay at his side, along with an empty jug of thick torch grease.

The sight stopped Sol in his tracks as he recognised the crest upon the old man's blue and gold robes, confirming what he had been told by the Deacon during their descent. He instinctively ran to the burning body, but the flames beat him back, singeing his hair and cloak. He hastily looked around, noticing several barrels of Bella-Pennu water stacked neatly behind the circle of onlookers.

"Quickly, the water behind you!" he shouted to the crowd, but his voice was lost to them. He pushed through them and pulled a barrel toward the body, with help from the Deacon. They came as close to the Archbishop as the heat would allow, Sol fumbling for his ceremonial scimitar sheathed upon his back. Smashing open the lid with the pommel, he dropped the sword with a clatter. "Deacon, help me!" Together they lifted the cumbersome barrel above their heads, dousing the burning body. The flesh hissed and crackled, spitting steam and black droplets, but strangely the body remained still. Dropping the empty barrel to the ground, both men faced the silent figure, waiting for the scented steam spiralling over their heads to clear. At once a breeze crossed the Square and removed the grey shroud. The flesh had partly melted away from the face. The lips, stretched in a curve around the mouth had split here and there, revealing the white teeth down to the roots, warping the dead Archbishop's expression into a sickening, elongated smile. His noseless, earless, boiled red and bone-white head tilted up towards the Trophy, staring with empty crimson sockets, tendons in the neck helping to support the skull's weight upon the thin, exposed vertebrae. Sol's legs gave way beneath him and he knelt and wept uncontrollably, and through the tears mouthed a silent prayer for his friend.

The crowd dispersed as four Deacons cleared a path for a highly decorated, canopied velocipede, drawn by two junior priests. Upon it rode Grand Cardinal Ugo Irrianna. The old man sat with his head slightly raised, his long white curly hair falling around his shoulders. His hands, smooth and well-manicured for a man of his age, rested upon his walking cane made of bone and branch, inlaid with thin intertwining spirals of gold and lapis lazuli.

The vehicle stopped and two Deacons helped the Grand Cardinal down.

"Cardinal Timmerman! What has happened here?" he exclaimed.

Sol was busy carving blessings into the air with both hands.

"Cardinal!" shouted Irrianna.

Sol's head turned. "Grand Cardinal," he said, straining to maintain a level timbre to his voice.

"Your Holiness. Archbishop Arramosa," he said, gesturing to the blackened mass before him. "He – he has taken his own life. He..."

The Grand Cardinal turned his head away from the horror, noticing Sol perform another blessing. He limped over and waved his cane in front of Sol's gestures, erasing their meanings from the air, then rapped Sol's knuckles with the cane, glaring. "What are you doing, Cardinal?" he snapped. "Think!" He pushed the words through his clenched teeth, whilst managing to maintain a half-smile for the crowd.

Sol opened his mouth to explain, but the old man cut him off, "You cannot be seen blessing a man who has taken his own life. If all paths to death led to the Garden of Contentment, then we'd have hundreds of misinformed peasants leaping off the city walls by nightfall, shouting 'My eternal soul is saved! Cardinal Timmerman will bless me!'" He turned to his junior priests who simply looked Sol up and down with disdain. His face was streaked with blackened tears, his hair brittle and curling where it had been singed, his robes splattered with patches of black water, his hose damp and stained from the knees all the way down to his sandals, his cloak smouldering at the edges.

The Grand Cardinal continued loudly, speaking for the priests and the crowd, but keeping his eyes firmly fixed on Sol. "I trust it was his friendship for the Archbishop that momentarily caused him to forget that suicide is a crime against life." The priests nodded once in unison, their faces emotionless, and the crowd responded with a mixture of muttered agreements and condemnations.

"Is that correct, Cardinal?"

"Yes, Your Holiness," Sol whispered.

"Answer for the crowd, Cardinal," said Irrianna quietly, leaning impatiently on his cane, "not me."

"Yes, Grand Cardinal," said Sol, struggling to return the usual calmness to his voice, "Suicide is a crime against life."

Irrianna hobbled closer. "If the Kaltesh catch word of this, they'll turn our celebrations into a mockery of all we believe," he said behind a smile. "Speak to no one of this." He turned slowly. "He was a good man," he continued, raising his voice and slowly lifting his head to direct his words to the onlookers. "A good man who, sadly, will not pass over to the Garden of Contentment, as will all of you believers here." He waved his cane casually around the circle of onlookers, while motioning his Deacons to attend him. "Remove your cloaks and cover this. Take it to the Holy Citadel; I'll be along soon." He faced the crowd as the Deacons took the body away, distracting the curious latecomers who chanced a peek beneath the robes with a brief prayer chant. "We will all pray for the forgiveness of his soul," he ordered. Instantly the people dropped to their knees. Once he was satisfied the crowd had settled he turned to Sol. "Finish this prayer for me, Cardinal, I have urgent matters to attend to."

Sol nodded once. "Your Holiness." He continued the prayer as the old man climbed aboard his velocipede, disappearing into the crowd with his entourage.

Everything had happened so quickly, realised Sol. Only now, as the true impact of what had happened sunk in, did grief knot his stomach and send a quiver through his voice. He knew he hadn't been given time to ask a single question, wasn't even allowed to explain his actions, and this angered him greatly. He replayed the events in his head as he blessed the people. Irrianna had appeared quickly on the scene. Grand Cardinals hardly ever left their chambers, and, on such occasions, Bishops announced their excursions well in advance through the religious publications, allowing the people to pay their respects along his route. In addition, they usually travelled in pairs. He hurried the litany along and slowly the people dispersed. Several approached and thanked him as he stood and bowed vacantly, mumbling his thanks. Gradually the Square returned to normal as if nothing had happened.

"Cardinal? Cardinal Timmerman?" The Deacon spoke softly and Sol looked up at the burly guard.

"Cardinal, your son. He is still inside *Oosah*. Shall I fetch him for you?"

Sol struggled to regain his thoughts. "No. No, thank you," he replied, and began to walk to the lift.

The Deacon bent down then hurried after him. "Cardinal, your scimitar."

Sol took the weapon vacantly, frowning once more at what he had seen. "Thank you. Oh, one task, Deacon. My wife, Roanne, should be at the Holy entrance soon. Please look out for her and tell her to wait for me there. We will be along shortly."

"By all means, Cardinal. One question though."

"Speak."

"What happened, why did the Archbishop... " he fell silent, unable to form the words.

Sol shook his head, unable to speak.

"The Grand Cardinal, what—"

"You said one question. There will be an official announcement from the Twelve, certainly. I believe all our questions will be answered then, don't you?"

The Deacon bowed and turned to leave.

"Deacon."

"Yes, Cardinal."

"Your name?"

"Sef, Sef Windmarsh."

"Thank you for your assistance today, Sef Windmarsh" said Sol, sheathing his scimitar. "I will remember your diligence."

The Deacon nodded his thanks and hurried away.

Rillian tied her ganapti to a holding post as Roanne patted its neck.

"If you feel the walk may be too much, mother, I can hire a velocipede to take us to the Trophy?"

Rillian squinted over the crowds up at the object lying distant. "It always seems closer than it really is. Distances are deceiving in your city. Hire your velocipede."

Roanne took a few paces forward when a thin figure stopped in front of her. "Wheels to take the strain and ease the pain from your tired limbs? Speed and comfort to anywhere, for anyone. An agreed price will grant your destination." The velocipede's driver grinned and rested his forearms against the rickshaw's yokes.

"How much to the Trophy, driver?"

"Who for?"

"My mother and myself," said Roanne, as Rillian joined her.

He looked between them, estimating their combined weight, then noticed Roanne's crest and her mother's Kaltesh apparel. "Fifteen tokens for you and your mother."

"Fifteen! I'd rather walk," answered Roanne angrily.

"But you're the wife of a Cardinal," said the man with a toothy grin, "and your mother a rich Kaltesh trader, unless you've stolen those robes and crest."

"Eight is a fair price for the distance," answered Roanne, ignoring the insult.

"Twelve is a fair price for the wife of a Cardinal, or a thief. Every driver in the city will tell you that."

Rillian squeezed her daughter's arm and nodded to her.

"Then be sure the ride is smooth and swift," said Roanne, helping her mother into the vehicle.

As the driver hauled up the wooden yokes and made his way into the crowd, Roanne shook her head. "The more Sol earns, the more we seem to be worth to the people. Although he ignores the value of tokens, I can't."

"One of the disadvantages of your position, Ro," said Rillian, lowering her veil over her face. "But surely Sol is right to ignore the value of tokens. After all, he is working toward the truth of enlightenment, and not for payment earned from deception?"

Roanne ignored her mother's sarcasm. "Sol works too hard. The Kaltesh way is different, mother. Wealth doesn't have so much importance to the people of this city; they have everything they need."

"Tell that to the driver of this velocipede. He recognises an opportunity to earn over and above a fair price when he sees it. Perhaps your people are changing their ways. There is a price for everything, and the driver is quite right to ask for more, knowing you can afford it." The old woman tilted her head ever so slightly towards her daughter. "You must have noticed the price of food increases with every festival we attend. Even as the price of the food the Kaltesh eat has remained the same for as long as I can remember – simply the energy expended during the hunt and its preparation."

"Differing ways, mother."

The velocipede skilfully negotiated the crowded maze of stalls, heading towards the Trophy. After a short distance the driver stopped abruptly, jolting the couple forward in their seats.

"Driver! What are you doing?" shouted Roanne, "Mother, are you alright?" she asked, holding Rillian's shoulders.

"It caught my breath, nothing more," wheezed the old woman, removing her veil and breathing deeply.

The driver reversed the vehicle between two stalls as Rillian spoke. "A funeral procession approaches," she lifted her head. "I can smell death on the air."

"Nonsense. Abeonian treatment of the dead is different, mother, you know that."

As the driver halted he turned to face them. "Look, a Grand Cardinal. Now that's something you don't see every day." They watched as Irrianna's cavalcade went slowly by. The two Deacons carrying the body of Yan Arramosa marched at the rear, Irrianna waving blessings to the people as he passed.

"There!" said Rillian, pointing, "A procession for the dead, the soul returned to the winds by fire."

Roanne remembered the plume of black smoke she had seen through her telescope. "Driver! Hurry on," she urged. "If you run all the way you can have your fifteen tokens." He nodded and hastily pulled the rickshaw into the lane left by the cavalcade.

"You see, Roanne? You are beginning to realise the value of Sol's position."

But Roanne was looking behind her, wondering what was hidden beneath the capes.

They had not travelled much further when the velocipede stopped once more.

"Roanne Timmerman?"

She turned quickly as the vehicle halted, to see a Deacon blocking their path.

"Yes, what is it, Deacon?"

Deacon Windmarsh bowed. "Your husband informed me you have arranged to meet him at the Holy entrance. He wishes you to know he has been delayed and requests that you await him there," he said, breathlessly.

"My son and husband, are they alright?"

"They are. Please, allow me to escort you to the Holy entrance," he said, taking hold of the driver by the arm.

Roanne jumped down from her seat. "What's going on?" she asked, pointing. "Why was there an unannounced Grand Cardinal alone in the Square, and what were those Deacons hiding beneath their cloaks?"

Windmarsh was unsure of her authority over him. He understood instructions from a Cardinal had to be followed to the letter, but a Cardinal's wife? He glanced over his shoulder, stalling for time. "Perhaps it would be better if your husband explained the incident. I'm not sure what happened."

Rillian lost her patience, "Oh, please! Why not simply tell us what you saw? Surely that's the simplest course of action?"

He looked over the two women's heads, avoiding their eyes. "I don't know what I saw. I mean... I think, it was so – Archbishop Arramosa... he was on fire, we tried to help – but he..."

Roanne seized the Deacon by the arm. "Yan Arramosa?"

He nodded, and as he looked down at her she understood.

"I'll take it from here." She glanced behind the Deacon and saw her husband. As he approached, his eyes seemed to look straight through her, his expression blank and free of any discernible emotion. She noticed his usual, purposeful stride had slowed to a helpless shuffle, and as his eyes focused upon hers, his expression slowly changed, the muscles in his face twitching, as if he were reluctant to publicly express his emotions.

He brushed past Deacon Windmarsh, and as Sol's perception of his wife dawned upon him, he could see a burden of loss in her eyes. He tried to push his pain aside to concentrate on hers, but it had built up with such ferocity that, as their bodies touched in an embrace, he released it, sending ripples of pain to show itself in a flood of tears as they held each other tightly.

"I know, the Deacon just told me. Poor Yan," she said, caressing his cheeks. "What happened?"

His mouth quivered but he could not speak.

The old woman joined them and he noticed her as she placed a hand on his shoulder.

"Rillian?" he mumbled, glancing between them both.

Roanne bowed her head and nestled into his chest. "Mirrimas is dead, Sol. Hulneb is High Celebrant now."

"Where's this fine young man I've heard so much about?" asked Rillian, holding Sol's forearms.

Sol gulped back his tears and Roanne felt him steady

himself against her, his grip tightening on her back as he struggled to put the events of the day in order. At last he spoke in a high-pitched tone Roanne had never heard from him before.

"The Trophy . . . our son has been claimed by *Oosah*. I left him in the auditorium of the one hundred seals, but when I returned for him, he'd gone."

EIGHT

DECISIONS

"Gone? What do you mean, *gone*? He *must* be in there somewhere!" Roanne shook her head and glanced over to her mother, then back to him. "You've made a mistake, Sol." She headed off towards the Trophy but Sol seized her arm, whisking her around to face him, holding her by the shoulders.

"There's no mistake. I went back inside, shouted his name, searched every area and pounded on the seal where I'd left him, until my fists were numb. He's not in there, Roanne. I checked with the lift Deacon – he didn't come down on his own. Opi is gone, as I said. He has been summoned – carried off to the Garden of Contentment by Tal Salandor."

She brushed his grip aside. "You took him inside? You never mentioned you were taking him inside – I would *never* have let him go with you if I'd known that! Was that your intention all along? Is that why you didn't tell me?" She glared at him as he held her again. With a sharp tug she broke free of his grasp and ran through the crowd toward the Trophy, tears clouding her vision.

"ROANNE!" He shouted, running after her. But her slight frame and agility left him negotiating a wake of irritated individuals, bowing apologies after swearing at her.

Finally, he caught up with her at the lift gates. The lone Deacon there had drawn his sword and stood poised to strike upon seeing this agitated, tearful individual, who appeared like many others he'd seen before, determined to gain access to *Oosah*.

"DEACON! Sheathe your sword!"

The guard looked up and relaxed upon seeing Sol. In a flourish, the Deacon's sword disappeared beneath his robes and he stepped back one pace, keeping his eyes firmly fixed on Roanne.

Sol slid to a halt as her knees gave way, kneeling in front of her, holding her tear-streaked cheek next to his. "Opi begged me to take him inside. I made a mistake. It's no use, Roanne. He's gone."

Her body shook with grief as he held her shoulders, trying to help her to her feet. But she was a dead weight and screamed up at him as their eyes met.

"You fool! He's your only son and all you can do is spout your religion!" She brought up her clenched fists and pounded his chest. "We must get back inside and help him! He's only a little boy." Her voiced trailed off and she buried her head in his chest as his eyes denied her. "Only a little boy."

They returned to Rillian, then took a velocipede back to the ganapti holding posts, all three remaining silent with their own private thoughts.

Sol paid the driver and they mounted their rides, heading back along the busy thoroughfare. As the animals walked side by side Roanne broke the silence, her voice now level and determined, retaining its anger. "You'll start an investigation right away."

He answered without taking his eyes off the thoroughfare ahead. "Is that what you want me to do? You do remember what I told you? Opi has been blessed. He has passed over, he–"

Roanne pulled her ride to a halt. "Passed over! *Passed over*? You idiot! He's your son, your flesh and blood, barely eight cycles old. Is it your intention to simply sit back and accept his disappearance without taking action? Is that what you're going to do? Pretend nothing has happened?"

He pulled his animal around to face hers. "Roanne, please, you must understand. Something *has* happened, and you have to accept it. Opi has moved on, transcended this existence to join Tal Salandor in the Garden of

Contentment." He bowed his head and mumbled a short prayer.

"Garden of *Contentment*? What about the seals? You said you left him in the auditorium of one hundred seals. Obviously he accidentally opened one and is trapped on the other side!"

"Yes," added Rillian, "he must be trapped, you must go back for him."

Sol shook his head, gritting his teeth. "Both of you – remember his age," he waved a hand in the direction of the Trophy and raised his voice. "Theorists have worked on those seals for centuries without success. Do you expect me to believe he's achieved something men and women, four times his age, with twelve times his education and five hundred times his experience have failed to do, attempt after attempt, time and time again?" He looked from one to the other, his eyes pleading for them to see the common sense of his statement.

Roanne's eyes narrowed on his. "It is far easier for me to believe that Opi opened a seal accidentally, than it is to believe he was spirited away to an invisible garden beyond this existence. What do you expect me to believe? You're a scientist as well as a Cardinal. Which is the more likely? You're asking me to believe in sorcery. *You* must do this! You're the most gifted Cardinal this city has ever seen – you must know in your heart only you can save him." She sat back in her saddle, aware she was pushing him to the limit. Would he break? They had never argued over belief before. She had always accepted his faith and never questioned any of the doctrines he held so close to his heart. She knew they were both at a defining point.

Sol thought deeply. If the populace and, more importantly, the other members of the order saw him taking action contradicting sacred beliefs and truths, it would be considered the height of sacrilege. He and Roanne could be put to death for such actions, his name struck from the records of Holy achievement, his staff, friends and colleagues interrogated and perhaps banished from the city, and no one would ever acknowledge his existence or breathe the name of Timmerman again. He had seen it happen before. He looked away from them both as his insides churned with his dilemma, the rushed activity of the thoroughfare bombarding his senses. Life's foundation of factuality and theology seemed to be crumbling before his very eyes, just as over the past few cycles it had settled as a comforting mantle supporting everything he held dear. He could feel Roanne's eyes probing him, waiting for his decision, and he knew if she spoke again her words would be lost in a flood of emotion. Rillian regarded them both intently, relaxing against the high backrest of her saddle, as though she knew Sol's thoughts, as if she had already completed their unspoken conversation in her head like a game of squares, with all its possible permutations and countermoves carried through and brought to their obvious conclusions. He found his gaze wandering back to Roanne, and as their eyes met the decision was made.

"I'll conduct an investigation," he heard himself say quietly. "A situation such as this has never been recorded; no one has ever been summoned by Tal Salandor in such a manner, this could be a portent. That is all I have as leverage. I will insist I oversee an extensive investigation immediately, to search for and gather any clues left behind by the Almighty that could further our understanding of *Oosah*. " He steered his ganapti around them as Roanne spoke.

"Will they allow you to do this?"

"My position entitles me to start a preliminary investigation into any area of *Oosah* I consider worthwhile, and at any time." He pulled sharply on the reins to direct the animal. "I will take my demands to the Twelve immediately." He dug his heels into the ganapti's ribs. "I'll be home after dark," he shouted, as the animal galloped away.

NINE

THE HOLY CITADEL

The late afternoon sun cast long shadows over the Ravine District as Sol approached across the Divine Bridge of Emakurow. In this lower part of the city, the pace of life was far more relaxed and religion was foremost in the people's thoughts. Peasant traders led their tired animals home, dragging behind them carts containing unsold fruits and vegetables. Beggars huddled in groups arguing and comparing their profit, while street preachers orated the lessons of Tal Salandor to the passersby.

Beneath the bridge huddled thousands of tiny slum dwellings, the original homes that had been built for the workers during the city's construction. To Sol's right, twenty giant buttresses reached up from the perpetual torchlight of their foundations, holding the dam wall in place. Built inside these colossal constructions were networks of small accommodations, housing for the most part the manual workers of the city. Beneath them, the pipelines carrying the water networks began, filtering and channelling clean water to every home and business, replenishing artificial lakes, rivers and canals. The sewer pipes and tunnels meandered beneath the streets, coming full circle to deposit the waste into the river through the opposite city wall, a dozen leagues distant.

Ahead lay a fork in the roadway where smaller roads spiralled downward from the main highway, to left and right. At this junction a fortified garrison building, housing five hundred Deacons, sat behind two tall, ornate metal doors. As Sol dismounted, a figure lit torches atop the battlements, and he turned and watched as Deacons throughout the city followed the signal from the garrison. Gradually the city's thoroughfares became illuminated by torchlight.

A wicket gate opened in the right-hand door and a Bishop slipped through, hurrying over to him.

"Cardinal Timmerman?" he said, removing his hood. "What is your business here?"

"I request an audience with the Twelve. I must speak with them immediately."

The Bishop shook his head. "Oh, no no no. All appointments must be arranged through the correct channels, you know that. Your cleric should deliver your request to me in writing. Then–"

"I haven't time for small-minded bureaucracy, Bishop," said Sol, taking him by the arm. "I have urgent business of a personal nature. The primary entrance to the Citadel is now closed for the night. You must allow me an audience with the Twelve."

The Bishop looked down at Sol's hand clutching his arm, and Sol released his grip.

"Come back tomorrow, Cardinal, via The Eliyas Bridge as per protocol." he stiffened and jerked his head up. "I will go so far as to take your request to the Twelve personally. You'll have an answer by midday tomorrow, or the next." As he was turning to leave, a Deacon hurried over to him, holding out a piece of folded paper. The Bishop took it and waved him away as he unfolded and read the note.

He spoke without looking up at Sol. "Hmm. It seems you're expected." He turned, clicked his

fingers and the gates responded, crawling apart. "Follow me, Cardinal."

'Expected?' thought Sol, leading his mount as he walked behind the Bishop. The last time he had visited the Citadel via this entrance was on his day of elevation. The fears of that day came to haunt him again. He was just a priest, a young man burdened with the weight of adult responsibilities, his family, his ambition and hunger for truth. Back then he worried whether he had the strength to honour all his commitments, and how a man in his position balanced duties such as committing to memory ancient

reports from Cardinals long since dead, lest he waste his time repeating their mistakes, preparing his son for the world, loving and keeping Roanne happy, while they both came to terms with the gossip and speculation concerning their marriage.

The garrison's formal courtyard had seemed much larger during his last visit. A cloistered stable to his left housed ganapti, with a fenced grazing area with bales of uncured Farrengrass tops stacked neatly in the far right corner. A stable lad ran over, took the reins from him and led his animal to a nearby trough. To his right the Deacons' accommodations were arranged over six levels. The ground level contained the armoury, several blacksmiths' workshops and a kitchen; behind this, a dining hall and classrooms. The next two levels contained the Deacons' quarters, and above them were the law library and private study rooms. Off to the far right corner of the courtyard a team of carpenters and blacksmiths worked on what appeared to be the base of a huge, wheeled tower, carving an ornate balustrade to fit a spiral staircase that sat, half-finished, inside the skeletal construction. The bright ringing of hammered clasps, hinges and split pins the size of a man's arm echoed discordantly off the walls of the garrison.

An imposing, angular, five-storey granite tower dominated the courtyard's rear boundary wall. At its base, a tall, arched passageway was barred by a heavy iron portcullis. Above the archway stood double doors of ornately carved oak, deeply figured with illustrations depicting the construction of the building. These doors sat behind a deep balcony of basalt, its face glittering as it reflected the flaming torches either side of the doors. This balcony was reached by two curving, basalt staircases, sweeping upwards as if to embrace the portcullis. This was the senior Archbishop's residence where he sat in solitude, editing and compiling theories before he passed them on to the Citadel for analysis by the Twelve Grand Cardinals.

"I'll see to it the bridge is lowered immediately, Cardinal," said the Bishop with a sudden change of attitude. As Sol watched, the Bishop ascended the stairs and entered the building, slamming the doors behind him. A tired, metal groan filled the courtyard, accompanied by a vibration beneath his feet. As the portcullis slowly rose, he ducked beneath its pointed teeth, which yawned like a great metal beast. He stood in the arched passageway, the mouth to the Citadel, as a drawbridge unfolded in front of him. Three black metal hinges set into its top squealed their complaints as the mechanism was manoeuvred by thick iron chains to complete the walkway. Behind the tower's stone walls, cogs and gears embraced, pulling the wooden roadway up and out into the open air.

He stepped forward onto the wooden construction, hurrying as best he could without appearing to be desperate. The edge of the second half of the drawbridge had come to a rest upon a misshapen stone atoll, standing high above the slums. As he stepped onto this island he took stock of his situation. How would his request be received? He theorised as to the refusals the Holy Twelve could present to him. He was just one man, pitting himself against the twelve greatest minds in Abeona. He shuddered at the thought of his own transgression, his sudden contradiction of all he had learnt and believed in. But now, perhaps, his circumstances would awaken an unnourished curiosity dormant in the minds of the old Theorists, invigorating *their* hunger for truth. He turned sharply as a screech broke his reverie; and watched the drawbridge fold back upon itself.

The monolith he stood upon was the Pinnacle of Judgement, far more ancient than the towering edifice he now turned to face. He remembered the history lessons from school, and how the architects of the Holy Citadel had stood in this very place centuries ago, drawing up their plans for the magnificent building. Seven hundred cycles later, the pinnacle had become a place of judgement for heretics and criminals alike, following its retirement as the Citadel's primary, defensible entrance. After sentencing, malefactors would be stranded here, for if, as they claimed in their defence, their actions were the bidding of a higher power, it was believed this higher power would come to deliver them from their predicament. They were left, without food or water, to await their saviour's arrival.

If they sought atonement for their sins and repented of their crimes, then, upon receiving a Grand Cardinal's absolution, their souls would be rewarded, welcomed to reside in the Garden of Contentment. This could only be attained after voluntarily casting their bodies into the boneyard surrounding the base of the pinnacle, half a league below.

Sol stood upon the roadway in the centre of the pinnacle now, apprehensive of his position and the meeting awaiting him in the Citadel. He could only imagine the horror of being stranded on this precipice without food or water, awaiting an inescapable fate. The Pinnacle, a quarter of a league in both width and breadth held a few remains of foundations from an ancient pavilion. The majority of its surface, a mosaic of uneven flagstones, some cracked, others crumbling, tilting upward at their corners.

The wind was cold now, blowing hard across the dam wall several leagues distant, carrying with it tiny droplets from the imprisoned river. He closed his eyes and turned into the wind, enjoying both the distraction and refreshment it gave. After a few moments he opened his eyes, catching sight of several birds soaring high above the distant water. They plunged beneath the waves in turn, each emerging with fish that they carried back to their nests, hidden in the Goraknath mountains, far to the north. A creak filled the air from the silent building to his left, and he turned to see the drawbridge from the Holy Citadel reaching over to him, unfolding from the mouth of the building's entrance like a stiff tongue. This was not an accident of engineering, for it was believed all truths were spoken from the Citadel, a building said by scripture to have been originally constructed for Tal Salandor and his servitors, in thanks for leading the people to the Trophy to defeat the invaders.

The light from the Citadel's opening illuminated the way, and as he looked down in a final moment of concentration a glint caught his eye. He bent down and prised a small, hooped, golden earring from between the damp flagstones. He studied the intricate design, twisting it between his fingers for a moment before the thump of the drawbridge impacting upon the pinnacle urged him forward.

The Citadel loomed above Sol's head as though growing from the stubby remains of the mountain. Beneath the building's façade, a sheer wall fell to the depths of the ravine. Before that and to his far left, protruded the bridge of Eliyas, connecting the Citadel to the city as its primary entrance, reaching over the buildings before spiralling down to ground level, half a league away from the Square of Remembrance.

Records told how the entire building had been carved into the stump that was left of the mountain after the city was constructed. The city's master stonemasons had hewn from the rock a network of passageways, porticos, grand halls and apartments, toiling for seven hundred cycles until the building was complete. The Citadel's corridors were highly polished and arranged to reflect sunlight deep into its network of passageways, ensuring every room was blessed with sunlight during some part of the day.

The Bishop at the garrison had been quite correct, thought Sol, with some concern; it was a breach of protocol for a Cardinal to visit the Citadel without prior arrangement. He tidied himself as best he could, brushing down his robes and arranging their folds, but this did little to improve his mood or appearance.

Waiting for him in the mouth of the building was a short figure wrapped in a black cloak with gold edging.

The cloak's purple designs entwined in a forced perspective, giving the figure an unnatural depth. Sol took one last look up at the Citadel as he neared the entrance. Twelve minarets reached high into the air above one hundred smaller priest's prominences. The quality of the workmanship was unique, and as he walked nearer he noticed grotesque gargoyles huddled together beneath the minarets. The huge, ugly demons seemed to watch his every step with their lifeless stone eyes, their expressions contorted as if they were aware of some dark encounter waiting for him inside the building, and were gloating at his imminent misfortune. He ignored such dark imaginings and looked to the frieze carved above the doors. The first panel depicted herds of Gen'hib-Maun grazing on grassy plains attended by a single shepherd, the next, the discovery of *Oosah*, then the building of the wall and the ascent of the mountain. In the final panel, an invader, a bizarre, six-limbed creature battled Tal Salandor beneath *Oosah*.

"Cardinal Timmerman?" asked the figure in a chirpy voice.

Sol looked down at the chubby little man and bowed. "Yes."

"My name is Gar Ommus." He returned the respect. "Senior Archbishop, retired." He held out his hand and Sol shook it, then the little man looked Sol up and down, frowning at his dishevelled and smoke-stained clothes. "Oh dear. Well, never mind, you'll have to do." He cleared his throat. "I am personal assistant and scribe to the Holy Grand Twelve. They are expecting you. Please, follow me."

Sol hastily unbuckled his sandals, placing them in a wooden tray upon the top step as Ommus pushed open a small doorway set into the metal gates, stepping through. Sol followed and closed the door behind him. They walked across a smooth-cobbled courtyard of grey gabbro, patterned with patches of light green moss spreading out between the stones, affording occasional comfort to Sol's bare feet. He smiled inwardly at the sensation, aware it reflected his trepidations – unsure as he was as to the outcome of his meeting.

An ancient wooden temple sat to their right, dedicated to Ouy Leva, Theorist and subsequent first Grand Cardinal, self-appointed custodian and oral historian from the first age. The temple, nothing more than a rickety shell, had been removed from its original position, adjacent to *Oosah* in the Square, to protect it from the elements. It was surrounded by dwarf fruit trees and herb bushes. Here, several young priests pruned the greenery, supervised by a Deacon. Beyond this, twelve stone stairways of striped gneiss reflected the glow cast by lanterns perched high in the ceiling. The rock sparkled with thousands of tiny flecks, mirroring, in Sol's eyes, the night sky. Each staircase, appointed for the sole use of a specific Grand Cardinal, writhed and twisted around the others like snakes, untangling themselves as they terminated at a landing high above. Sinuous vines, rich with ripening yellow hayberries, entwined themselves around their balustrades, forming a lofty canopy of green. There, songbirds roosted between the large, triangular, mottled green and yellow leaves, singing to each other in melodic counterpoint. Sol looked up, noticing the glass roof occupying the centre of the ceiling, its leaded panes arranged as a pyramid with a cradle of lighted candles dangling from an iron chain at its centre.

The retired Archbishop hurried ahead, nodding and mumbling to himself. Sol followed as Ommus climbed a staircase, stopping for a moment to pluck two ripe hayberries and offering one to Sol. He shook his head, managing a half-smile. The old man tilted his head to one side, raising his eyebrows as he sniffed the fruit before popping both into his mouth.

When they reached the landing, Ommus turned right, through a high arch leading to a vaulted colonnade of gold and marble walls lined by tall, painted, limestone pillars.

The little man stopped and turned. "I trust this area of the Citadel is new to you?"

Sol nodded. "I remember the garden; my elevation to the Cardinalship took place in Ouy Leva's Temple of Pronouncement, several cycles ago."

Ommus smiled. "Yes, I remember, but that is just a tiny part of the Holy Citadel. Now. Wait here." He pointed down the vaulted corridor. "When I reach the doors at the end, walk the centre line upon the floor and face straight ahead – no matter *what* you see. Keep your head level, eyes fixed ahead. Do I make myself clear?"

Sol looked down at a thick strip of dull silver, set into the ebony floor. "You do."

"I will wait for you at the doors," said Ommus, hurrying down the colonnade. He waved Sol forward as he reached the far end.

"Don't look down!" called the little man, sternly. "Keep your eyes straight ahead and feel the cold metal beneath your feet."

Sol stood upon the line, then looked up and began to walk, staring directly ahead. Suddenly he noticed movement in his peripheral vision.

"Look straight ahead!" The little man's voice echoed around the colonnade.

With some difficulty, Sol's concentration remained fixed, resisting the temptation to look left and right at the movement on either side of him. After eighty paces he finally reached Ommus.

"What did you see?" he asked, placing a hand upon Sol's shoulder.

"There were figures watching me. They seemed to be shaking their heads; some drew swords and held them forward, preparing to strike. Then, as I reached the halfway point, they sheathed their swords, bowed and began to kneel. When I finally reached you they were all kneeling with their heads bowed."

The old man quickly clapped his hands together a few times and chuckled "Mmm, interesting."

Sol glanced back down the colonnade, surprised to see they were alone. He turned. "Who were they?"

The old man grinned and raised his wispy, grey-streaked eyebrows. "Oh, just paintings around the pillars and upon the walls behind them, that's all."

Sol frowned. "Paintings?"

"An optical illusion, drawn by the individual's view of reality." The old man tapped his left temple a few times with a forefinger and winked once. "What you see depends on how well you kept to the line. Your height, width of vision, and how clear your perception of colour is are all contributing factors. Everyone sees something different." He took Sol by the arm and began to walk to the door behind him. "I've tried so many times, but because I'm somewhat, ahem, shorter than average, and my sight's not what it was in my youth, all I ever see are fish talking to loaves of brown bread and playing games of chance."

"So what is all this supposed to mean?" asked Sol, with a little impatience.

Ommus shrugged. "Well, officially, it could be said the Citadel is wary of your visit, but respects your motives and acknowledges the authority of your position."

"And unofficially, how does this illusion work?"

"Unofficially? The old man thought for a moment. "I've theorised the paintings play tricks on the brain, reflecting the state of mind of the individual viewing them. So unofficially, you saw your subconscious desire for the Twelve, or perhaps everyone, to ultimately bow down to your requests," his eyes narrowed upon Sol. "whatever they may be."

Sol ignored the question implied in the other man's words and looked back down the colonnade once more. The walls and pillars were covered in a multitude of swirling colours with no discernible pattern.

Ommus grinned, clearing his throat and lifting his head

a little. "The rule is – you must walk back the way you came, with your eyes closed. If you keep to the line all the way to the doors, then what you saw on the way in is the truth and will prevail, no matter what the outcome of your meeting. If you stray from the line, well... I will be waiting to escort you back to the Pinnacle of Judgement when your meeting with the Twelve has concluded." He produced a cord from around his neck and chose one of the many bronze keys threaded upon it, unlocked the door and ushered Sol through.

"Wait on the balcony at the end of this corridor. Good luck," and with that he closed the door behind him.

At the end of a narrow, alabaster passageway Sol found himself on a low balcony overlooking a large, shallow, rectangular pool. The water was flat and clear as glass; beneath it a mosaic map of the ancient city as it was when first built. The tiny tiles of the mosaic were cut from precious stones, which shone in the light of a hundred or so candles mounted on sconces around the walls. High above him another, smaller, pyramid of glass revealed the dark blue of the early evening sky.

He impatiently thrust his hands into their opposite sleeves. Both the silence and the flickering candlelight reflected beneath the water wove a soothing tranquillity into his head, and he struggled to shake it off, wanting to stay alert, knowing he would need all of his faculties at their sharpest for the meeting. Determination was a highly respected and encouraged attribute for a Cardinal, but this trait was usually exercised during their work, and not during their meetings with their superiors. He had to tread lightly and with the utmost respect.

As he watched the water, four young priests appeared from the cloisters surrounding the courtyard. He estimated they were around twelve cycles of age, and each of them struggled with a large brass urn containing steaming water perched upon his shoulders. Together, they walked barefoot to the water's edge and slowly tipped the hot water into the pool, breaking the silence and mixing the colours of the mosaic map into a shimmering kaleidoscopic haze. He recognised the blue Bella-Pennu water, scented with citrine and jade entante oil, for relaxation of mind and body. He held his breath as the sweet, musky aroma drifted up from the pool, preventing its potency from interfering with his concentration. The priests hurried back into the cloisters and silence fell over the scene once more. He exhaled as the water began to settle and from under the balcony two figures appeared directly beneath him, dressed in full-length, hooded white robes. They walked slowly to the water's edge and stopped as others, identically adorned, joined them from the three remaining sides of the bathing area. Sol counted them. Eleven figures stood around the pool, three at each side and two directly beneath him. They looked to be well-built and powerful individuals beneath their robes, although their long hoods hid their faces from the candlelight.

"Welcome, Cardinal Timmerman."

The voice startled him. He whirled around to come face to face with Grand Cardinal Oen Zoloth, the most senior of the Grand Cardinals and public spokesperson for the Holy Church of *Oosah*. He was dressed identically to the figures below.

Sol bowed deeply. Beneath his robes, his fingernails slowly traced around the edge of the earring he had found. "It is a great honour to visit the Citadel again, Your Holiness."

Zoloth detected the nervousness in Sol's voice and a slight frown creased his brow. "Attend me, Cardinal, there is much to talk of." Sol followed his superior down the steps towards the pool, as Zoloth continued.

"It was our intention to summon you several days after the festival, to evaluate the impact of your closing speech, but following recent events and much deliberation, we have decided to inform you of your next assignment immediately." He stopped, pulling his hood back from his face and Sol noticed how much he had aged since their last meeting. His mottled neck sprouted from the robe like gnarled roots of an ancient tree, exposed from the soil. He had lost his hair, and lines creased his face in memory of many mixed emotions. Despite these signs of age, his light grey eyes remained clear and alert, vibrant as they reflected the shimmering pool. He spoke quietly but confidently, his soothing voice having an unusual melodic and rhythmic quality.

"Archbishop Arramosa's untimely death has already cast a shadow over the upcoming festival." He sighed. "The Kaltesh tongues are already wagging, creating speculation among themselves and our citizens alike, but we can use the Archbishop's passing for the greater good of Abeona."

They reached the bottom step and Zoloth motioned for Sol to wait. "There will be a moment of silent prayer." As Sol bowed his head, Zoloth took up his position at the water's edge. He waited for a few moments and then, as if responding to a command only they could hear, the Grand Cardinals simultaneously removed their hoods and dropped their robes. As they stood naked, Sol opened his eyes and saw how their illusion of youth was created. Each robe had a network of wire sewn into it, creating a padded cage that sat a few inches above the body, exaggerating the physique and helping to keep the wearer cool. A thicker piece of wire ran up the spine to keep the posture correct and a hoop extended into the hood of the garment to maintain its shape. These discarded robes now lay like ghosts of youth at the feet of their withered owners, and as Zoloth stepped over his robe and into the ankle-deep water of the first step, Sol noticed how well-muscled the Senior Grand Cardinal was for his age. He was obviously an individual who took great care of his body, and rumour had it he had been a champion swordsman in his youth. The remaining Grand Cardinals followed his lead, and when they were all submerged up to their necks, Zoloth spoke.

"Cardinal Timmerman, please kneel at the water's edge." He turned back to briefly speak with Grand Cardinal Irrianna, then waded back to where Sol waited.

From the cloister behind Sol, three priests appeared carrying trays of refreshment. They knelt and placed the trays at the edge of the pool, then hurried away as the Grand Cardinals came over one by one to take the hefty golden goblets and several glass jugs of red wine waiting there.

Zoloth took a goblet and motioned to a priest, staring at Sol as he spoke.

"A goblet for our guest. The finest Vinifera from my personal vineyard."

Zoloth watched the Grand Cardinals wade back to the centre of the pool before smiling and speaking softly. "I understand Grand Cardinal Irrianna has already made our position clear to you concerning Archbishop Arramosa's suicide?"

"Yes, Your Holiness."

Zoloth nodded slowly. "Good. We can be sure the majority of the people will want to know the truth behind this incident, so we have already planted theoretically possible rumours concerning motive and reason for his action into key city locations. Not one of these fictions will overshadow the other, as all have an average believability score of between forty-two to fifty-nine percent. This will prevent the populace from reaching a hasty judgement, until you deliver your findings."

Beneath his robes, Sol's little finger found the earring's centre. "My findings?"

"We have decided to inform the people that your duties during the festival will be to conduct an investigation into Yan Arramosa's death. Obviously, this task is purely for the public's peace of mind, as there is no need to waste resources on an investigation. We have theorised and concluded as to the cause, without any fear of possible inaccuracy. We must, or rather you must, as our most prolific Theorist, be seen to represent the Church's determination to unearth the truth of his death and our dedication in this matter."

The priest returned with a tray bearing a single goblet.

Sol took the offered refreshment, thanked him and took a sip. "Why not simply make an announcement in the religious papers concerning your findings? Why deceive the people, Your Holiness?"

"This is not deception, Cardinal," said Zoloth, raising his eyebrows at the implication, "simply misdirection. Immediately following your 'investigation,' you will make an announcement concerning your recommendations for the future of the city and its people."

Sol shook his head, "I don't understand."

"You see, I was recently blessed with an epiphany." He drew an oval shape on his chest with his left index finger, making the sign of *Oosah*. "The culmination of this sacred event? We have decided to abolish the Theorist grades, gradually, over the next three cycles following this festival. Grade One Cardinals will then adopt the new position and title of Constable, overseeing the Deacons encompassed by his or her diocese. Your speech, which you will now have to re-write, will allude to these changes." He shook his head. "I'm afraid poor Yan Arramosa couldn't bear to be part of this new order." He sipped his wine, studying the Cardinal for any reaction his expression might betray.

Sol frowned and looked across the water to the eleven, "Surely the people will object. Why abolish the order? The people will revolt – they are eager for the truth of *Oosah*."

Zoloth closed his eyes and breathed deeply, savouring the perfumed vapour rising from the water, exhaling slowly through his nostrils with his eyes still closed. Sol took the opportunity to drain his goblet, hiding his unease.

The Senior Grand Cardinal opened his eyes. "The city's population continues to grow, and with it, the people's awareness of their need to expand." He brought his arms out of the water and held his hands as far apart as possible.

"The people are becoming cramped behind the city walls. The Twelve have theorised and concluded, with a ninety-two percent certainty, that protection from the Kaltesh is no longer needed. Our recent studies prove that worship of *Oosah* is beginning to dissipate considerably among all public sectors. Sales of the religious papers have dropped significantly, to the point where they are no longer cost effective to produce." He took a few paces forward, revealing his shoulders. "A new creed is required, a focal point for the populace, a doctrine to govern the people and provide them with law and protection in the guise of faith. We cannot sit back and wait for this fateful day to arrive by any hand other than our own, Cardinal. We must act now and introduce this day ourselves, before the people realise they have nothing, and anarchy ensues. From this anarchy, only false idols can possibly emerge to mislead the people, enticing them along a dark path to a malignant deceiver."

Sol could not believe his ears. "But surely–"

"We need to move outwards if we are to evolve – some have already realised this. Cartography is becoming more popular by the day," he waved a hand absently toward the balcony, and Sol detected the volume of his voice increase a little. "The people want to know what lies out beyond the desert. More than fifty-six percent of the population have a Kaltesh map upon their walls. Faith in *Oosah*, promises of answers to hidden truths, salvation from the invisible unknown, by the invisible unknown?" He smiled. "The people are realising these just aren't enough any more."

Sol looked down and thought for a moment, unconvinced by his superior's euthenics. "But what if the people refuse this new way? Wouldn't this also lead to anarchy?"

Zoloth drained his goblet, placing it on the poolside to refill it slowly, his voice returning to its usual melodic calm. "They will follow you. Obviously a minority will refuse, but the clerics will instruct them and the Deacons will ensure heresy will not be given a voice to distract the majority. Your duties will be altered to complement this new Imperial Age. The people will not need 'theories,' so you will become a Truthsayer. You will be obliged to govern your sector of the city and have a seat at the table of the ruling body, reporting directly to us. You will be encouraged to develop new laws by direct contact with the people." The Grand Cardinal lowered his head slightly, narrowing his eyes. "Sol, only a man of your high profile can walk amongst them, hear and see where problems live, breed and grow. A man like you can make a difference; a family man, a man for a greater community. A true *leader*."

At once he understood Zoloth's use of the word 'family.'

"You're talking about unifying us with the Kaltesh, aren't you?"

The Senior Grand Cardinal suppressed a smile now. "In good time. As they quite rightly say, 'patience is the key to joy, haste the key to sorrow.' In a way, you have already started this unification by taking a Kaltesh wife, have you not?"

He nodded.

"The joining is an inevitable step in the evolution of our cultures. If we do not take action now, eventually the people will tear down the walls of Abeona in a violent surge as they struggle to grow. The people need a new challenge, just as our ancestors had the challenge of building this city to protect their Trophy. Eventually we will encounter the Kaltesh, and we will need you and your wife to bridge the gap between our two beliefs, orchestrating a unity between our differing ways. In time we will all be as one under God."

"God? Who or what is a *God?"*

"For the moment, just an acronym. Guided Organised Doctrines, a code word for the new teachings, in the tradition of three letter names we use to honour Tal Salandor. All will be explained to you in writing. I believe the documents are already awaiting your return at your estate. Commit them to memory, then destroy them."

Sol sat down cross-legged on the stone floor, forgetting to ask for permission. He struggled to ignore Zoloth's revelations and concentrate on his purpose for being there, but this news needed clarification for his own peace of mind. "Then I trust our beliefs will remain intact for a time under this... God? Surely *Oosah* will dominate in our teachings of this new creed, Senior Grand Cardinal?"

"For a time, the Garden of Contentment will remain, as it is a Truth. We realise the transition will be difficult for closed minds, as the core of our new creed is to teach the people the worth of their own selves. This is the primary teaching, and this will dominate. After an indeterminate length of time our guided organised doctrines will become irrefutable. We intend to teach the young that our bodies are our own trophies, and the discovery of our true natures hiding inside to be more important than the discovery of what lies inside an ancient, foreign artefact."

Sol's eyes widened. The words washed over him as smoothly as the scented water washed over the naked bodies of the Twelve. Now his entire life was stripped bare, exposed to upheaval, and he felt as naked as the old men before him. Vulnerable, alone, lost. His heart began to pound, heavy in his chest, and after a few moments he found his voice once again.

"So when do you intend to set all this in motion, Your Holiness?"

Zoloth looked surprised. "It is already in motion. The process will take cycles in its entirety, but you will light the way for us all. When they see your face, they will see the face of their future, the face of fulfilled promises and optimism. When they hear your voice, they will hear the voice of our god."

Sol spoke quietly. "I trust I have no choice in this matter?"

Zoloth walked up the steps to place a hand on Sol's

shoulder. "Sol, let me reassure you. This is the only way forward. You will begin the preparations from Yan Arramosa's classroom; Ommus will give you the key. The people will see you as investigating Yan's death, whilst you are in fact drawing up the details of our future plans. We suggest you settle yourself in immediately. If you need further reassurance, then bear this in mind. Your new position will allow you to retain your estate and the benefits therein. You have my word there will be no loss to your standard of living – should you decide to accept the position offered. If you decline, then another Cardinal will be appointed Constable of your sector. Obviously he or she will require the accommodation which befits such a highly respected position." He returned to the warmth of the water as Sol looked down and exhaled slowly, his anger rising.

"Grand Cardinal, there seems to be a misunderstanding concerning my reason for being here. I have not come to ask permission to investigate Yan Arramosa's death. My visit concerns my son, Opi. I took him into *Oosah* this morning. I was called to the scene of the Archbishop's suicide, and when I returned inside to collect my son, he'd vanished. I respectfully request the Twelve allow me back inside, and command all Theorists to work on the seals alongside me to help find my son – before you introduce this new order. There may be evidence left behind that could lead us closer to the truth of *Oosah*, thus rendering the new order unnecessary."

Zoloth held his gaze for several moments then turned, wading back to the eleven bathing in the candlelit water. The mumbled deliberations of the Twelve travelled across the rippling water as Sol's heart pounded in his chest. He looked up to the early evening sky. The sun was beyond view and it would soon be dark. Below him, part of the pool hid in shadow, and the crisp red crests of water from the Twelve's motion had dulled beneath the torchlight to tiny teardrops. He looked back to the heavens. In the sun's place, the planet's satellites glowed behind the hazy twilight, sluggishly drawn through their timeless orbits as night approached. The celestial pathway stretched directly overhead from horizon to horizon, giving the void a twinkling beauty. This narrow line shone brightly, reminding him of the jewels at the bottom of the pool. This was the path to the Garden of Contentment, but seeing it gave Sol little comfort. His eyes slowly crept along its length, wondering if Opi was walking it now. It was believed there were many hidden dangers along the route, but Opi was a clever boy, he would be fine. Besides, Tal Salandor would look after him, once he reached the Garden.

The splashing of water trespassed on his thoughts. He looked down to the pool to see Zoloth leading the Grand Cardinals towards him. Once they had taken their positions behind Zoloth and the water had calmed, he spoke.

"You are correct, Sol Timmerman, there has been a misunderstanding, but it is entirely yours. Your son has passed over toward the Garden, you know that as a Truth." He looked up briefly, "I saw you looking up but moments ago, searching for him treading the path. He can see and hear us even now. Do not put doubt concerning your beliefs into his heart, Sol. He is a very lucky boy; it is a very small minority who pass over, chosen at such a tender age. His is the blessing of learning and growing to manhood in the Garden with Tal Salandor." Zoloth turned his back on Sol to face the eleven. "All that has transpired is as Tal Salandor said. *'A child will join me,'*" he said. "*'I will care for him in the Garden as his father leads the people into a new, prosperous era.'*" As the eleven made the sign of the Trophy on their chests, Zoloth turned back to Sol. "You will see him again, when it is your time. However, we all fear that if you continue this fantasy of your son being trapped inside *Oosah*, then it *could* come to pass your son will shun you upon your arrival at the Garden. This would lead to your solitary banishment to the lower plains, and we do not wish that for you. Remember this, Sol. In the new creed you will prepare the people for their way of life, until the day they are judged fit to walk the celestial path. Once their journey comes to an end, your son will be there to greet them and invite them into the Garden of Contentment. His passing over whilst inside *Oosah* is the first step of the new creed. Tal Salandor, the first son and father, has blessed the new order with this act of appropriation. Everything is as it should be."

Sol felt the tears in his eyes as his stomach churned. The Twelve stared at him from the water, penetrating, reverent eyes unblinking and confident. They nodded in unison and smiled up at him. At last he found the courage to speak. "Please, Senior Grand Cardinal, allow me just one day. My son *could* be trapped behind a seal. Allow me to–"

"Trapped? Is that what you *believe*?" Zoloth's eyes widened in disgust as the others began mumbling behind him. He raised a hand and they fell silent. "Have you learnt nothing? You're still a Cardinal – you dare utter words bordering on Kaltesh sacrilege! What purpose would the Almighty have for imprisoning your son?"

"I... I don't know." He looked over to the eleven, "Grand Cardinals, please – one of our most sacred rules states – *'he that nothing questions, nothing learns,'* I cannot understand–"

Grand Cardinal Irrianna stepped forward. "Kaltesh men have greater faith in things they cannot understand," he spat, his eyes full of anger. "That is why they do not question, why they do not have a Theorist grade. You must realise this truth. It is impossible for your son to have opened a seal, insanity to believe such! Moreover, the Almighty does *not* leave clues or evidence for us to use to prove a Truth. The occurrence in itself is all the truth that is needed."

"Grand Cardinal Irrianna is correct," said Zoloth quickly. "Surely you don't want to be remembered as the last Cardinal of your order to be declared insane, immured here for the remainder of your life?"

Sol shook his head.

The candlelight hinted at a smile touching Zoloth's face. "Only Tal Salandor possesses the ability to open doors from the other side of existence. Return to your wife; comfort her, if that's what her frail beliefs require. I trust yours do not?"

Sol spoke quietly, struggling to stop his voice faltering. "No, Senior Grand Cardinal, they do not. One other matter. My son is the nephew of Hulneb Vela, now Kaltesh High Celebrant. Would our inaction concerning his nephew be taken as an insult?"

'So, what Irrianna's Kaltesh friend told me was true,' Zoloth thought, hiding a little disappointment. He paused for a few moments. "We are already aware of their new leader. Since *Oosah* creates the backdrop for his personal concerns, his position as High Celebrant prohibits any interest he has in this matter from being brought to the fore by Kaltesh law." Zoloth looked to the darkening sky. "It will be night in a short while. Leave us now, we have duties to attend to. You have until the commencement of festivities to inform us of your decision." He turned in unison with the other Grand Cardinals, and Sol found himself rising to his feet, surprised to see two Deacons of the Trophy standing a few paces behind him. The Deacon to his right pointed toward the steps, "By the same way you entered, please, Your Holiness." Sol nodded, walking slowly up the steps as a line of young priests and priestesses hurried from the cloisters to his left. He glanced at them as they trotted by, their bare feet slapping the marble of the poolside. They were between the ages of fourteen and eighteen, he estimated; fresh-faced and alert, but he noticed the lack of purity in their eyes as several watched him walk by. They seemed fiercely resolute, as if their naked innocence of youth and its vulnerabilities had been replaced by an impenetrable shell, created by the false superiority of promised enlightenment. Their faces saddened him, they had lost so much at an early age,

trading their puerile beauty to become harbingers of the new creed. He looked away and wearily trod the shallow stone steps, eager for the noise of the streets and the purity of the evening air. As he reached the balcony the splashing of water, throaty laughter and high-pitched giggles broke the silence of the Citadel. He turned to watch the revelry, but the two Deacons stood shoulder to shoulder, allowing only a glimpse of the distasteful frolics of the naked bodies in the pool.

"If you don't mind, Your Holiness," said the Deacon, nodding to the corridor ahead, and Sol felt a chill in the serene glow of twilight. He hurried on, ignoring the sounds behind him, taking comfort from his image reflected in the walls and floor of the smooth alabaster corridor.

Ommus was waiting for him at the entrance to the colonnade.

"Everything went well, I trust?"

Sol shook his head, aware the effects of the Vinifera were beginning to take hold. "So much for the Citadel's respect for me."

Ommus raised his eyebrows and slowly shook his head. "A Cardinal's trials are ever mounting, Sol." He handed him a heavy envelope. "The key to our tomorrow, I believe."

Sol stared at the envelope for a few moments then took it, tracing the heavy contours beneath the paper with his fingertips.

Ommus noticed his disappointment. "Not your tomorrow, it seems."

Sol shook his head, tucking the envelope beneath the folds of his robes.

"I know what you're thinking," said Ommus. "Cast the key into the boneyard when you reach the pinnacle."

"You're an observant man, Ommus," said Sol, placing his feet either side of the metal strip.

"There's always more to learn." The old man turned and walked the line, stopping when he reached end of the colonnade. "Come forward. I'll tell you when you can open your eyes."

Closing his eyes he took a deep breath, his head spinning with anger and Vinifera. He took a few paces, noticing his balance was not as it should be, and squinted toward Ommus. The peripheral figures appeared again, peering around the columns and talking to each other behind cupped hands. They pointed at him and appeared to be laughing. He tried to ignore them, but had to keep his eyes open to retain his balance. Then a figure ran just ahead of him to his right. This newcomer was much smaller than the others, and they tried to stop him as he ran past them. As Sol came within ten paces of Ommus he closed his eyes, just as the running figure stopped and held out its hands to him, pleading for assistance, mouthing words he couldn't hear.

"Stop. Open your eyes and look down."

He had kept to the line perfectly.

They made their way through the garden in silence. Ommus spoke to a Deacon at the front gate and had the Citadel's drawbridge lowered onto the pinnacle. As they walked over to it, the garrison drawbridge creaked over toward them in the darkness.

"Before you leave, please, tell me what you saw on your way back down the colonnade?"

Sol looked down at him, but the old man stared ahead. "Be quick," he said, shuffling, "it's cold. I know Zoloth laced your goblet to throw you off balance, it's an old trick he still hasn't grown out of." He wagged an accusing finger at Sol. "And don't think I couldn't see you peeking; my eyesight's not that bad."

"Is what I think I saw important to you?"

Ommus blew into his cupped hands and rubbed them together briskly. "I know why you came to the Citadel, so yes, it is. Besides, it was important enough for you to peep, to ensure you stayed on the line, cheating yourself so you could confirm what I told you on the way in as the truth."

The drawbridge slammed onto the pinnacle and Sol turned. His eyes remained fixed upon it for a few moments, then he looked swiftly back to the old man.

"I saw my son."

Ommus smiled up at Sol, "No doubt." He turned and headed toward the drawbridge and beyond, the Citadel, awaiting his return.

"Why did you come onto the pinnacle with me, Ommus? By talking this way, aren't you risking everything?"

The little man stopped, then turned slowly. "Everything? It seems to me you've already lost more than I ever had. I wanted to ensure the Deacons in the garrison remembered to lower the drawbridge for your return home." At once his voice adopted a serious tone. "I wouldn't want Zoloth to abandon you here. And, if that were the case, I, and only I, know a way down into the slums." He looked around in the darkness, pushing the dust aside with a sandal. "My predecessor ensured I knew of a stairway beneath one of these flagstones, leading up from an alehouse built next to the boneyard. I've led many a whore, other 'guests' and certain *supplies* into the Citadel by these means, during my tenure." He tapped the side of his nose and grinned. "Part of a Scribe's duty is to maintain discretion, protecting the honour of the Citadel. Deacons guarding the Eliyas Bridge entrance can be somewhat, *officious*, shall we say?"

Sol took a few steps back onto the drawbridge. "Why don't you come with me, Ommus?"

"You must understand, Sol, I haven't seen so much activity in the Citadel since the day of your elevation. Before you came along, the Twelve usually spent their time in solitude, but since your success all attention has been focused upon you. The Twelve meet every single day behind closed doors. Zoloth and Irrianna have both become impatient and short-tempered, arguing like schoolchildren when they think no one can hear them. It really is quite amusing. We're both safe for the time being, besides, I'm of more use to you in the Citadel, and for the first time in a long, long time, I'm enjoying life again. When the time is right, I'll join you."

"But you don't know my intentions."

"Humph, really? A short time ago you told me I was an observant man!"

Sol gave a weak smile as the Archbishop's voice became distant.

"If you're uncertain of my motives, be assured, Yan Arramosa was a good friend of mine. I'll get word to you if need be. Take care."

Sol began to walk across the drawbridge, then turned on his heels. "One thing I must know," he shouted, "who painted the walls and pillars of the colonnade?"

The old man stepped onto the drawbridge, turned and shouted back across the pinnacle.

"If you believe in legends, then someone called Tal Salandor," and with that he hurried towards the mouth of the Citadel.

TEN

HERESY

The streets were beginning to empty as Sol approached his estate, the oil burning in the torches lining the way giving the air a welcoming aroma. Ahead, his estate walls clad in a blanket of patchy green and yellow ivy, his family tower glowing with warmth. He glanced up to a balcony, noticing a single torch illuminating the vacancy where usually Roanne and Opi would be awaiting his return. He coaxed the tired ganapti into a trot.

Two burly Kaltesh guards flanked the door at the estate entrance. They were dressed in uneven weaves of a dark, coarse cloth and both wore fixed expressions of indifference. Upon seeing him they drew their short-swords and stood shoulder to shoulder, trying their best to block the wide entrance doors.

"Relax, gentlemen," he said wearily, in their native tongue. "I expect you're Rillian's personal guards? I'm Cardinal Sol Timmerman, and this is my estate."

They mumbled to each other then stood aside, sheathing their swords.

Sol nodded his thanks, dismounted and pulled out his key. Once the doors were locked behind him, he led the ganapti to the stable area and tethered him next to old Ganu, snoring in the corner. He hurried across the gardens, then crept silently up the winding stairway into the family tower, becoming aware of a murmured conversation coming from the formal reception room above.

Standing just short of the open doorway he watched the scene with interest. Roanne sat next to Rillian. Both women had their arms folded and stared vacantly at the unfinished evening meal on the low table before them. He recognised Tulteth, playing with Ebe on the three shallow steps leading up to the balcony. Sol smiled grimly, remembering how much Opi enjoyed the little animal's company. Ebe sniffed the air then turned and looked over in his direction, and for a fleeting moment Sol thought he detected the semblance of a smile touching the animal's tiny face. A trick of the flickering candlelight, he decided. He looked around the room as the creature scampered onto the balcony, followed by Tulteth.

To the right of the balcony steps sat Hulneb. The large man proud and motionless, empty goblet held loosely in his right hand like a king on a throne from a children's fairytale. He belched loudly and wiped his damp beard with the back of his left hand, ruining the illusion of nobleness his posture created. The candles dotted evenly around the room cast a gentle yellow light against the darkness, the High Celebrant's dark outline seeming comfortable, almost part of the structure of the room. Sol walked in and cleared his throat.

"Sol!" Roanne jumped up and ran over to him, flinging her arms around him. "We were just wondering where you were." She spoke quickly, "When do you start? How many Theorists have the Twelve assigned to you to look for Opi? Twenty, thirty?"

He held her tenderly, caressing her face and gently pulling it up towards his. At once her beaming smile faded as she caught the disappointment in his eyes, the weary rhythm of his breath and slump of his shoulders. He heaved the words out. "The Twelve will not allow me to search for Opi – they are convinced he has passed over."

"*What?*" she mouthed, breaking their embrace.

A shadow from the balcony slowly rose to dim the candlelight.

"Passed over – do they mean my nephew is dead?" demanded Hulneb.

Sol and Roanne parted, she remaining at his side as he squared up to the High Celebrant.

"I am told congratulations and commiserations are in order, Hulneb," said Sol, holding out his hand. "Mirrimas was a man of great integrity."

Hulneb took the offered hand but remained impassive. His dark eyes gave no hint of emotion while his wiry, auburn beard hid any muscular twitch or spasm of regret he had no control over. He nodded rather than bowed. "Commiserations to you also, my brother-by-union."

"Opi isn't dead – I'd know," said Roanne, tearfully.

Hulneb glanced at his sister and then back to Sol. "Agreed. She would know. The Kaltesh have a spiritual link to their children." He turned slowly and returned to his seat.

Sol greeted Rillian with a bow and a kiss of her hand, taking a seat to the left of the balcony, opposite the High Celebrant. The old woman said nothing also, helping Roanne light more candles.

"I have grown tired," said Rillian, finally. "Come visit us at first light tomorrow, Roanne. We will discuss this, and the choices you now find before you." The old woman collected her things, then looked at Hulneb. "I'll take my guards with me. Shall I send yours to escort you back to the caravanserai?"

He shook his head and stood, kissed her on the forehead and sat back down. "I'll be fine here, mother. There is much to consider and talk about."

As Rillian passed Sol, she held both of his hands tightly and whispered. "Be sure you do the right thing, Cardinal."

He simply nodded, unsure if she would take any action regarding her grandson, or if she could under Kaltesh law.

"Come, Tulteth,'' she said, raising her voice, "the remainder of the evening is not for your ears."

"Won't you stay, mother?" asked Roanne, but the old woman simply shook her head. "I'll see you to the stables, then," said Roanne, pulling her shawl around her shoulders.

Sol watched them leave, and when he was sure they were out of earshot, he spoke.

"Listen, Hulneb. I know you think me weak and stupid, and that my curiosity is wasted–"

"Your curiosity is not only wasted, it's restless, endless and useless," he said, pointing a finger glittering with rings of gold and precious stones as he thrust it forward. "You're a myth-maker, bastardising a recognised legitimacy with your own illegitimate conjecture."

Sol stood and forced a laugh. "And how long have you been rehearsing *that* speech?" he replied, removing from beneath his robes the earring he had found, placing it in a wooden bowl on an occasional table beneath an oval mirror. He looked at his reflection and noticed how tired he appeared, then turned and began to remove his outer robes. "Hulneb, if your manners were as finely honed as your vocabulary, you'd have credibility as a priest in any religion, except Abeona's." He shook his head and dropped his battered cape unceremoniously to the floor, ready for the High Celebrant's reply.

But Hulneb simply smiled and spoke in a soft whisper. "When I seek your credulity you'll be the first to know about it." He walked onto the balcony to stare out over Abeona. As Sol joined him he turned. "There are more important things at hand now, Sol."

"For you, as High Celebrant – or for us, as a family, as you've just said, my brother-by-union?"

Hulneb's gaze lingered on the Cardinal, failing to suppress his agitation at the question by shifting his weight as his eyes narrowed upon him, before his focus returned to the city.

"For us. For family," he finally said. "Even you, as a non-blood relation are essentially family. Opi is my blood nephew. Always, for family. That is our way, our responsibility. Surely yours is no different?"

They both turned upon hearing Roanne's voice.

"This came for you." She handed a letter to Sol, then carried the dinner plates into the kitchen area.

Sol slumped into a chair, facing the city. Reluctantly he broke Zoloth's seal on the envelope and examined the contents. The new creed was laid out meticulously. There was no mention of *Oosah*; only Tal Salandor and the Garden of Contentment tenuously connected the traditional ways to the new guided organised doctrines. Opi filled his thoughts as he dropped the pages onto the flagstones beside him, clasping his hands together and staring across the city. An uneven, broken curve of flaming beacons dominated the city centre to illuminate the Trophy from beneath, and he found himself wondering about Opi's fate, and what part he himself had played in the whole affair. He had not told Roanne everything. How it was believed the inhabitants of the Trophy had taken prisoners inside to dissect them during the war, their bodies opened and exposed whilst they were still alive, their pain threshold tested, their organs examined, their body parts discarded from the Trophy once their usefulness was at an end. How some Cardinals believed the scriptures that told of men, women and children taken from their beds during the nights by strange lights in the sky, never to be seen again. He looked down at his singed and stained tunic as drunken laughter filtered up from the streets beyond the estate wall, feeling as though there was a hint of truth to Yan's concerns. Perhaps the people were indeed losing sight of the real reason for the festival: the gift of language and the written word from Tal Salandor, the victorious end of the war and respect for the tens of thousands dead. All at once he felt self-conscious, his robes of office and official adornments meaningless against the steady stream of moneymaking masses flooding the Square. A wave of anger smothered him as he realised he was just like one of the costumed entertainers there, playing a small part in a misleading charade, and he did not like it, not at all.

Roanne came onto the balcony carrying a plate of boiled meat and steamed vegetables, placing it upon his lap. "You must eat," she said, quietly.

"I'm not hungry," he said, keeping his eyes fixed on the city.

She sat beside him. "What was in the envelope?"

He picked at the vegetables then turned to her. "The future, for some," he said wearily. He motioned for Hulneb to take the remaining seat on the balcony. "I've been sworn to secrecy by Zoloth, but none of that will matter in a short time." Taking a deep breath, he looked from one to the other, sitting forward and waiting. Roanne crossed her legs at the knee, holding her hands upon them, nerves causing her supporting leg to gently bounce at the ankle. Hulneb remained proud, but as the evening breeze stroked the flaming torches set into the walls, Sol was certain he had at last allowed a wave of sorrow to grace his features. He recounted his meeting with Zoloth to them in full, before bowing his head. "I'd like a goblet of wine, please, Ro."

When she returned with the wine he had forced half the meal down. Hulneb sat in silence, filling a large pipe with thick black Kaltesh Farrengrass. Sol watched him as Roanne uncorked the bottle of Vinifera, wondering what Hulneb's slender, curved pipe had been made from. It was ornately carved, and the bowl had been deeply hollowed out to take a large amount of the herb. Satisfied the pipe was sufficiently loaded, the High Celebrant held the bowl in the base of the torch flames to his right, until the Farrengrass smouldered. He quickly put the pipe into his mouth and sucked, causing the embers to glow. Puffing a few clouds above his head, he took the pipe from his mouth and smiled, gazing over at Sol.

"It belonged to Mirrimas," he said, aware of Sol's curiosity. "It was his favourite pipe and it gives the smoothest and coolest smoke of Farrengrass I've ever experienced. It was carved from the upper leg bone of a warrior Gen'hib-Maun, by my great-grandfather." He drew on it again before passing it to Roanne, as Sol poured wine into three goblets.

"It's said Kaltesh Farrengrass is the strongest there is, in its cured form, and helps you to see the world more clearly," said Hulneb, leaning over to take a goblet.

Sol took a sip of his wine. "I don't need a narcotic to

help me see clearly. My course of action is clear and straightforward."

Roanne sat back and closed her eyes.

"You're being used," said Hulneb quietly, pointing at the papers lying on the flagstones "As soon as you speak in public about this new religion they'll have you executed for heresy."

"And what purpose would that serve?"

"It would legally remove you from your religious hierarchy. You're forgetting, you're more of a threat to their way of life than a benefit. There's a great deal of corruption behind the walls of the Citadel, of that I'm *well* aware, from listening to my father. Your own rules state any Cardinal responsible for opening a seal in the auditorium of the one hundred will take up residence in the Citadel as a junior Grand Cardinal, taking a position at the table of Twelve when one becomes vacant. You? Sitting there, with access to all the ancient records of the catacombs! Imagine if you find something they've overlooked, and that leads you to open a seal of significance, immediately promoted as your law demands, an extra gilded throne for a master craftsman to build. Thirteen chairs at the table – no more stagnation when it comes to a vote. Zoloth can't have that! Your voracity for truth is well known, Sol. As is your tenacity."

"Why not? After all, every member of the church is working toward the same objective."

Hulneb leant forward, squinting for a moment as the pipe smoke found his eyes. "Sol, you've become something of a celebrity, even amongst the Kaltesh – despite your inaccurate use of the *Ticandra* during the last festival's team combat games. Zoloth was right about one thing – taking Roanne as a wife was a bold step in everyone's eyes, and has brought both of you much respect from my people. You're too clever for your Holy Twelve and they're aware a man of your veracity could expose them for the perverse idiots they obviously are." He chuckled and took a sip of wine. "How a governing body of twelve men, elevated mostly by succession and very few by their achievements manages to remain intact in this city over all these hundreds of cycles is beyond me. I'll say it one more time. If you rise to Grand Cardinalship, you'd introduce change, and the Twelve are scared of that."

"Succession is the way it has always been, Hulneb. Hardly different from the Kaltesh way – your position was arrived at by succession. One of our fundamental truths; The skills of a Cardinal are passed down to his children. This is a blessing from Tal Salandor."

Hulneb nodded. "Yet had Roanne been born before me, she would now hold the position of High Celebrant, for we, at least operate equality." He sat forward. "Listen, the truth is simple. You are this city's finest Cardinal, but so far have not found one shred of evidence to prove *Agasanduku* was constructed by a foreign race." He gulped down some wine, pointing absently over the balcony with his left hand. "Consider this – if that object had been the product of another species, as your dogma teaches, then our minds would have no comprehension of its mechanisms." He chuckled to himself as he drew on his pipe, sitting back in his chair. "We would be as infants, lost in the desert – no, worse, like a throd fish riding a ganapti. Impossible!"

"You know a great deal about my husband's faith, and take every opportunity to preach your own, Hulneb," said Roanne, reaching over and taking the pipe from his mouth.

He shrugged. "As High Celebrant it's my business to know a potential enemy's belief system, and to present alternatives. It's all too obvious to me, *Agasanduku* is nothing more than a hollow shell, built by the Kaltesh twin brothers, Alamala and Unamanu, to reassure fools who cannot accept their solitary existence among the stars. I'm sure the Twelve Grand s*eniles* are aware of this fact, and they're taking every precaution to prevent Sol from opening the final seal which exposes their 'Trophy' as nothing more than an empty carcass." He smirked, bringing the goblet close to his lips to hide their movement. "Imagine the impact of *that* little truth on the people of this city."

Sol looked up at the night sky for a moment. "All you've said has crossed my mind hundreds of times before, Hulneb, but none of your beliefs give me concern now. I *know Oosah* is as *I* believe. My only concern now is Opi, and where do I turn to voice this concern? My own church has forbidden me to search for him, and by the time the Twelve have deliberated over a request from you to look for him, he could be dead."

Hulneb turned. "Then all is lost for you, your son, family, and your way of life."

Roanne looked sharply at Sol. "So you do believe he's still inside, and not carried away?"

He turned slowly to her and nodded.

"So, how do we get him back?"

Hulneb gulped his wine. "I'll assemble one thousand of my finest warriors. Five hundred will storm the Citadel and I will lead the remainder triumphantly into *Agasanduku*. Then we'll–"

"Be slaughtered when you're forced back outside for food after you discover there's no way to break the seals with weapons, and the five hundred storming the Citadel will be picked off, one by one upon the Eliyas bridge. The same outcome once they're marooned on the Pinnacle of Judgement, or cornered in the garrison. No, we must use more surreptitious means. I have an idea, but it's dangerous, and no one must know our *true* intentions." He looked from one to the other. "No one." They both nodded as he pulled out the envelope given to him by Ommus, tore it open and examined the heavy iron key to Yan Arramosa's classroom before placing it beneath his tunic. "We'll have to be swift. Once I'm inside *Oosah* you must destroy the lift and gantry entrance. I must not be disturbed while I work." Sol took the pipe from Roanne and puffed a plume of smoke from the side of his mouth over the balcony, staring at Hulneb.

"I'm coming with you," she said, as a matter of fact.

He knew there was no use in arguing with her, "I would expect nothing less." He looked back at the burly High Celebrant. "Tell me, Hulneb, are you as skilled a craftsman as your great-grandfather?"

"I've made many a pipe, if that's what you mean?"

Sol stood and walked into the living area, returning in a few moments with his official seal. He handed it to Hulneb, then passed him the envelope from Zoloth. "Could you cut down my seal and carve into it a replica of the seal on that envelope?"

Hulneb leaned into the light, examining both. "It could be done."

"Could it be done by morning?"

"Hmm. How much wine do you have?"

"Hulneb!" exclaimed Roanne.

"Fair exchange is no robbery!"

"We have an entire cellar, I'm told," said Sol. "Just don't drink so much that you can't see what you're doing."

Hulneb produced a dagger from his sleeve and began whittling at the seal as Sol relaxed back into his seat.

"Well, my brother-by-union, how would you like to join me for a ride into the city centre early tomorrow morning?"

"Are you asking for my continued assistance?" said Hulneb, without looking up.

"I am. Your resources, your influence, anything you can offer to help me."

"And what will I receive as payment for my services?"

"What do you want?"

Hulneb blew onto the seal to remove tiny shavings, then angled the seal into the torchlight to inspect his handiwork. Finally he looked over at Sol, glancing up at his sister for a moment before speaking. "Let me see inside. Let me see the truths there – help me prove my faith, once my nephew is found. I want to see the heart of *Agasanduku Oosah*."

Sol's eyes narrowed and he finally managed a

smile, "You have my word," he said slowly, "For family."

Grand Cardinals Zoloth and Irrianna breathed deeply as two junior priests dried the sweat and water from their bodies with hand towels. When they were both satisfied, they were helped into layered silk robes. They dismissed the juniors, leaving the remaining Grand Cardinals to the entertainment of the pool.

Hidden in the walls behind the archways surrounding the poolside, a wide, wooden door was set back into the shadows, and Irrianna silently pushed it open. Beyond, laid out beneath a huge canopy of glass and metal, stretched twenty square leagues of grassy slopes, terraces and rolling hills – a scaled down interpretation of the Garden of Contentment.

"Will he fall in with our plans?" asked Irrianna, as he secured the door behind them.

Zoloth stepped onto the grass, enjoying the warm, springy sensation between his toes, before hurrying towards a lone fruit tree occupying the top of a gentle hill. He plucked two ripe apples from the low branches and handed one to Irrianna, sitting with his back against the trunk as he regarded the fruit.

"Timmerman has no choice," he said, as Irrianna sat beside him. "I made that clear, did I not? Above all else he is still a Cardinal. The tenet was sewn into his head long ago. He will do our bidding." He bit into the apple.

Irrianna placed the fruit by his side. "You're forgetting, Yan Arramosa was like a father to him. His assassination may motivate Cardinal Timmerman toward an unfortunate course of action."

"I neither forget, nor overlook outcomes of motivations. There are no unfortunate courses of action, Ugo, my friend. It does not matter now what Arramosa knew, all of his paperwork has been taken care of. Be assured, every possible consequence has been considered. Arramosa was a fool; he could have held a position of esteem and authority after the Grand Event. Now his demise will serve us by distracting Timmerman, causing him to either mourn, or more likely conduct an investigation from Arramosa's office, if he refuses to commit to memory the falsifications we've provided him with. After a time, his persistence will dwindle and, don't forget, he is only one man." He looked to his confidant, "And how does that Kaltesh saying go? *'The fish that nibbles at every bait will soon be caught'* ? Something like that. If he takes one step beyond his jurisdiction, he will be ours under the law."

Irrianna nodded. "I suggest a state funeral is in order for Yan Arramosa, and Cardinal Timmerman should have an integral part in the proceedings. A eulogy perhaps? That task will keep him busy. We can keep an eye on him then. Shall I make the necessary arrangements?"

Zoloth nodded. "An excellent proposal – forgiveness from Tal Salandor for Arramosa. Make it absolutely clear his wife attends also. Her motivations are uncalculated. We cannot allow her the freedom to introduce unforeseen elements."

"Agreed."

"Then this discussion is over."

"One more thing. What of his son, Oen? Men are unpredictable when it comes to their families. If he proves to be as determined and resourceful over this matter as he is in his work... well!"

"What of him? I suspect Timmerman has him hidden somewhere in the city. You didn't believe his story, surely? Trapped behind a seal? Simply an excellent attempt at manipulating us, as it's a certainty Arramosa hinted of our plans, and he now needs us to allow him back inside to further his studies. Be reassured. If anyone in this city is to have the knowledge and glory that comes from deciphering the key to the next seal, then it will be us. I suspect his son will soon be found alive and well, hopefully just in time for the Grand Event." Zoloth turned. "Speaking of which. The numerical conclusions?"

"I've collated the information from my extensive tour of the city during the past cycle. Everything will be ready in good time."

"Projected death toll of the irreligious fools?" asked Zoloth.

"Between eighty-seven and ninety-eight percent."

Zoloth's eyes widened as he placed his unfinished apple upon his lap. "This is too good to be true. I expected seventy-six percent at the most. You have done extremely well, Ugo." Zoloth smiled to himself. "I will never forget the Almighty speaking to me during my sleep, telling me of his plan. Over three nights he visited me, detailing the Grand Event. Glorious!"

Irrianna picked up his apple and bit into it as Zoloth relaxed back against the tree trunk, clasping his hands behind his head.

"There, you see, Ugo" he whispered as he closed his eyes. "There is absolutely nothing to worry about."

ELEVEN

A MURDERER'S MEMORIES

They had talked for a further two measures, discussing Sol's plan. And when the third bottle of wine was emptied and the fifth pipe of Farrengrass extinguished, Sol and Roanne took to their bed, leaving a satisfied Hulneb to sleep on the stone balcony beneath the scattered stars.

Sol fell into a restless sleep, twisting and occasionally kicking against an unknown assailant as Roanne lay awake for a further measure, silently sobbing for the loss of her son while the past evening's events repeated themselves in her head. Instead of the usual playing and reading with Opi before bed, there was an awkward visit from her family to occupy the time before Sol returned.

She sat up, slowly climbing out of bed as Sol's movements became too much for her, deciding to walk the silent corridors and gather her thoughts. Finally she found herself in Opi's room. There the moonlight illuminated a few toys lying on the floor, along with the clothes Opi had decided not to wear for the day out with his father. The bed was still unmade and Ebe lay asleep, curled up between the folds of the bedclothes at the foot of the bed. She moved the sleeping creature onto the blanket beneath the window and found herself climbing into her son's bed. His smell was still fresh on the sheets and pillow and she cried again until her exhaustion forced her to sleep, and she dreamed.

The morning was young and fresh and she found herself staring out across the ocean. The low sun warmed her face as the rippling tide caressed the rocks at her feet with a soothing whisper. She noticed the water was receding. Here, just a few feet from the beach, young balias shells had uprooted themselves and now hid in tide pools, huddling together in little clumps, awaiting their fate. The rocks and seaweed had dried quickly, forming a maze of stepping-stones above the water, stretching half a league ahead of her until they vanished beneath the crashing waves. She found herself walking out across the maze, and then all at once everything vanished...

Now the sun was higher in the sky. The ocean, in all its expansive glory, spat its white foam at her as it crashed against the rocks, as if angry she was brave enough to venture this far into its territory. But this salty spray served only to cool her face; she licked her lips and wiped her eyes as the roar of the ocean filled her ears.

He looked out over the water. Ahead of him, half a dozen rocks briefly showed their faces as the waves wiped watery hands to smooth their contours. As these fingers of foam receded, the rocks revealed adult balias shells feeding on the thick, fleshy green seaweed entwining them.

Her head was level with the back of his neck and she felt the weight in her hands and the muscles in her forearms tense as she heaved the rock high above her head. She stood motionless for a moment, the rock shading her eyes from the sun, and she noticed how old Mirrimas had become. His long, knotted white hair twisted in a horizontal line in the air as the sea winds blew across the delta, revealing a patch on the back of his head where his hair had thinned. There, the skin was dry and mottled and she concentrated on that patch, staring hard. As the rock came back over her head she tried to scream to warn him, but could not summon her voice. The rock was brought down swiftly. She heard the crack of bone and a whimpering cry as his body jerked forward and his arms came up.

Now the spray was warm and red as she licked her lips once more, dropping the bloodied rock into the water.

Early the next morning, before Roanne awoke, Sol and

Hulneb approached the Archbishop's longhouse. Opposite this forlorn structure, the Square of Remembrance glowed with smouldering fires and torches from the previous night's revelry. Sol rode his ganapti past the Holy Entrance to the Square, directing the animal through a long, torch-lit tunnel that opened into a courtyard of blue slate flagstones.

They dismounted, securing their animals beneath the longhouse. Sol headed for the stairs at the front of the building.

Beyond the door, a vaulted corridor stretched over the stables, running the length of the longhouse with the classrooms opening from it. Candles hung from the ceiling every ten paces, creating pools of yellow light as they hurried along, their shadows growing and receding around them. As they reached Yan's classroom Sol held up a hand.

"Wait," he whispered, "the doors are ajar."

A few paces ahead of them the room was shrouded in darkness. Then candlelight appeared briefly at the crack between the double doors, returned and stopped. They both heard the unmistakable sound of a falchion sword drawn swiftly from its sharpening sheath.

"Sol Timmerman, Grade One Theorist," shouted Sol, "conducting official business on behalf of the Twelve Grand Cardinals. Sheath your weapon, show yourself, and state your intention!"

The candle went out with a brief hiss, and the falchion blade briefly caught the candlelight from the hallway as a figure took a step closer. Sol drew his scimitar, Hulneb producing two highly decorated short-swords from beneath his long black cloak, standing ready.

"This isn't your fight," said Sol, his eyes remaining fixed on the doorway.

"Agreed," answered Hulneb, "but I have no intention of returning to my sister with more sad news."

The double doors burst open, and with a swift movement the falchion came whistling through the darkened doorway toward Sol's chest. Sidestepping the thrust, he parried the attack, sending the blade into the wall of the narrow corridor. Twisting from the splintering impact of the blade on the wood panels, the falchion sliced the air above Sol's head. He crouched, bringing his scimitar up from his right flank, catching the blade near the grip-guard with a melodic metal note. The falchion took a step back into the classroom and Sol advanced, holding his scimitar before him. "I am a Cardinal in service of the Holy Church of *Oosah*!" he shouted, "Sheathe your weapon!"

Now Hulneb stood at his side, his short-swords twisting around his wrists in a threatening display of skilled swordsmanship. As they advanced into the dark, a broad swipe at knee height forced both men apart, Sol sidestepping left, Hulneb remaining close to the doorway. The falchion, now aware it was outnumbered and escape unlikely, darted between them, running between a row of desks toward the back of the classroom. Hulneb pursued, holding his short-swords in front of him at arms length, their tips meeting an inch from his forehead. "Take the right," he barked to Sol, "he won't get past me."

"This is your final warning," said Sol, flanking the falchion along the aisle.

The blade darted toward him and he ducked behind a desk as the attack took a large chunk of wood from a chair back. Hulneb leapt forward, slicing the air at chest height with both blades as the falchion leapt upon a desk, jumping to the next.

Sol lunged forward, but the assailant predicted the move, leaping to the next desk then the next, somersaulting in mid-air to land facing them at the top of the aisle.

Hulneb was moving fast now, knowing the enemy's escape was just a handful of paces distant, readying himself, breathing deeply, concentrating. But the falchion had already recognised him as the more capable swordsman, blocking both blades as they attacked at head and thigh height successively. Bringing his blades in an arc to strike again, Hulneb felt a foot in his chest, timed to catch him just at his moment of imbalance, sending him backwards into the aisle.

The glow from the hallway now welcomed their attacker, and as he glanced to the door to check his position Sol ran forward. A flourish of steel and the falchion sliced Sol's left forearm. Hulneb ran forward, noticing Sol's scimitar falter as the falchion continued on its trajectory towards him. The big man took a step backward, tripped and hit the floor, knocking the wind out of himself. Now the falchion saw its chance, swiftly altering its attack, angling its tip down towards Hulneb's chest.

Instinctively, Sol threw himself toward the High Celebrant's body, bringing the flat of the scimitar's blade down onto his chest. An instant later, the falchion tip met it, shrieking to a halt, finding the blood groove running along the scimitar's blade. Slackening his grip on the sword, Sol brought his knees together, allowing momentum to do the rest as he kicked out. His feet found the side of the swordsman's head, sending him crashing into the oak door frame. Hulneb turned, scrambling over the injured assailant, holding both short-swords like scissor blades against their attacker's neck. The body tensed beneath him as it felt the cold blades, then relaxed back against the floor breathing hard, aware it was defeated.

"For a moment, when your sword came down, I thought all this was just a ruse to eliminate me," said Hulneb, catching his breath.

Sol stood and sheathed his scimitar, then held his arm as it began to throb. "It's about time you trusted me, despite my *Ticandra* mistake. Hold him there. If he moves, remind him who has control of the situation."

"*Ti-can-dra-esh-roo-neth*!   *Ti-can-dra-esh-roo-neth,*" said Hulneb in his rich Kaltesh tones. *Ti* - turn, *can* - behind, *dra* - you, *esh* - and, *roo* - level, *neth* - strike! You need to understand it and learn how to pronounce it before you shout it. And you missed, *esh-roo-neth*."

Sol shrugged, then winced at the pain in his arm as he

picked up the dropped falchion, placing it onto Yan's desk. He strode into the corridor to bring two candles into the room, then set about lighting all he could find, until the classroom was bathed in candlelight.

Hulneb looked around the classroom. "What do you call the move, saving my life?"

"Desperation. Someone's beaten us to it," said Sol, his eyes wandering across the papers strewn among the overturned bookcases. Yan's pictures had their backs cut from them and the stone model of the Trophy lay on the floor amid its shattered glass case. Students' desk drawers had been removed and scattered over the floor along with their contents.

"I'm sorry I fell, tripped over my cape, of all things," said Hulneb, pulling the assailant to his feet. "It belonged to my father, and he was a head taller than I am." He sheathed a sword and gripped the stranger around the neck, holding the tip of the remaining sword to the stranger's stomach.

Sol waved the apology aside, glaring at their attacker. He was in his mid-sixties, standing slightly shorter than Sol. His dry skin wrinkled, his head sporting a silver ponytail from the back of his otherwise bald head. He was dressed entirely in a tight-fitting, thickly-padded, black weave. Despite his age, his frame was broad and muscular.

"Are you responsible for this?" hissed Sol, looking over the papers strewn across the classroom. The old man simply looked relieved upon seeing him and bowed slowly in silence. "See if you can find something to tie him up with, Hulneb." As Sol turned away, the old man shook his head and reached out for him, mouthing words silently.

"I'm going to have trouble here," said Hulneb. "I think he's trying to say something to you."

Sol turned back to the stranger. The old man opened his mouth, sticking out, as best he could, the stubby, ragged remains of a tongue.

"Now that explains a lot," said Hulneb. "Okay, we've

seen enough." But his mouth remained open and Hulneb brought up a large hand to close it.

The old man's eyes darted toward Yan's desk and he reached out.

"So you want to try your hand again, do you?" said Hulneb, moving his grip to the stranger's throat.

"Let him go," said Sol, pulling up a chair and positioning it behind the black-clad figure.

Hulneb pushed him down onto the seat as he continued to motion toward the desk.

"It's not the sword he's after," said Sol, glancing at the table, snatching up a sheet of paper and a quill. The old man nodded, reaching out for them.

"Okay, but move for that sword, and I'll gut you," spat Hulneb.

Gnarled fingers wrote quickly upon the paper and held it out to Sol.

"What's he trying to say?" asked Hulneb.

"'Apologies'" read Sol. "'I am Tyn Narrat, book carrier to Cardinal Ana Zoloth.'" The name caused Sol's heart to pound. Ana, a colleague and lover from so long ago. They had trained together as junior priests, under Yan.

"What's a book carrier?" asked Hulneb, interrupting Sol's memories.

"Before the library was built, Cardinals employed junior priests to carry their reference books," Sol said, absently. He peered at the words and continued. "'She must talk with you.'"

Sol glared up from the paper, "Ana's dead," he stated forcefully. "What are you playing at, old man?"

Tyn Narrat shook his head as Sol stared at him, bringing his hands up to his ears, pushing his palms hard against them, moving them backwards and forwards.

Hulneb peered into the stranger's left ear where a large red scar snaked into the ear canal. "By the Brothers, he's performed Hathranelzra!"

Sol seized the large Kaltesh by the arm and turned him

around, remembering the speaker in his dream of yesterday. "*What* did you say?"

"Hathranelzra," replied Hulneb, surprised. "It's an old Kaltesh punishment ritual, although it hasn't been used for many cycles. The convicted criminal had a choice – they either perform the ceremony, or they're put to death, along with their family." He replaced his short-sword and took the paper and quill from the old man, then wrote the word down on the paper, holding it up to him.

The old man nodded and bowed his head slowly with regret.

"He's cut his tongue out and had his ears ruined," said Hulneb quietly. "*'I'll speak not of my innocence, hear not words of pity, but see for my remaining days the world following my crimes.'* That's the old ritual passage, if I remember correctly." He shrugged, "Something like that. Rillian would know for certain, she's seen a few performed in her lifetime. Anyway, have you heard of it?"

"No," said Sol, picking up the paper and quill.

"There's no need for all that. If you'll allow me," said Hulneb, pulling back his sleeves. "If he's really Hathranelzra, then he should know the language of hands. We still use it to communicate with each other during a hunt." He began making shapes in the air with his fingers and the old man's eyes lit up, watching carefully. He gestured back to Hulneb, his fingers swiftly forming contours and tracing figures.

"He's going too fast for me," said Hulneb, jabbing his fingers together, then dropping them slowly to the ground. The old man nodded, then started again.

"What's he saying?" asked Sol, eager to understand.

"He's sad – no, that's *sorry* for attacking us, but thought we were responsible for this mess, and had returned. He'd surprised whoever did this earlier, but they ran off. He says he came searching for yesterday's admittance register into *Agasanduku*, or proof of Yan Arramosa's murder, but someone had beaten him to both, it seems."

"Yan's murder? Tell him to explain *exactly* what he means, and all that nonsense about Ana."

For the next few minutes Hulneb and the old man spoke in the language of hands, while Sol sifted through the papers littered around Yan's desk, listening to Hulneb's translations.

"Apparently, Yan Arramosa had vital information for you and was on his way to deliver it when he was murdered." Sol turned to him, aware he had stopped in mid-sentence.

"What's he saying, Hulneb?"

"He says he witnessed it, but didn't recognise the murderer. Hold on, he's going too fast again. Okay, yes. He says Ana may know more. She's in an asylum in the... no, that's *near* Gal Bapsi Park."

"An asylum? But I attended her funeral!" whispered Sol in disbelief.

The old man bent down, picked up the stone model of the Trophy and placed it upon Yan's desk, then began signing to Hulneb once more.

"He says Ana told him this is important. He was to deliver it to you."

Sol stood behind Yan's desk, watching the morning twilight creep across the city. "I must speak with Ana. Take the model back to my estate and explain everything to Roanne. I'll be back in a measure." He scribbled a note on a piece of paper and found Yan's seal under the desk, placing the paper in an envelope and sealing it with wax.

"Can you write, Hulneb?"

"In my language or yours?"

"Mine."

"Difficult, as you Abeonians insist on writing backwards. What do you need?"

Sol smirked. "It's the other way around, we write from the left to the right, to be right. Just an admittance pass from Grand Cardinal Zoloth. Only a few words, but the handwriting needs to be different from mine, lest both are checked together."

Sol watched the old man as Hulneb sat behind the desk, his tongue sticking from the side of his mouth as he drew the quill across the paper. He looked up. "This Ana Zoloth, is she by any chance a relation–"

"Grand Cardinal Zoloth's daughter, one of the most successful Cardinals the city had ever seen. Everyone believed she'd unlock the truth of *Oosah* in her lifetime, but she submitted several heretic papers to her Bishop, insisting a four-armed deity, a daemon with five eyes, had spoken to her inside *Oosah*. Her Bishop passed her reports on to the Twelve, there was a preliminary investigation carried out by Yan and my father, but the matter was taken out of their hands. The Twelve interviewed her, *extensively*."

Hulneb understood by the tone of Sol's voice how extensive their interview techniques must have been. "And she was declared insane," he said, dropping the quill into its well.

Sol nodded without looking up. "Indeed. Her published papers were destroyed. A few fakes have found their way into the library over the cycles, so no one knows *exactly* what she wrote." He lowered his voice, struggling to speak. "My father told me to stay away from her, that she'd insisted she had visited the Garden of Contentment with that daemon, in a floating chariot made of mirrors. She said there were no souls residing there, that we are not rewarded for our faith in Tal Salandor with rebirth, as he simply does not exist." He quickly checked Hulneb's work, using Hulneb's copy of Zoloth's seal to make the document seem authentic, before placing it in an envelope. He turned his back, hiding his emotions. "It was reported that she hanged herself in her cell, the night before her trial."

"So," began Hulneb, standing, "who decides what constitutes insanity in this city?"

"The Holy Twelve, under the recommendation of the Senior Grand Cardinal," Sol replied.

"Don't tell me," said Hulneb, closing his eyes and holding up his outstretched palms. "And at that time it was Zoloth?"

But Sol was already through the doorway and striding down the corridor, the Hathranelzra following close behind, leaving Hulneb alone to the chaos of the classroom as he opened his eyes.

TWELVE

CONVERSATIONS WITH THE DEAD

The Hathranelzra had pointed out the building from some distance, before running off into the waning shadows of early morning.

The building hid in plain sight amid a network of meandering alleyways, sitting with its back against the fringe of Gal Bapsi Park. From the outside, its appearance was that of a merchant's villa, displaying a similar architectural style to the older buildings surrounding the Square of Remembrance. Its sharply-angled, red-tiled roof held five tiny, shuttered windows jutting out along its length, the white-painted wooden frames peeling from neglect, ground floor windows closed to the day, thick drapes preventing any glimpse of the interior. Its neighbouring buildings were now merchant's warehouses, their high walls projecting over the pavement, helping to keep the customer dry during the rainy season, and valuables from the view and temptation of the criminal. The building gave no clue as to what it really held – how its purpose had been altered without the knowledge of the populace. It wore a disguise of familiarity amid a street of regularity.

As Sol approached, a group of children walked next to his mount, patting the animal, holding out hands for tokens. Laughing, they shouted up to him, but he was oblivious to them, his mind dwelling in youthful memories of Ana Zoloth.

They laughed as they ran and fell into the grass, just short of the walled orchard.

"I've never heard such contrived rubbish," she said, flicking her long red hair back over her head and turning her back on him. "Would you be so kind?" She held a thin yellow ribbon between her thumb and forefinger.

He took it from her sheepishly. Her neck was slender and blemish-free. Her hair smelt of rose petals, shining, each strand a conduit for the fading warmth of late summer. He delicately tied a neat bow and she turned with a smile. "Thank you, Sol," she said, motioning for him to sit.

She broke the small block of soft white cheese in half and handed him a piece.

"Thank you. Well, that certainly gave fat Arramosa something to think about," he said, tearing a bread roll in two. "'My name's Ror Kanf, and this is my dissertation,'" he mimicked, trying his best to impersonate the Lower Fourth Quarter accent of their fellow second-year student. "'The Trophy, Oosah Agasanduku *– obviously constructed by an off-world species – displays traits obviously inherent only to non-city dwellers or Kaltesh tribespeople.'"*

They turned to face each other. "Obviously!" they said in unison, lying back into the soft grass, laughing at Kanf's battology.

"How many times did he say that?"

"I lost count after eleven."

She took half the roll from him. "Seriously though, my friend, it's my dissertation after lunch, and this will make or break my dreams for the future."

He propped himself up on his left elbow and looked at her. "Don't tell me you're nervous?"

Her face strained to remain impassive, but the security of his companionship warmed her heart. Her eyes betrayed the false mood she attempted to create: her pupils dilated, her plucked eyebrows elongated and her cheeks rose. "Obviously," she said, through her laughter. . .

The ganapti bellowed as two women emptied effluent from an iron bathtub into the narrow channel between the cobbled walkway and the road. The animal began to rear up and Sol calmed her with a soothing whisper, patting her on the neck as she snorted, shaking her head.

A tall, bedraggled gatekeeper, clutching a pike half as

tall again as himself, sat on a wooden stool, his back slumped against the asylum wall. Upon seeing Sol he stood slowly, scratching at his fartleberries, wiping his nose and sniffing at the mephitic air. He finally spoke. "Your business?"

Sol dismounted, placing his hood over his head to hide his face. He handed the gatekeeper the document he had prepared at Yan's office.

He took it reluctantly, breaking the seal with grubby fingers to read the information written there.

"I heard a whisper Arramosa was dead?" he said abruptly, looking up from the document. "Doused himself with grease and set himself alight, right in the middle of the Square." He spat on the floor, adding to the puddle he'd accumulated there.

Sol jabbed a finger at the paper. "Well, if you look carefully, you'll see this document is still valid, for today, and today only."

The gatekeeper shrugged, turning to the iron gates to push them open.

"You can leave your ride here," he said, holding out a hand for the reins, and Sol obliged.

The small courtyard was in ruins, with many of its flagstones cracked or missing, allowing a thin-bladed grass to add colour to its otherwise bland palette. Propped against one of the fifteen pillars that supported the narrow, red-tiled veranda roof rested a velocipede with a broken wheel and axle, several piles of roof tiles stacked in its seat. In the centre of the courtyard sat a low, circular wall protecting a thick iron mesh set into the ground below. A cloud of steam rose from it, carrying the odour of boiling fish. Sol looked about in the silence as he headed for the veranda, noticing the window shutters were nailed closed and all the doors, bar one, boarded up. He marched purposefully towards this door as it creaked open, revealing a thin, sharp-featured woman in her late fifties, he estimated. Her long black hair was swept over her head and tied tightly back by a blue scarf. Around her waist was a thick brown belt with a bunch of keys dangling over her right thigh. Upon seeing him she bobbed at the waist rather than bowed, studying him with a superior air as she closed the door behind her.

"I'm here to visit Ana Zoloth," declared Sol, joining her in the shade of the veranda.

The woman adjusted the yellow and green sash hanging from her shoulders and frowned. "We have no one by that name here, Archbishop...?"

"My apologies – Cardinal... Osterley. My documentation from Archbishop Arramosa says otherwise." He handed her his forged paperwork and stood squarely in front of her.

She stared at the document. "As I said, Cardinal Osterley, there is no one by the name of Ana Zoloth residing here." She looked up and handed it back. "Obviously, your information is incorrect."

Sol sighed. "More likely she is known by another name. If I could come in and look for her, Madam...?"

"Zannus, head carer. I'm sorry, but the guests cannot be disturbed without the proper authorisation." She smiled sharply and stood her ground, folding her arms.

He produced the envelope purportedly sealed by Zoloth himself and held it out to her. "Then perhaps I should return to the Holy Citadel, to inform Senior Grand Cardinal Oen Zoloth he was mistaken, and that he should take this matter up with you personally, when he has the time?"

Zannus gave a weak smile and dropped her arms to her sides as her eyes fixed upon the seal. "Oh, I see. I'm so sorry for my abruptness, but you're several days early," she said. "Just to make sure you're here for the right guest – as we do not refer to the guests by their names – the woman you're here to visit, does she have dark red hair, brown eyes, standing roughly at your height?"

He suppressed a grin. "She does."

"Then your visit is not in vain and your timing is just

right. Her medication has just been administered."

Beyond the front door and two darkened rooms within, a narrow iron stairway spiralled down beneath street level. Zannus led the way with a torch, the sound of dripping water giving counterpoint to the rhythm of their footsteps against the metal.

"You'll excuse the stench once we're inside, Cardinal. Some of our elderly guests refuse to use the facilities provided for their personal hygiene. They are bathed every other day, their accommodation cleaned in between."

The basement at the bottom of the stairway opened out into a small, square area with an arched wooden door set back into the wall ahead. Barrels of water were stacked to the ceiling at the left of the door, and to the right a frail old woman sat at a child's study desk, eating a plate of cold fish and ripe blackberries.

"Mother, this is Cardinal Osterley. He's here to deliver Number Fifteen's supplies." The old woman stood, wiping her oily mouth with the back of her hand and pulling open a drawer set into the desk. She passed a key to Zannus, then sat back down to continue her meal.

Zannus opened the door ahead with the key. Once through the door she turned sharply left into a damp stone corridor, which curved gently to the right. To Sol's left stood heavy oak doors spaced at intervals of ten paces, with small inspection hatches set into them.

"We're directly under the courtyard," said Zannus, casually pointing upward. Behind the wall on your right are housed our kitchen and staff quarters." She stopped at an open door where several women were preparing food. "This wing has just eaten. Would you like breakfast? The churchman who usually delivers Number Fifteen's paper makes time for our pickled fish and sweetbreads."

Sol peered into the large room where all manner of food was stacked against the far wall.

"I've already eaten, but thank you anyway."

"I see." She walked on slowly, toying with the keys between her long fingers. "Below us are four circular areas identical to this. They are reached by an interconnecting stairway in the kitchen. The whole complex was built as a prison to house captured Kaltesh warriors during the war, holding a maximum of two hundred and fifty. We keep the, ahem, *less cooperative* guests in the lower levels." She continued along the corridor as a scream filled the air. The voice trailed off into a gurgled cry of profanity. Then all around them rose other voices, their screams echoing along the corridor in a wave of anger and distress. Fists pounded the door ahead, and as Sol passed the inspection hatch a man's face appeared. He clutched the grille with dirty hands, dribbling from a toothless grin. Upon seeing Sol's robes he began laughing.

"Cardinal, CARDINAL!"

Sol stopped, facing the man and at once he calmed.

"Yes, Cardinal, come in, come in here. I've all the answers you're looking for. I know the truth."

"Ignore him," said Zannus. "He's a murderer and defiler of old women."

"NO," screamed the man. He pointed to Sol. "HE'S the murderer. I'm the real Cardinal, not him. Don't you understand?"

Sol hurried along as the man's screams followed him.

"Don't worry," said Zannus. "He says that about everyone he sees. His medication should take effect soon."

She stopped several doors along the passageway. "It's this one. Allow me." She unlocked the door, pushing it open to stand on the threshold, hands clasped together in front of her. "You'll be quite safe with Number Fifteen. I'll light the candles, but be sure to put them out and lock the door when you leave." She stepped into the room and set three candles aglow. "You have just a short while," she said without turning. "I'll lock the door behind me." She turned, her expression exaggerated by the candlelight, harsh and angular, superior, matching her tone. "Here," she reached into a purse upon her belt, fanned out a few keys in her palm and selected one, passing it to him. "Make sure you lock the door on your way out, and hang it on the hook to the right of the door. The cleaners will need it soon." He bowed to her and she bowed in return before retuning to her business.

"You're late," said a shape huddled in the corner, with a weary croak.

Sol locked the door. It took his eyes a while to adjust to the dim glow, so he took one of the candles from the wall and crouched down. "Ana?" he whispered. "Is it really you?"

The figure sat forward holding a pewter plate of fish bones, the small sphere of candle glow illuminating her face with an all too honest flicker. Her once long, straight hair was cropped into short and uneven spiky clumps, her face was drawn with deep lines. Large, dark rings hung beneath her left eye, while her right eye was hidden by a large leather patch. Her gown hung from her right shoulder, stained and threadbare. She sat up, crossing her legs, baring blackened knees and feet.

At once he recognised her and his heart sank. Shakily, he placed the candle onto the floor in the small space between them, slowly holding out his hands to her face. But she turned fast, out of the candlelight to rest her left cheek against the cold, damp wall.

Her lips quivered as she whispered to him. "Are they all dead? I expected to hear fighting. You're too late. I'm still eighteen, eighteen cycles old *and* a Cardinal! You should have been here a long time ago."

He swallowed hard, sure his voice would fail. His throat dry, his thoughts dwelling on all the cycles she had lost. Finally he forced himself to speak. "Ana, if... if I'd known, I wouldn't have let this happen."

"You've never been in a position to prevent anything!" she hissed behind clenched teeth, her voice suddenly level,

"Including your ambition for your lost son. They told me, it's only now, since you lost him you've started acting like a man." She laughed. "Your face, Cardinal Timmerman! Same expression, no wiser, simply older."

He sat down cross-legged opposite her. "Who have you spoken to, Ana?"

She gazed around the room, stretching her arms wide. "The... the wall, of course, the wall tells me everything that happens outside. I'm well informed. I'm still a Cardinal and can theorise better than any, including you. Tiny voices tell me everything."

Sol clasped his hands together. "Ana, I was met by someone claiming to be your book carrier. He told–"

"Shh!" she interrupted, waving her hands at him rapidly. "They're talking." She placed her left ear against the wall and covered her other ear with her right hand, her eyes narrowing as a smile touched her chapped lips. "You left him inside, didn't you? I expect your Kaltesh wife came close to slitting your throat while you slept," she said with a childish giggle, turning to face him.

"Ana, your father will pay for this. I'll get you out of here and insist you're reinstated. I have a friend in the Citadel – he will help us."

"Reinstated?" Anger clouded her features, lines becoming darker, staring. "My position was *never* revoked. I died, and I'm still eighteen. Such a tender age to die, don't you agree, Sol Timmerman? The walls do." She frowned and waved an accusing finger at him. "They say Opi's not very happy at you leaving him alone."

"Ana, please. Don't play games with me. Your book carrier, Tyn, or whatever he is, told me my life is in danger and that you wanted to see me."

She coughed. "Perhaps it is, perhaps it isn't. Perhaps I do, perhaps I don't. Besides, what's wrong with games? Don't tell me you've forgotten how to play games. We played games yesterday, remember? On the grass in the junior priests' quarter, running and laughing during lunch, dreaming we were Grand Cardinals, agreeing that together *we* would discover the ultimate truth. The walls remember that day, they watched us, thought we'd be together forever and we'd have children. By the way, how is your half-Kaltesh son?"

Sol stood and turned away, unable to listen any longer. He knew the cycles of incarceration had taken their toll on her once strong and noble mind, turning it into a fragile object uncertain of reality or itself. His eyes fell on the walls where she had drawn pictures: childlike, fragmented impressions of the past. The Trophy sat in the Square, and above it, in the clouds, likenesses of them both, he assumed, smiling down together with elongated mouths and large, circular eyes. Beneath this, an uneven line of theories was scribbled, down to the floor. Some had faded, others had been crossed out and arrows pointed to circles and boxes of other ideas. He recognised some as having been refuted cycles before they became Cardinals. Upon the bed was a pile of neatly stacked papers sitting next to a quill and a bottle of ink. He studied her scribblings for a moment before realising none of it made any sense. With a hollow feeling of sadness that angered him, he realised it was no use trying to release her – she'd only scream and raise the alarm. He walked to the small barred opening set into the centre of the wall to his right. Beyond a small courtyard's high wall, Abeona was slowly being illustrated by the dawn, its silhouetted buildings showing colour and substance as the sunlight caressed them. To his right, he could just make out the branches and budding leaves of a fruit tree, realising this was her only view of the outside world, teasing her with the freedom lying beyond, measure after measure, cycle after cycle.

She laughed behind him. "Didn't you play a game with your son? Hide and come seek, and he won."

He turned quickly, his impatience replacing his regret. "Tyn – your book carrier – said the model of *Oosah* was important. Why?"

She shook her head, looking down at her hands, her fingers stretched wide apart. "I don't know. Why would I? Besides, Tyn didn't say anything, probably wrote it all down, poor old friend." She nodded toward his bloodstained sleeve. "I see he's still skilled with that old falchion. He always drew first blood. Surely *you* didn't manage to kill him?"

Sol held his arm. "Tyn's alive. There was a misunderstanding, that's all. What of Yan's model, Ana?"

She leant forward on all fours, like an animal, and shouted at him. "That's *my* model, and don't let Yan Arramosa's unholy ghost tell you otherwise!" She stared up at him open-mouthed, a string of saliva dangling from her lip. "He should never have found me, never come to question me. He would still be alive today if he'd just stuck to filing papers. Once a Cardinal, always a Cardinal!"

"Ana! The model! Why is it important?"

But she only gaped at him; it seemed to him her medication was only now starting to take effect.

Sol slumped to the floor, easing his back against the cold brickwork. "How can you know so much, Ana? Who have you been talking to?"

She sat back, her head rocking from side to side as she picked at a dirty thumbnail. Her eyes became glazed and she stared at the ceiling. "I made the model to remind me of *Oosah's* beauty." Slowly her eyes met his, her head tilting to one side. She smiled with a sadness he'd never seen before, as though behind that smile there were a hundred things she wanted to say, but couldn't. "I... I spoke to Mya before she died. She wanted you to know she loved you very, very much, at... at the end."

"Impossible! My mother died during the collapse! I saw her body!"

Her smile became a brief, bitter laugh, edged with pain. "Did you? Then I spoke to her ghost, held in the cell opposite mine, many years ago." Her gaze returned to the ceiling.

He spoke again, realising Zannus could return at any moment, ignoring the suggestion Ana planted, determined to concentrate. "I left Opi in the fifth alcove in the auditorium of one hundred. Is there anything you can tell me that would help me find him? Please, anything at all, however trivial?"

"Your half-breed son? I suggest you take my precious model and break it over your wife's precious head. That's how important they both are to me, *Cardinal* Timmerman." She placed her ear against the wall once more and he stood, brushing himself down. As he turned to leave, she raised her voice.

"Do you remember when I tried to teach you how to swim, in the lake by my father's house? How afraid you were! Timmerman, Timmerman, you must learn to swim again." She giggled and repeated the phrase over and over, rocking back and forth in time to her ramblings.

Opening the door just wide enough, he squeezed through into the corridor, locking it behind him.

Her face appeared at the grille with a metallic clatter, chewed, dirty fingernails poking through the small gaps in the metal straps. For the first time, she spoke with a level of calm lucidity. "My bastard father stole everything from me, stole my theories, my life, and opened the seal with the cipher the daemon gave me, after they burnt it out of me, cutting me, in that filth, that unholy Citadel of liars. He should have let me die!" She nodded fast, urging him to agree with her, eyes wide, smiling maniacally. "Yan knew this – he was on his way to tell you this truth, and *so* many others. Your robes are a mask to the truth, Sol. The city outside, with its high walls, that is the real asylum." She began to sob as her forehead rested upon the grating. "If you only knew the truth behind the hundreds of lies!"

"I'm so sorry, Ana," said Sol, turning away as tears filled his eyes. "Yan committed suicide, that is the word of the Church, and your father opened a seal long before you became a Cardinal. He wouldn't need to steal your theories." He stared down at the key in his hand, then reluctantly hung it on the hook next to her cell door.

"Idiot! You must learn to swim, Tim, Tim, Tim," she sang over and over again, louder and louder. But her voice was lost amid the sea of other tormented pleas as he hurried away.

Zannus was waiting with her mother beyond the arched door.

"I trust you found everything in order, Cardinal?"

"Everything. One question. What was the name of the last Church official to visit Number Fifteen?"

"It was an unscheduled visit a few days ago. An elderly, chubby gentleman, an Archbishop, a tutor, I believe. Very polite but in a dreadful hurry. He didn't give his name, just documents."

"Thank you. I must be on my way."

"I'll see you to the front gate."

"No need," said Sol, "I know the way," and with that he bowed and hurried up the winding staircase.

THIRTEEN

REVELATIONS CAST IN STONE

As Sol entered the living area. Roanne, Hulneb and Tyn were sitting around a table about to begin breakfast,

"Was it her?" asked Roanne, as the housemaid placed food on the plates.

He pulled up a chair and sat opposite Hulneb, waiting for the housemaid to leave before answering. "Not as I remember her, no. She's suffered a great deal and has lost her grip on reality. Zoloth's kept her locked up for many cycles, and has been forcing medication of some sort on her. Also, it seems Tyn was telling the truth," he said, nodding to the Hathranelzra, "and that Yan was murdered, having discovered her whereabouts."

"Murdered! Why? Who could be responsible?"

Hulneb cleared his throat to speak, but Sol cut him off. "I theorise Yan only recently discovered that she's alive, and was coming to inform me when he was killed. He was trying to tell me something during our last meeting, but was strangely reluctant, as if there was too much to say. As to who is responsible..." He shrugged.

"Oh, it's obvious!" said Hulneb, flatly.

"I'll not entertain such theories without evidence," said Sol.

"Go clean yourself up and I'll see to that wound," said Roanne. "An Archbishop, Ommus, came to see you soon after you'd left. There's a letter and a package for you – he asked if I would leave them on the balcony."

"Did you tell him where I was?"

"No. He was in a hurry, and didn't seem that interested in conversation."

Sol took himself outside where a small wooden box with holes in its sides was set upon his chair. He picked it up and peered inside, where a homing bird with blue feathers looked back at him.

He came back into the room, studying the letter.

"A homing bird to communicate with Ommus." He raised his eyebrows, "It seems the Twelve have changed their decision concerning Yan's death, stating he was murdered, and have organised a state funeral for the city to pay their respects to him, later today. I'm to give the eulogy, and we're all commanded to attend, showing our unified respect." Then his face grew pale and he closed his eyes, slumping into his chair.

"Now what?" asked Hulneb. "Oh, and turn and face us so Tyn can read your lips. My hands will start talking in their sleep if I have to sign much more."

"It says work began this morning dismantling both the public observation platform and the lift and gantry leading into *Oosah*. The lift is to be reassembled in a newly-built memorial square, a monument in respect of the many Cardinals who have died in service over the cycles. After the festival, a new system of entry will be built, honouring Yan's life, and named after him."

Hulneb raised his eyebrows and his chest rose and fell as he heaved a long, slow, thoughtful sigh. He folded his arms, sitting back and staring at the floor. "So, that's it. So much for our plans. Now we have absolutely no way into that carcass."

Sol stood, pacing back and forth beside the low table.

"You'll have to think of another way! There must be one!" said Roanne.

Sol stopped pacing, turning to look between both of them as he spoke. "There is no other way! All is lost now. I'll be officiating at Yan's funeral while Opi's life ebbs away." He knelt, peering closely at the model of the Trophy which Hulneb had brought from Yan's classroom and placed in the centre of the table. "Ana said this was important, and told Tyn she wanted me to have it. I must know why!"

"It's just an idol," said Hulneb, casually looking up.

"Like the cheap little silver trinkets sold in the Square – pay it no mind Sol. I'm hungry, can we–"

"Your disagreements are taking us nowhere!" spat Roanne. "That thing has cursed us! Cursed everyone! All the cycles wasted, everyone's lost in their own beliefs, rather than concentrating on what's really important!"

Sol held his hands wide, just short of the model, marvelling at its accuracy. "This, this is important, and I must discover why."

Roanne pointed at Sol across the top of the model, her finger almost touching his forehead, forcing him to look up. "You, all the times you should have spent with your family, instead of worshipping this... this...deceiver, this *all-silent distraction from reality*." Her anger rose to boiling point and as her temper burst she stood, snatching up the stone model and holding it above her head.

"Roanne! No!" shouted Sol and Hulneb in unison. For a brief second, as she brought it swiftly down, she was reminded of the image from her dream. As it hit the table, a crack appeared along its centre and she quickly picked it up to slam it down again.

Hulneb and Sol shielded their eyes as the model shattered into pieces upon the granite table, fragments tumbling onto the floor.

"You'd do well to attend our birthday festivals," said Hulneb, coughing, waving the dust away from the table.

As the pieces came to rest, Roanne stepped forward, the disturbing dream of her father's murder replaced by what she saw. She picked up the largest fragment. "Look, it's not made of stone. It's plaster, stippled to look like stone, and sandpainted. This section is hollow."

"Been saying that all along," said Hulneb, absently picking up a piece and turning it over in his hands.

Sol examined the section Roanne held.

"But it's not *empty*, Hulneb, there are passageways and rooms in minute detail," said Sol, quietly. He began searching the floor on his hands and knees for the section containing the entrance he had used with Opi. Scooping it up, he peeled away the exterior coating. "The floor and wall sections are made of paper-thin wood veneer." He held the section out to them in turn, pointing. "Look, here are the corridors I walked with Opi, here and here, leading into the auditorium of one hundred seals." His eyes widened. "The interior continues beyond the known open seals." He snatched up all the fragments and tore the plaster coverings away, then began piecing it back together.

"It's just a toy," muttered Hulneb, absently handing him a piece, "as I said, pay it no mind, Sol."

Sol looked between them. "But don't you both see? This proves Ana was telling the truth. She must have built this model as a visual reference, rather than make notes or draw a diagram someone could find. Then, covered it over to look like a simple stone idol, but keeping the truth, the proof, hidden within."

"You should return to the asylum – she'll be able to help us," said Roanne.

"She said she couldn't remember why the model was important. There's no chance she'll remember how she managed to unlock these seals. Besides, we're forgetting. This is no use to us," he sighed, placing the broken pieces upon the table. "We still have to find a way up to the entrance."

"If your Ana Zoloth knew this much about the interior of the Trophy, then it makes sense Zoloth knows just as much, if not more," said Hulneb.

Sol thought for a moment. "I don't believe so. That possibility has already crossed my mind. But then why would he keep that knowledge to himself all this time? *That* course of action *doesn't* make sense."

Hulneb leant forward, resting his elbows on his knees. "How about *down* into the entrance?"

Sol examined the entranceway again. "Looking at the curve..." he traced it slowly with his index finger, then nodded. "It may be possible – *if* this is completely accurate.

But, we still have to find a way up above it."

Hulneb yawned and stretched. "Well, I think better on a full stomach, and since breakfast's covered in a layer of dust, I suggest we find a street vendor."

Tyn smiled and nodded, signing his agreement.

Roanne stood, signing to Tyn for a few moments. He signed back quickly, interrupting her, and she smiled. "Hulneb, Tyn knows the of best Kaltesh street vendor in Abeona. He'll take you there. Besides, Sol and I must talk. We'll be here when you return."

Hulneb stood, brushing himself down. "I'll tell mother about the funeral for your Archbishop, and return with her at the twelfth toll." He looked at Tyn. "Perhaps we'll take breakfast with her?"

Tyn smiled.

"Come on then, old man, lead on. Let's get some real Kaltesh food."

Tyn sniffed then signed at, rather than to, Hulneb.

"There's no need for that! Of course I'll pay," he said as they crossed the room. He looked back to Sol and Roanne as he reached the doorway, giving her a wink. "Just as well he can't talk."

They watched from the balcony as the two unlikely companions vanished into the early morning crowd.

"I must study that model and make detailed notes," declared Sol.

"Before you do that, I'm going to look at your wound."

He sat and began tinkering with the model while she sat beside him, rolling up his sleeve, aware he was almost oblivious to her presence.

"You can study that when you're bandaged up properly," she said, as he tried to pull his arm away.

"It's not too deep, just a nick."

She disappeared into the kitchen for a few minutes, returning with a poultice of herbs, a bowl of boiled water and a muslin cloth. Sitting beside him, she began cleaning the wound. "Any deeper and he could have severed a tendon. Your sword arm would have been useless. You could have been killed so easily, and all for a misunderstanding."

He winced as she pressed the herbal mixture into the clean edges of the cut.

"Sol, I don't trust Hulneb," she said quietly, wrapping a bandage tightly around the poultice. "He's suddenly become very helpful – and I can't help thinking he has his own agenda."

"Oh I'm sure he has, but I don't believe we'll know exactly what that is until all this is over and done with. We can trust his loyalty for now. He's certainly taken with that old man, though."

"Tradition. Hathranelzra demands great respect from my people. Besides, he told me you were both almost bettered by him in combat. Best to keep such a man at your side where he can be seen, rather than where he cannot."

"You're beginning to sound just like Hulneb, Ro. Besides, Hulneb wasn't bettered, he simply tripped backwards over that black cloak he inherited from your father."

She tied a knot in the bandage and stared at him. "Tripped?"

He nodded. "He said Mirrimas was a head taller than him – he was just excusing himself."

She stood and looked sick.

"Roanne?"

She held her hands up to cover her face. "Of course."

"What?"

"Sol, I dreamt last night I saw my father's murder. In a way, I did. The Kaltesh blood relations have a curse. Whilst asleep, our dreams can invade each others'. It's very rare for this to happen – but... Hulneb was sleeping out on the balcony, and I saw my father murdered in my dream. I believe it was Hulneb's memory dream. The murderer stood a head shorter than Mirrimas."

Sol frowned. "You don't honestly believe Hulneb killed him, just from a dream, surely?"

She thought for a moment. "Sol, my head's so full with worry over Opi, I don't know what to believe, who to listen to or trust. I can tell you that when we were young, Hulneb's dreams sometimes found their way into my head at night. I taunted him for being a late developer; he couldn't grow a full beard until his twentieth year. I remember once dreaming he was strangling me, and when I woke up screaming he was standing over my bed. I ran out of our caravan and fell into the sand in the darkness. It just so happened, that night Mirrimas had decided to travel by moonlight. He heard my screams, saw me fall and ran over to pull me clear of the caravan flanking ours."

"How can you tell it wasn't simply your conscience influencing your dream?"

"I can't. Hulneb says to this day he heard me scream and came in to wake me. From my point of view, it just seemed like an ideal opportunity for him. He could have murdered me, thrown my body into the sand and by morning the caravans would have been almost a hundred leagues away and my bones picked clean by sand rats. The following morning Mirrimas helped Hulneb begin building his own caravan, while our mother selected a team of ganapti for him."

Sol shook his head and folded his arms gingerly. "But you have no proof Hulneb intended to murder you, and you must know you can trust me, surely?"

She stood and shot him a look of anger. "You took Opi inside the Trophy – despite all the arguments we've had about that."

"I simply wanted him to follow in my footsteps, Roanne. I wanted the Timmerman name to be spoken of in hundreds of cycles' time as the family who achieved enlightenment, celebrated as saviours of our world. If I'd have thought–"

"I've heard this a thousand time before, Sol! You've spent your entire life theorising – then when you really needed to think clearly, you were unable – or unwilling!"

"There was nowhere for him to go – I told him not to touch anything, that I'd be back soon. While I was running along the gantry, I was thinking I had given him freedom for a few moments, given him responsibility. If I'd found him playing with seal panels when I returned, I'd have been proud and disappointed in equal measure. I wanted to see what he would do; I decided at that moment I wanted to give him that chance. The decision was made so quickly! I left him alone for just a short while."

"Far too long!" She walked around the table, unable to look at him any longer. "Sol, when all this is over, I'm leaving this city and, if he's alive, I'm taking Opi with me, to live with my family."

He sat back in the chair, bewildered by her statement.

"So what do you expect me to do?"

"Whatever you want to do, that's what you've always done, isn't it? But if you remain here, this city will destroy you – and I'm not going to sit around and wait for that day. Look what it's done to us already! We've lost so much in such a short space of time." She looked toward the balcony.

He stood. "I thought I was doing the right thing. I wanted to prepare him for life here. I wanted to harden him against the harsh reality he'll meet once he's on his own out there – and not sit back and hope he'd be strong enough to deal with everything life throws at him. What would you have had me do?"

She shook her head. "All for your obsession with being right, with trying to be someone every stranger in this city should look up to and admire." She turned to face him. "Your family's love was never enough for you, you always had more time for this... this," she picked up a piece of Ana's model and threw it across the room where it shattered against the wall, "stupid fixation."

"My family's love has *always* been enough. It's my love for you, Opi and all the people of this world, be they Kaltesh or Abeonian, which has motivated my search for the truth." He clenched his fists and raised his voice, unable to control his anger. "I became a Cardinal for everyone's salvation, not for myself, not for my father, not for glory and admiration, but for the possibility of enlightening all." He realised his good intentions had only brought pain to everyone he had ever loved. His wife sat beside him as he held his head in his hands, unable to explain further. She placed her arms around his shoulders and nestled into him, holding him tightly. Then her body trembled as all the bottled-up emotion struggled to the surface in a wave of tears.

They sat there in each other's arms for a long while in silence, just as they used to when they had time on their hands, simply enjoying the warmth and closeness of each other as the city bustled beneath them. Eventually, Roanne fell asleep and he made her comfortable. He sat forward and examined the model, going over every detail time and time again. Then he drew a detailed plan and, folding it, tucked it beneath his bandage.

It was late in the morning when Roanne stirred.

"This meat is past its best," Sol said, pushing it around his plate.

She yawned and stretched, running her fingers through her hair. "I'd planned to order fresh today."

He stared toward the balcony for a few moments silently, his eyes vacant with concentration.

"We'll need at least a sackful. And it must be freshly slaughtered."

She stared at him, wondering if the poultice she had applied contained too much antiseptic and it had found its way into his head. "What for?"

He removed fruit from a large, hammered iron bowl,

placing the broken pieces of the model inside, then set it alight with a candle. Satisfied every piece was burning, he picked up the homing bird sent to him by Ommus. He placed the cage on Roanne's lap, sitting beside her and warming his hands over the burning model. "I must send an important message, but before that, there's one thing I must do." He stood and hurried into his study, then returned carrying a large, leather-bound book. The cover was intricately decorated and was embossed with both the Cardinal and Timmerman crests in high relief, interwoven in gold and silver respectively. He sat for a moment with his father's heavy tome upon his lap, staring at the cover. Finally he opened it, tearing out the first page. Roanne watched as his brow furrowed, his mouth silently forming the words he read, his eyes occasionally skipping to his father's annotations in the margins.

In his head, he heard his father's voice as he had read the words to him as a child. His rhythm was measured, neither high nor low, but now and again that noble voice would emphasize words and phrases, bringing the passages to life, adding colour to the musty book, creating images in his head of great adventures and achievements from the otherwise formal, historical recountings. Sol closed his eyes as he knew every word, as he listened to the memory, relishing it, reliving it. Suddenly he was a little boy again, the same age as his son, tucked up in bed safe and warm, realising that's exactly where his son should be now.

As Roanne watched, he opened his eyes, quickly wiping away a tear with the back of his hand before he scrunched the page into a ball and dropped it into the flames. He stared as the page blackened before igniting, continuing until every page of the book was no more.

FOURTEEN

A FUNERAL FOR THE FAITH

The Hathranelzra, accompanied by Roanne's family, arrived at the Timmerman estate at midday. Roanne watched Rillian holding Tulteth's hand for support as they walked across the courtyard, noticing Hulneb had changed into flamboyant red and black robes, ornately decorated with sinuous threads of copper. His beard and moustache had been trimmed, and his hair was smoothed back with an aromatic mixture of fat and crushed deltham buds. Tyn looked uncomfortable beneath his Kaltesh attire and kept pulling at the folds of the loosely fitting tunic. When they entered the living area, Sol picked up the caged bird and escorted Hulneb onto the balcony to explain his plan.

Roanne watched them closely. Hulneb belched and picked at his teeth, nodding, laughing, his eyes studying her husband with great interest as he listened. He patted Sol on the back and said. "Ale, at this time of day? When do we leave?"

"Just one flagon, Hulneb, that's all. Roanne and I spent much of our time in the Ravine District when we first met. She told me you'll feel right at home in the refreshment houses there."

As Rillian signed with Tyn concerning the importance of the folds in his tunic, Roanne took Tulteth by the hand and sat down with him.

"We haven't had much time together, Tul. I'm sorry." She wanted to tell him of her plans to rejoin the tribe, but something in the back of her mind told her to wait as she half-listened to Sol and Hulneb's conversation.

She looked her younger brother up and down. His features were more like Mirrimas' than either her own or Hulneb's. His light green eyes were clear and healthy, his skin smooth and his high cheekbones made him appear overly alert. "You're looking more like a young man now than a child, Tul." She smiled and leant closer to him. "I'd wager you've had many girls dancing beside your caravan during the early evenings. The First Son's colours suit you."

He lifted his head proudly, running his fingers over the fabric. "Yes, they dance. And when Hulneb's in a drunken sleep, I pull one or two up onto my deck and tell them how beautiful they are. Don't worry about not seeing the family." He grinned, revealing his pure white teeth. "Things will be different one day. I'm looking forward to becoming High Celebrant, Ro. I've so many ideas for the tribe."

Roanne smiled grimly, remembering how Hulneb had said exactly the same to her many cycles ago. "Patience–"

"Is the narrow path to old age. Mirrimas told me that so many times, I could hear it in my head when I tried to sleep at night. Life's experiences are wasted on the old. All they talk about is the past because there's no future for them."

Roanne chuckled, surprised by his damning words, but dismissing them as nothing more than adolescent intolerance. "Tulteth, I'm sure you'll find you can learn a great deal from older people. Father taught you many valuable lessons, I'm sure?"

He made a disapproving noise with his lips. "Only that everything I did was either wrong, or not quite good enough." He smiled and held her hands. "You've taught me so much more."

"Me?" she said, taken aback. "But we've hardly seen each other." She frowned. "What have you learnt from me?"

He looked around the room. "To take what you want, and chase happiness. After your Alonetime in Abeona, you left the tribe to be with Sol. That took a lot of courage."

"Not really. You must remember I was very young."

"Only a few cycles older than I am now."

She held onto his hands and stood, leading him to face

the mirror on the opposite wall. Standing behind him, she placed her hands on his shoulders. "Look at yourself, Tulteth." She rested her head on his right shoulder. "When I was your age I knew, as you do, exactly what happiness was. Later, when I met Sol, I chased another happiness, then another, when I wanted a child. You'll find the happiness you seek will change over the cycles, so don't be too eager to put yourself into a position you'll regret later. Our father had a great deal of responsibility on his shoulders. That was something he wanted dearly and studied long and hard for. Hulneb inherited his position," she lowered her voice and turned her head to his cheek, whispering, "and to be honest, I don't think he enjoys it very much, despite all he says. When it's time for you to be High Celebrant, you won't be allowed to dance in the sand, or invite girls up into your caravan, or any of the other things you do now. Your days will be filled with decisions, planning, harvesting, meetings and rituals. That's why father always took time for himself up in the mountains. I think he secretly longed to be simply the nomad from time to time, and not the leader everyone looked to for help."

The boy's shoulders slumped and he stared hard at his reflection, then his eyes fell to the wooden bowl on the table beneath the mirror.

"I wondered where I'd lost that," he said, picking up the hooped earring Sol had found. "I *knew* it had fallen out when I was playing with Ebe yesterday."

Roanne carefully pulled his long, black, curly hair back, exposing his ears. "My handmaiden must have found it. Here, I'll fix it for you. Which ear?"

He handed it to her. "The left, the third hole above the hoop at the bottom. They all used to belong to father," he said proudly, tilting his head to the right. "Hulneb gave them to me."

She fixed the earring, ensuring it matched the position of its twin in his other ear, then pulled his hair back down over his ears as the frantic beating of wings caused everyone to turn to the balcony. There, Sol was pushing a piece of paper into a tiny wooden cylinder attached to the homing bird's leg. Hulneb released the bird into the air and they both turned.

"If everyone's ready?" said Sol, and he strode towards the doorway with Hulneb at his side.

They all rode to the Square where Sol hurried them through the Holy Entrance.

Rillian, Hulneb, Sol, Tulteth and Tyn made their way to the Trophy and joined a small group of Kaltesh kneeling in front of a priest reciting *The Building of Agasanduku* in their native tongue.

"What are you up to, Hulneb?" asked Rillian in a whisper as they knelt. She closed her eyes.

"Mother?"

The old woman shuddered. "Don't give me that innocent tone. I know you're planning something, you've been in far too good a mood of late."

The High Celebrant grinned. "Shh," he said quietly, "All in good time, mother, all in good time."

"Is your co-operation just a ruse? Have you finally come to your senses and realised we can conquer these fools?"

His expression changed as he turned to her. "Conquer Abeona, and then what? Forcing others to fight over a belief is stupid. Killing in that belief's name? Especially so, if that belief cannot be proven." He turned away. "All in good time mother, all in good time."

Roanne quietly made her excuses and hurried through the market area. She hired a velocipede and, producing a sack from beneath her robes, purchased a variety of fresh meat on the bone from several different stalls. When the sack was sufficiently full, she instructed the driver to take her to the Ravine District.

"My apologies, but I have instructions to join the

procession from the Citadel," said Sol, looking between Hulneb, Rillian and Tulteth. The old woman nodded. "We will see you after the ceremony. May the Brothers share their purses of good fortune with you." she said, before beginning her prayers.

Sol waited a few minutes for Hulneb to make his excuses. They left the Square separately, meeting outside to ride to the Ravine District, both covering their robes on the way with the cheap, roughly-woven capes worn by street traders.

Tulteth turned and scanned the crowds. After a few minutes, he and a group of other youngsters crept away to explore the festival's many entertainments, leaving Rillian with Tyn.

"One thing still puzzles me, Sol," said Hulneb, above the noise from the street, "That book carrier – he knows a great deal about Kaltesh ways. You should have seen him at breakfast. He even asked if we had an old preserve, one that my mother herself enjoys. Vile stuff made from gantric root balls and ground dendratell pepper stalks. He's obviously Kaltesh, but how did he end up in the service of your Ana Zoloth, carrying a Deacon's sword? I've a feeling there's more going on here than we've been made aware of."

"Oh, I don't doubt it, but time's limited. We have to make the best with what we have. Obviously there's more to discover concerning Ana, her father and this Tyn Narrat. But I can tell you one thing for certain – he was not Ana's book carrier as he claims. Cardinals ceased using book carriers a dozen cycles before Ana became a Cardinal. But it's not his identity that concerns me, only his objectives. Other issues are more important now. Perhaps Rillian can find out more from him?"

"Perhaps." Hulneb's thoughts returned to Sol's plan. "But three of us against an entire city, Sol?"

"I theorise we have more chance as three, rather than three hundred."

Hulneb shrugged. "So, what are the chances of Zoloth secretly being Kaltesh?"

"Zero. His family lineage is well documented. His ancient ancestors had an important role in the building of this city, and a few generation ago, its defence. And I can tell you, he is no lover of your people, or their ways."

"Well, I look forward to making the man's acquaintance."

On the Emakurow Bridge they took the right fork down through the wide, spiralling thoroughfare. Hulneb fell silent, finding himself reining his animal to a sudden halt.

"Hulneb?"

"I know this place," he said slowly, dismounting.

"Hulneb, we haven't time for sightseeing."

But the large man was walking to the edge of the roadway, staring out into the abyss toward the far distant dam wall. "I've been here before," he whispered to himself, as the wind slammed into his face.

Sol stood beside him. "Come on," he pleaded. "We've less than a measure. You probably remember this view from a previous visit."

"No," said Hulneb. "I've never ventured this far into Abeona."

"With your parents, as a child perhaps?"

"No. Mirrimas never took me anywhere other than the Square. Mother escorted Roanne around the city a few times." He tugged at his beard then turned, walking back to his animal. "That's strange." He looked over at Sol with a smile as they mounted. "I've got it," he said. "I dreamt about this part of the city the other night whilst asleep on your balcony. A memory dream from Roanne, for certain. Thank the Brothers for that. I hate mysteries."

As they reached ground level, Sol kept his eyes fixed on the mountainous Pinnacle of Judgement and headed for its base.

They found the alehouse, built partly around the foundations of the pinnacle. It was a large, three-storey building with a traditional, blue-tiled, oval roof that followed the gentle curve of the giant blocks of the pinnacle's base. Ivy twined around the building, curling over its roof and partway up the pinnacle, giving the monument the appearance of a gigantic stone phallus.

"This place has seen better days," said Hulneb, tying his ride to a holding post.

"It's only an alehouse," said Sol.

"No, not this monstrosity, the whole area," he said, looking around. "I never thought this city could be so ugly. Children wrapped in rags, people sleeping in the street," he looked down at his boots. "ganapti crap practically everywhere you step. Are you sure this is the right place?"

Sol nodded. "Come on."

Inside the alehouse, a long, thick bar, fashioned from a single trunk of ebony dominated the far end of the room, itself lined with small, wooden bowls containing aspic appetisers. The air was thick with Farrengrass smoke, carrying a pungent odour of sour ale and wine. To their right crackled an open fire, where a young girl stood barefoot, slowly turning a spit holding an unrecognisable carcass. In the right-hand corner, a trio of musicians struggled to hold a melody together with two flutes and a guitar, as numerous drunken men and women attempted to dance. Several patrons watched from their tables, clapping along out of time to the display, creating an effect like a slow applause, while the remainder huddled in pairs in shaded corners, engaged in various levels of bavardage.

Hulneb pulled out his pipe and began to fill it as they sat down at the bar.

"Two flagons of Dreamer's ale," shouted Sol to the barman, who was leaning on the bar top, talking with three street cleaners, sitting six stools away.

Hulneb lit his pipe from a candle on the bar and exhaled through his nostrils. "Dreamer's?"

Sol nodded to one of the many barrels stacked in pyramids of ten behind the bar. "Seemed fitting," he said, looking back to the barman. "I used to drink barley wine around here in my youth, but that's just a little too strong for me nowadays."

"You used to drink *here*?"

"No, around here. The area's changed a great deal since my younger days, when on occasion I'd try to find my father. This part of the city's now a refuge for all the visitors who decide to stay, but have nowhere to sleep. They can find casual work harvesting, planting, stacking, cleaning and the like, for merchants. But during the growing season there's little else for them to do other than watering and weeding. The city should have made provision for them." He turned his back to the bar and looked around. "I remember this used to be a fashionable eating place when I was courting Roanne."

"It's a shit hole," said Hulneb, resting his elbows carefully on the bar, lest they find a puddle of beer.

"So, act like you're used to it," said Sol, tilting his head toward the big man. "We need to blend in. Remember, we're here to present the owner with a business proposition."

Hulneb raised his eyebrows, sucking on his pipe.

"She's here," said Sol.

Roanne appeared at the door holding a small backsack. On seeing them she waved Sol over. "It's outside," she said quietly.

He kissed her on the cheek. "I'm still not happy with you doing this, Ro."

She squared up to him. "I have to. This has to be as convincing as possible – you told me

yourself, whores are usually the last course of a banquet, and I must at least appear palatable."

He knew he couldn't argue with her. "Go sit with Hulneb, and remind the barman I'm waiting for two flagons. I'll bring the sack inside."

She crossed the room, watched by several pairs of eyes, and sat next to Hulneb.

The barman ambled up to them, wiping his hands on a greasy cloth draped around his neck.

"What was it?" he said to Hulneb.

"Two flagons of Dreamer's. Roanne?"

"Barley wine, please."

The barman turned and hurriedly poured the drinks as Sol walked in with the sack on his shoulder. He placed it beside Hulneb's stool, then stood next to Roanne.

As the barman placed the drinks on the bar, Sol tossed him a couple of tokens, ignoring the considerable ullage. "Do you like her?" he said, tilting his head to Roanne, smiling wide-eyed. The barman placed the coins in a tray behind him, tossing Sol a small copper coin for change."No," he growled without looking at Roanne, hurrying back to his conversation.

"No!" said Hulneb, clasping his flagon. "What kind of an answer is that?"

"An honest one," said Roanne, sipping her drink.

"We don't have time for negativity, however honest," said Sol, moving to Hulneb's right shoulder. He walked up to the barman and interrupted his conversation.

"Oh no, here we go again," said Hulneb. "I've only been here a short time, but that's long enough to recognise that look on his face. There's going to be trouble, I just know it."

"The question was a serious one," said Sol calmly.

"I don't give a shit what it was," said the barman, placing his hands wide upon the bar and leaning forward. "Me friends and me are having a business meeting, so go back to your girlfriend and leave us alone."

"I don't think you understand–"

"Yes, he understands. It's you who's having the problem," said the shortest of the three men, turning to face Sol with his hand on the hilt of a dagger at his waist. "Now move along the bar before I carve you an extra nostril." He turned and smiled at his friends, who smirked as he took a gulp from his flagon.

"Your husband's turning out to be a troublemaker," said Hulneb, straining to hear the exchange. "I'm becoming quite fond of him."

"This sort of trouble's new to Sol," said Roanne with a little concern. "He's used to arguing points rather than facing them. I hope he knows what he's letting himself in for."

"I know what *I'm* letting myself in for," said a voice directly behind her.

They both turned to see two workers, their faces and clothes caked here and there with patches of damp sand.

"So do I. We like her, even if the barman don't," said the taller of the two to Hulneb.

The shorter man took a step forward. "Sure." He reached over and placed a dirty hand on Roanne's shoulder, his forefinger reaching up to stroke her neck just below her ear.

She brought up a hand and slapped his away. "Leave me alone."

The worker instantly lost his temper. "If the barman is good enough for you, so are us!" he shouted, pointing a finger at her.

"Yeah," grinned the other worker, aroused by his friend's anger, "and at the same time."

Hulneb downed his flagon and whirled around on his stool, sucking on his pipe. He regarded the workers, weighing them up without attempting to hide the fact. "Gentlemen, are you saying you can only please a woman together? Or is it that neither of you can bear to be alone with the opposite sex for fear of inadequacy?"

The workers looked at each other, each waiting for his colleague to answer.

"Barman, this will only take a moment," said Sol,

reaching beneath his tunic and pulling out two gold tokens, holding them between the thumb and forefinger of each hand. "For your time," he said, tossing them across the bar, turning to the barman's associates. "There's plenty of work for you gentlemen outside. I suggest you tend to it," he said, raising his voice as he pulled back half of his grey cape, revealing the Church emblem of *Oosah*.

The barman looked over to his friends and motioned for them to turn their backs.

"The girl is a *guest* of the occupants of the Holy Citadel," began Sol, his eyes lingering for a moment upon the three, "and I've brought meat for their banquet." He looked at the barman. "It's in a sack, here, and it must be delivered along with her."

The barman nodded and picked up the coins. "Okay. Come back after dark and I'll let you out back."

Sol's smile vanished. "No, I don't think you understand. She's the pre-banquet entertainment for a handful of select guests, following the state funeral later today. I trust you've heard about that?"

"Mutterings."

"I see. Well, we'll need to deliver the goods as soon as possible, won't we?" he said, grinning. "You know – settle the girl in, a few drinks–"

The barman sighed and held up his hands. "The usual, I get the message."

When realisation dawned on the taller of the two workers, his expression immediately betrayed the fact, and Hulneb was ready for the reaction that came as a wide, sweeping fist.

Blocking the blow with his forearm, he pushed the worker away with his left boot, holding out his pipe to Roanne, "Here, quickly! Take it!" She snatched it away as the second worker came forward, arms outstretched for Hulneb's throat. The High Celebrant reached forward, seizing the man by both wrists, sidestepping while pulling him forwards. The impact against the bar broke two fingers, and the worker crumpled to the floor in agony.

Now Hulneb's head went back, a fist catching him squarely under the chin. Tumbling against the bar, sending his flagon clattering into the serving well, he cursed.

Sol turned upon hearing the uproar.

"Oh no," said the barman, producing a dagger from his belt. "It's a bit early for all this." Sol reached out and grabbed him by the wrist holding the dagger, shaking his head. "Perhaps it would be better if I took care of this for you."

Hulneb felt clawing hands upon his chest as he was pulled forward and thrown to the floor. The worker took a hammer from his belt, pinning Hulneb's arms to the floor with his knees.

Roanne cursed in Kaltesh, unable to move as the broken-fingered worker seized her throat with his good hand, pushing her against the bar. As she was bent backward she placed Hulneb's pipe into her mouth, holding the worker's wrist with both hands, the pain in her spine reminding her of Rillian's combat training. To the surprise of her adversary, a smile found her lips. Looking to her right she stretched, reaching out to seize a flagon. In a moment it was empty, and before the ale spilled over the bar she thrust it against the worker's left ear, forcing the air it contained into his ear canal, rupturing his eardrum. Releasing his grip, he expected her to straighten, but instead she brought up her knees and hips, looking at their shadows on the ceiling, grasping the edge of the bar tightly with both hands, curling her body back, coiling like a spring to kick out with her heels to the middle of his chest as he took a step back in pain. Her perfectly-timed strike caught him just when his shadow told her he was in mid-step, his weight not fully transferred to his right foot. As her feet found the floorboards she watched him grimace with pain and lack of breath, his brain unsure which pain receptor required the most attention as he stumbled backwards.

As the hammer came up above Hulneb's head, Sol ran over, his scimitar struggling from beneath two layers of clothing as Hulneb's fingers fumbled for the worker's eyes. A wooden stump came down hard on Hulneb's chest as the metal head thumped against the floor an inch from his left ear. Bewildered, the worker stared at the clean cut which had severed the head of his hammer. He felt a foot in the side of his head as Sol kicked him off Hulneb, helping him to his feet with one hand, while holding the tip of the scimitar at the worker's groin with the other. He glanced up at Roanne. "Take care of him, Hulneb. I need to help her." The big man stopped him with a firm arm across his chest as he took a step forward. "No need, and, I must add, an insult to Kaltesh women in the throes of single combat, unless assistance is requested. Watch. *Hool Napresh* should be next."

Removing the pipe from her mouth for a moment to breathe in the stale air, Roanne leaped forward, aware that her opponent would collide with a table where an elderly couple sat trying to enjoy their breakfast of sweet hot pastries and ginger tea. Grabbing his broken fingers with both hands and leaning back, she pulled him towards her, halting his momentum instantly, squeezing his fingers as hard as she could. Feeling bones grating together beneath her grip as she twisted her hands, she thrust her head under his right arm. Peering beneath his armpit she smiled at the bewildered couple across the table, clenching the pipe stem between her teeth. "Excuse me," and with that, as the worker screamed again, her right palm came up swiftly under his chin to silence his screams, sending his head back, his mouth now with two shattered teeth. Pulling him forward a few paces, ensuring his feet wouldn't tangle with the table, she hoisted him over her head to land him face down on the floor behind her, his combined pain from the accumulated injuries rendering him unconscious.

Hulneb shrugged. "Fine, *Neelas Napresh* it is then. Result's the same."

Roanne walked over to them, fixing her hair. "On your way out, remember to take your friend," she said calmly to the worker on the floor.

"Here," said Sol, picking up the severed head of the hammer, "a souvenir." He tossed it to Hulneb who glared at him as he caught it.

"You left it a little late again," said the big man, rubbing his chin.

Roanne puffed a cloud of smoke above her head. "All this Farrengrass has slowed your reactions, brother," she said with a smirk. "I suggest you give it up. My husband may be *too* late, next time."

Hulneb snatched the pipe from her mouth, wiping the damp stem on his sleeve as the bewildered worker hurriedly dragged his unconscious friend outside. "What of the barman?"

Sol nodded, sheathing his sword. "This is the right place."

The barman led the group to an expansive storeroom behind the bar, where an ancient wooden door, splintered and stained, adorned with metal studs bleeding rust into its surface dominated half of the far wall. Beyond this, a courtyard with high walls on each side hid beneath the slanting shadows of the adjacent buildings. From fifteen enormous vats dotted around the courtyard, a network of hissing copper pipes of varying thicknesses snaked, eventually finding their way into the rear wall of the alehouse.

They followed the burly publican as his body effortlessly negotiated the hot copper tubes.

"Be careful – don't touch the pipes. They'll sear you to the bone."

Beyond the metal maze, against the courtyard's wall, stood forty oval, wooden barrels, each of them three men wide by two men high. The stench of fermenting ale and spirits filled the air. The barman took a small ladder from between the first two barrels and propped it against the third. As he reached the top of the ladder, he pushed against the barrel, and with a damp groan a door opened, revealing a Stygian interior.

"Through there," he grunted. "A corridor runs through, leading into the base of the pinnacle."

Sol handed the barman another gold coin as he joined them at the bottom of the ladder. "Your service to the Citadel and the Twelve is noted and appreciated, sir."

The coin disappeared into a pocket. "Just keep the Deacons away from my brewery and alehouse, as agreed."

Sol nodded as the barman returned to his business. When he was satisfied they were alone he nodded to Roanne. "You first. Be quick, I'll be right behind you."

"I'll keep watch," said Hulneb, turning to face the storeroom door.

Yan Arramosa's funeral procession crept through the city streets. The coffin rode atop an ornately carved oak cart, decorated with yellow garlands of wild flowers. Three incense burners projected from either side of the cart, swaying leisurely from the motion, leaving a wake of blue mist carrying a subtle fragrance of lemon and cinnamon. Eight priests pulled the cart along, six more walked behind it with heads bowed, the whole ensemble following behind an Archbishop who led them, waving blessings before him. The Twelve Grand Cardinals brought up the rear, sitting in pairs, expressionless, aboard a six-wheeled carriage drawn by four ganapti yearlings.

The unannounced procession drew small groups of respectful onlookers as it passed, their numbers increasing steadily as it neared the Necropolis of the Holy. Rumour had spread swiftly through the Abeonian streets of Yan Arramosa's funeral.

"Ommus is late," whispered Irrianna. "He's never late.

You should not have trusted him."

Zoloth smiled. "You worry needlessly. His presence is required elsewhere. He'll be along shortly." He inclined slightly towards Irrianna, unable to conceal his anticipation. "The wait is over, my friend. Ommus and I have studied the illuminations. We agree that we now have all the information required."

"*All?*" exclaimed Irrianna, slightly louder than he intended.

"Save your excitement for the appropriate time. My daughter's work is indisputable. *Oosah* will be ours on the last day of the festival. The culmination is now nothing more than a formality."

The cavalcade approached along a winding, gravelled roadway, lined with fruit trees laden with white blossom. The early afternoon sun, almost directly overhead, cast but a few shadows, with only the distant sounds from the city and the tender breath of the desert to give the trees occasional movement. The scene took on the air of a half-completed tapestry, lacking neither depth nor passion, as if waiting for an event to give the day meaning and colour.

The procession topped a rise in the landscape, revealing the Necropolis of the Holy: a wide, deep, circular amphitheatre hewn into the rock. Around the circumference of this huge bowl, waterfalls emerged from the inner corners of twelve pairs of giant stone eyes. The Fall of Tears represented the founding Twelve Grand Cardinals, forever keeping a parental watch over their deceased successors. The water gently cascaded from block to block, down into a shallow, circular pool at the bottom of the amphitheatre. At the centre of this pool sat a wide, circular island, with an ornate altar at its centre reached by six shallow circular steps. A gently-arched bridge of polished white marble spanned the pool, ornately carved balusters and coping stones reflected in the still water beneath. Between the falls, hundreds of tombs sat upon the stepped sides of the amphitheatre, a statue atop each, depicting the occupation of the deceased interred within. Narrow steps separated these tombs, allowing loved ones to pay their respects.

The two vehicles halted, the Grand Cardinals watching as the priests slid the coffin from the cart and hoisted it onto their shoulders. Following a brief pause, the Archbishop led them down the steps towards the pool, followed by the Twelve.

After changing her clothes in the barrel at the rear of the alehouse to those fit for a funeral, Roanne climbed out of the sack Hulneb had carried her out in, explaining to the barman it contained rotting meat. Passing Hulneb a backsack containing the whore's clothes, she climbed into the saddle behind her husband as Hulneb tied the backsack to the hobble strap of his saddle.

"Are you okay?" Sol asked, as she wrapped her arms around his waist.

"I'm fine. Let's go. I just hope your contrived plan works – should we find ourselves needing to carry it through."

He rubbed his heels along the ganapti's flank and it bellowed, moving onto the roadway. "We've accounted for all outcomes. What I meant to say, Ro, was, I never imagined you'd, that you–"

"There has never been an occasion when I've needed to show my combat skills. My people are taught from an early age. I enjoyed it."

"That fact was obvious."

They galloped through the city toward the Necropolis, with Hulneb close behind.

The priests placed the coffin of Yan Arramosa onto the marble altar at the centre of the island.

"Timmerman's not here," murmured Irrianna, his eyes

searching the growing crowd.

Zoloth gazed up to the entranceway where a steady line of mourners poured into the amphitheatre. Cardinals, Bishops, clerics, junior priests and their instructors walked side by side with commoners. Then two ganapti appeared, stirring up a cloud of yellow dust, their three riders quickly dismounting.

"He's here," said Zoloth, under his breath whilst turning his back to them. "And he's brought his Kaltesh wife and brother-in-law. This should be very interesting." Zoloth nodded to the Bishop standing over the coffin who nodded back before instructing everyone to take up their positions.

"What is this place?" asked Hulneb.

"The Necropolis of the Holy," said Sol bluntly. "A burial place for high-ranking Church officials and Abeona's most successful individuals."

"So your father's buried here somewhere?" asked Hulneb, looking around.

Sol's eyes remained on Yan's coffin. "No. That drunken fool's body is buried elsewhere."

"Hmm. Searching for truth can drive a man to drink, as much as discovering lies whilst doing so can. Tell me, Sol, why..." But before Hulneb could continue his question, Roanne's frown and slight shake of the head forced him to bite his tongue. "I see," he said, pointing below. "Is this somewhat overdressed individual struggling up the steps with a cane Irrianna? He has an expression like that of a ganapti about to give birth! Since when has he carried a cane?"

Below them, holding his robes clear of the ground with one hand, came Irrianna, followed by three musicians carrying long brass horns.

"Word has it he fell from his ride, breaking his leg, some time ago – he uses the cane for support," said Sol.

Irrianna halted ten steps below them and waved his cane

at Sol. "You're late, Cardinal Timmerman. Yan Arramosa's family are waiting, as are we!"

Sol approached the Senior Grand Cardinal until he was three steps above him, the crowd flowing around them to join the others gathering at the edge of the pool. "My sincerest apologies, Grand Cardinal, but my ganapti threw a shoe halfway here, and I was forced to ride Roanne's."

"Come on!" said Irrianna, turning and waving the musicians away. "You can make your apologies afterwards."

When they reached the bottom of the steps, Roanne and Hulneb joined the back of the crowd as it parted for Sol. All eyes were fixed upon him and silence fell as he stepped onto the stone bridge, mouthing a prayer for the thousands of individuals who had died whilst in the service of the church. There, the twelve Grand Cardinals seated around the circumference of the island faced the altar. He saw they were mostly grim-faced, some with their heads bowed and eyes closed, others mumbling prayers as the scene gradually filled his peripheral vision. He took a deep breath and prepared himself, then approached the coffin, kneeling before it, bowing his head and closing his eyes. Emerging from the darkness, the expression on the corpse inside came forward, and he realised this single memory, from only a handful of measures ago, had manoeuvred him to this point, taken him like the wind plucks a leaf from a tree, depositing it where it will. He recalled in detail every event since that moment, asking himself if he had taken the correct course of action – questioning if he was about to take the correct course now. Then his memory travelled backwards, past the horrific moment of Yan's death, and he found himself staring into Opi's excited eyes, upon seeing *Oosah*. Then came that final, terrible moment, that brief glance he had given his son as he told him to wait, and for the first time he remembered Opi's expression. It was an expression that silently begged him, *'Don't go! I'm afraid. Let me come with you! Please dad, don't leave me here on my own.'* He realised he had seen it in his son's eyes then, but chose to ignore it, insisting Opi face his fear, to mature faster, to be more the youth he wanted him to be, to become as infatuated with *Oosah* as he himself had become at his age. And as he remembered, a tear swelled in his eye.

"Cardinal Timmerman, we were beginning to think you had fallen foul of an accident on your way here."

Sol slowly stood and Zoloth noticed the moisture around his eyes. "I grieve for him also, Cardinal. Yan was one of our finest Archbishops, a brilliant analyst, archivist, teacher, and a dedicated soul. He will take his great wisdom to the Garden to benefit the souls who reside there."

Sol struggled to remain calm, clearing his throat before speaking. "Undoubtedly. Senior Grand Cardinal, I have given your offer considerable thought. And I can say without any shred of doubt, I have reached a conclusion, thus, making a determined decision that will benefit everyone concerned."

Zoloth raised an eyebrow. "And your decision?"

"With your permission, I'll inform you after I've conducted Archbishop Arramosa's service, Your Holiness."

Zoloth bowed as Sol descended the steps, "Acceptable, Cardinal."

Irrianna signalled the trio of trumpeters and three notes sounded, forming a minor triad.

Silence fell around the auditorium in a gradual wave, a few conversations trailing off in whispers. As Zoloth took to the podium above the coffin, the chord ceased. Bowing his head and turning slowly around on his heels he blessed the entire congregation, then looked up to the sky momentarily, waiting for silence.

"Tal Salandor said; *'There is but one way to enter this life, but the black gates to death are many.'* And so those numerous gates, for the righteous, for the souls which hold the truth in their hearts and believe, without a shred of doubt in the glory of the garden, *know* they will find a path beyond that gate. Whatever that entrance to death may be, however painful, however difficult to comprehend, however swift or however slow." He paused for a few moments, picking out faces in the crowd, nodding to them with a half-smile. "Yan Arramosa knew this," he continued, raising his voice, holding his arms up to the sky, "and Yan Arramosa treads that path to the Garden as I speak to you all now, you who have gathered here to honour his life." He waved a sign to the sky, then closed his eyes and intoned a short prayer. After a few moments he silently left the podium and motioned with a wave of his hand for Sol to take his place.

Sol's expression remained impassive as he stepped forward. He glanced at Roanne and Hulneb, managing a slight smile. He looked to his right beyond the pool. Sitting in their ranks were his colleagues, their robes of office creating rows of ordered colour behind the front row of Yan's close friends and family mourners: Archbishops attired in azure and gold, Bishops in emerald and silver, Cardinals in burgundy and emerald and the various priests behind them in grey and white, public onlookers sitting in rows to their left and right. It looked to Sol as if the entire Church membership had come to pay their respects. He turned back his sleeves slightly to reveal his hands and placed them together in prayer, fingers interlocked, pointing toward the dusty base of the podium and the earth beneath, the source of all life. He looked down, for a few moments touching his wedding bangle, rubbing it slowly with his left thumb.

His head finally jerked up, his voice strong with authority. "Yes, Tal Salandor said this, and it is the truth. It is also a truth that Yan Arramosa was my most trusted and loved friend in this city of thousands. A man whose warmth, generosity and kindness were second only to his integrity, honesty and dedication to the truth." He looked over the congregation, clasping his hands behind his back, finding his wedding bangle once more. "Yan instructed me as a junior priest, as he did many of you here today." He paused once more, walking slowly around the podium as he continued. "He helped me to develop into the man I am now, instilling in me the importance of my position and the responsibility and respect it demands. Now, sadly, the influence of these fine attributes Yan freely shared has been taken from us all, and I ask each and every one of you: can you, as individuals, exhibit just one of his noble characteristics? Can you be as gracious and selfless as he, during *your* lives? Can you look into the eyes of a friend, neighbour, relative or complete stranger and treat them with the same level of grace and good will as Yan did, all throughout his life?" He paused and looked over the congregation, returning to his original position behind the coffin, his voice now conversational, but commanding. "Try it. Go on. Look at each other now and ask yourself this as you gaze into your neighbour's eyes. If you can give as Yan Arramosa did, then you too will be rewarded as he." He looked to Roanne.

"I ask Grand Cardinal Oen Zoloth to join me now on this podium for a brief moment, so we can share as Yan Arramosa did, throughout his life."

Zoloth opened his eyes, raising his head, surprised to be called to the podium. Suppressing his eagerness to be part of the ceremony once more, he stood, failing to notice Roanne staring nervously at Sol.

Her heart began to pound, recognising the expression of regret her husband failed to contain. She tilted her head up to her brother. "What is he up to?" she murmured. Her voice faltered, "This isn't part of the plan."

The big man shrugged, narrowing his eyes on Sol as he puffed on his pipe. "I have absolutely no idea, but I'm sure it'll be worth watching," he answered with a grin, folding his arms.

She looked back to her husband, hoping he would look her way once more, affording her a reassuring smile, but his eyes were firmly fixed upon Zoloth.

As the Senior Grand Cardinal stood next to Sol atop the narrow podium, both men bowed slightly toward each other. The congregation began to whisper, aware this was a breach of protocol, but eager to see the city's two most significant religious personalities together.

"Grand Cardinal Zoloth," began Sol, as he held up his hands for silence. "I will share with you *my* truth and integrity, for all to see."

As complete silence fell around the auditorium, Zoloth's eyes met Sol's, and for a brief moment he saw in them something he had not seen in a very long time. His brow quivered as he recognised the hatred, the fearless resolution that had built up in his most successful Cardinal as Irrianna's words echoed in his memory.

'Men are unpredictable when it comes to their families.'

"Grand Cardinal Zoloth," began Sol, his voice raised so it would carry to the very fringes of the congregation. "I hold you personally responsible for Yan Arramosa's murder, deception and complicity with the Grand Cardinals over this matter, and the abduction of my son..."

A wave of gasped disbelief swept from the front of the mourners to the back. As Zoloth understood what had been said and his jaw slackened, Sol's hands leapt from their prayer position and seized the old man around the throat. The auditorium erupted, colours intermingling as ranks were broken. Zoloth's two personal Deacons drew their swords, hurrying forwards from behind the seated Grand Cardinals. Several onlookers fainted, others stood waving fists, mourners cried, Irrianna struggled to his feet barking orders. Roanne and Hulneb pushed their way through the ranks of onlookers towards the bridge as Zoloth dropped to his knees, desperately pulling at Sol's wrists as the lead Deacon ran up the steps. Sol glanced up, pulling Zoloth to his left, twisting at his waist to kick the deacon squarely in the chest. Tumbling back down the steps he collided with a seated Grand Cardinal, both falling into the pool.

Sol continuing through clenched teeth as Zoloth struggled to cough. ".....subversion, perversion, heresy, a betrayal of our most sacred beliefs...." Then a gloved hand seized him by his braided hair, pulling his head back, the sunlight finding the lustre of the polished steel blade as it came to rest against his throat. His grip on Zoloth lost, he held up his hands in surrender, the blade still at his throat.

Roanne screamed, pushing forwards past Hulneb, finding four Deacons, swords drawn, blocking their entry to the bridge. He pulled her back, aware the Deacons would not hesitate to prohibit her interference at any cost as she struggled against him.

Irrianna took to the podium, waving his arms around, directing his Deacons into the crowd to quiet them. "Stay calm, everyone!" he wheezed.

Zoloth stood and coughed, one hand holding his throat, the other waving away a few junior priests who sought to attend him.

"Congregation! Congregation! Please, stay calm! Cardinal Timmerman's emotional outburst is but a symptom of his grief, nothing more. I will allow him to explain." He turned, nodding to the Deacon to pull Sol to his feet. His hands held behind his back, his scimitar removed from its sheath and taken out of reach, he was escorted to the front of the island.

"Cardinal Timmerman," barked Zoloth, "will you retract your accusations, or do you stand by them?"

Sol lifted his head defiantly. "I stand by them firmly and hold them in my heart as ultimate truths," he shouted, struggling against the Deacon as another two joined them.

"And what proof do you have to support these allegations?"

"None, other than your own words. Your plans to change our religious beliefs and–"

"Cardinal! You are obviously delusional with grief. I have stated no such fantasies. Without proof, your accusations are empty." Zoloth shook his head, looking over the congregation as they muttered among themselves.

"This is a serious crime against all we believe, Cardinal, and demands to be punished as such by our laws. You will be stripped of your official title and accommodation, as required by your crime of heresy and my attempted murder. You and your family will be banished from this city and your name struck from the records of achievement." He nodded to the Deacons. "Remove his official robes." They pulled him to his feet, stripping him of his cloak, robes and hose, passing them to Irrianna who folded them over his arm.

Sol turned and glared at Zoloth, and the old man saw his hatred had not dissipated.

"I accept my punishment under the law, but request under this law for an ancient rule to be enforced. This is my right. I demand to be placed on the Pinnacle of Judgement. Let Tal Salandor prove my claims!"

Zoloth raised an eyebrow and glanced sideways at Irrianna, who shrugged slightly.

"This is your right, Sol Timmerman, but your family will suffer the same punishment under that rule."

"My family?"

Zoloth smiled. "There is a sub-clause, pertaining exclusively to members of the Holy Church of *Oosah*. Or were you unaware?"

"But my family are not guilty of any crime against you or this city! My wife, she–"

"Then choose banishment!" Zoloth took a few steps towards him. "The rule stands, as it has been written, since the laws were first passed. Your wife? She is your closest relation, and from this day forward she can only infect the loyal citizens of this city with *your* heresy, as you have undoubtedly infected her."

"That's not true!" shouted Roanne. "My beliefs are not on trial here! I don't recognise your authority over me!"

Zoloth turned on his heels, ignoring her. "Hulneb Vela, High Celebrant and spiritual leader of the Kaltesh," he shouted. "Is this not the lawful rule of Abeona?"

Hulneb took a step forward and the Deacons allowed him past, blocking Roanne as she tried to follow.

"It is the written law of Abeona, yes," said Hulneb, stopping where the bridge met the island.

Zoloth's gaze scanned the congregation; most of them had left their seats and were now gathered in front of Sol. "And you would not call upon any member of your tribe to act on this judgement, even though Sol Timmerman's wife is your sister?"

Hulneb turned to look at Roanne. "If my sister chooses to live within these city walls, then she must live by its laws – she understands that. To think otherwise is foolish. My Kaltesh brothers and sisters will take *no* action, you have my word. The people of this city will suffer no retribution. This is conditionally guaranteed, Grand Cardinal Zoloth."

Zoloth frowned, "Conditionally?" He waved him forward, "Please, clarify your condition?"

Hulneb approached Sol slowly, swiftly drawing a dagger from his sleeve. He seized a lock of hair braided with blue ribbon from the back of Sol's head, laying it across his blade.

He stood astride Sol, looking defiantly out over the congregation, before bending down to speak to his brother by union. "I told you I'd eventually have my Trophy." He stood, paused, and with a swift movement cut the braid of hair at the scalp, leaving a bloodied wound. "This is my condition, Grand Cardinal," said Hulneb, holding the braid out to him, then up to show the congregation as some shouted their objections.

Roanne saw her chance as the Deacons blocking her way had become distracted by this unforgettable spectacle. Gracefully she weaved her body between them, being careful to minimise physical contact. "You bastard, Hulneb!" she screamed as she ran along the bridge, "You can't–" A Deacon seized her from behind, and she turned swiftly, clubbing him squarely on the jaw with the fingers of both hands interlocked, kicking him to the ground as he stumbled back. A second Deacon came forward from the altar, but she had anticipated him as being eager for a fight, elbowing him in the temple once, before a punch to his throat sent him choking to his knees, his sword clattering upon the granite.

Hulneb watched her advance, standing his ground. Her hands were claws now, outstretched, and as she swiped for her brother's face, he simply bent backward at the waist as a Deacon wrapped his arms around her waist, picking her up and pulling her aside. She spat at Hulneb, but it fell short into the dust. "You're murderers, both of you!" She screamed, kicking back, tearing at the Deacon's gloves as he pushed her right arm behind her back, forcing her to shriek in pain and finally remain still.

Zoloth closed his eyes for a moment and nodded to the High Celebrant. "Your condition is a fair price for peace." He walked over to Hulneb, placing his hands on the large man's shoulders and speaking loudly. "Both the people of this city and the Kaltesh would see it as an act of peace if you would join the Holy Twelve in our Citadel, to cement this agreement in writing."

Hulneb bowed slightly, tucking the scalp under his belt. "I will assemble my personal honour guard – simply as a measure of my respect for your hospitality, you understand – and attend you within the measure."

Roanne glared at Hulneb, whose face had taken on a gentle smirk, and at once she realised Sol's plans were no more. She looked over at her husband, breathing hard, unable to speak, noticing he had grown pale, defeated and frail now his official robes and adornments had been stripped from him. His white undergarments were hanging in creases around his thin, muscular frame, stained with sweat and a streak of blood. The sunlight caught his face and through the tears clouding her vision, she understood how vulnerable he was at last.

FIFTEEN

JUDGEMENT

The funeral ceremony continued, concluding peacefully under the respectful mumblings of Irrianna, once Sol and Roanne had been taken from the auditorium under guard. In the Holy Citadel, Zoloth made them as comfortable as their crimes allowed – a damp cell situated in the bowels of the building.

Zoloth locked the cell door, taking a few steps backwards out of arm's reach and dismissing his personal guards. Satisfied no one else could hear, he spoke through the thick iron bars as he placed the key beneath his robes.

"You're a fool, Timmerman. You've thrown away everything: your life, your family's lives, their future. For what? Simply because you didn't agree with the way the future must be?" He seemed genuinely interested and craned his neck as if that might make Sol's answer all the more comprehensible.

Sol turned from Roanne, who was bandaging his head with a strip torn from her robes.

"You wouldn't allow me back into *Oosah* to search for my son. I believe Yan's murder was a distraction to lure me away from him, so your Deacons could kidnap him and you could hold his life over my head as leverage, forcing me to fall in with your heretical new god order."

Zoloth looked bewildered. "What? That is nothing more than a foolish, contrived fantasy. My belief is that your son is alive and well, and in the care of your wife's mother. You clearly believed telling us that preposterous story about his disappearance would allow you back inside *Oosah,* under the pretence of searching for him, while all along you simply wanted to further your ambition to become a Grand Cardinal *before* the new order was introduced and your position abolished. I'm sure Arramosa informed you of our plans, prior to our meeting?"

"No," said Sol abruptly, remembering the letter Yan had wanted to give him. "Is that why you had him murdered, because you believed he exposed your planned heresy to me?"

Zoloth shook his head. "What was to be the next stage in this sick fallacy? That perhaps your son is special, being of mixed, or rather *tainted* blood – that this is the explanation for him opening a seal in the auditorium of one hundred?" Zoloth chuckled and folded his arms. "Perhaps you would have me believe your son is our divine saviour, a chosen one, holding the key to the truths hidden inside *Oosah*." He shook his head and looked at Roanne. "Your husband should have written fables; sadly he has missed his true calling in this life."

She held his gaze but said nothing, so Zoloth looked at Sol once more. "Perhaps you'll be more careful when choosing your vocation in the next, if there is such for you." He turned and hurried into the darkness.

"I'll expect to see him with us on the Pinnacle, Zoloth!" shouted Sol, stepping up to the bars and clutching them. "I demand it!" he screamed. "You must release him to us. Zoloth! ZOLOTH!" But only his own voice echoed back to him as the door to the cells slammed and locked behind the Senior Grand Cardinal.

"Why didn't you tell him you know about his daughter?" asked Roanne.

He took a deep breath and rested his forehead upon the bars. "It wouldn't have done us any good."

"So now we know for certain Opi is inside the Trophy," said Roanne. "There's no reason for Zoloth to keep him from us. Do you believe he opened a seal *now?*"

But Sol remained silent, his eyes fixed into the darkness where Zoloth had stood moments before. Deep in thought, he closed his eyes, his theory concerning recent events now shattered by Zoloth's admissions, struggling to see where the truth really hid. It seemed it ran from him, purposely evading his focus. Like an animal aware it was being hunted it scampered and scurried though his memories in a blur. Never quite seen, but leaving clues as to its destination for him to follow. "I will find you," he muttered. "I will not fail you."

Hulneb stood upon the wide balcony dining area, provided with an expansive view of the city. Below, he could just make out the Pinnacle of Judgement. From this lofty position, it appeared as just a small, roughly circular area amid the surrounding darkness, illuminated by ambient light from the Citadel. Beyond that stood the garrison buildings, and far to the pinnacle's left, the dam and the river meandering up to the far distant Goraknath mountains. He turned his gaze back to the city. The wall curved smoothly away and disappeared into the haze as smoke drifted from the torch-lit streets. Looking directly beneath him his stomach quivered. The sheer drop of smooth-cut stone vanished into darkness, its distance measured every eighth of a league by four rows of flaming torches three men in length, jutting from the face of the Citadel's front wall. The heat from them warmed his face as Zoloth spoke, his voice adopting a silky, fatherly tone, his masterly measured rhythm precisely regulated as he lit candles set upon a long dining table of highly polished mahogany.

"Hundreds of cycles ago, proclamations were spoken from that balcony, High Celebrant. Bishops were placed along the halls of the Citadel, a Cardinal upon the pinnacle, another in the garrison, then at measured distances, five hundred or so priests throughout the city. They spread the holy words to the populace and the news would reach every ear during the same measure."

"An interesting way to communicate," muttered Hulneb, as he focused on the tiny points of light reaching up from the depths of the dam wall.

Zoloth nodded. "Interesting, yes, but ultimately impractical. Sadly, on several occasions, the words were misconstrued along their way, and messages were wrongly orated to the people – either on purpose or accidentally. All news is written now, removing any chance of creative embellishments by those seeking to advance their own agenda." He finished lighting the candles, throwing the taper into the fireplace. Producing a parchment from beneath his robes, his voice took on a warm, friendly tone. "I do not wish to appear disrespectful, but can you write?"

Hulneb turned, remembering forging the document for Sol. "I can make my mark in Kaltesh, if that's what you require?" he replied, slowly walking down the shallow steps towards his counterpart.

Zoloth held the parchment in front of him. "This document declares the sentence carried out today to be lawful and immutable, guaranteeing no retribution by you, or any Kaltesh, on behalf of your sister." He stabbed the paper twice with a spindly, white finger. "You should place your mark next to my name, here. This signifies your responsibility in this matter."

Hulneb took the parchment, studying it carefully, walking slowly to the long ebony table elaborately set for them with silver plates and utensils. A long silence followed as Hulneb remained still.

The Senior Grand Cardinal shuffled uneasily, then checked himself. "You appear unhappy with this. Perhaps a beneficial amendment is in order, High Celebrant?"

Hulneb looked up and turned to face him. "Beneficial?"

Zoloth angled his head toward the two Kaltesh guards standing in the lounge area in front of the double oak doors. "If we could speak in private?"

Hulneb sat at the table, easing his weight into the back of a chair decorated with gold leaf. Satisfied with the creak it gave, he barked a throaty order in Kaltesh, and the two men hurried through the doors to wait outside. As the doors closed behind them he looked up at Zoloth, his brow creasing with curiosity. "What do you have in mind?"

Zoloth remained impassive, purposely keeping his distance as he placed his hands behind his back. "We need to discuss the future for our respective people, Hulneb. May I call you Hulneb?"

The High Celebrant nodded once.

"We've all spent far too long separated by our beliefs and fears. I believe it is time to cast aside those ancient, foolish restrictions, and unite everyone under one philosophy."

Hulneb shook his head, his mouth creasing into a thin, disrespectful smirk. "You honestly expect my people to discard thousands of cycles of ritual, overnight? For what?"

Zoloth walked forward, his eyes fixed upon Hulneb's. "For a far more comfortable, safer and more prosperous way of life."

Hulneb was unable to stifle a chuckle. "Forgive me, Senior Grand Cardinal, but if you refer to your abundant supply of water with your ornamental fountains and pools, your man-made river and canals, your roofs for shelter and your walled areas of grassy slopes, planted flowers and caged singing birds, then I'm sorry, but my people would laugh at you, as I have done." He gestured to the balcony. "I mean no disrespect, but far beyond Abeona the rivers are clear and cold, our tents and caravans cool, and neither the grassy slopes of the Goraknath foothills, nor the western forests of rain far beyond require walls." He placed the parchment on the plate in front of him, clasping his hands together over his stomach. "We have all the comfort, safety and prosperity we need."

Zoloth pulled on a tassel protruding from the wall, and Hulneb was sure he heard a bell toll in the distance. He placed his right hand next to the pommel of a short-sword, unsure if his two bodyguards would be enough to stop an assault from Zoloth's highly trained Deacons, remembering Rillian had pleaded with him not to meet the Grand Cardinal on his own territory. *'Abeonians cannot be trusted,'* she had said, *'especially Zoloth. Be wary of him at all times.'* He had brushed her concerns aside with a casual shake of his head. Now he began to feel uneasy, his palms sweaty and his throat suddenly dry.

Zoloth sat at the table opposite him, delicately arranging his robes over his chair. He smiled.

"I understand," he said softly. "But what of you, Hulneb? Do you intend to spend the rest of your life wandering the wilderness?" he gestured to the balcony, "Do you not covet all you have seen here today, and more?"

He held Zoloth's stare as the double doors opened quickly without a respectful knock. Gripping his sword, Hulneb stood, sending his chair back onto the carpet with a clatter.

Upon seeing the combat-ready Kaltesh, the three priests stopped in their tracks, taking a step back in unison as if they were tethered at the waist by an invisible rope. Their eyes darted between him and Zoloth.

"Relax, my friend," reassured Zoloth, ignoring the priests' ungainly display, "Simply a banquet for us both. A man thinks more clearly on a full stomach, don't you think?" He waved the hesitant priests forward with a single gesture.

Hulneb sheathed his sword. "We believe a man thinks clearer on his feet," he said, picking up his chair.

The three priests came forward in small, measured steps, carrying golden platters of roasted game, grilled fish, boiled vegetables, fruit, steaming bread and pastries. There was enough fare for six men. They laid the table in silence as a fourth entered and placed two silver goblets and a large bottle of wine in front of Zoloth.

Their task complete, they stood in line facing the table and bowed in unison, waiting for Zoloth to wave them away. He stood, clasping his hands behind his back, walking the length of the table, inspecting the banquet in fine detail. "The wine?" he barked.

The shortest of the four uncorked the bottle and filled both goblets. Zoloth nodded once towards the doors. The priests bowed and hurried out, and as the doors closed, he picked up a goblet and held it under his nose.

"No doubt you've noticed the work upon the city walls?"

"I can't say I have," lied Hulneb.

Zoloth took a sip and paused for a moment, then swallowed and passed Hulneb a goblet. "I'm preparing the walls so they can be safely dismantled; we will utilise the blocks to expand. It is our intention to construct new thoroughfares, homes and schools and places of business. But walls will no longer contain our community. We'll build roadways out across the sand, bridges across valleys out into the green areas, past the fringe settlements and to the ocean, constructing habitats wherever we choose."

"And why do this?"

"To invite your people to join with us, to become one tribe with no boundaries. To come and go as we both please, but to *always* have a home here if we desire to worship the Trophy *Oosah Agasanduku.*"

"My people? Living here?" Hulneb shook his head, "I'm pleased to say our ways are different, Senior Grand Cardinal. The people of this city are governed by routine, and no doubt you'll take your routines with you. You eat when a bell sounds, telling you it is time. We eat when we are hungry. Your people are forced to work to a toll's measure, before hurrying home to seize a few precious moments with their loved ones. We all work together only to sustain our lives, and the lives of those who cannot fend for themselves. Your city has beggars and the poor running barefoot alongside the rich and greedy, riding upon golden carts." He looked away with self-assured smugness. "We prefer Kaltesh equality."

Zoloth responded instantly. "My people have a standard of living reflecting their position in society. This is how it has always been, and can only ever be. You can't expect a street cleaner and a merchant of the finest silk to share the same table of fare."

"They both contribute to make this city the perfection you claim it to be, so why not?"

Zoloth glared at him. "Wealth must be distributed by worth. If a merchant sees a beggar equally rewarded for sitting in the sun day after day, then where is the incentive for the merchant to rise from his bed before dawn, to work until dusk, and employ the beggar?" He chuckled again, but this time made no attempt to hide the fact as he looked his counterpart up and down. "Why, we'd all be walking around in rags, Hulneb."

The High Celebrant shrugged. "Then at least provide the poor with enough to narrow the void between effluence and affluence. As I understand it, the pleasures of the Abeonian poor are simply sex, and for the most part, sex alone. They have more children because your social structure provides them with a certain amount of free food and accommodation. Therefore, the more children they have, the better off they are. Utter stupidity! Why, you're heading toward a society where the only adults you'll have walking the streets will be the lower classes, with lower-class values, skills and behaviour. Is that what you're offering to share with my people, Senior Grand Cardinal? Your inadequate, decaying social structure?" He smiled up at his opposite, confident now. "You really should ask yourself what possible benefits you are offering my people from this new way of life. The Kaltesh would begin at the bottom of your social ladder, elevating your poor to a middle class. The Kaltesh would spend their days performing menial tasks, hard labour and the like." He sat forward and stabbed the table with his finger. "More to the point, what benefits can you *personally* reap from this amendment?"

Zoloth relaxed, determined not to lose his composure. "For myself and everyone it's simple. The eradication of fear. The Kaltesh have many useful skills to enrich this new society, regardless of your surprisingly low opinion of their worth. An equality neither the Abeonian nor Kaltesh has ever seen would soon arise from this bonding." Zoloth smiled genuinely for the first time. "Hulneb, your early arrival for this season's festival was surprising. The concern this caused could be felt in the streets like a pandemic. The old fears are still felt here; it's no secret among my people. The apprehension that your warriors will attempt to take control of *Oosah* once and for all, fulfilling your ancient ancestors' ambitions, is a great intimidation, moreover, ultimately terrifying. Only when you appear with open arms and empty hands, can the city slowly return to its usual state of contentment. So, what if we both agreed to turn away from our mutual object of desire, and instructed our people to do the same? Together we could do this. We could end fear and religious jealousy, uniting every man, woman and child under a new order. I agree, the social structure will need much work to perfect it, but just think of the endless possibilities it could lead to, once agreed and implemented by us."

Hulneb sipped his wine, studying Zoloth over the rim of his goblet for a few moments before replacing it upon the table, turning it slowly in the wet ring that had formed there. He kept his eyes on his jewelled fingers as he spoke. "So, Timmerman's accusations were true?" He looked up to gauge his counterpart's reaction.

Zoloth raised his voice. "Sol Timmerman's punishment is proportionate: for attempted murder, his accusing me of murder, and his breaking of the sacred vow *not* to mention any of what I have just told you, until the appointed time." He sighed and calmed himself. "Hulneb, listen. I wanted to make this offer in person to your father." He pointed toward the balcony. "I learnt a valuable lesson from the priests misinterpreting the proclamations hundreds of cycles ago. I knew I had to make myself completely understood, without any likelihood of a misunderstanding."

Hulneb stopped turning the goblet and took another sip,

producing his pipe and lighting it from one of the candles on the table. Satisfied the pipe was sufficiently alight, he drained his goblet and replaced it, wiping his mouth with the back of his hand. Puffing a green cloud with satisfaction, he spoke slowly through the smoke. "And you and I would be equals governing the people under this new order?"

Zoloth nodded and leant forward. "Bring your entire tribe into the city and we can all, standing side by side, working as one with a common goal, remove the city walls and create a new era for the people of this world. We can turn our backs on *Oosah*, advance across the land, explore, forge a new way as we venture together beyond our known boundaries." He gestured toward the balcony once more. "Within a few hundred cycles the sand will consume this city, and *Agasanduku*. They'll both be nothing more than a child's bedtime fairytale." He paused, studying Hulneb's face in the flickering candlelight, but Hulneb just puffed on his Farrengrass.

"All my people are in this city, Zoloth."

The Grand Cardinal smiled broadly and sat back. "Now we both know that isn't true. I am aware a considerable percentage of the Kaltesh tribe remain to guard your crops and water caches, for fear of an attack by my Deacons. If we are to unite everyone, then everyone must be brought together. It would be unfortunate if a minority were left to create their own sect," Zoloth grinned and scratched his cheek. "Trophy revivalists, if you like. Such a movement would seek to undermine our collaboration with treachery and subterfuge. Both of us would be seen as legitimate targets by such a faction, and soon we'd be in the same position our ancestors were hundreds of cycles ago."

Hulneb looked at the fare before him. "If I agree, you must understand – it will take time to summon every member of the tribe."

"Then I would respectfully suggest you send word immediately. I intend to announce this new system during my closing speech on the last day of the festival, the last festival this city will see conducted for the false idol in our midst. You have until then."

Hulneb shuffled uncomfortably in his seat. Zoloth's new order had a certain attraction, not only for his people and their well-being, but for himself also. The winters seemed colder as he grew older, the work harder: arranging harvests and distributing food, caring for the elderly and the young, repairing the caravans and tending the animals, ensuring the breeding stock and livestock for slaughter were maintained to the optimum levels. He sighed. The arbitration processes for serious crimes and petty disagreements between neighbours that were brought before him were becoming all the more frequent and irritating. Once the committees had debated, researched and presented him with their lengthy evidence, the final decision always rested upon his shoulders. All too often the convicted party had threatened his life, and at the back of his mind he knew it was only a matter of time before some drunken idiot decided he should end his High Celebranthood, once and for all.

However, making that life-changing decision for his people held the greatest lure for him. *'If they look to me to decide right from wrong for them, then this could be the ultimate decision I make,'* he thought. He straightened himself up in the chair, looking hard at Zoloth across the candlelit table.

"And what will you put in place as a substitute for *Agasanduku*? Surely our new society will need to worship?"

Zoloth stood and picked up his plate, studying the banquet before him as he slowly walked the table's length.

"The people need to value their own lives, and not an idol that takes valuable time and resources, giving nothing in return but self-deluding comfort. We will teach the people to worship themselves."

Hulneb closed his eyes and shook his head. "The

worship of oneself wouldn't be enough. Everyone needs to look higher, for comfort and support."

Zoloth plucked three ripe, red grapes with his thumb and little finger, dropped them on his plate and licked the juice from his thumb. Cheese followed, then he tore a roll of brown bread in two. He glanced over to Hulneb and offered him half. "After many centuries of devoted reverence, no, not at first."

Hulneb shook his head. "Then what do you suggest they worship until they learn the value of themselves?"

Zoloth continued to place food on his plate. "Why, us, of course," he said casually, convinced his aporia was finally making an impact upon his guest.

Hulneb stood and picked up his plate, scanning the table for the best cuts of meat, finding they were all without fat or sinew. Ignoring the utensils, he scooped up several slices of game, along with a handful of small, filleted fish, then walked to the balcony and began to eat as he looked over the city.

Zoloth joined him. "Imagine being a key part of such an historical event, Hulneb. Your name would be recorded as the architect who led your people in from the wilderness." He paused for a moment, lowering his voice and leaning forward. "In the eyes of countless generations, you would be... *immortal*."

Hulneb glanced at Zoloth standing to his left, remembering the faces of his tribe as they caught sight of the city walls. The cheering and laughing, hugging each other, singing ancient songs and crying tears of happiness. The occasion brought them all together, kept them all together, working as one for a common goal. Could he end all that and replace it? Would his people be content under combined rule? The festival was always eagerly anticipated. It was known a few saw it as just an excuse to line their purses or to overindulge. But underpinning all this there was still *Agasanduku* and the hallowed memory of the twin brothers who had constructed it for *his* people.

He was aware that respect for those brothers only showed itself in Abeona as mocking nursery rhymes or late-night folk songs, and he suddenly realised as he ate that he didn't have the confidence to turn his people away. Indeed, their reactions could manifest as, at best, his banishment from the tribe to, at worst, his execution. He found himself looking at Zoloth, whose eyes were eager and wide, and at last he saw the insanity in the man who ruled over this city of fools.

'One swift, continuous movement of my arm,' he thought. His heart began to race. *'He's a tall man, his balance point at roughly the same height as the balustrade. I could end this right now. The remaining eleven Grand Cardinals are said to be simply puppets under him. I could have my warriors storm the Citadel within the measure, rescue Roanne and Sol, liberating the city and returning rule to the people.'* He smiled broadly at his thoughts, as he imagined the concept. To what end? He remembered the beauty of the world outside the walls, and his breathing returned to its measured pace as his gaze drifted over the city and the darkness of the desert. He shook his head slowly. His nephew. The Trophy. An empty shell, but it provides the comfort of the unknown to everyone. Another Zoloth would soon crawl from the dark corners of the city. There would always be men like him, where there was gain to be made from the hearts of those seeking spiritual comfort.

"I can see by your expression my offer holds a certain attraction for you, Hulneb."

He smiled at Zoloth, who stooped slightly, pregnant with anticipation, Finally he spoke. "I will give this considerable thought."

Passing Zoloth his half-eaten meal, he turned to the table to make his mark on the parchment. "You will have my answer on the first day of the festival," and with that he strode to the doors and hurried out, leaving a billowing cloud of smoke in his wake.

Zoloth pulled on the tassel once more and began hurriedly pacing the length of the table.

Finally Irrianna appeared at the doorway.

"I saw him leave. He looked pleased with himself."

"He didn't commit, Irrianna," said Zoloth, stopping to drop the plate onto the table with a clatter. He began to pace once more. "We'll just have to do this the hard way. Have our Deacons ready to remove all remaining after the Grand Event."

Irrianna was taken by surprise. "All?"

Zoloth stopped at the centre of the table and stared hard at his colleague. "Have all this taken to the stables, and have some incense brought in here. That Kaltesh stench catches the back of my throat."

In the cell far below, dirty water dripped from the drains overhead, creating a steadily growing puddle of effluence around their naked bodies.

Roanne sat with her arms over her knees, watching the droplets fall and splatter the dust into brown mud. She looked dejected and weary, her eyes vacant, her eyebrows twitching to the despair of her thoughts.

"All we have to do is wait until morning, when we're taken up onto the pinnacle." whispered Sol. "By evening we'll be ignored – left for dead, and in the darkness can begin our search for the opening."

"But I wasn't supposed to be with you – I was supposed to release you," she mumbled.

"I theorised Zoloth may insist upon you being imprisoned with me – an ancient rule – there was a forty-two percent chance he'd remember it. However, I'm sure we can count on a friend," said Sol with a smile.

She looked up at his bandage. "You heard what Hulneb said, you saw his face, how he gloated over all this. How can you rely on him?"

"Hulneb played his part to perfection. For a moment

even *I* was convinced of his motives."

She stood, astounded at what he had said. "You mean that was all *arranged* – and you didn't tell me?"

"I'm sorry, Roanne," offered Sol, "but we needed your reactions to be convincing. It was his idea, you must understand that. If Zoloth suspected this was all a ruse, then Tal only knows what his response would have been. But no, it's not Hulneb that will release us. He has too high a profile, and I'm sure Zoloth has eyes watching his every move."

She looked down to the puddle once more. "Is there anything else you haven't told me?"

He shook his head and winced at his throbbing wound, turning to face her. "Ommus is to release us as soon as the first torch is lit tomorrow night." He held her shoulders and smiled. "Everything will work out well, trust me. This will all be over very soon, and then we'll search for our son."

The sound of a key sliding into a lock caught Sol's attention and he clasped the cell bars, peering into the dark corridor. The far door creaked open, then closed gently, followed by shuffling footsteps.

A torch grew steadily brighter and at last revealed a rounded face, smiling broadly.

"Ommus," whispered Sol.

Roanne joined him at the bars.

"Oh, my oh my," started the little man. "You really are one for theatricals. Yan would have been proud of you today."

Sol managed a weak smile. "I'm sorry I offended his family."

Ommus raised a finger. "He would have understood, as would they. Don't worry yourself needlessly, Sol."

"What news do you have?"

"Hulneb Vela had a lengthy conversation with Zoloth, which ended moments ago. I couldn't hear all that was said, but I did see Irrianna visit Zoloth just after Hulneb left." He shook his head and his gaze became distant.

"Irrianna looked troubled. Here," he held the torch out to Sol, "hold this." He began fumbling through his robes and their numerous pockets. At last he produced a key and began unlocking the cell door.

"What are you doing?" asked Sol.

Roanne looked up at him, "Isn't it obvious?"

Ommus stopped and looked at them both. "I've come to get you out of here, why else would–"

Sol shook his head. "No. We must stick to the arrangement. If Zoloth sees we've escaped he'll have the Deacons tearing this city apart to find us."

"We'd be safe in mother's caravan," offered Roanne, her intolerance growing.

Sol answered quickly. "Would we? It would be the first place he'd insist on looking. No, we keep to the plan."

The little man reluctantly withdrew the key, replacing it beneath his robes. "Then I will see you both tomorrow evening, as arranged. I have two junior priests I can trust with my life, and yours – they will help us." He took the torch from Sol and hurried back into the darkness.

They said nothing as they lay together in the damp, dark air. Sol, the first to sleep as Roanne huddled close to him, unable to quell the fears circling in her head. Then she slept and, much later, dreamt.

She watched as he looked out over the water. Ahead of him, half a dozen rocks briefly showed their faces as the waves wiped watery hands to smooth their contours. As these fingers of foam receded, the rocks revealed adult balias shells and the thick, fleshy green seaweed entwining them.

Her head was level with the back of his neck. She felt the weight in her hands and the muscles in her forearms tense as she lifted the rock high above her head. She stood motionless for a moment, the rock shading her eyes from the sun. As the rock came back over her head she tried to scream to warn him, but could not summon her voice. Then the rock was brought down swiftly. She heard the crack of bone and a whimpering cry as his body jerked forward and his arms came up.

He fell head first into a shallow pool, as it began to calm it was invaded by growing blooms, colouring the water red. He turned quickly for an old man, gasping for air. She jumped in after him, sure the blow had been enough – but somehow it had not. His face cleared the pool and surprise momentarily replaced his anger. Her hands clasped his neck, pushing him under. He screamed a name beneath the water, expelling his breath in a torrent of red bubbles. His arms came up and grabbed her wrists, and for a moment she thought she would lose her grip amid the slippery mess. He tried to raise his body but she knelt on his chest now, using her weight to force the last breath from his lungs. His grip began to relax, his head tipped backward...

Roanne awoke, screaming.

"It's okay," said Sol, holding her head to his chest, "it's okay. I'm here. It was just a dream, only a dream. You're safe. We'll be out of this soon."

She caught her breath and opened her eyes, suddenly aware of her surroundings.

"It was Mirrimas – the dream I've had before – his murder." She began to sob. "The... the dream was different – went on further. I saw him strangled, Sol. It was horrible! It was Hulneb. It all makes sense to me now. He must have been sleeping in the Citadel above us."

A voice from behind the bars startled them both.

"It is time, Sol Timmerman," said the Deacon.

The drawbridge lowered into position in front of Sol and Roanne as they stood together aboard an old hay cart drawn by a single ganapti, led by a junior priest. Beyond the pinnacle, a crowd had been allowed into the garrison to view the spectacle. The garishly attired onlookers lined the battlements, the wind carrying their distant cries of abuse and curses across the abyss. Behind the cart walked the Holy Twelve, led by Zoloth.

As the procession halted on the lonely pinnacle, Zoloth instructed two Deacons to help Sol and Roanne out of the cart, their hands bound, both shivering from the early morning chill.

The eleven bowed and chanted a short prayer of respect and regret, then turned to hurry back to the protective walls of the Citadel, leaving Zoloth as their sole representative. The two Deacons pulled Sol and Roanne across the dusty flagstones, then drew their swords, taking a few steps back to stand either side of Zoloth, as the empty cart was led away.

"I've been informed a substantial amount of money is changing hands among the peasants of the Ravine Quarter," began the Senior Grand Cardinal. "It seems the odds are that you will both starve here, and not leap to your deaths below." He chuckled. "The odds are one thousand to one against Tal Salandor coming to your aid." He looked from one to the other and held his hands out, palms up. "Do either of you have a token?" he said with a grin, "I'm willing to place a wager on your behalf. Then again, if Tal Salandor does come to your aid, you wouldn't need currency in the Garden of Contentment, and would have no way to collect your profit."

"There'll be others like us, Zoloth," said Roanne, taking a step forward. "Your time will come sooner than you think. The people of this city won't stay silent forever."

"A revolt? How very romantic of you," said Zoloth. "Then again, there's a certain romanticism emerging from these wagers, for almost everyone agrees you will stay together to the end." He nodded to Roanne then looked at Sol. "I for one believe she will take her chances and jump, rather than watch the man who led her here wither to a dry husk. Don't you find it strange that peasants somehow find money to waste on wagers, rather than feed their children?" He paused for an answer that never came, so he cleared his throat and continued. "I suppose poverty is the enemy of good manners. Have either of you any thoughts on this?"

"I'll take a wager," said Sol, "that I'll see you again, Zoloth."

"And I'll see you dead," added Roanne, her voice wavering from the chill.

Zoloth tilted his head to one side and looked at Roanne with a gentle, almost fatherly smile, mistaking the quaver in her voice for fear. He raised his eyebrows and placed his hands into their opposite sleeves. "A wager? I'm terribly sorry, but as you've already made clear, neither of you has anything to offer in the way of collateral."

"How about your life?" said Sol, "I will spare it upon our next meeting, if you answer one question."

Zoloth's eyes widened slightly and he suppressed a smile. "One question? That's all you ask? I would have expected more from you, considering your circumstances." He shifted his weight as the cold found its way through his sandals. "Never mind. Ask, and be quick about it."

"On your way back to your chambers, walk the colonnade of painted pillars. Then act upon what you see. Can you do that, Zoloth? Do you have the courage?"

Zoloth could hide his amusement no longer. "Courage? Hah! Why would I need courage when I have absolute power?" He nodded to a Deacon who threw a large sack tied with string at their feet.

"A little reminder of your loss, and to help you through the cold nights. They'll help to keep you warm, but will no doubt prolong the agony of starvation."

Roanne stared at the bundle in horror, expecting Opi's dead form to come tumbling from the sack, as the second

Deacon walked forward to cut their bonds. With that, Zoloth turned and walked back to the Citadel, the Deacons watching Sol and Roanne until the drawbridge was raised.

Now the cheering began, and they turned to see a few youths throwing stones that fell short into the abyss. Sol untied the sack and took out his crumpled robes and cloak, placing the latter around Roanne's shoulders, holding her tightly to him.

Zoloth sighed deeply with satisfaction as the doors to the Citadel slammed behind him. He nodded sternly to the two Deacons, who hurried ahead. Composing himself, he walked on proudly, lifting his head in defiance as he passed the statues of Grand Cardinals long since dead.

They had all been fools, he thought. They had toiled and sweated through their short lives, always searching for the answer – an answer they had never received. As Cardinals, they had put forth their theories, debated and researched until that one shred of either luck or brilliance had promoted them one small step closer to their goal.

He stopped at one ancient statue and looked up at the stone image. This figure also stood proud and defiant, clutching his stone Book of Truths to his chest. Zoloth wanted to laugh out loud in the silence, wanted to dance around the statue and shout at it, longed to scream at all of the stone effigies occupying the garden, informing them *he* would be the one – *he* would break the next seal, and that their pathetic achievements for a lifetime's toil were nothing more than a tiny fraction of what he would achieve. He calmed himself, reading the inscription carved into the statue's base. He'd read it a hundred times before, but now it only served to amuse him.

Sur Orison
Grand Cardinal
Theorist of Armour
Author of: *The Defensive Attributes of Oosah*
Born 183157 - Promoted to Grand Cardinal 183239 - Died 183334

And he'd been proven correct, thought Zoloth. After a lifetime of experiments with all types of alloys, swords, spears and arrows, the conclusion was finally reached that the Trophy was impenetrable by any means known. He grinned and whispered to himself. "Now, almost three hundred cycles later, I know better."

"Contemplation, Senior Grand Cardinal?" said a voice behind him.

He turned to see Ommus, followed by two junior priests, heading toward the Citadel's lift, leading down to the bridge of Eliyas.

"Ah, Ommus, I was told you would be attending to your duties in the city shortly. How have you been? These past few measures must have been very upsetting for you?" He looked at the priests and spoke. "Thank you for your recent acts of clarity on my behalf. You can return to your studies, until summoned for your rewards."

Ommus wondered exactly what he meant, then shrugged. "No more than usual, Grand Cardinal," he said, watching the priests shuffle away, one turning to look back over his shoulder with a smirk. "What makes you think so?"

"Walk with me, Ommus. Our time has nearly come, but there is still much to talk of, a few tiny but nonetheless significant details to clarify."

"Your Holiness."

"Have you finished illuminating the manuscript?"

"Yes, Senior Grand Cardinal. It is sealed, in the hands

of your cleric, awaiting perusal in your chambers."

"Thank you. Now, I understand you will pay your last visit to my insane daughter tomorrow and copy her final illustrations, then release her from the contract she has with us. Is that correct?"

"Yes, Your Holiness."

"Well, strange news has reached my ears, Ommus. It seems a Cardinal... *Osterley,* visited her on my behalf recently. Do you have any idea who that might have been?"

Ommus frowned. "Osterley? There is no Cardinal by that name in the ranks of the Holy Church. Besides, only Your Holiness, Grand Cardinal Irrianna, and I know of your daughter's whereabouts."

"Or so we thought, Ommus. This impostor carried official documents, complete with my seal. I find this very upsetting, and this news has caused poor Irrianna an immense amount of concern. We're so very close – we can't afford any interference, now the Grand Event is nearly upon us, can we?"

"None whatsoever," said Ommus gravely, wondering if Zoloth would soon reveal to him exactly what the Grand Event entailed.

Zoloth placed a hand on the little man's shoulder and stopped. "I feel it is time for spiritual guidance over this matter." He held the bridge of his nose between his thumb and forefinger, closing his eyes. "Forgive me, but I grow weary from rising so early and overseeing the recent sad events, and need to relax in the pool. Would you be so kind as to join me?"

Ommus paused and glanced in the direction of the lift to the bridge of Eliyas. "I have urgent charity business on behalf of the Church Aid organisation, which shall be occupying my entire day in the Ravine Quarter. There's food to be–"

Zoloth removed his fingers from the bridge of his nose and opened his eyes. "Oh, I insist," he said. "This will take but a few moments of your time. Besides, waiting a measure or so longer will not cause the starving to become any more hungry."

Ommus thought for a moment. All the arrangements had taken careful planning. The task of formulating every detail had almost always fallen upon him, and at times he had thought the Grand Event, whatever it may be, was nothing more than a fantasy. They had come such a long way together, and it seemed he had always been Zoloth's servant in these matters. It was time he was rewarded for his endless toil. He turned to Zoloth and bowed slowly.

"Then perhaps you would walk the line of the colonnade of painted pillars, maybe a vision will enlighten you as to our next course of action concerning Cardinal Osterley?"

"Forgive me, Grand Cardinal," he said with a light chuckle, "but many times I have walked the colonnade with no result worth mentioning." He grinned. "Other than those for a light-hearted tale after a meal and a few goblets of wine."

Zoloth put his arm around the little man's shoulders and began to walk slowly towards the colonnade's entrance. "But the new age is almost upon us. Surely you would agree Tal Salandor would grant you a vision now, after all the cycles you've spent in devotion to *Oosah*, and our triumphant Grand Event?"

Ommus thought for a moment. "Well.... yes." His shoulders slumped, he was eager to relax in the pool. "I will try, Your Holiness, I will try."

Zoloth hurried to the end of the colonnade and turned to face him.

"Have faith, my friend. You must *believe* you will see beyond these walls and the path to your future. At the end of this brief walk, your doorway will open."

The old man removed his sandals and stood upon the cold line of silver. Concentrating hard he took a step forward, then another and another, struggling to keep his head level and his eyes focused ahead.

His eyes widened. At last a vision slowly emerged from the pillars. A lifetime of belief, he thought. Three dozen times he had walked the silver line, and three dozen times he had seen absolutely nothing worth mentioning, nothing which could be regarded as a divine message. This time it was different. A tear found its way into his left eye, clouding his vision for a moment before he wiped it away with a trembling hand.

He could see figures watching him as he walked, staring at him, waiting. There was one at either side, both with swords drawn and held by their sides.

As he reached the halfway mark, Zoloth smiled. "Yes, you see. It is possible. I can tell by your expression, Ommus. Finally you have been blessed."

The figure to the right remained at the halfway pillar and disappeared from view as the little man advanced, but the figure to the left followed, moving from pillar to pillar almost in the blink of an eye.

Zoloth bowed as Ommus was three paces from him, then looked over the little man's shoulder and nodded.

The sword exited his chest just below the breastbone, causing him to cough and splutter on blood forced into his throat by his heart's excitement. The figure from the left came striding in front of him, drawing a blade swiftly across his neck.

Zoloth took a step back as the advancing pool of blood threatened to soil his sandals.

"There Ommus. Now you have seen your future."

The day passed slowly upon the pinnacle. The jeering crowd dissipated by midday, leaving Sol and Roanne to lie together, sheltering from the sun in the shade provided by the stubby remnants of an ancient, decayed structure. Sol placed stone chippings in front of him at equal distances apart, watching as the shadow from the pavilion wall they lay against crept slowly around. As the measure bell tolled he placed a larger stone adjacent to the corresponding stone chip, level with the shadow's line. "We have a few measures before the hottest part of the day," he said, looking to the sky. The sun is warming the other side of this wall. It's best we move to the other side at sundown. The heat absorbed by the flagstones and brickwork will help keep us warm during the night."

They were both surprised and horrified at how quickly the body missed food and water. One day in the baking heat and their lips, free of any protective balm, became dry and split into sore creases. The sides of their mouths began to crack and their limbs ached. Roanne's spirit was the first to break; her nightmare, having robbed her of sound sleep during the night, playing repeatedly in her head throughout the daylight measures. After a time it was all she could think or speak of.

As soon as the sun dipped beneath the mountains, Sol began searching for the flagstone that would lead them to freedom.

"Come on, help me. The loose stone is here somewhere. We'll have to move fast once Ommus arrives." Blowing dust and scraping debris from around each flagstone, he crawled around on his hands and knees, trying to find the passageway he knew was there, Roanne helping him. They searched long into the night to no avail.

"This is useless. He's not coming," Roanne said, shivering from the chill.

"It's here, I know it is. Keep looking. Perhaps we can lever it up from the outside."

"But we've been searching all night. My fingertips, Sol. I can't feel them."

He looked at his own bloodied nails. "Then sleep. I'll wake you when Ommus arrives."

She curled up beneath his cloak, and after a while drifted into sleep.

His arms came up and grabbed her wrists, and for a moment she thought she would lose her grip amid the slippery mess. He tried to raise his body but she knelt on his chest now, using her weight to force the last breath from his lungs. His grip began to relax, his head tipped backward, the last breath exhaled, rising to the surface of the pool as foamy red and white bubbles.

Her hands remained tight around his throat, fingers waiting for that tell-tale pulse to cease, for she did not trust him, even this close to death. The water began to calm, the blood gathering at the bottom of the pool as she waited.

As the night waned, Sol continued to search for the flagstone which led to safety, cursing Ommus and his betrayal, while all through this, Roanne's restless moans joined the sounds of his fingernails scraping at the joins between the stones. The approach of day saw Sol's spirit fade. He had crawled over the entire surface of the pinnacle dozens of times, his knees and forearms bruised and bleeding, his stomach throbbing with hunger. He lay on his back, staring at the fading stars above him.

Roanne lay motionless.

The Monitor's morning bell tolled, rousing Sol from a fitful doze. Was it a memory, he wondered? An echo from the last day he had seen his son? He crawled to the edge of the pinnacle and stared into the abyss. Perhaps the stories were right, perhaps a few imprisoned individuals had flung themselves to their deaths, lest they die painfully from starvation and thirst. The bell continued for a while, then faded, and he slipped back into unconsciousness.

SIXTEEN

VISITORS

Hulneb kept vigil from his throne atop his caravan, searching the thoroughfare leading from the centre of Abeona with Mirrimas' telescope. He lowered the device and turned to Tyn, sitting at his side. "This is pointless, Hathranelzra. There's no sign of them!"

Tyn signed back.

"No, Sol insisted we stick to the plan – I gave him my word." He lifted the telescope to his eye once again, chewing at the stem of his pipe. The light was beginning to fade.

"Pray to the Brothers they return during the night. Perhaps the city is too busy for them to travel unnoticed."

He noticed the sudden silence first as he placed his saddle on the ganapti. The caravanserai was always a hive of noisy activity: traders entering or leaving, children running and shouting, youths gathering around musicians performing. A perimeter guard breathlessly ran over to him. He stopped, waiting for Hulneb to wave him forward, but the big man walked over to him as Rillian appeared upon the rear deck of her caravan, watching as the guard caught his breath before cupping his hands to whisper into the High Celebrant's ear. Hulneb nodded, waved him away, then called him back to give more precise instructions, stabbing his finger at the dusty ground to enforce the seriousness of his commands. The guard nodded, bowed and hurried off.

"Hulneb?" croaked Rillian.

He turned. "An unscheduled visitor has just entered the encampment. Someone of importance, it seems."

Flanked by Kaltesh guards, ten Deacons entered the

circle of caravans surrounding Hulneb's. They took up positions around the perimeter, shuffling to keep the spaces between them as equal as possible. Hulneb watched with a frown as a priest entered the enclosure, pulling a rickety velocipede behind him. Setting the rests down into the dust he unbuckled his harness and ran to the vehicle's door. Once he was in position, a figure appeared from beneath the canopy, dressed in a pure white silk robe and hood. The visitor took the priest's offered hand, stepped down into the dust and pulled back his hood.

"Senior Grand Cardinal." Hulneb bowed, trying his best to sound welcoming and calm as Zoloth walked over to him. "This is an honour."

Zoloth's face was expressionless as Hulneb began securing the saddle's buckles.

"I feel I must apologise for the early measure of my surprise visit, High Celebrant, but there is a matter of the utmost urgency which requires your immediate attention." He looked over to Rillian, who regarded him from the shade of the caravan's rear deck canopy with her arms folded across her chest.

Hulneb quickly picked up a backsack from the dust beside him, the contents spilling out onto the ground. Before he could gather them up, Zoloth bent down to retrieve them, turning them over in his hands.

"Cyprian accoutrements and enticements, Hulneb?" said Zoloth, raising an eyebrow. His fingers slowly pushed up beneath the black lace, his other hand allowing the cheap jewellery to dangle between his fingers.

Hulneb took them back, stuffing them into the backsack. "They must be returned to their owner as soon as possible, I wouldn't want her to be unable to find work today, especially as I escorted her from the encampment, adorned in Kaltesh trader's clothes, late last night."

Zoloth nodded his agreement. "So, you enjoy the flavour of Abeonian women, as much as your sister enjoyed her Abeonian man. How charmingly consistent your family has become." He looked over to the caravan as Hulneb secured the backsack to his saddle.

"And Rillian," he said, raising his voice slightly, "how beautiful you are, as always."

The old woman slowly nodded once.

"If we could talk inside, High Celebrant?"

Hulneb patted his animal, "Follow me, Your Holiness."

"Allow me to offer my heartfelt condolences concerning your loss, Rillian." began Zoloth, as he reached the caravan. "Mirrimas was a worthy leader." Walking up onto the first step he nodded back to Hulneb as he took her hand. "As, I have discovered, is his successor." He bowed, then kissed the back of her hand, smiling up at her.

"Senior Grand Cardinal," said the old woman quietly, "you risk a great deal coming here unannounced, following your treatment of my daughter."

"Shall we continue this conversation inside as you requested?" suggested Hulneb, stepping past them to pull aside the entrance drape. "You must find it a little hot being so exposed, Senior Grand Cardinal?"

"On the contrary," said Zoloth, keeping his eyes fixed on Rillian, "there is an unseasonable chill to the air I find somewhat refreshing. I will accept your hospitality, however."

Rillian led them into the circular reception area, where Zoloth made himself comfortable amid the cushions as Rillian ordered a handmaiden to fetch water.

"Your daughter is, in fact, the reason I am here," began Zoloth, looking at Rillian. "I fear many of your tribe may consider my treatment of her unlawful," he turned to Hulneb, "despite your agreement in writing and your announcement during Archbishop Arramosa's funeral, High Celebrant."

"You understand correctly," said Rillian, bluntly.

"Indeed. Then perhaps it would be beneficial if you were to publicly announce to your tribe that you have absolutely no objection to my decision?"

"Beneficial?" asked Rillian, "And exactly who would benefit if my son were to announce this?"

Zoloth sighed. "Why, everyone. Neither of us can allow an outbreak of misinformed violence before the festivities officially commence – or after, for that matter."

Hulneb thought for a moment, thankful the handmaiden had returned with water to interrupt the uneasy silence. He took the jug and sipped slowly to prolong the quiet as his mind raced, then passed it to Rillian. His eyes levelled upon Zoloth as he spoke quietly. "So, you're here to ask me to call the tribe together and explain my reasoning?"

"I would respectfully request you summon your tribe to explain in detail the events leading up to your sister's imprisonment upon the pinnacle. I'm sure we wouldn't want words from gossiping tongues reaching your remaining tribe members' encampment deep in the desert. Would you not agree it would be best for them to hear the details of this sad, unfortunate occurrence from you, first hand?"

"Are you afraid for yourself, Zoloth, is that what you're saying?" asked Rillian with a half-smile, hiding her amusement by sipping the water.

Zoloth looked surprised. "Hardly. I'm too well protected, by my Deacons and Tal Salandor, high above, to worry about personal harm, Rillian. No, it is the repercussions against your people from *Abeonians*, following any attempted violent act upon myself, my Church, or my people – or an effort by your tribe to rescue your daughter, to which I refer." He sat back against the cushions, relaxing. "*My* people are loyal." He looked hard at the old woman, and Hulneb watched uneasily as they held each other's unblinking stares.

Zoloth continued. "These fanciful future possibilities – and let us all hope they are just that – are exactly what I am here to present to you, and hopefully, prevent," he lowered his voice and adjusted the cushion behind his back. "I'm hesitant to suggest this, but equally unsure if you would have considered all the ramifications of every possible reaction over this matter."

"Are you threatening us, Senior Grand Cardinal?" enquired Rillian, sharply.

He looked surprised and sat forward. "Threatening? No, Rillian, I do not threaten. I merely offer my unique view into a possible future and, as I just said, present you with preventative choices."

"So, simply put – you want me to recall the tribe and explain what happened?" said Hulneb, impatiently.

"If you are confident no action will be taken by misinformed individuals, then there is no need. On the other hand – and allow an old man to be so bold when I say, and I'm sure you'll both forgive me when I do – Kaltesh behaviour is at best governed by passion and not by clear-minded deliberation, with the end results of such actions the last aspect to be considered."

Rillian passed the jug back to Hulneb, returning Zoloth's insult in silence. Hulneb took a sip out of turn to seal the insult, and said nothing.

Zoloth looked between them, shaking his head slightly, aware of the offence. "I am willing to come to an arrangement for this small act of transparency on your part, and peace of mind for my city, and its people."

"And that arrangement is?" asked Hulneb, biting his bottom lip.

"I'm prepared to remove your sister from the pinnacle. Her disappearance will be explained easily: that she jumped to her death, embracing Kaltesh beliefs, rather than starve to death next to the man who led her there."

Rillian leant forward, her eyes narrowing on his. "You are sure you can do this? The other Grand Cardinals, what do they say of this proposal?"

Zoloth pulled up his sleeves and placed his fingertips together, forming a cage with his hands. "Rillian, I take the responsibility of my position *very* seriously. I will do, can do, anything to ensure this city and its inhabitants function the way I see fit. The other eleven know nothing of this meeting," he grinned. "But I digress. Sol Timmerman has been punished for his crimes. Your daughter's treatment, however, I now offer back to you, her family." He looked quickly back and forth between them. "I will officially present you with a body you can burn, and thereafter arrange for your daughter's safe delivery to you. I am willing to do this under two conditions."

"Which are?" asked Hulneb.

"Firstly, that you instruct your entire tribe to hear my closing speech on the last day of the festival. Hulneb, you will take the stage with me, and together we will inform the populace that my treatment of Roanne is lawful, and that you exonerate myself and all Abeonians of any culpability over her death. Secondly, that Roanne will never, under any circumstances, return to this city, or make her well-being or true identity publicly known. I will complete my obligations under this arrangement after the upcoming festival, upon the morning you depart Abeona. I will guarantee she is kept alive and well until returned to you."

"No," said Hulneb, flatly.

"No?" blurted Rillian, her heart racing.

Hulneb closed his eyes and shook his head, "No."

"We must discuss this," said Rillian, without looking at him. She lifted her head defiantly. "You will leave us, Oen Zoloth. Wait outside until we have spoken."

The Senior Grand Cardinal paused for a few moments, then shrugged and stood. "I will await your decision in my velocipede." He bowed to them both sharply, and was gone.

Rillian sighed, placing her hands in her lap. "Hulneb, what *are* you thinking? I believe his desire for peace is sincere. Why can't–"

"We *have* peace! He simply craves control over us all. Remember what I told you – his ramblings in the Citadel. He's addicted to the prospect of absolute power. He talks a lot but says very little."

"But if there's a chance he can return Roanne to us, why not agree?"

"I'll not have the minds of the tribe poisoned by his madness. It's an attempt to convert them, as he tried to convert me in the Citadel, citing benefits for us in a society he controls. No, mother, I'll not agree to this, never. You told me yourself, he cannot be trusted," he took a step forward. "What justification do you have for saying this – is it from personal experience?"

She glared at him and he saw her anger. "He's Abeonian, our sworn enemy. They are the thieves of *Agasanduku*," she said, holding her arms wide. "This entire city, the walls, nothing more than a thief's bloated purse!"

"Your hatred is clouding your reasoning, mother. I'll not sit in my caravan, brooding over the ancient past as you do. Long have you taught me to do so, but recently I have seen with my own eyes the reality of this city. They open their gates to welcome us, sharing equally, respecting our different beliefs. They do not ridicule or condemn us; the people simply want to live in peace. You must cease this obsession over right and wrong, over ownership of *Agasanduku*, over passed-down, unsubstantiated stories! Is clinging to hatred all you have left in your heart, now Mirrimas is dead?"

The old woman stood, pointing at her son. "My great, great, great-grandmother was murdered by them, Hulneb! And that murderer's kindred line live comfortably here. Can't you *see*? Roanne can–"

He held up his arms in disbelief, letting them fall to slap against his sides, turning away from her for a moment. "I know, you've told me *so* many times. But that was *her* war, not ours, and not yours. Can't *you* see the utter idiocy of punishing the innocent descendants of a murderer, a murder committed *during a war?* How far are you prepared to go back with your punishments? Hundreds, thousands of cycles?" He laughed. "And at which point do you stop dealing out your retribution, and who do you select in this kindred line to receive it – a child? Do you stop at the beginning of time itself, with the very first coupling that gave rise to us all? How do you choose what to believe to bolster your viewpoint, to justify your revenge? An angry ancient scroll, a hate-fuelled, biased campfire story – where's your compassion, your impartiality? Only an utter fool would act so violently being so ill-informed! No, mother. I will *not* allow my sister to be used to further Zoloth's agenda. Even if that would mean her life is saved! I will maintain the peace as long as I am the decision-maker for the Kaltesh, respecting the wishes of my father, his tireless work to achieve this goal, and respecting his memory."

She smirked at her son, surprised by his speech, unable to feel proud, blind to his integrity. "Do you believe the tribe would be so easily convinced by Zoloth's speech, is that what you're afraid of, Hulneb? Losing control over our people?"

He leant forward. "I'm afraid of hatred and revenge, of mindless stupidity disguised as righteous retribution against an imagined injustice or oppression. And what comes from victims of revenge? What would you expect or how would you react? I'll tell you – more of the same. You cannot take up arms against the past, but you can lay them down for the future."

The old woman took a long, deep breath. "These recent events have kept me awake. You cannot trust them, any of them! Think for once, Hulneb, and please, *please* listen to me." She held up her clenched fists to him, raising her voice, speaking slowly. "We only have Sol Timmerman's word Opi is trapped inside *Agasanduku* – his telling of events *cannot* be confirmed, as his is the only voice. Who was the last person to see Opi? Yan Arramosa, we were told! And what happened to him? What did he see, or hear? Who *really* killed him, Hulneb. And why?"

He stroked his beard then placed his hands on his hips.

"What are you suggesting?"

"In a moment. We have to ask ourselves, where is Opi? He's been missing for three days now without food or water. If he's trapped inside, he's dead. If not inside, then where is he? And why has he been hidden from us?"

"Are you suggesting Sol is responsible, and has done something to Opi, mother? That he would harm his own son? That is one of the worst crimes known to both our peoples – as heinous as a child murdering their own parent. Surely you don't suspect Sol of such treachery?"

She met his disbelieving stare, her hands now relaxed into a pleading gesture. "He is the only consistent factor in all this. Obsession will drive a man beyond rationality – look what happened to his father. Who really knows what Sol would contrive? I'll answer my own question and tell you – Sol."

He pulled out his pipe and began to fill it from a pouch on his belt. "But, to what end?"

"To allow him more time inside their 'Trophy', to finally seize the fame and glory his father sought, but primarily to act on behalf of *their* truths. Can't you see? He's working against us, *with* Zoloth. I believe these circumstances we find ourselves in are nothing more than an elaborate ruse. They want the tribe here to witness their triumph. Imagine, *Agasanduku* rising above the Square, not walking, as we believe, its legs tucked away like a sleeping ganapti's. Such a grand event would destroy our beliefs, and they know once belief is crushed the Kaltesh will be lost, purposeless. It will be our ultimate defeat, Hulneb, worse than our extinction, having to live with the heaviest of burdens in our hearts, the knowledge that *we were wrong all along*, and that thousands had died fighting for a lie disguised as a truth." Her voice trailed off as she lowered her head. "Subjugated, ridiculed, beaten."

Hulneb lit his pipe. "I cannot, will not, believe that of Sol." He exhaled a plume of smoke. "No, mother, we will only find the truth with both Sol and Roanne alive.

Besides, the entrance gantry into *Agasanduku* has been demolished – there's no way into it."

"*So you've been told*, by Timmerman! What is his plan to find a way in?"

He lowered his head, feeling ashamed. "He didn't tell me."

"Because there isn't one he's willing to share! Hulneb, these circumstances do not need your belief, it's what's more probable you need to concern yourself with. We, or rather *you,* are not in a position to demand *both* of them are returned safely." She held him by the wrists, shaking. "Look carefully at the actual position you find yourself in, son. Of your own doing? No. You've been swept along with all of this, tricked, along with Roanne. Manoeuvred into a position you cannot possibly escape." His eyes couldn't meet hers and he began to think, *'Could all this be true, have I been just a puppet since I arrived here? Has my brother-by-union used me for his own ends?'* Her voice snapped him back to the moment. "Ask yourself Hulneb, what is the actual cost of Roanne's life returned? The answer, possibly the death of all we believe. Plead with Zoloth and agree to his terms, but have Roanne returned to us now, insist on this! If we are to maintain our cultural identity, we must flee this festival before it begins, all of us, before our entire race is poisoned by the Abeonians. It's all so clear to me now, they only seek to welcome us to convert us, as we, thousands of cycles ago sought only to invade Abeona to kill them all. We cannot live together."

Hulneb puffed a cloud of smoke then removed the pipe from his mouth. "I cannot believe this. We've moved forward, evolved beyond such childish behaviour to respect each other. However, I'll assemble the elders and you can voice your insane conspiracies to them. If they agree with you, every member of the tribe will be informed, to decide if they stay for this festival, or leave. After all, it's far easier to escape from the city than invade it. That's my final say. It is done."

Before she had time to reply he was pulling the drape aside and hurrying outside.

There Zoloth, from the shade of his velocipede, was speaking with a Deacon. The Senior Grand Cardinal glanced up, speaking urgently as the Deacon turned to glare at Hulneb before rejoining his comrades. He watched him walk away as he strode up to Zoloth.

"High Celebrant. I trust the discussions with your mother were thorough?"

"Of course."

"And?"

Hulneb paused, relishing Zoloth's anticipation, rehearsing his speech in his head. "I'm afraid it is you who have failed to consider all the ramifications of every possible reaction over this matter. You're lacking clear-minded deliberation, with the end results of such actions the last aspect to be considered."

The Senior Grand Cardinal was left speechless as Hulneb continued.

"If Roanne is returned to us, we will never be forgiven for agreeing to this *beneficial arrangement,* as you put it. An arrangement leaving her husband to die alone? He is her only hope of finding Opi – as it's clear neither you, nor any of the other *Grand* Cardinals have the ability to open seals inside *Agasanduku,* or assist him in any way. As you are solely responsible for the death of her son and husband, she would not rest until she had murdered you – following your abduction and a lengthy Kaltesh ritual of abuse and torture, fitting for such a crime." He leant into the velocipede, his forearms resting on the carriage door, lowering his voice. "Make no mistake, Zoloth, she would find a way here, plan every detail carefully, ensuring her objective is completed, no matter how long it took her, no matter what the cost." He straightened. "So, again, the answer is *no*. I'll not have Roanne responsible for murdering you, leading us into a war. " He smiled and brushed down his beard. "Look at it this way, I'm saving your life. Now, if you'll excuse me," he gave a respectful nod, "I have an appointment of my own to keep. Good day, Senior Grand Cardinal."

Zoloth opened the door of his velocipede to reply, but Hulneb was already in his saddle, digging his heels into the animal's ribs. Shielding his eyes from the early morning sun he watched Hulneb gallop away. He cursed Irrianna under his breath for befriending Tulteth. If the young lad had seen the entrance to the Citadel in the Goraknath foothills, and informed Roanne... He knew he couldn't defend a Kaltesh assault on all fronts. His Deacons would be spread thinly, allowing her to pick her point and moment of entry. Remembering the determination in her eyes at the funeral he realised Hulneb was correct – she would find a way to confront him. He looked down into the dust and shook his head. Irrianna was right; there were unforeseen circumstances.

"Zoloth, are you certain she's still alive?...Zoloth!"

He stepped out of the velocipede, distracted from his concerns. "Rillian, I don't have time for–"

"There never will be a better time. Answer me. Is she?"

"You of all people must know, surely? I'm here, am I not? She is fine."

"Answer me! Are you certain?"

Zoloth hesitated, looking back in the direction of Hulneb's departure. "I must leave, Rillian."

"You're doing this for me, aren't you? Can I see her?"

He smiled and shook his head. "For you? Yes." He faced her, "And, as I said, my people. But I am truly sorry. It is impossible for you to see her now."

She held onto his arm with both hands as he turned to leave.

"I worry constantly, Oen. Is that not what a mother should do?"

He glanced down at her hands. "Yes, that is what a mother should do. That's why I came here today – I could not allow you to lose another member of your family,

Rillian." Reaching down, he took her hand and kissed it again.

She turned slowly and walked back to her caravan, watching from the steps as Zoloth and his Deacons filed out of the caravanserai, too caught up in her thoughts to notice Zoloth's entourage now consisted of only nine Deacons.

Two figures sat opposite the alehouse, enjoying the morning twilight, the older of the two scanning the torch-lit streets, searching for any uncharacteristic movement that might signal their exposure. The second, considerably younger and larger than his companion, sniffed at the air, picking at food stuck between his teeth with the tip of a small dagger.

Across the street, a woman draped in rags picked up a few vegetables that had fallen from a passing cart. She hurried on her way, cradling her bounty in her arms, followed closely by her three young, rasorial children, clawing and shouting at her with their small, hungry voices.

Slowly the street awoke. Beggars followed merchants on their way to market. Window shutters opened to allow the dusty stench inside, figures sifted through the streets like rats following the reek of decay.

"He's definitely not coming," said the younger man, stretching and replacing the dagger into his sleeve. He licked his lips and spat into the dust beside him.

The first said nothing, maintaining his vigil as the dawn sunlight brought everything before them into focus. The second stood and helped the first to his feet, placing the sack he had used as a pillow upon his right shoulder.

A handful of workers had gathered at the alehouse door, waiting for entry so they could eat before the day's work. They chatted idly, filling their time with lies, complaints and anecdotes.

The doors to the alehouse opened and the two figures hurried in behind the workers, the larger of the two heading straight to a woman who stood carving a freshly roasted joint of meat upon the bar.

"Supply delivery," barked the larger man, winking at the startled cook. The second man said nothing, tossing a coin onto the bar which she quickly picked up.

"Wait. What do you have there?"

"Just the usual. We're here to deliver fresh meat and escort the other night's entertainment

home." Nodding toward his companion, he smiled. "The entertainment's his sister, and he's waiting for his share of the profit." He heaved the sack onto the bar top and opened the neck, revealing cuts of meat on the bone. He took out one and handed it to the cook. "Here, for you."

She reached inside and pulled out another cut. "These will do. Be quick and quiet."

"We know the way," he said tying the neck closed before hoisting the sack back onto his shoulder.

They hurried through the maze of pipes, up into the barrel and along the dark, low corridor that opened out into a narrow well. An iron ladder vanished into the darkness above them.

The larger man climbed, while the other drew a sword and followed.

A flagstone split open along a crack across its centre, its two halves separating on hinges to reveal a wide opening into the dusty sunlight. A sack came through the opening and landed to the left, then another, empty, to the right, closely followed by Hulneb's dirty face.

Sol and Roanne lay motionless.

Hulneb jumped onto the pinnacle, hiding beneath a Kaltesh hunting sandcloak. The heavy fabric, sealed with sand took on the appearance of the surroundings. Peering beneath it he looked around, then ran over to Roanne and checked her breathing. It was shallow, and she moaned as he picked her up, hurrying back to the opening, picking his route to hide behind the low remains of the pavillion. He passed her to Tyn who climbed back down with her over his shoulder as Hulneb closed the flagstone hatch and followed.

They reached the empty barrel. "Give her a few sips of water then clean her up as best you can, Tyn." He handed Tyn the backsack containing the whore's clothes that Roanne had worn on their previous visit to the hostelry. "And dress her in these. I'll be back as quick as I can."

The Hathranelzra gently laid her down then signed to Hulneb.

"I don't know – use ale and a rag to clean her face, there's plenty around here, but keep her quiet!"

He returned to the pinnacle and removed Sol's clothes, stuffing the cloak with the meat from the sack, roughly arranging it in the shape of a body. Then, with some difficulty, he carried the Cardinal back down to Tyn. Once again he climbed to the pinnacle, this time burdened with the meat they had previously left in the tunnel, collected Sol's robes and repeated the process with the now ripe-smelling meat.

When he returned, Sol had regained consciousness. His sunken, vacant eyes circled with dark rings, his fingers caked in dust and dried blood, his hair matted with sweat and dirt. As he noticed Hulneb crouching next to him, he squinted, trying to focus.

"Ommus?"

"He didn't show up," said Hulneb, putting the spout of a waterskin to his lips. "Just a few sips, Sol. Slowly now."

"Roanne – is she okay?" he mumbled.

"She's alive. We need to get you both out of here, now. I'm going to put you into a sack and carry you out. Keep quiet and we'll soon be safe."

Sol nodded as he focused on Roanne, who began to stir.

Hulneb held her cheeks, gently lifting her head up to

his. "You'll need to walk, Roanne, it's the only way we can get you out of here." He gently slapped her cheeks. "Roanne! Can you make it?"

She nodded and he helped her to her feet.

Tyn reached into a pocket and passed Hulneb a handful of jewellery.

"Worthless trinkets from one of this city's traders. You'll need to wear these if the barman and regulars are to recognise you as the whore that visited the Citadel," said Hulneb, fitting the earrings.

Tyn pulled the sack over Sol's head, tying the neck over his feet. They made their way back into the bar.

"Where did you come from?" barked the barman, having just started serving, surprised to see strangers appearing from behind the bar.

Hulneb turned with faked surprise. "We were here the other day, if you remember? We came to collect the Citadel's guest." He nodded to Roanne, who did her best to smile.

The barman walked over to her. "You look a little worse for wear."

She leant over to whisper in his ear. "For old men they have a lot of stamina. I'll think carefully before taking this job again."

He bellowed with laughter. "I've heard that before." He patted Hulneb on the shoulder. "And what do you have there?" he asked, placing his hands on his hips, nodding toward the sack.

"Stale meat," said Hulneb, turning to face the door. "We'll return later with fresh."

The barman held his arms. "No, wait. Has it been paid for by the Citadel?"

"Of course," answered Hulneb, without thinking.

"Then I'll take if off your hands."

Hulneb hesitated. "I really don't think you'd be wise–"

"Nonsense. I insist." said the barman, grabbing the sack and turning Hulneb around.

"Well, in that case..." Hulneb placed the sack onto the floor and opened a small hole at the neck.

"Go on, smell it," he offered.

The publican placed his nose over the small opening and breathing deeply, coughed, waving a hand in front of his face as Hulneb tied the neck closed. "I did warn you," he said, winking. "I'll find you something special next time."

The barman returned to his place behind the bar as Hulneb hurried for the door, dragging the sack behind him. As they walked out into the sunlight, two figures stood up from a table and followed.

"'Ello again."

Hulneb wheeled around, vaguely recognising the voice.

"I can't earn cos o' you," said the worker, holding up his damaged hand, which had now been splinted and bandaged. "Can't feed me kids," he pointed at Hulneb with a dagger held in his good hand, "so I'll take that sack, and whatever other valuables you three 'ave."

As Tyn turned to see why Hulneb had stopped, the other worker joined the first, and Hulneb felt Sol shift slightly in the sack.

Tyn reached for his falchion, but Hulneb held his arm and shook his head. "Gentlemen, I can assure you the contents of this sack will leave a bad taste in both your mouths. Best let us be on our way."

The second worker seized Roanne by the wrist, pulling her over to him, holding a dagger to her throat. She struggled until she felt the blade on her neck.

Hulneb's anger rose as he looked at his sister, his free hand instinctively reaching for a short-sword, but he checked himself, placing the sack upright onto the ground between them.

The worker snatched Roanne's cheap earrings and necklace. "These will help," he said to his friend, "see what food they 'ave in that sack, they won't move while I've got 'er."

Broken Fingers struggled to untie the cord and swore, then pushed his blade under the cord to sever it with a single upward movement. The neck of the sack sagged and he replaced his dagger into his belt. As he opened the neck wide and bent down to peer inside, a whisper found its way up to him.

"It's *hello* again," said Sol from the bottom of the sack, bringing his right foot up hard to catch the worker full in the face with his heel. The impact broke the worker's nose, sending him backward into the dust.

Tyn saw his chance as the second worker froze in surprise, dropping his blade as Roanne elbowed him in the stomach. The falchion shone in the sunlight as Roanne struggled free, stumbling towards Hulneb who, stepping in front of her, advanced on the sprawled worker who clutched his bloody nose with his good hand, his other elbow resting on the ground. Hulneb kicked the elbow away and drew a sword as the worker's back hit the dust.

The falchion was on its way back to its scabbard before the worker knew what had happened. He looked down to his dagger and screamed as he realised his severed fingers lay on the ground beside it, his arm terminating in nothing more now than a bloodied palm with a thumb. In shock, he turned and ran down the street.

Hulneb's boot came down on the strapped hand, and the worker's face contorted in agony, unable to utter a sound as the High Celebrant stood over him. "Your actions alone have brought about your family's empty table." He placed the tip of his sword at the worker's throat. "You're confused as to who is the guilty party here – for you and your comrade are responsible for your inability to provide."

The worker nodded, and as Hulneb took a step back he scrambled to his feet.

"If by chance we happen upon each other a third time," said Hulneb, "I will end your grievance with us once and for all." The worker ran after his friend as Hulneb sheathed his sword and turned to Tyn. "You were lenient,

Hathranelzra." He looked at his sister. "Roanne?"

"I'm fine – just need water," she said shakily.

Tyn signed and Hulneb laughed, then peered into the sack where Sol lay unconscious, exhausted by the exertion in his weakened state.

"We must move quickly," said Hulneb, hoisting the sack back onto his shoulder.

"What did he say?" asked Roanne, nodding toward Tyn.

Hulneb glanced her way as he led her across the street toward a waiting cart where one of his personal guards posed as a merchant. "He says he's getting too old for combat. He meant to sever his hand, not just the fingers."

Following breakfast, Irrianna sat beneath the fruit tree in the garden. Zoloth had spent the first meal of the day brooding, his conversations with the other Grand Cardinals uncharacteristically short, his thoughts obviously elsewhere.

Irrianna yawned and rubbed his eyes as Zoloth strode up the hill and sat beside him. "Oen, are you sure you want me to do this?" he asked.

Zoloth nodded as he dried between his toes with a white cloth. "You are the only person I can rely on in this matter. Deacons brag to each other in their barracks and bars, and whisper secrets to whores in their beds. *You* can be trusted." He held Irrianna's disbelieving stare. "I cannot stress enough the importance of this task. Release her, allow her the freedom she deserves."

Irrianna ran his fingers through his damp curls. *'No,'* he thought. *'If she survives, I'll not have the possibility of her eventually taking my place at your side. A poison will be used, the same that was administered to Arramosa's killer. She will simply sleep and not wake.'* "Of course," he answered, "She deserves freedom, as she has served you well." *'No. There must be no trace of her body. I've learnt one useful lesson from Yan Arramosa's death. Fire is the only way. I can poison her first, but to be sure, a fire must accidentally find its way into her cell. There must be nothing left of her. As for the staff, if the fire does not kill them also, then by the time they have finished arguing which of them should bring me the news, it will be too late.'*

Zoloth slowly put on his sandals, then stood. "Our festival procession will leave at first light and travel slowly to the Square, taking the longest route through the city, encouraging the people to pay their respects. We will stop in the Ravine District to hand out food to the indolent masses. You will have plenty of time to slip away during our display of charity, release her, and return before the procession continues."

Irrianna stood and ambled down the hill in silence.

Roanne fell asleep next to Sol on the way to the Kaltesh caravanserai, both hidden beneath cut flowers in the back of the cart.

Hulneb drew up outside his caravan and carried Sol inside, with Tyn carrying Roanne close behind.

"What in the name of the Holy Brothers are you doing?" asked Rillian, as Tyn lowered Roanne onto the old woman's bunk.

"They were close to death. I did what I had to," replied Hulneb, easing Sol onto Mirrimas' bunk.

"But you had an agreement with Zoloth!" she croaked, standing between the unconscious couple. "This will be the first place he'll look once he finds they're missing!"

Hulneb straightened and rubbed his right shoulder. "We have nothing with Zoloth apart from exchanging a few idle words. You told me yourself, he wasn't to be trusted, so, I haven't. The agreement he proposed breaks his own laws, so I refused it." He grinned to his mother. "We'll simply hide them and claim innocence if they come marching in here. The twelve wouldn't start a war over just one man."

"You're a fool, Hulneb!" shouted the old woman, stepping forward. "You've lied to me and learnt absolutely *nothing* from your father! Wars always start with just *one* man."

"I didn't lie to you, I said, 'It is done.'"

Sol had regained consciousness and turned his head toward her, "Hulneb's not to blame – most of this was planned. I'll be gone by morning."

"Go attend to your duties, Hulneb," said Rillian, kneeling over her daughter. "Tyn and I will care for them."

As he turned to leave, Sol spoke. "Thank you, Hulneb."

He paused at the drape, giving Sol a sideways glance, nodding once before thrusting the drape aside to leave.

The old woman looked at Tyn. "Fetch boiled water, towels and food." The Hathranelzra bowed and left them alone.

"Sol, I told you to do the right thing."

"I have," he said slowly, staring wearily at the canopied ceiling.

"Have you? You'll bring death to the Kaltesh with your disregard for authority. Your union with Roanne was a mistake and I was wrong to give you my blessing. I realise that now."

"Mirrimas gave his blessing, that was enough for us," said Sol. "It should still be enough for you. Hulneb's motivations are honourable. Mirrimas would have done the same."

She turned from bathing Roanne's face. "You know nothing of the real Mirrimas. He wouldn't have condoned Hulneb's actions. I've a good mind to summon Zoloth right now and end this before–" she felt a hand on her arm and turned to see Roanne staring up at her.

"Before what?" asked Sol. "What would you have done if it were one of your children lost inside *Oosah*, and you were denied the right to search for them?"

The old woman stroked her daughter's hair as tears welled up in her eyes. "Everything," whispered Rillian.

"War will always start with just one."

That evening Rillian summoned Hulneb.

He hurried into the compartment to find Sol and Roanne sitting up in their bunks, enjoying a light meal of fruit and bread.

Sol placed a hand on the back of his head and looked up, wincing. "You were *too* convincing at the Necropolis, Hulneb."

"There's no need for further thanks." He turned his attention to his sister. "I'm sorry we didn't tell you about our arrangement, Ro. It was my idea. Sol wanted to tell you, but I thought you would be more convincing if–"

"I've been told," said Roanne, sharply, finding it impossible to look her brother in the eye.

"Are you feeling better now, sister?" asked Hulneb, almost tenderly.

"Apart from a recurring dream – and being kept in the dark over all this – fine," she said bluntly. "Is there anything else you haven't told me?" she asked, finally finding the strength to face him.

He shook his head as Sol looked between the four of them. "From now on, we'll have to move fast. Hulneb, did you learn anything during your meeting with Zoloth?"

Roanne watched him carefully as he replied, waiting for a telltale sign, a twitch of a nerve to reveal a lie, a change of timbre to his voice to conceal a truth.

"Nothing that I didn't already know or suspect. He's insane and holds too much power for his own good, and your food is bland and your wine's kept cold to mask its flavour. But that's not all of it." He recounted their recent meeting in detail.

"So what did you say?" asked Sol, finally.

"I agreed. The remaining tribe members will arrive by the end of the festival." He took a step forward and jabbed a finger at Sol. "You should have allowed me to have him killed on his way back from the funeral, as I suggested."

"I must enter *Oosah* tonight. Prepare your warriors; they may be needed. If Zoloth wants to conduct a search for us, then welcome him, I'll be inside before daybreak." He tried to stand but became dizzy, held his head and sat down again.

"You're in no condition to move," said Rillian. "You must rest if you are to have enough energy to rescue your son."

Sol stood again, slowly and shakily. "There's not enough time. The festival begins the day after tomorrow."

"We wait one more day," said Hulneb. "Look at yourself, you're a mess. You couldn't defend yourself against Tulteth, let alone anyone else. I'm not carrying you to *Agasanduku*."

Sol looked over to Roanne, who nodded reluctantly. "Hulneb's right, you'll need all your strength."

He took a deep breath before sitting back down. "Tomorrow's festival eve. We'll make our move then, during the evening curfew."

SEVENTEEN

PARENTAGE

Much later, when Sol had fallen asleep, Rillian summoned a handmaiden. Together they helped Roanne into Rillian's private compartment. There she slept for a few measures, whilst the old woman watched over her.

When she awoke, Rillian gave her a bowl of medicinal broth.

"Your brother has much of his father in his ways. He continues to surprise me in his choice of action, in spite of his boasts."

"That's something I need to talk to you about," said Roanne, sipping the thick liquid. "Since you arrived, I've been having terrible dreams of father's death."

The old woman looked uneasy. "You have suffered the dreaming memory, that's what you're saying, isn't it?"

Roanne nodded. "The dreams are horrible, so vivid – but I must tell you."

After Roanne's description, Rillian struggled to her feet, then walked into one of the adjoining compartments. She returned with a handmaiden carrying two large jugs of scented water. She handed her daughter a cloth and a large, soft towel.

"You can wash behind the screen," she said, waving her hand. Roanne pulled a drape to one side and took the jugs and cloth in with her. Set into the floor of the caravan was a wide, circular, wooden mesh which she stood upon. She closed the drape, undressed and began to wash.

"This news saddens me, Roanne," began the old woman, "but it does not surprise me. I have had an almost identical dream since we arrived in this city."

"So who do you think is responsible?" She hesitated for a few moments, unsure if she should voice her accusation. "I'm certain it's Hulneb."

Rillian's answer came quickly. "Oh, I don't think so, Roanne. If you had seen his face when he returned from the delta that day. Your brother's not a murderer – he'd like everyone in the tribe to think of him as the hardened warrior, but the worst I have seen of Hulneb was when he was a child." She grinned as the memory became clear. "He discovered this city takes its water from the river, so he took half the youths away from the cavalcade one night as we camped in the Goraknath foothills. Mirrimas followed him and found them standing on the banks of the river, pissing into it." The old woman chuckled to herself. "Really, Roanne, deep down he's as gentle and inoffensive as a newborn, and that is his problem. It's mostly a front with Hulneb, and always has been. That comes from your father telling him stories as a child. Kaltesh this – Kaltesh that. Just stories, in the end. Your brother's quite the romantic – as was Mirrimas. They both lack the fight to reclaim what is ours."

Roanne shook her head. "Then how do you explain the dreams? The murderer stood a head shorter than Mirrimas in my dream, and Sol told me during their confrontation with the Hathranelzra, Hulneb tripped back over Mirrimas' cloak. It has to be Hulneb – he is the right height."

The old woman sighed. "Has to be? Or should be? No. Someone else is responsible for Mirrimas' death, and there's only one way to discover who that someone is."

Roanne's head appeared at the drape, her hair dripping with water. Rillian held out the towel for her and she hastily wrapped it around her damp body and sat down, pushing her hair back over her head.

"Tell me."

The old woman paused. "You'll have to fight against waking, Roanne – however upsetting the nightmare is. You said the water in the pool was beginning to calm where Mirrimas lay." She held her daughter's hands. "You must wait in that dream, hold onto it and don't let the horror force you to wake. When the water calms and is completely still, you'll see the murderer's face reflected back at you."

Roanne stared vacantly into her mother's pleading eyes.

"You *have* to do this Roanne – I must know the truth, but my mind is not strong enough any more. My dreams are mostly forgotten by morning, they're just fragments, like pieces of broken pottery discarded in the sand."

"Alright. I can do this," Roanne whispered. "If I had not chosen to stay in this city, then Mirrimas would still be alive today."

"You don't know that for certain," said the old woman sternly. "You can't carry that guilt around inside you, it's unhealthy. You stayed here because of your love for Sol, and to be true to yourself. I could say my love should have forced me down to the delta with Mirrimas, and now he'd still be alive – then I think what could have happened. Would we both be dead? I will not allow you to take the blame for this. In time, we'll know where the guilt lies, but I'm sure it's not with Hulneb."

Roanne exhaled quickly and bit her bottom lip, looking away. "I'm so unsure of him, I just don't know," she said quietly.

"He was a just a youth when we left you here with Sol, now he's a man. A man you hardly know."

After a few seconds of silence, Roanne managed a gentle smile. She held her mother's cheeks and kissed her. "You're right, as you always are in family matters." She shook off her uncertainty and her voice found its optimism. "Now mother, more favours to ask. I'll need new clothes – just normal daywear, nothing special. And could you help me cut my hair?"

Rillian took an ivory comb from a box by the side of her bed and sat behind her daughter.

"Are you certain your best choice is to be with Sol tomorrow night?"

"There's no other place for me. I must help him find Opi. I must be there."

"Why not wait here with me? Opi may not be lost

inside, as Sol believes. Would it not be best to remain in safety? If Opi were to return on his own and you were both killed whilst looking for him…"

"No, mother. I must go with Sol."

Sol had cleaned up and changed into Kaltesh trader's clothes, then spent the morning watching the city from the high observation deck of Hulneb's caravan. Ebe sat at his feet, having followed Tulteth to the caravanserai, the little creature sniffing the air and seemingly also enjoying the view.

Nothing had changed since his imprisonment. The people continued their day-to-day business, either oblivious or uncaring of the past day's episodes. Children ran and played on their way to school, happily aware it was the last day before the festival, merchants stopped to buy and sell with Kaltesh traders, women gathered to gossip, city workers dragged their feet.

He scanned the horizon, holding up a hand to shield his eyes. *Oosah*'s faint outline appeared like a ghost to him in the mid-morning heat, barely visible above the buildings, and he found himself thinking of it as a malevolent spirit, forged from the hundreds of thousands of souls lost over thousands of cycles for its sake. For the first time in his life it appeared unsightly against the city, and this sent a shiver through his body. This forever-silent entity, expressionless and emotionless, seemed to be gloating at the fools swarming beneath it, and he couldn't shake off the feeling that it waited for him, that their next encounter would ultimately destroy one, or perhaps both of them. He ignored his irrational fears and concentrated, running his ideas over and over in his head, planning his movements, working out exactly how he was going achieve his objective. Roanne walked up behind him in silence, to stand at his side.

She held up a hand to shield her eyes and spoke quietly.

"When are we going to make our move?" He turned and at once was surprised. Her hair had been cut and was now just below her ears, framing her face and accentuating her beauty with spiky cuts smoothed with scented balm. Her eyes seemed more penetrating than before, and he noticed the pencil-thin, black painted lines around them. He raised his eyebrows as her perfume found its way to his nostrils. She was dressed in a short purple skirt of silk, and a black tunic decorated with red Kaltesh symbols hung precariously from her upper arms.

"You look as you did when we first met, Roanne. You're absolutely beautiful," he said, touching her face gently with the back of his hand. She held it with hers, enjoying his tenderness.

She shook her head and her hair fell back into place. "I just hope Opi likes it," she said, running her fingers through it.

Sol smiled and turned back to the city. "I promise I won't tell him. I'll let him see for himself when we return."

"Sol, I'm coming with you!"

He shook his head. "You know that's impossible. I'm fully responsible for this situation, so it's up to me to make things right. It's going to be difficult and dangerous enough for me on my own, very tough physically if my idea works. You're far better off waiting in the safety of your mother's caravan."

She stood beside him and gripped the deck rail, leaning over to face him. "It's up to *me* to decide how I'd be better off, not you. I'm not going to sit here and wait when I *know* I can help."

"You must understand, you can't help. Wait with Hulneb and Rillian until I return."

"No. I don't feel comfor–"

"Hulneb's not waiting anywhere," said a voice from behind them. "Not when there's a chance of adventure ahead, and the prospect of proving an Abeonian truth is a lie."

They turned to see Hulneb, with Tyn by his side, holding a jug of water. The High Celebrant looked at Roanne with a faint smile, appearing to her like a chastised adolescent, and she was instantly reminded of their childhood together. He looked at his feet momentarily, clasping his hands behind his back. When their eyes met moments later, his smile had vanished and he cleared his throat. "Roanne, I've decided to start an investigation into our father's death," he said quietly, having removed the husky, authoritative tone he usually forced. He nodded to Tyn, who passed the jug to him. He took a step toward her and then drank deeply before holding the jug out for her. For a moment he stared, unsure of her reaction, but she stepped forward, took the jug from him and sipped.

"Thank you, Hulneb."

Tyn stepped forward and made several flamboyant signs to Hulneb, before taking the jug from Roanne.

"Good point, Tyn," said Hulneb, his voice regaining its commanding bass. "Sol. As High Celebrant of the Kaltesh, I am hereby officially requesting to be escorted into *Agasanduku*, as is my right by position and treaty."

Sol sighed. "You know my title has been stripped; I have no jurisdiction over treaties. Your request should be taken before an Archbishop, for due process."

"Then escort me to a Church representative who can deal with my request."

"You know I can't do that either. I am no longer a member of any church."

Hulneb folded his arms and looked to his sister.

"We thought you'd try this alone," said Roanne. "You won't get away with it – we all have to do this. We've come this far together."

Hulneb took a step forward before Sol could speak. "If she goes, then so must I, to ensure her safety. No arguments. Plus, I have a duty towards you. You've saved my life twice. I owe you a life-debt twice over."

"Ensure her safety! But she's as good a fighter as you or

I, perhaps both of us together!"

"Then a good enough reason for me to join you, ensuring both of you are safe."

Sol shook his head at the inevitability of the situation.

Tyn stood to one side and made a few quick gestures.

"He says he can't come with us – he has business elsewhere," translated Hulneb.

"And what business is that?" said Sol, looking at Tyn.

The Hathranelzra stared back at him. His expression was set and determined, defiant. He slowly bowed then gestured with his hands once more.

Hulneb nodded, and when he had finished, spoke.

"For now, my duties with you are at an end." As soon as Hulneb finished, Tyn bowed once more to all three of them in turn, then hurried away.

Sol closed his eyes slowly, in acceptance, "Let him go." He knew there was no use arguing with them. If he tried to slip away unnoticed during the night, he'd only be followed. He realised there would be no use in trying to coerce Rillian into supporting his cause, either. He shook his head and stared back at the siblings who now stood together, resolutely, side by side.

"We'll need the strongest knotted climbing ropes you have, Hulneb, knots at ten paces apart, Roanne, some Kaltesh pilgrim's clothes, a thick towel, short-swords and a belt for each of us. We leave on foot as soon as the first torch is lit. If you both insist on coming with me, then I insist you do everything I say."

Hulneb nodded. "I'll make preparations," he said, departing.

Sol looked back to the city once more and something inside told him he was making a mistake by allowing them to join him. He shook the absurd feeling aside, scanning the people below, his eyes falling upon a stationary figure staring up at him. The Hathranelzra made three signs, then quickly disappeared into the crowd.

"My mother's set aside a compartment for us both,

Sol," said Roanne, placing a hand on his shoulder. "We'll need to get as much rest as possible before tomorrow."

She took him by the hand and led him away, unaware he had not heard a single word she had said, as Ebe followed.

EIGHTEEN

THE DEAD

There was never enough time. During these past few cycles, it seemed this somewhat imaginary but nonetheless precious commodity had visited them in fleeting episodes. After a long while they had learnt to recognise these instances of privacy, and seized them to be alone together. Their love for each other was always present in their hearts, but their work took its toll, and for a time, it seemed they were two separate entities simply sharing the haven of a comfortable bed. Their love would surface in little gestures and actions they both recognised subconsciously throughout the day, while their communications dwindled into triviality. Gradually their lives took different paths...

Sol would arrive home late; Roanne's evening meal for him would be ruined. He'd eat and exchange superficial conversation, to return to his books and sit brooding over his lack of progress.

When Opi was born, time became all the more transitory. Sol's work began to suffer. The goals he set himself became impossible to reach within his allotted time frame, and he became solitary. A few of his colleagues spun malicious rumours that Roanne was part of a Kaltesh master plan, to distract the Theorist and prevent him from discovering the ultimate truth. The baby would wake them at night, disturbing the dreams that somehow seemed to fuel his progress with their strange voices.

Then Opi began to talk to his father, and Sol recognised the character rising to the surface in the little boy. It seemed as though Opi Timmerman had become an individual overnight, with a personality all his own.

Late one evening Sol sat at his desk, brooding over a string of problems that he couldn't connect. He fumbled through his notes and study books, cursing as the papers arced from his cluttered desk to the floor. As he bent down to snatch them up, he saw Opi, ready for bed. The little boy picked up the papers and handed them to his father.

"Don't worry daddy," he said. "It's okay." His expression was copied from his father, as were his words. Sol had told him this time and time again, when the child became impatient with his toys and puzzles. Looking at him then, with mock despair colouring his voice, Sol realised his mistake. He had brought his frustrations home with him and missed his son's development.

The boy held up his arms for a cuddle, and Sol picked him up to sit him on his lap. Opi smiled back and held his father tightly, then turned to the desk with all the big old dusty books, papers, quills and drawings, and began to play. At once Sol felt his cloud of depression lift. The little boy always managed to bring the happiness back into his life, and lift the dark clouds that hung heavy over his father's head. For this reason, Sol had a name for his son: my little Master of Clouds. It was a name he kept to himself, for himself, and never spoke aloud. A name to remind him of his mistakes and near-failure as a father.

After that evening his obsessions took a back seat, and for a while at least, Opi became the most important part of his life.

Roanne lay naked upon the handmaiden's bed, studying the pendant Rillian had given her, tracing her fingers around its multifaceted design, feeling the complexity of texture of its metal surface. She hoped closer examination would reveal a clue to its origin, but then realised Mirrimas had undoubtedly tried this countless times before. She wondered how he had felt upon first finding the object, if indeed it had found its way into his possession by chance. She closed her eyes, imagining the scene as he caught a glimpse of a shining *something* from atop his ganapti, an object glinting far off, as bright as the sun, peering out from the sand ahead. How he ordered his ride into a gallop with a single utterance, jumping down from his saddle and carefully removing the object from its tomb of sand. After returning to the caravans following his solo trek into the vast wilderness, he would have sat in front of a fire after a meal, producing the object as the epilogue to his tales, to elaborate how he had found it. Much later, he and the tribe would have ruminated as to its purpose until sunrise. She remembered those half-drunken nights filled with laughter, coloured by music, the smiling faces of her friends and their parents illuminated by the licking flames of the campfires. Their exaggerated reactions to the tales told on those nights were so clear in her memory. It was a comfort she realised she missed such a great deal now, and she pulled the gold chain taut between her fingers. Then another possibility was conjured up in her imagination: an ugly scene of Mirrimas stealing the pendant from a Kaltesh trader, perhaps murdering him and his family for the strangely intricate object, burying his body in the hot sand and setting fire to his caravan. Perhaps that was why Mirrimas was murdered – revenge for his stealing this trinket of beauty and unknown purpose, and she wondered if perhaps her dreams of his murder were nothing more than a misleading fantasy, fuelled by her worry over her son. She shuddered in the heat as her eyes fell upon the pendant again, feeling suddenly alone amid the sumptuous silk bedclothes of her youth, realising both her imagined circumstances surrounding the discovery of the pendant were equally possible. She shook the feeling away, turning onto her side, concentrating on the more urgent issues. Now it was just herself and Opi that mattered. He was the only person in her entire life she could trust to be honest with her and to communicate without having a personal agenda. Be it over the ownership of a trinket or the discovery of a truth, it appeared there was always a hidden schema, and the older the individual, the more convoluted and distorted were their truths pertaining to the perception of the past. Opi's innocence prohibited such deceptive machinations, and his expectation of honesty from the adults around him was reflected back to everyone he met. She felt a twinge of sadness touch her as she realised eventually these noble qualities would evaporate, infected by the lies of adults. *He will become one of them*, she thought. It was inevitable. His purity would eventually be diluted, like the colours of a banner bleached by constant exposure to the sun; his morals would be eaten away if he remained in this city of liars.

At once an idea came to her and her heart quickened. *I will take him away with me, away from the tribe, just us, together, alone. Yes. I can do it, we will manage. I know all there is to be known about the desert – how to survive – I will show him, teach him. I know where the Kaltesh water caches are, the timing of the harvest tides at the ocean. We will travel together and explore, free of infectious greed, of Abeona and the Trophy, of the Kaltesh, of the treachery that seems to run through everyone's adult heart.* She allowed herself a smile as she placed the pendant beside her bed, happier now to be free of its mystery, content now she had at last seen a new future for her and her son.

As Sol walked in, she rolled onto her stomach, surprising herself at her instinctive reluctance to be seen naked by her husband. Then she remembered him, as if his entrance had just been a sliver of memory of a long-dead friend, realising even now, after all that had occurred, deceit and lies were characteristics she had never experienced from Sol Timmerman. She remembered the conversation through the cell bars between him and Zoloth. Where was the truth? Had Sol hidden his son to further his career, as Zoloth had surmised? No. She knew that was a lie, as much as she knew then Zoloth was speaking the truth when he insisted he had nothing to do with Opi's disappearance. That left just one possibility. He was still alive, trapped behind a seal. One more question nagged at her. Did she still want her husband after Opi was found?

Even throughout his priesthood, Sol had remained true to himself and his family. *Foolish,* she thought. *You have delivered us into this predicament by your honesty and your naive trust of your associates. I should have realised sooner, our son is very much like you. You both share the same sincerity of innocence.*

Sol removed his Kaltesh attire, sitting on the bed for a moment before lying down next to her.

"I've spoken to Hulneb," he said, almost to himself. "Through him, Zoloth's managed to entice every Kaltesh into the city for the festival, to announce his new order on the final day."

"Perhaps he intends to slaughter us all?" she murmured, as if not at all concerned by the suggestion.

"Us? Don't you mean them?"

She remained silent.

"I've discussed this with Hulneb. There simply aren't enough Deacons. If any armed conflict were to ensue, the fatalities on each side would not be worth the battle. Both sides learnt that hundreds of cycles ago."

She frowned. "Shouldn't you be more concerned with rescuing Opi?"

"This is all related, Roanne. Hulneb has spoken to his personal guards. They will remain in the city after the festival, if need be, and supply us with food and water for as long as the search takes."

"I'll talk to Hulneb later," she said. "When we find Opi, these guards you speak of can escort me back to the tribe. You too should leave the city when this is over. There's only death waiting for you here, Sol."

He moved closer to her and placed a hand on the back of her head, slowly stroking her hair.

"Not necessarily. I can't stop you from taking Opi away. I could live here alone, in hiding. I've given it a great deal of thought. I know Abeona as well as anyone. I could spend the rest of my days here." He moved towards her, trying to gauge her reaction, wondering if she still held a place for him in her heart.

She avoided turning over to look into his eyes. Would his obsession with *Oosah* prevent him from leaving Abeona? Now she became aware there were two possible futures for her. Then, as she imagined those two futures, she saw them meld into one, saw him standing with Opi perched upon his shoulders.

"I'll come with you if you want me to, I promise," he whispered.

She turned over to lie on her back and his hand found her cheek. She reached up to embrace him and their tension of the past few days gradually transformed into passion.

After a while, their bodies perspired beneath the Kaltesh canopies and burning incense. Entwined as one, their love for each other returned with a renewed energy and sense of purpose.

After a measure they slept, and for once, Roanne was free of her nightmare.

NINETEEN

SHARING WINE

Feeling a weight upon his chest he rolled over, sending Ebe to the floor with a high-pitched shriek.

He stirred as the little creature climbed back onto the bed to wake him by sitting on his chest once more.

"Roanne! Get up, quickly! Now!" She slowly sat up, squinting at the dull glow of a lantern Sol held in front of her. "We have to get out of here now. Come on!"

She nodded and yawned, still half asleep, then slowly began to dress, coughing from the humidity. "What's going on?" she mumbled, then she noticed the smell.

He turned. "There's no time to get dressed." She snatched up the pendant as he grabbed her by the hand and pulled her across the bed, stumbling over the cushions littering the floor. Throwing aside the curtain into the living circle he picked up his pace, straight into Rillian's bedroom. It was empty.

Roanne could hear the shouting and screaming outside. "Sol, *what's* going on? Where's my mother?"

"Not here," he coughed, dragging her towards the rear of the vehicle.

Roanne shouted for Rillian at the top of her voice, but no answer came.

Sol pulled her out onto the rear deck where the heat slammed into them.

For as far as they could see, the caravans were blistering with fire. People were running blindly, shouting behind the tall flames, colliding as they searched for loved ones. Burning bodies, dead or dying, lay in the hot dust. Children's cries rose above their parents' voices and animals ran in panic, having broken free of their flimsy enclosures, bellowing and trampling individuals as they went. Embers spiralled into the air like swarms of fireflies, and on the fringes of the settlement the fire had caught several Jalinprabda banners that now waved the orange flames high into the night sky.

Their caravan was surrounded on all sides by burning vehicles, vehicles set there to protect it.

Sol turned towards the steps that led up to the centre deck and observation platform high above. The flames had already consumed the canopies, and now hungrily lapped around the poles supporting them.

Ebe appeared at his feet, shaking with fear, and he picked the animal up and held it in his arms.

"Is there any water on board?" shouted Sol to a bewildered Roanne.

But she simply stared.

"Roanne!"

"My mother! Where's my mother?"

"We need water!"

She looked around, suddenly aware of their situation. "Barrels are under the caravan in the shade. I–"

Thrusting Ebe into her arms he crouched to look under the vehicle. The flagstones were damp, and in the flickering firelight he could see the barrels had all been broken open. He hurried back to her.

"The barrels are smashed. Come on!"

To their right, the sound of splintering wood preceded a billowing cloud of smoke and sparks as two burning caravans were violently pushed aside to collapse into piles of burning planks. As the smoke cleared, Roanne pointed.

Forty warriors, creating a narrow channel between the blazing caravans, were pushing a low wagon through the flames. They were beaten back by the heat as the front axle of the wagon splintered in two from the impact, upending it. A figure scrambled from beneath the timbers and layers of steaming banners and blankets that were in the back of the wagon. He ran towards them, his head wrapped in soaked rags. He threw three bundles tied with string onto the deck and they landed with a wet thud.

"Quickly," said Sol, "untie these and wrap them around your head and shoulders."

They jumped and ran as the angry flames licked at their ankles, just as the observation deck splintered and fell, levelling the vehicle in a deafening crash of splintering wood.

The narrow valley of flames seemed endless, and the plaintive cries from the fires on both sides filled Roanne's ears. Her limbs ached and her chest heaved as her body struggled to take a breath. She fell to the ground and Sol and the figure seized her by the arms, dragging her to safety. They fell on all fours, coughing uncontrollably, Sol retching his last meal onto the flagstones, Ebe scampering clear of them both.

Hulneb removed the steaming blanket from his head as Tulteth joined them, picking up the small animal in his arms.

The High Celebrant spoke between sharp breaths, almost coughing the words out as his eyes streamed with tears. "Have you seen Rillian? We can't find her."

But Sol's eyes were now firmly fixed upon the pendant swinging from Roanne's neck.

The Hathranelzra moved across the rooftops unseen, hugging the shadows and choosing one of the many routes he had trodden a thousand times before. Passing beneath open windows where families sat at their dining tables, he was an inconsequential sound, ignored amid twilight's many, as the city's timbers creaked. Glimpsed from the corner of a single, sweat-soaked eye as couples entwined upon their beds, he was disregarded as twilight's shadow of a swaying branch as they rolled in their passion. He manifested himself as a single footstep from a wandering ghost, past children's cramped bedrooms, adding credence to a bedtime story, or the belief adults knew only a fragment of the nefarious misadventures conducted throughout the night. He knew the latter was true.

The courtyard was quiet as he jumped down from the red-tiled roof, remaining still for a few moments to catch his breath, watching for movement on the veranda. A ganapti stirred in the stable.

He hurried to the locked front gate.

Rillian stood in the shadows on the other side of the narrow street. On seeing him she took a step forward and made a sign. He nodded, took a handful of fat from a pouch beneath his cloak and smeared it over the gate hinges, silently unlocking the door to let her in. He took her by the hand, leading her along the veranda toward the front door.

Silence. He ran to the circular grating and lowered himself down. The fat he had smeared on the hinges three visits ago silenced the rusty inspection hatch as he pulled it open to climb down the chimney into the kitchen. A few moans filled the air as he pushed open the unlocked kitchen door, and within moments he was back upstairs, opening the veranda door for his charge.

They hurried down the winding staircase, the Hathranelzra leading the way with a long, black-bladed dagger held out in front of him, the other hand clasping Rillian's tightly.

Soon they were at her cell. Tyn pulled the inspection hatch aside to reveal Ana's face waiting there.

"They told me you would come," she whispered.

He took the key hanging on a hook beside the door, unlocked it, replaced the key and they hurried in, pulling the door closed.

It was Zoloth's favourite day. He had been washed and dried, his toe and fingernails had been cleaned and shaped, and now his attendants dressed him in the Senior Grand Cardinal's resplendent garment of office, a garment which legend told had once belonged to Tal Salandor. Minute strands of gold, silver and bronze had been woven into this white silk festival robe and precious stones of the highest quality and shards of alabaster and marble decorated the garment. The night before, three junior priests had polished every single facet of the garment until it reflected light. The design was indefinable, said to be an exact copy from the most ancient painted room from deep within the Citadel, the room that Holy Scripture told had once been Tal Salandor's private place of contemplation. It was said some saw malevolent evil hidden in the design, and if stared at too long it could awaken untold wickedness hidden within the depths of the soul, hence many bowed their heads at the sight of the garment. Others could not take their eyes from it, telling of feelings of divine enlightenment and the comfort it provided. In truth, the garment had tailored itself to fit each Senior Grand Cardinal perfectly, altering its cut and fit to complement anyone who wore it.

Zoloth lifted his leg so his foot could be guided into a white, fur-lined leather sandal. "This is an auspicious occasion, Irrianna," he said with a smile, as he admired the workmanship of his garments.

"Indeed."

"I trust everything is in place and prepared for today's itinerary?"

Irrianna nodded. "Passes have been issued to our personnel with the seal of Ommus, lest they are questioned or stopped whilst attending to their duties, as you requested, Your Holiness."

"Excellent." He made some final adjustments to his clothes and waved his priests away.

"Then let the day begin."

The cavalcade of the Twelve shone brightly and glittered myriad colours in the torchlight. Some said in daylight it was as if invisible torches illuminated it, others believed it was the divine light of Tal Salandor's love, watching from above, but to literalists it was simply the quality of the precious metals and stones decorating the twelve carriages that caused this effect. Some concluded the carriages were covered with metal found beneath the Trophy upon its discovery, and this metal had fallen from the object as a gift to the original Twelve Grand Cardinals, others believing the carriage's supple white leather seats were formed from the skin of heretics, sacrificed for their idiotic beliefs, and, if viewed from a certain angle, the horrific forms of male and female bodies could be seen, stretched and padded in an obscene, misshapen display. Few supposed the ganapti drawing the vehicles knew their way to the Trophy, as the carriages were without drivers, and the path had been inbred into the animals over hundreds of generations, while many simply pointed out that the lead carriage containing the Senior Grand Cardinal was indeed led by a single priest, and that the blinkered ganapti behind merely followed his lead. Stories were wild and numerous concerning the festival cavalcade, and with each passing celebration a new myth would surface in an alehouse or upon a street corner, to become a truth for those needing improbable legends to believe in.

This festival, it was the turn of the Senior Grand Cardinal to be the subject of idle storytelling from wagging tongues. *'Zoloth will lead us all to the ultimate truth,'* some claimed, clutching their chests. *'I was told Tal Salandor's garment fits him as if it were made for him,'* whispered others. *'He will change our lives forever,'* many boasted. *'He's harbouring the souls of all the dead cardinals in his head – he's mad,'* mumbled his few critics, whilst those critical of such comments recounted how Sol Timmerman had challenged Zoloth, and failed in shame.

For the man himself, these ideas simply amused. The attention offered him was welcome. But he knew one overheard opinion *was* a truth, and *would* become legend. Zoloth tried to recall when the idea had come to him, or in fact, if the speculation concerning him had given rise to the idea in the first instance. He couldn't remember, and honestly didn't care, for he knew no one in the city – not even Irrianna, his trusted confidant – knew everything he had planned.

It was straightforward for a man in his position. He looked upon his colleagues, subjects and servants as merely toys to be manipulated. Blindly they followed his instructions, like trained ganapti, unaware their reactions had been plotted and accounted for in his head. How he enjoyed watching the results unfold before him: a whispered comment in one ear, a forged letter left to be read, a conversation intentionally overheard, a piece of evidence found here, a damning meeting exposed there, a bribe, a warning, a promise, a murder. This manoeuvring had begun many cycles ago. As a child growing up near the Arovam Lake he had controlled his friends, forcing them, without their knowing, to carry out his wishes. As a priest, this choreography of personalities had continued, and now his manipulative skills were at their peak.

The cavalcade waited as the drawbridge lowered onto the pinnacle, and Zoloth and Irrianna stood by their carriages, discussing the day's schedule.

"Look!" exclaimed Irrianna, pointing.

A huge cloud of black smoke drifted over the city, the early morning breeze teasing its edges into wisps of grey against the blue.

"Ah, excellent," nodded Zoloth. "A guarantee the Kaltesh will send for their remaining tribe members."

"Guarantee?"

"They'll require new caravans – or individuals to help rebuild whatever remains of them. They'll call for materials, fresh animals to draw them for their departure. I have sent word I will supply a limited amount of resources – labour and animals to assist following this... *accident*, a small token of my goodwill, but sadly not enough to complete their task."

"You think of everything, Senior Grand Cardinal."

Zoloth smiled as his eyes fell on the pinnacle. "Indeed, Irrianna. But that is nothing," he said, allowing himself a smug grin as he gestured to the shapes huddled on the ground before them. There, black-feathered carrion birds had gathered, tearing at the crimson flesh beneath the rags with their yellow beaks.

"I had hoped Timmerman and his wife would have lasted a little longer." His voice was tainted by honest regret, "I had so dearly wanted to see them one final time, or rather, wanted them to see me." He looked down at the sleeves of his robe and sighed. "No matter. Everything has been considered and accounted for. It is time. You had best board your carriage, my friend."

Irrianna shuffled away as Zoloth climbed into his carriage, assisted by a Bishop, who then took the reins of the lead ganapti.

The cavalcade trundled onto the drawbridge, and as Zoloth's vehicle came to the centre of the pinnacle, he shouted. "Halt. Attend me."

The bishop reined his animal in and helped Zoloth down. The Senior Grand Cardinal adjusted his robes, striding over to the body lying near the edge. The birds were reluctant to withdraw, which pleased him, but the smell was not what he had expected. It was potent, but held a hint of something he had experienced before. The Cardinal's cloak was in tatters, stained with blood and urine, and Zoloth held a silk, hayberry-scented handkerchief to his nose, stopping a few paces short.

Then he looked more closely, and, with his staff, lifted the cloak to find the heaped ganapti cuts where the head of Sol Timmerman should have been. He turned, motioning Irrianna to attend him.

"Check the other body, Ugo, now!"

"What is–"

"Do it!" he spluttered, through the handkerchief.

He turned back to the birds' feast, covering it once more with the cloak, before waving a blessing into the air, carving lines with the tip of his staff and shouting his grief for the people to hear.

Irrianna stopped at his side and waited for him to finish.

"It's just rotting meat – she's gone."

Zoloth gritted his teeth, his eyes narrowing. "Then they're alive. Our arrangements must be brought forward; we cannot wait until the last day of the festival. The Grand Event will be introduced today. Inform the priestesses immediately."

Irrianna's jaw dropped. "But there's still confirmations needed. We have to–"

Zoloth glared at him. "We need *nothing* more; we have everything we need. We will head for your engagement first, Irrianna. Complete your task. The sooner we reach the Square, the better. The Preferred, are they safe?"

"The fifty Preferred are several leagues north of the city, protected by twenty Deacons."

Ana embraced Rillian tightly. "I can't believe you're really here," she whispered. "You've put yourself in great danger. It's almost daybreak; the staff will be awake soon."

The old woman shook her head slowly, ignoring her concerns. "I can see Tyn has cared for you as best he could, Analissa. Believe me when I say I'm so sorry. You have suffered a great deal. I had no idea you were being kept in such conditions."

The two women parted. "My father continues to administer his drugs in an attempt to take my sanity from me, claiming my ideas as his own, undoubtedly in exchange for my 'care'." She trembled and held her arms across her chest. "But I have only given him tiny fragments of my true knowledge – the remaining theories are all in my head. His drugs won't tear them from me fully."

"You must come with us now," said Rillian, trembling. "Zoloth has become unpredictable."

"I seem to remember Sol Timmerman hinted at that a few days ago."

Rillian looked to Tyn, then back to Ana. "Things have changed." Her voice wavered. "Mirrimas died seven seasons ago and Hulneb now holds the position of High Celebrant."

Ana nodded, "My father's work, I expect?"

But Rillian turned to the door as moans from the neighbouring cells filled the air.

Irrianna stepped down from the carriage, donning a festival mask but also keeping his head and face hidden by his long hood. He hurried down an alleyway as best he could until he came to the gates, fumbling in the flickering torchlight for his key. Unlocking them in haste he strode across the courtyard to pound upon the door.

"Alright, alright!" came an angry voice. The door swung open and Pol Zannus showed her face. "We're not open for visitors until the–"

Irrianna silently raised his mask for a moment and just as swiftly replaced it.

"Grand Cardinal! This is an unexpected visit!" she said, lowering her voice and bowing.

"Thank you, but I have little time. I apologize for the earliness of the measure, but must speak with Number Fifteen, in private."

She nodded. "I was readying myself for the festival, there's no need for apologies."

"I will let myself out. Return to whatever you were doing," he said.

'Release her?' he thought to himself. *'And provide her with freedom and the chance of replacing me at her father's side? Never!'*

Tyn clicked his fingers once and turned to them as Ana began to speak. He held a finger to his lips for silence, then signed quickly to Rillian.

"Someone's coming," she whispered.

Ana huddled back into the shadows, as Rillian lay on the bed beneath the covers. Tyn stood in the narrow gap between the wall and door frame.

The door opened slowly, and Irrianna came in, locking it behind him.

"Ana? Ana, are you awake? I have a gift for you from your father. Ana?"

She leant forward into the dim candlelight.

Taking a step forward, Tyn moved silently behind Irrianna as the old man removed his festival mask. "Your father feels you should celebrate the festival as best you can," he said, forcing a smile and producing a small bottle of wine from a pocket in his robes. He placed his mask at the bottom of the bed. "It is your favourite grape, I understand," he said, running a finger across the hand-painted label. "But first, I have something else for you to enjoy," he said, undressing. "There's not much time, so I'll make it quick."

As he placed his cloak, tunic, hose and cane next to his mask, his eyes noticed the shape beneath the bedclothes move as Rillian sat up. He stumbled backwards and Tyn seized him, holding his blade at Irrianna's throat, pulling his left arm up painfully around his back. The old man clutched Tyn's right forearm with both hands as the blade touched his skin.

"A gift, from Zoloth?" said Rillian, with a mocking croak. "Unlikely."

Ana stood and, taking the bottle from him, uncorked it.

"What are *you* doing here?" spat Irrianna.

Ana put a finger to her lips. "He doesn't know, does he?"

"Know what? What's going on here?" He demanded.

Ana ignored the question, and Tyn tightened his grip on the old man. "A toast to the festival and my father's generosity, then," she said, holding the bottle out to him.

The Grand Cardinal shook his head, puzzled by the company he found himself in.

"Oh, not to your taste? But as I understand it, all Grand Cardinals enjoy the finest wine Abeona produces. You are a Grand Cardinal, are you not?" She glanced at the bottle, "And this, the finest wine?"

Irrianna's mouth tried to form words as he looked between them – then slowly his mind began to piece together cycles of clues picked up during his long association with Senior Grand Cardinal Oen Zoloth.

"It was in my day," she said, looking at the label, taking a step closer to him. "Or have the grapes soured that much, over all these cycles, Grand Cardinal?"

Irrianna's eyes widened, and he began muttering involuntarily, aware he should be saying something in his defence, but unable to form any coherent sound. Then his brow creased as events slowly took shape in his memory. He began to realise, and calmness came over him.

Ana grinned at him. "You can cry out if you want, but no one will come. They'll just think it's another inmate cursing the fact they've lived through the night."

Rillian stood, searching his robes, finding two skins filled with ganapti fat slung upon his back. She sniffed one and turned away sharply.

"Torch wax? So you're here to deliver torch wax on the first day of the festival? A Grand Cardinal delivering wax?"

"It was needed, so I brought it with me. It is that simple." He stared hard at Rillian, and then he remembered the notes passed on to him by Yan Arramosa a while ago. Everything had been so confusing, and Zoloth had insisted upon collating all the documents Arramosa had brought together, despite Irrianna offering to share the heavy workload.

"Then let's celebrate the festival," said Ana, breaking his concentration. "My esteemed guest first." She thrust the bottle in front of his face.

Then he remembered the envelope Arramosa had spoken about, just a few days before he was murdered. What was it he had said? *'All the information has been cross-referenced and collated. There is an eighty-nine percent accuracy rating for my theories, and they are sealed in an envelope to ensure my safety.'*

Something like that.

"This is foolish. You must let me go," spluttered Irrianna. "If I am late, your father will know something is wrong. You will be discovered and executed, all of you. Let me go now, and I'll escort you all out of here." He smiled at Rillian and Ana, nodding slowly. "Yes, listen. You'll all be safe and I'll not mention any of this. You have my word."

"Drink!" shouted Ana.

Irrianna took the bottle and held it up level with his lips as he felt the grip from behind tighten, feeling the blade on his neck slowly stroke the tiny grey bristles there. The wine's perfume was welcome above the stench of the cramped cell. And for a fleeting moment, he considered drinking the wine, until he remembered the agony on the face of Yan Arramosa's assassin during the private meal Zoloth had arranged for him as a reward. The way he had torn off his tunic, clawing at his stomach with his fingernails, gouging at his skin, causing narrow, bloody rents to appear, as if trying to remove something from deep within him. Then his body had suddenly stiffened, his breath drawn in with quick short gasps without exhaling, like a suffocating fish free of the water, writhing uncontrollably in a net. Then he tried to remember to whom Yan Arramosa said he had addressed the envelope.

In a swift movement, he brought the bottle back to throw at Ana, but she took a step forward and held onto it with both hands, prising it from his grip. He shouted, then felt the cold pressure on his neck as Tyn drew the dagger slowly across it, cutting his tendons and transforming his cries into a pathetic, gurgled moan. He dropped onto all fours, clutching his neck, and Rillian turned away as Tyn struck again, thrusting the dagger into the back of his neck, slamming his palm onto the pommel with a crack of bone.

The Hathranelzra took Irrianna's robes, tunic, hose and

cane, passing them to Ana, then thrust the dying body onto the bed and covered it with a blanket. As it writhed, he removed the golden sandals and found Irrianna's keys in a pocket of his cloak.

He signed at the two women, then began dressing himself in Irrianna's clothes.

"We'll never make it," said Rillian.

He shook his head and signed again.

"He's right, mother," said Ana. "We have only a few moments before this place comes to life."

Silently they unlocked the door, Tyn leading the way with his face hidden by Irrianna's mask. They hurried up the stairs and into the living quarters, around the veranda and out through the gate into the streets.

Irrianna's head swam toward death as his life soaked into the soiled bedclothes. Had he heard correctly?

"He's right, mother."

Then he understood, just before he died.

The peasants cheered as food fell at their feet. Mothers frantically waved their babies' limp arms as they bounced them up and down, others bowing and praying, some turning away. Zoloth waved to them, smiling and nodding reverently as he concluded his speech, allowing Irrianna plenty of time to complete his task. But all through this, a nagging feeling crept up on him. Timmerman, and the words Irrianna had spoken days before, came back to him. He found the muscles in his face had relaxed, and he forced his hidden smile for the crowd once more.

He gratefully sat back into his seat, as a masked figure walked past his carriage, bowing to him as it went.

Zoloth found his smile once more, waited a few moments for Irrianna to take his seat in the carriage behind him, before ordering the cavalcade forward.

TWENTY

BENEATH

The Kaltesh set to work repairing their homes with assistance from a troop of junior priests, Deacons and Abeonian craftsmen. The dead were covered and set upon funeral carts to be taken into the desert for cremation. It was an ordered scene of concentrated single-mindedness. Gradually, new homes found the daylight.

In the midst of all this, Rillian galloped her ganapti up to Hulneb, sharply reining in the animal in a cloud of dust. The High Celebrant excused himself from discussing the repairs with three tribe elders, waving the dust from his eyes, watching as a warrior helped her down. He strode over, hands on his hips, face set with a mix of pale anger and relief. "We've been searching everywhere for you, mother. Are you alright?"

She nodded, looking at the burnt remnants being drawn away by the cartload. "I saw the smoke at daybreak. An accident?"

Hulneb shrugged, following her gaze. "Who can tell for sure? We've no idea how it started." He turned back to her and hesitated for a moment as she took his offered arm. She was trembling. "Where have you been?" he asked bluntly.

"I had a few final preparations to make in the Square before the festival."

"In the middle of the night?"

The old woman glared at him. "They were of a personal nature. Are you questioning me as High Celebrant, Hulneb, or as a concerned son?"

He shook his head. "I'm sorry."

She lowered her voice as they walked though the workforce. "I suggest you, Sol and Roanne ready yourselves for tonight. They are safe, I trust?"

"They're both fine, hidden from the tribe. Tulteth is with them."

"Good. Then take me to them. I can oversee everything that needs to be done here, after I have led the people in prayer."

He nodded and returned to the elders, explaining she would attend them later.

"This is a tale to be told around campfires for generations to come," said Tulteth enthusiastically. "I just wish I'd been part of it."

"Oh, I'm sure over the cycles you'll be able to add yourself to the story," said Roanne, packing her backsack as Ebe watched.

"Not at my expense," said Hulneb sharply, as he entered the tent with Rillian on his arm.

Roanne ran to her and they embraced, Rillian kissing her on the cheek.

"We've been so worried! Where have you been?"

The old woman paused and glanced at Hulneb. "I always spent one evening alone with your father – walking the city streets and talking. We enjoyed taking in the city together, alone and anonymously, walking freely. Tyn came with me for protection, and I could talk to your father again in Tyn's presence."

Roanne hugged her mother again, as Sol took a step forward.

"Rillian, I need to ask you about Roanne's pendant."

Mother and daughter parted and Rillian looked at Roanne, as she produced the object from beneath her tunic.

"How did Mirrimas come by it?"

She thought for a moment. "I have no idea, Sol. He told me he would give it to Roanne as an anniversary present during this visit."

He became impatient. "You must have some idea! Didn't you ask him how he came by it? It's a very unusual object."

The old woman was unconcerned by his questions and sat down on the nearest pile of cushions. "Sol, when I say I have no idea, that's exactly what I mean. Why is this so important to you?"

All eyes were fixed upon him now, and to everyone he suddenly took on the air of a Cardinal, his cold, fact-seeking, superior air interrupting the warmth of their family reunion. He continued, ignoring Roanne's depreciative scowl and folded arms.

"If I'm not mistaken, the designs on that pendant are identical to those within the deep levels of *Oosah*. Even the material it is fashioned from appears to be the same."

"Which means?" asked Hulneb, impatiently.

"Which means Mirrimas either visited the deep levels, or came into contact with someone who had." He paused, glancing at Roanne, choosing his words carefully before continuing. "Only Grand Cardinals are permitted into the deep levels now. It has been recorded that long ago, several Church officials were driven insane by what they had witnessed there. Perhaps Mirrimas was permitted entry, though an act of mutual benefit, with a higher member of our Church?"

Rillian sighed, taking a seat. "Well, I can tell you that Mirrimas never went inside *Agasanduku*, nor was he insane." She stared at him, unfazed by his insinuations. "Many times he was offered the opportunity to venture inside, but found the very idea of it disturbing, sacrilegious, even." She managed a slight chuckle as she looked between Hulneb and Roanne. "The Kaltesh need not see inside your *Oosah* to know what's there."

Sol opened his mouth to argue the point, but Roanne cut him off.

"Are you suggesting one of the Twelve was somehow connected to my father, Sol," she asked, placing the pendant back beneath her tunic.

"I'm not suggesting anything, for now. The sad facts

remain: there's a possibility your father was murdered, and he had an object connected to *Oosah* in his possession."

"If I find Zoloth had something to do with–"

"You're jumping to conclusions, Hulneb," said Rillian. "Don't make accusations based on assumptions. Believe me, you'll regret them later."

He turned his back as Rillian continued. "Sol, what exactly are these deep levels?"

"Eight levels, or floors, if you like, near where I left Opi. They're areas of great wonder, containing objects so extraordinary, with walls of glowing gems, shining in unison and by themselves. Some Church members have said they've heard voices of the dead speak to each other there, and, as I said, many Cardinals were supposedly driven insane by what they experienced whilst working on the deep levels' seals."

"Hmm. Well, I'm sorry I cannot help you further," said the old woman, standing. She held out her hand and Hulneb took her arm once more. "Now, I must attend the elders and prepare my people for the festivities." She lifted her head and paused for a moment, studying the Abeonian. "Good luck, Sol Timmerman. I'm sure you'll return with my grandson, safe and well. In return, my children will take care of you. I will lead the elders in silent prayer for you all." As her gaze lingered, Sol was sure there was more she wanted to say. He took a step forward, but Roanne stepped in front of him to kiss her mother on the cheek.

"We can continue this conversation when you return," Rillian said quietly, looking at Roanne.

"Can I stay and hear what you're going to do?" asked Tulteth, looking at his brother.

Hulneb shot him a glance.

Tulteth looked between Roanne and his mother. "Can I? Please?"

"We'll tell you everything when we return with Opi. You'll be the first to hear," promised Sol.

The young boy's shoulders slumped.

"If you were a little older and stronger, Tulteth, you could go with them," said Rillian, "but their quest is a dangerous one. You'll have your own adventures one day, and must stay safe today to experience them tomorrow. This day, and whatever it brings, is for them, and them alone."

The young boy sighed and headed for the open air, but Hulneb seized him by the arm.

"Don't forget to look after our mother while we're away. That is the most important task of all for you, brother. Oh, and be sure you don't tell your friends you've seen Roanne and Sol. This is not the time for bragging."

"Why?"

"If Zoloth were to discover they were alive, then…"

"Then what?"

"Don't play games with me, Tulteth," said Hulneb, letting go of his brother's arm and crouching down. "I know you're not stupid. Remember, I've visited the Holy Citadel. I heard the screams of the heretics as I walked its corridors. Men stretched until they snapped like dry twigs, their teeth pulled from their skulls, their skin seared with white hot irons as our families mark their livestock. The smell of the–"

"Hulneb!" said Roanne.

"That's okay, you can tell me more later," said Tulteth, and with that he ran outside.

"He's not as innocent as you think, daughter," said Rillian, watching him run across the encampment. "He will make a fine warrior one day, soon."

"True, but Hulneb shouldn't take away what little innocence he has left with his horror stories."

Hulneb shook his head and looked over to Sol for support, but he shrugged.

"Return safely, all of you," said Rillian.

Hulneb hugged her, kissing her on the forehead, then Roanne came forward to embrace her before the old woman turned to follow her son out into the sunshine.

"Reassure me, Sol. How exactly are we going to get into the Square tonight without breaking the curfew?" asked Hulneb.

"We need to position a caravan over the drain at the centre of the camp, then we simply open the grating and climb down."

"Climb down into what?"

"Just follow your nose," said Roanne, opening the neck of her backsack for Ebe to climb in. "Failing that, follow the gullies you tip your waste into."

The large circular stone waste-well held a narrow row of steps jutting from its side, leading down to a metal grating. In the middle of this sat a square inspection hatch, just wide enough for a man to climb through.

The grating was loose, and to Sol's surprise the metal hinges opened silently.

"Looks as though someone's used this as an exit recently," Sol called up to Hulneb and Roanne. Holding a torch into the darkness, he looked down.

"Perhaps whoever was responsible for the fire?" offered Roanne.

"Then we must be wary," said Hulneb. He waved one of his personal guards forward. "Fetch five warriors and have them stand guard over this grating when we leave. If anyone comes out other than the three of us, hold them until I return. Keep them alive at all costs."

The warrior grunted and ran off as Sol stepped down onto the metal ladder beneath the hatch, followed by the brother and sister.

At the bottom of the ladder they found themselves in a tunnel barely large enough to stand upright in. Sol took the lead, holding his torch ahead of him at arm's length as he walked down the gentle slope. The shallow wastewater flowed ankle deep around their feet, and Hulneb muttered curses and complaints in Kaltesh as he felt the chill around his ankles and the shit between his toes.

After several hundred paces the tunnel widened. They came to a junction where two more tunnels converged, identical to that which they had travelled. Ahead of them, atop three circular steps sat a domed hatch, a wheel at its centre. "This is it," said Sol, seizing the wheel. "Give me a hand, Hulneb, turn it to the left." Slowly the wheel turned with a screech of tired metal. Sol gripped a handle set into the front of the dome and pulled the hatch open. "Now watch your footing on the ladder; there's quite a drop."

Following a long descent, they found themselves on a square metal island three storeys high. Its surface was constructed from a metal mesh, and Hulneb at once felt uneasy as he looked through the small holes surrounding his feet. Steadying himself he looked up, gasping at the size of the tunnel. Illuminated by a row of blazing metal cradles the size of a velocipede, each hanging from three thick chains through a hole in the ceiling. They created pools of flickering light, shadows dancing upon the tunnel walls, disorientating him. As all three watched in silence, the fires spat embers into the darkness, some surviving the long fall to hiss into the foul black water beneath. The damp tunnel walls were encrusted here and there with barnacles and colourful shells, feeding on the refuse from the city high above. Mosses gave the ancient stonework a green tinge of varying hues, dangling in damp clumps from crevasses in an assortment of lengths, some dangling like threadbare curtains into the black river that steadily flowed beneath them, hiding what lay upstream.

"What are those?" asked Hulneb, pointing, using the respite to light his pipe with his torch.

Roanne looked at the walls of the tunnel where stone faces, five men high, with mouths wide open, were carved into the stonework at regular intervals. They were uncannily realistic, and their eyes seemed to stare back at them as the shadows weaved across their faces. Just beneath them, a narrow stone maintenance walkway jutted from the wall, barely wide enough to traverse.

As if in answer to his question, a mass of dark sludge leapt from the mouth closest to them, to fall clear of the walkway into the black water with a spatter. He coughed a cloud of smoke in surprise, the sound echoing back to him.

"Household waste," said Roanne. "And have you noticed every face is different? These are the faces of the original house owners, when the city was first built. It helped the workers identify which house had an obstruction in their drains. The workers enter the mouth of the homeowner who reports a blockage, to clear it. Since Abeona's population has grown, these outlets are shared by various buildings."

Hulneb shook his head, sucking at his pipe until it was burning to his satisfaction. "What a wonderful way to spend the day."

"We'll take a service barge as far as we can. It's slower, but safer than the maintenance ledge," said Sol, looking below. "Come on."

He led them down two flights of narrow metal stairs to the bottom tier. There, a squat jetty sat above the water where a thin, flat-bottomed barge designed for two workers, was moored alongside.

"If we're lucky, we won't meet any workers – but if we do…" He looked at Hulneb, who nodded his understanding by patting his short-sword hilts beneath his cloak.

"This place reeks," complained Roanne as her feet felt the cold water again.

"What do you expect?" said Sol, stepping into the small craft. "We'll have to row upstream towards the Square. There are several drains situated there, and we'll need to exit not too far from, but not too close to *Oosah*."

"How do you know where you're going?" asked Hulneb, suspiciously.

"These tunnels are built under the main roadways, so

we just need to follow the central thoroughfare west to the Square," answered Sol, looking above. "The thoroughfare to *Oosah* is always illuminated, even down here, as a mark of respect, so we simply follow the cradles above us."

"So why were these tunnels built on such a gigantic scale?" continued Hulneb as he climbed into the barge.

They helped Roanne down into the bobbing craft, and she answered him as she took a seat at the bow, aware his constant questions were his way of masking his trepidation. "Probably to allow the waste to build up. A series of valve doors allow water in through the dam wall, beneath the ravine floor, to flood the tunnels. It's part of the water network that irrigates the city's crops, and channels the fresh water to the buildings. The waste material is filtered and a small percentage reused for farming, before the remainder is dumped through the city wall into the river, to flow down to the ocean."

Sol looked up. "These tunnels are flushed once a day. It's not really necessary, but this was carried out during the conflict with your people, Hulneb, lest any of them breached the defences where the waste is dumped, and entered Abeona by those means. It's now more of a ritual cleansing than anything else, as the defences have been heavily manned and fortified since then."

"One warrior for every household," said Hulneb, looking up at the stone faces. "They could enter through these mouths and slit the throats of everyone in the house while they slept in their beds."

Roanne and Sol turned in unison, glaring at him.

He grinned, "I'm only thinking aloud for a change, Just a little joke. But you both must admit, this regular flushing is a waste of precious water," he said, taking Sol's torch from him and placing it at the stern of the craft.

Roanne slotted her torch into a holder at the bow of the craft then made Ebe comfortable among the towels in her backsack, "It would take more than a ritual to cleanse this city of its sins," she muttered under her breath, as she untied the bow rope securing the barge and turned. "Okay, we're clear."

"Just one more thing," said Hulneb, placing his oar into the sludge, "When will the next flushing take place? Have you taken that into account?"

Sol grinned. "Don't worry. We've plenty of time to reach our destination before then."

"You're sure about that?" persisted Hulneb, exhaling a plume of smoke.

But Sol just smiled and looked ahead as he began rowing through the sewage.

High above them, the festival eve streets were far from quiet. Just before the curfew bell, a few groups of drunken men and women zigzagged across the thoroughfares, avoiding hurrying carriages and velocipedes, singing and laughing whilst heading home. Street cleaners collected the debris from the heightened activity of the day, whilst the strong Deacon presence rushed people along.

The evening curfew was a mark of respect for the many thousands who had given their lives during the war against the occupants of the Trophy, as it was believed their ghosts walked the streets of Abeona throughout the night, on a pilgrimage from the Garden of Contentment, revisiting the city of their deaths. Anyone found wandering the streets without written authority was publicly shamed; paraded upon the festival stage for all to see.

The tiny barge moved at a steady pace.

"Remember Hulneb, I'll need a Deacon's uniform once we're in the Square," said Sol.

"Why didn't you tell me that before we left?" complained Hulneb.

"I did! And I told you it has to be the uniform of a Deacon of the Trophy for this to work."

He shook his head, muttering under his breath. "I'll do my best."

"Any less and it will be the end of us all, Hulneb," said Roanne. "Wait! There's someone in the water up ahead," she stood as best she could, pointing. "There."

"Paddle backwards," ordered Sol. "Maintain our position."

As it drifted past, Sol recognised the bloated body lying on its back, noticing the gaping wound across its neck. "Ommus. That explains why he didn't come to our aid, poor fellow." He waved a brief blessing into the air before returning his oar to the water. "Come on. We must hurry now."

The tunnel curved gently to the left and they found themselves at another junction.

Ahead, a huge bronze, naked, male figure appeared to be pushing against a closed circular door twenty men high. Bent at the waist with one leg behind him for support, his arms outstretched, fingers splayed apart, head bowed to the tunnel floor as if exerting great effort, keeping the way to the tunnel beyond sealed. Hulneb studied the figure's joints, noticing they were constructed from huge bolts, glistening with grease in the cradlelight. The forearms had been forged to appear muscular; the hands and fingers spreading across each half of the door had been intricately fashioned with veins and creases in the metal skin.

"And that is?" he asked, pointing with the wet stem of his pipe.

"Eli Eliyas. He perfected the water filtration system. You're looking at one of several doors, designed to hold back the water from the river," replied Sol.

"And of course, there would be another set of these doors at the other end of that tunnel, with the water beyond that?"

"Oh, there are many beyond this door before the dam baffles are reached, of course," said Sol, giving Hulneb a reassuring grin. "We're many leagues from the dam wall, don't worry. The workers maintaining the system are trained from a very early age in order to thoroughly learn all its intricacies. They know what they're doing."

Hulneb looked at the figure and shuddered, "Which way?" he asked, "This place doesn't feel right. It feels as if there's a lightning storm coming, like the ones of the plains."

"To the right, then on to the next junction. There's another pier there, that's where we proceed on foot. But you're right, my father had a similar feeling on many occasions, as if two cycles have overlapped, and down here we're in between them. Neither yesterday, today or tomorrow."

Roanne turned with a smirk. "It's just the smell, the smell of many cycles in one."

To Hulneb's relief, a short while later Roanne caught sight of another three-tiered structure rising from the sewage in the far distance, behind a pillar which seemed to grow from the water where the tunnels converged. As they steered around it, the big man stared in disbelief, their torchlight casting a dull light onto the object of which the three-tiered structure formed the base. Its middle deck sat at the ankles of a gigantic bronze, female figure, twice the size of the statue of Eli Eliyas. Behind her, the walls were blanketed with moss, ancient and thick, having never required removal. It too shone in the light, deeply layered with different hues of green and brown, dripping with foetid water. The figure's arms were stretched out from her sides, each hand identically splayed against circular doors set high into the walls. The figure's craftsmanship was astonishingly intricate and detailed, the folds of her bronze dress perfectly realised, her long, wide sleeves draping around her arms as if made of silk.

"The statue of Kay Varanack. She designed the sewer system, tunnels and bridges. This is the main junction," said Sol with some relief. "At the top of that figure are the central well tunnels leading to the Square. There's an access ladder inside, rising all the way to the top."

"How do you know so much about this system?" asked Hulneb.

Sol replied following two slow strokes of his oar. "My father was obsessed with this network of tunnels. Not only because of its function, but also due to its craftsmanship," he looked up, "and particularly these functional bronze statues."

The High Celebrant regarded the towering figure ahead. Her head bowed, her expression forlorn, sorrowful, her hair falling across her shoulders, bronze filaments entangling, reaching down to follow the curves of her breasts. "Well, I can honestly say I can't blame your father for that. I wonder if that's how she really looked? Never, never have I seen such a beautiful woman."

Roanne made a disproving sound with her mouth, as Sol turned with raised eyebrows. "We're nearly there," he said. "It's not too far now." He remembered his father's preoccupation with this area of Abeona: the scores of detailed sketches of the tunnel network adorning his study walls, the long lists of hastily scribbled questions and theories he'd prioritised numerically alongside them. *The tunnel of no purpose,* as he had called it, where a bronze statue of Kay Varanack as a child, sat atop a small tunnel's arch, holding her hand across her brow as if searching for something in the distance and shielding her eyes from the sun, the shallow tunnel leading only to a brick wall. There were so many mysteries, it seemed.

Something invaded the memory, catching his eye and he looked up. A shaft of light penetrated the dank air from a crack in the ceiling. He bit his lip, glancing back to the pillar in the centre of the waterway, then up to the shaft of light which had diminished a little as they made progress.

'The lone pillar occupying almost the exact centre of the tunnel before Varanack has no supporting function for the

tunnel ceiling, no markers or inscriptions, no reason for its placement, logically, religiously or architecturally,' he remembered his father had written. *'Two identical pillars can be found in the network, haphazardly placed in comparison to the functional beauty of the network's overall support construction. One pillar is barely noticeable, its straight face jutting almost unnoticed from the curve of the tunnel wall, its differing arrangement of brickwork betraying its age. What purpose could these pillars possibly serve? Did ancient Abeona enjoy a similar water filtration and sewage network to that which exists now, despite Ulu Varanack making no mention of this in* A Stonemason's Life? *Could it be Abeona existed as a settlement long before the dates currently taught and recorded in our holy scriptures? Many of the city's older structures bordering the Square of Remembrance share similar craftsmanship to these pillars, but are off-limits to investigation through excavation, as scripture forbids such. It's becoming more and more apparent scripture – and in some cases, the reluctance to further question its accuracy by the historians and archaeologists – is prohibiting the exploration of ancient Abeona and discovery of knowledge and hence understanding of its history. I am growing more and more fearful such narrow viewpoints could infect and ultimately influence the teachings of the Holy Church, more fearful that perhaps they already have, and this is how it has always been; that this is the true nature of our perceptions of life from when the very first word was written in* The Books of Truth.'

He heard a sound behind them and spun around, looking up to the mouths lining the walls, trying to make out if one had just deposited waste. "Did anyone hear that?" he asked.

"What?" said Hulneb, scanning the walls.

Another sound echoed around the tunnel, and from the corner of his eye, Hulneb noticed a shape moving into the shadows along the narrow walkway above. A few stone chips fell into the water with a splash, and Sol pulled in his oar. "Where did that come from?"

Silence fell around them now their oars were at rest; only the crackle of the fires above and the distant drips of water could be heard.

Hulneb leant forward, pointing to the walkway. "In the shadows," he whispered. "Someone's up there; they must have been hiding in a mouth."

The barge began to slowly retreat with the current.

"Keep rowing, Hulneb," said Sol, picking up his oar. "We've got to keep moving." They paddled through the water, alternating their thrusts either side of the barge.

The movement above came again, and Hulneb could see a flash of colour from a Deacon's cape as a figure ran through a pool of light. "There!" he shouted, pointing.

The Deacon ran as best he could along the slippery ledge and was ahead of the barge in a matter of seconds.

"If he makes it to that pier and up to the city..." said Roanne.

But Hulneb and Sol were pushing the barge through the refuse as quickly as their oars would allow, the little craft bobbing up and down as it proceeded.

"We're not fast enough!" shouted Roanne, turning to them momentarily. She watched as the Deacon jumped from the ledge, down onto the top tier, tumbling as he landed. He looked back at them briefly, spinning around to open a door set into the centre of the bronze figure's stomach.

A few moments passed, then a sound like distant thunder came from all around them, followed by a high-pitched, metallic screech echoing down the tunnel. The walls shook, sending tiny stone chippings splashing into the water, as above the burning cradles swayed, casting their shadows in a disorientating dance.

Slowly the left arm of Kay Varanack moved inward, the huge hinges forming the elbow and shoulder joints slowly turning.

"He's opening the valve inlet door!" shouted Sol.

"Come on!"

The sound of water rushing into the tunnel joined the cries from the metal as the barge began to lose ground.

Frantically they plunged their oars deeper into the water, paddling as fast as they could amid the froth. Their efforts were in vain. "We'll have to swim," shouted Sol, and with that he discarded his oar and jumped into the foul water. To his surprise and relief, the water only came up to his knees. Roanne and Hulneb jumped in after him, wading against the brown and white foam as the surge carried the little barge back down the tunnel.

The Deacon reappeared in the doorway and hurried down the stairway to the second landing as Sol reached the jetty, helping Roanne out of the sludge. The Deacon jumped down to the bottom tier, running over to kick Sol in the stomach. He keeled over, winded, falling back into the water as the Deacon turned his attention to Roanne, scrambling on all fours. He drew his broadsword as Hulneb pulled himself out of the water, his short-swords quickly in his hands. The Deacon's heavy blade came down towards the back of Roanne's neck, only to find the two blades crossed like scissors, blocking the strike. The Deacon sidestepped, pirouetted, his blade catching the light from the swaying cradles. Roanne was on her feet now, as Hulneb advanced on the aggressor.

Their eyes met and Hulneb noticed how young he was, a confident grin upon his fresh face, expertly carving the air between them with his swordplay. Then he recognised him as the Deacon he had seen Zoloth talking to at the caravanserai. Hulneb stood motionless, puffing on his pipe, squinting through the smoke at the shadows swaying backward and forward across his opponent. The young man was unfazed by his foe's relaxed air, his focus now darting toward Sol, pulling a Kaltesh short-sword from its scabbard.

"You cannot win, Deacon," gasped Sol as he caught his breath. "This city and all it holds sacred will very soon be betrayed by the Twelve you serve."

"I serve only Senior Grand Cardinal Oen Zoloth," said the Deacon, lifting his head, spitting into the water in front of Sol. He was breathing hard now, his body swaying slightly, readying himself.

"Now that's unfitting behaviour for a Church representative," shouted Hulneb above the noise of the rising water. He shook his head and tutted, "and in front of a lady."

The Deacon smiled. "I enjoyed watching your people burn," he said, returning his attention to the High Celebrant. "Now all three of you will drown."

With that, Hulneb jumped forward, blades arcing swiftly through the air. All three clashed in a silver flurry, impacts reverberating above the rushing water. With a broad, sweeping stroke at chest height, the Deacon's broadsword shattered both of Hulneb's blades as he blocked, sending the broken pieces splashing into the water, now ankle deep upon the tier. Discarding the jagged remains of his weapons, Hulneb stepped to the side as the broadsword was brought up and over the Deacon's head, to come down with a splash and a metallic ring where Hulneb had stood a moment before.

Sol saw his chance, diving at their attacker with his sword outstretched, its tip finding the Deacon's armpit beneath his armour as he raised his weapon once more. The young man cried out, dropping his weapon into the water, and at once Hulneb leapt forward, his weight knocking their assailant onto his back beneath the sludge. Now Hulneb seized the Deacon's throat with his large hands as his opponent kicked out, raising his hands above the water, grasping Hulneb's forearms, frantically searching for purchase. But Hulneb pinned the Deacon's shoulders down with his knees, as his head appeared momentarily above the foam, gasping for air, spitting out sludge as Hulneb brought his head down hard, smashing the Deacon's nose with his forehead. He cried out in a red gurgle as the blood flowed into his throat.

Roanne stared in horror at the contorted expression on her brother's face, the sheer determination and unyielding hatred that had suddenly transformed him. His arms shook as he concentrated all his strength and upper bodyweight into his hands, his teeth biting through the stem of his pipe protruding from the side of his mouth. The severed bowl fell into the water with a brief hiss and was swept away. He spat out the stem as the Deacon's hands lost their grip, kneeling on his chest, heaving his bodyweight down again and again, forcing a last breath from the Deacon's lungs. The body began to spasm beneath his weight, limbs flaying about uncontrollably below the rising water. Then he was still.

Satisfied he was dead, Hulneb released his grip then groped around in the water to recover the broadsword. He stood, watching as the water coursed around the limp body, threatening to sweep it away, an arm pointing with the current as if eager to begin the journey to its final resting place. Hulneb gave the body a kick to help it on its way.

"Hulneb, come on," shouted Sol.

He joined them. "Mirrimas' swords and pipe, all lost. Still, one debt repaid," he said, placing the Deacon's weapon through his belt before pointing. "I thought you said there was no water on the other side of these doors?"

Roanne grabbed her husband by the arm. "We have to close that door, or we'll be swept away with that Deacon and Ommus."

Sol hurried up the staircases and though the door set into the bronze figure's stomach. There, the slain bodies of two sewer attendants lay beneath a row of levers, each lever the length of a broadsword, protruded from the floor, set at a different angles. "There are so many, but only two doors!" he exclaimed, as Roanne joined him.

Hulneb shouted from below. "Whatever you're doing, you'd better be quick!"

"Why so many?" blurted Roanne, her eyes looking

along the row.

"My father couldn't work it out. He theorised perhaps they control doors we can't see, in other tunnels."

The roar of the escaping water filled their ears.

"We haven't time to theorise." Roanne crouched down, examining ropes looped around the bottom of two levers to Sol's far left. Her hands found a further loop connecting the two. "Look,

perhaps it's closed by four levers, all pulled together?"

He glanced over to her, "The Deacon was alone! That's it!"

Hulneb appeared at the door. "You'd better hurry up!"

Sol looked at the levers in turn, noticing two were damp to the touch at their tops. "He must have operated these," he said. "Ro, place your hands on the two that have ropes attached."

She did so and Sol nodded. "Pull them back as far as they go. Now."

The roar of surging water was met by the clatter of gears and screech of metal. Hulneb stood in the doorway, watching as Kay Varanack's arm pushed the door slowly closed.

As the water outside subsided and the door closed fully with a metal thud, Sol relaxed, letting out a deep breath.

Hulneb glared at them, nodding with relief, then looked at Roanne with a half-smile.

"Are you okay, sister?"

But she turned away from him in silence, to climb the ladder situated in the centre of the statue.

TWENTY-ONE

THE FESTIVAL

Analissa Zoloth lay awake in a tent in the square. The Kaltesh family she shared the tent with slept soundly to her left, but the skin stuffed with feathers she lay upon was uncomfortable, the tent cloth close to her face far too soft, and the expanse of sky just inches above her too daunting to give her comfort. She closed her eyes.

Rillian had introduced her to the family as a widow from the caravanserai fire, explaining her somewhat dishevelled appearance and distant air. They welcomed her, sharing an evening meal and wine with her before she made her excuses and took to her bed.

From the very first day of her imprisonment, she had prayed to Tal Salandor to see the city of her birth again, to be afforded one last glimpse of its majestic towers and boundary wall before she died. However, what she found as her mother guided her along the route to the Square a few measures ago both surprised and saddened her.

The canals she had known as a child, where colourful barges once sold fresh fruit and vegetables upon the grassy banks of cottage gardens, had fallen into disrepair. Only a few ramshackle craft sat alone on the still waters, frozen reminders of a time when the flavour of life was sweeter. Now, the busy thoroughfares dominated the city. Like stone scars they had cut through any obstacle that stood in their way, enticing the people to markets to purchase essential goods, directing the populace to favoured places of interest and points of sale, eradicating the quaint beauty of the original meandering streets and their picturesque simplicity. She had hoped to catch a glimpse of the playing fields she had used as a child, but only the black metal railings surrounding it remained. The once lush slopes of wild flowers and trees had been consumed by rows and rows of tiny houses where children sat upon doorsteps, dreaming, the former park's railings casting thin shadows across their faces, a barrier between them and the wheels of speeding carts.

For the duration of her imprisonment, she had survived by retreating into those happy cycles of her memory, shutting off the howls from her fellow inmates and the stench that filled her nostrils. She struggled hard to retrieve real memories as her consciousness swam against the tide of her 'medicine'-induced thoughts, threatening to sweep her away from that shoreline of sanity forever. She had fought, spitting out the poison when alone, thrashing against the undercurrent, crawling out of the water and pulling herself up onto the dry sand continually, following every 'treatment' forced upon her. Kneeling on the damp sand and gathering her memories up like discarded shells, she placed them in the correct order before her, remembering their emotions, identifying their levels of significance as that ocean of medicine she had escaped whispered enticements behind her. The little abalones – rare, beautiful and intricate – were of hot, carefree, childhood days when nothing mattered. Playing with her friends, watching the frenetic adult world from her open bedroom window as the summer sun warmed her face. Sitting on her father's knee as they relaxed upon the veranda by the lake, as he told her stories of great heroism and far-off lands, of princesses, warriors and wizards, of places only the imagination would ever see. Dotted around this, many tiny multi-coloured balias shells, representing the faces of the friends she had made, and places she had seen. They accumulated as she grew up, some left behind along that journey, never to be revisited but still in her memory. Her school, college, eating houses, landmarks and alehouses she had grown fond of as a young woman, places where she had stood alone in the evening twilight to simply marvel at Abeona's beauty. Then one shell shone brighter than the others in the sand, different from the rest, constant, sturdy and dependable. Her rival and lover, Sol Timmerman.

She looked further up the beach as something caught her eye and she stood, brushing the damp sand from her knees. There, the final memory shell, a giant white conch. She smiled, stepping over the tiny balias and ran to it. For her it was perfection, heavy and substantial in her hands as she reverently removed it from the sand. Its asymmetrical beauty and complexity showed her something new of it every time she held it. This was the Trophy, *Oosah Agasanduku*, her obsession, the indefinable mystery and centre of everything that had seized her wonder, amazement and curiosity upon first seeing it. She came back to it time and time again in her mind, turning it over in her hands, feeling its contours with her fingertips. Unable to let it go, she carried it up the beach with her, always part of her, a mystery that had kept her sane. She smiled, comforted by it as she cradled it in her arms, remembering the realisation of the trio. For she knew both she and Sol loved *Oosah*. Slowly they had become distant, separating as their obsessions for the object diluted their love for one other.

Then, further up the beach, she came across a broken shell, its sharp, jagged fragments protruding from the peppery yellow sand, threatening to cut her feet as she walked away from the water. Pulling the hair away from her face as the sea breeze sought to distract her, she carefully removed the tiny remains from the sand, to begin piecing them back together as best she could. When she had finished it lay there, a flat and incomplete precious wentle trap, a fractured representation of a recognisable whole. She realised then, part of herself had been lost to that expansive ocean, a portion that had succumbed during the battle and slipped away unnoticed in the tide, drowned by that medicine, buried by the memory-sediment beneath the waves. As she recognised that broken shell for what it was, she thought, '*Did I allow that painful part of me to pass on? Did I secretly wish for it to die?'* Now she realised, having seen Abeona once more – this broken shell was the time of her father's elevation, and how his wonderful stories abruptly stopped, how he slowly became someone else, an altered man wearing different clothes, speaking in a different voice. He became an unwelcome guest in the big house nestling at the side of Lake Avoram, until he left forever, his memory just a ghost, the house as empty as the shells on the sand before her. After her time of self-doubt, self-pity and self-recrimination, there was only realisation for her – the reality that there was nothing left to do but follow him in order to be part of his life, to hear his stories again, to love him and for him to love her in return, as he always had since her birth. The Priesthood beckoned.

On nearing the Square of Remembrance, her eyes had fallen upon the old priests' quarter and the Church publication tower. She recalled standing outside with other schoolchildren and junior priests on news day, waiting for the latest Theorists' publications to be issued. Everyone would wait impatiently, talking, laughing and arguing over the last issue's theories. She remembered, much later in life, looking down from a narrow window atop that tall, pencil-shaped tower with Sol Timmerman standing haughtily at her side, and how he had commented that the students below seemed like fluttering hens. *'They are there because of us. Us, Ana! Cardinals. We're grade five theorists at last!'* he had said, *'They crave our ideas as much as we crave the truth.'* As they watched, the Bishops filed out from the wide doors beneath them to stand on the steps in a line and announce which Cardinals' work they held. The students fell silent, before hastily assembling in orderly queues to purchase the papers as the names were called out in turn. Sol Timmerman would count how many waited for their theories, and she would come out just ahead of him almost every time.

The smile triggered by those far-off times evaporated as

she noticed the tower's pointed roof was now missing several tiles, its bare rafters exposing a skeletal confirmation of its redundancy. Its windows now dark where once she had seen the glow of a warm fire on a cold morning, a cluster of candles at a study desk, or incense drifting from an open window during a humid summer afternoon. She wondered how such a beautiful building could be left to decay in such a way, and then remembered all Church publications were now issued from the Holy Citadel. Beside this ancient tower sat a squat, smooth-faced white block with a low, sloping roof. The building offered no clue as to its function in its appearance, as its design was nothing more than a simple rectangle. It reminded her of a bloated toad, sitting in wait for the slightest sign of a loose brick, or crumbling plaster from its elderly neighbour, so it could then pounce at this first signal of decay, to consume the building and replace it with one of its own.

Just beyond this stood the Archbishop's longhouse. The building, with its many minarets and wide, vaulted front veranda, sat back from the pavement adopting, if a building ever could, a confident stance, she decided. The veranda's polished green slate floor shone in the bright sun, and there a few Archbishops talked, hands hidden in their robes, heads nodding. She looked up to Yan Arramosa's circular window. It too was dark, but this she had been expecting, shaking her head as the cart trundled past the longhouse and into the Square, suddenly aware with pride and relief she was now nothing more than a visitor from a superior and far more dignified past.

At once her heart trembled. Stepping down from the cart she stumbled, waving aside Rillian's concerns with a brief, "Thank you," while her eyes remained fixed upon it.

The crowd around her vanished and they were left alone in the Square together. It had fallen foul of neither progress nor neglect. It had remained unchanged, yet she realised its detail and scale had diminished in her memory, and it was almost like seeing the object for the very first time. It still maintained that unmistakable air of mysterious authority over everything around it. She found herself laughing, tears welling up in her eyes as her emotions took her back to her youth.

Behind her laughter she could hear her mother making excuses for her to the Kaltesh family she would share the festival with. "She's never seen the Holy Brothers' triumphant achievement before. Please forgive her ignorance."

And, she realised, that was exactly how she felt. Her mother was correct. She was ignorant, ignorant of it as she stared. It still hid from her secrets and truths, like the next instalment in a Cardinal's paper, held over for so many cycles, or one of her father's stories to be completed the following bedtime. She embraced her ignorance, for hers, compared to many others', was miniscule, and she knew soon this ignorance would finally expire.

She opened her eyes, crawled along the groundsheet and pulled the cover flap aside to peer out into the night. She smiled to herself, knowing it had waited for her. "Very soon," she whispered, "very soon, my dear old friend."

Hulneb levered the grating open with his broadsword and climbed up, helping Roanne up after him. Sol followed, replacing the grating in silence, joining them on the narrow stone steps jutting from the side of the well's circular wall. Roanne took the towels from her backsack and they cleaned themselves up as best they could, Ebe chattering away at the disturbance of his repose.

"Do you know exactly where we are?" asked Hulneb as he wiped his face.

It took Sol a few moments to orient himself as he looked around in the darkness. Tents, wagons and locked stalls surrounded them. Then he noticed the throbbing radiance above the stalls in the distance, and pointed.

"Yes. There it is. We're a little further away than I would have liked. Come on."

They discarded the towels and headed for the glow, picking their way carefully through the disorganized maze of vehicles and makeshift homes.

Gradually the distant glow grew brighter, the maze around them more complex, its fabricated streets and alleyways narrower. Finally they cleared the labyrinth and ahead of them loomed the Trophy. Sol sat on the low boundary wall, shuffling along it to match the view of *Oosah* he had seen as a child while sitting next to his father. Roanne sat to his left, and Hulneb to his right.

All around the Trophy, sixty paces apart, flaming beacons three men high illuminated the idol with a glow like twilight, crackling and spitting as the Trophy shimmered in the dancing flames reflected on its surface.

"Now what do we do?" asked Roanne.

"We wait," said Sol. "Once we see the Firekeeper and his assistant, we make our way to the lowest part of *Oosah*."

"You mean its feet?" asked Hulneb. "It's all too obvious it could walk across the land, killing as it went."

"You're suggesting the Kaltesh invented a walking mechanism, yet you continue to use livestock to pull your wheeled caravans?"

"Tradition! The feet have joints to walk."

"No. All six feet, or *megapods,* lead to sealed alcoves. We need to be exactly at its lowest point to the ground, unfortunately a considerable distance from the entranceway. The Firekeeper fuels the beacons surrounding *Oosah* at regular intervals, by the use of a ladder, and escorted by a lone Deacon. Once we take care of him, Roanne and I will pose as the Firekeeper and his assistant, you as the Deacon. When the time is right, we can begin our ascent."

"Just one point," said Hulneb, grinding his teeth. "If my information is correct, its lowest point to the ground has a steep curve rising to its outside edge." He drew an oval into the dust at his feet and turned to Sol, convinced the former Cardinal had taken his last small step into insanity. "A ladder will be of no use. It's just too large to be scaled by a single ladder," he said, stabbing his finger into the sand, "it won't reach beyond that curve."

Sol grinned confidently. "Trust me. One step at a time, Hulneb."

He rolled his eyes and sighed. "Okay. And how do you expect me to obtain a Deacon's uniform without raising the alarm?" He looked up at the beacons. "With all this light it's impossible to go unnoticed."

"They work in shifts throughout the night. We'll have to wait and hope one of them decides to take his break in a refreshment tent."

"Hope! How long do they take for their break?"

"One measure, usually."

They waited.

"It looks as if they're going to remain on guard all night," said Roanne. She looked at the sky. "Curfew is over. It'll soon be morning."

"It's like trying to catch a sand rat with bait and a line," said Hulneb.

"Patience."

At last Sol noticed three Deacons talking, just beyond the perimeter's glow. "Look," he said, nodding in their direction. As they watched, two Deacons ambled away into the relative darkness of the maze of stalls, whilst the other returned to his guard duty.

Sol turned to Hulneb, but he was already striding in their direction.

In a moment the Deacons had disappeared behind a wagon, with Hulneb not far behind.

"I should go with him," said Sol, but Roanne put a hand on his knee. "He'll be fine. Just wait."

The Deacons stopped beneath a red lantern hanging from the entrance to a long marquee. A burly figure sat asleep with his head resting upon a table, blocking the entrance.

The Deacons looked at each other and one drew his sword with a grin, slamming the pommel down onto the table with a clatter. The figure sat up with a start, sniffed and peered at them as they laughed.

They spoke for a few moments, the larger of the two Deacons producing a few tokens and dropping them onto the table. The seated figure scooped them up and stood, allowing the Deacon inside.

Hulneb watched from the shadows with interest. Silently he made his way round to the back of the marquee. Pushing his ear to the taut cloth he listened. The muffled sounds of laughter came from inside, and he lay on the ground, lifting the canvas slightly to peer inside. The marquee held a narrow corridor running along its centre, with eight tall, rectangular cubicles made from four posts with stretched material around them either side of it. As he watched, a Deacon entered an open cubicle for a moment, then returned to the corridor. Finally he found a cubicle to his liking, further along. A few moments later, the Deacon reappeared, completely naked, placing his clothes in a pile on a table outside, and Hulneb grinned, realising the purpose of the cubicles, then made his way to the front of the marquee.

"How much?" grunted Hulneb to the seated owner.

"Two."

He rummaged around, finding the tokens and dropping them on the table before heading inside. The marquee reeked of bodily pleasures, and Hulneb waved the stench away from his nostrils as he found the Deacon's uniform on the low table. Holding it up to himself he nodded, dropping the tunic back before slowly pulling the entrance cloth aside to peer in. His timing was good; the Deacon lay upon the whore, her eyes closed. Within moments a fist to the temple and another to the chin rendered the Deacon unconscious, Hulneb's large hand covered her mouth as she opened her eyes, wondering why her guest had decided to roll off her. He held his index finger across his pursed lips. "Shhhh, I won't hurt you. When he wakes, continue where you left off, and provide him with the *very* best of your expertise, understand?"

She nodded, wide-eyed, as Hulneb removed his hand from her mouth, reaching beneath his robes to drop a handful of coins on the thin, grubby sheet she clung to beneath her chin. As he stood, the whore lowered the sheet to reveal herself, an enticing smile touching her face. The High Celebrant raised his eyebrows briefly, head tilting to the right, then dropped a few more coins in her lap. "The very best, remember!" and with that he hurried out, scooping up the uniform and helmet, hiding them beneath his cloak.

As he passed the owner seated at the table he noticed his bewildered expression from the corner of his eye. "And, onto the next," said Hulneb, without looking back.

Roanne sighed. "This is all for nothing. We only have about a measure left before daylight."

"Then we hide in the Square and return tomorrow night," said Sol, with a determined stare as he drew patterns in the dust at his feet.

"But Opi has been without food or water for almost five days."

"He has his waterskin with him. He'll ration himself, of that I'm sure," he said, continuing to draw at his feet.

"And what if he hasn't, what then? What will we find?"

He failed to look at her. "We've both taught him the importance of his waterskin, don't worry."

She looked up to *Oosah*, letting out a long sigh. "What *are* you doing?"

He continued looking down. "Something Hulneb said has me thinking. There are two columns of unknown purpose in the sewer tunnels. My father was obsessed by them, believing they were possibly part of a previously constructed sewer system." He looked up and pointed to *Oosah's* feet. "If my calculations are correct, there are four more, as yet undiscovered. If that's the case, I theorise all six occupy positions directly beneath *Oosah's* megapods, acting as markers, or perhaps, supports."

"But why? History states the city was built around *Oosah*, it standing on the bedrock."

He nodded, returning his finger to the sand. "If we're to believe scripture." He bit his bottom lip, slowly drawing a circle. "The column we encountered before the statue of Varanack sits directly beneath this foot, *here*. I theorise with an eighty-six percent correct outcome that the Square, or at least the part of it beneath *Oosah*, is partially hollow. An as yet undiscovered sanctum, a hidden chamber, positioned directly beneath where we're sitting and above the ceiling of the sewer tunnel." He looked around, "There's much more meaning to this boundary wall, if I'm not mistaken. It's as though it was–"

A hand on his shoulder startled him and he turned to see a Deacon standing there. His heart began to race and Roanne placed her hand on her sword hilt as the Deacon crouched down and their eyes met. Sol noticed the wispy beard protruding from the helmet's faceplate, and he relaxed.

"Come on then," said Hulneb from beneath the helmet. "We have to be quick, I have no idea how good Abeonian whores are."

Sol stood, erasing the drawings in the sand with his foot, deciding not to follow up the statement. "Follow me."

He led them to the rear of the Trophy, where eight giant wings like those of an insect had folded in upon each other, stretching out to almost five times the length of the Archbishop's longhouse. "We'll wait back here in the shadows," said Sol to Hulneb. The High Celebrant strode into a pool of light from a fading beacon, pacing beneath it, awaiting the Firekeeper.

At last the three figures appeared, two carrying a ladder, with a Deacon bringing up the rear. Hastily they placed the ladder against a horizontal rest jutting from the tall metal pole which held a flaming cradle at its top. The Firekeeper's assistant stood on the bottom rung of the tall ladder to keep it steady as the Firekeeper carried up a basket upon his back, stacked with logs. As he began to place the logs into the cradle, Sol came up behind the Deacon standing guard. He tapped him on the shoulder. "Excuse me."

As their eyes met, the Deacon stared, slack-jawed with dumbfounded recognition.

Sol recognised him. It was Sef Windmarsh, the Deacon who had assisted him on that terrible day of Yan's death and Opi's disappearance.

Roanne appeared from the shadows, distracting the confused Deacon for a moment, and Sol saw his chance. He flipped his blade into his palm and swung the pommel into the side of the Deacon's head, knocking him to the ground, unconscious.

Hulneb took care of the Firekeeper's assistant at the base of the ladder, while Sol and Roanne dragged the unconscious Deacon into the shadows. There they rolled him under a cart as Hulneb appeared, carrying the Firekeeper's assistant over his shoulder. "His comrade has almost finished," he said, pushing the unconscious figure next to the Deacon. "Quickly."

"Coming down!" shouted the Firekeeper as he descended. As he reached the bottom rung, Hulneb smiled and hit him with a dagger pommel under his chin. "I'll take care of him," said Hulneb, supporting the little man with one hand. "You take the ladder."

Nodding, Sol pulled the ladder away from the beacon, walking backward and easing the top of it to the ground, hand over hand on each rung.

Roanne took the opposite end and they moved swiftly, Hulneb bringing up the rear.

Finally they reached Sol's chosen position.

"Quickly!" hissed Sol, placing the ladder so its top just met the curved underside of the Trophy. "Now, watch me," he called as he hurried up the rungs. At the top, he held his right hand back from the smooth, flat surface with his fingers spread wide apart. "Let us pray," he whispered to himself, bringing his hand rapidly forward. A metal hand reached out from the surface of the Trophy and he turned his wrist to seize it, clutching the metallic fingers with his own in an interlocking, claw-like grasp. The grip from the surface of the Trophy was as he expected, feeling minute imitations of every muscle in his fingers. Each subtle alteration he made was perfectly matched, allowing him to hang on without any discomfort.

Hulneb's jaw slackened. "The Brothers' magic!" he gasped. "He's using the Brothers' magic!" Sol repeated the process with his left hand. Gradually he pulled himself up, clear of the ladder, kicking downward and into the surface of the hallowed object to create protruding steps that vanished as he climbed higher. Slowly he made his way up its sheer surface. Roanne followed, and close behind her, Hulneb, who kicked the ladder away as he pulled himself up after his sister.

They climbed and climbed, Roanne beginning to struggle. "I'm not going to be able to keep this up for much longer," she said, the effort taking its toll on her slender limbs.

But Hulneb was right behind her now, kicking into the Trophy for footholds and climbing up to place his shoulders at her feet. "You can do it, sister," he grunted, pushing her upward towards Sol.

"That's it, Hulneb," said Sol, looking down. "Use your feet, Roanne. Kick down into it and the surface will support you."

As they continued, it became easier, and with practice just the right amount of pressure was found to grip the talon-like hands that repeatedly reached out from the surface to assist them. At last Sol, now clear of the curve, held out a hand for Roanne, pulling her clear onto the top as shouting from below filtered up to them.

The sound of metal upon metal distracted her as she joined her husband, and she felt the chain slide from her neck as her pendant bounced from the surface of the Trophy to slide and fall past her brother, to the ground far below.

"Roanne! Keep going!" said Sol as she looked helplessly back. "I'll help Hulneb."

She scrambled past him across the smoothly curved surface, towards the topmost area where it levelled out.

Sol turned to see Hulneb's head and shoulders appearing, his expression one of pure exhilaration. "I should have done this cycles ago!" he said with some shortness of breath, reaching out to Sol with his right hand. As Sol smiled back at him, Hulneb's expression changed and he screamed in agony, losing his left handhold. Sol instinctively reached down and seized his right arm with both hands, kicking into the surface for support. He pulled the big man clear of the curve as Hulneb kicked up footholds, revealing an arrow protruding from his right calf.

They made their way to Roanne, lying on her back and breathing hard.

Below them the shouting had increased, and as they looked around them the city lights began to fade as the sun peered over the distant city wall.

Ana ran unseen past the marching sentry Deacons to hide in the shadows of the gigantic megapod. It was cold against her back, refreshing as she splayed her long fingers wide against the surface, enjoying its texture, watching for their return. She froze, holding her breath, becoming part of the surface, as Tyn had explained to her with his language of hands time and time again. When she was sure she could not be seen she climbed a little, then froze again, forcing her body into the contours of the mechanisms, folding herself into an inconspicuous silhouette. There, in the shadows of yesterday she absently traced a forefinger over the marks he had scratched into the metal with his dagger, '**A** + **S**.' *So very long ago*, she thought, remembering, telling him to hurry as she kept watch, stifling her giggles as he concentrated on immortalising them both, making them part of it. *Different people now, after all that's happened, all those adolescent dreams torn asunder by others.* She smiled grimly, unwilling to chart the directions both of them had been forced to take, *not again, not now.*

Slowly she climbed, little by little, hiding for a few moments, scared she'd somehow be seen, as they both were back then by Yan. Just a quick telling off from their instructor, for he didn't see the marks Sol had made so high up. 'Get back in line with the others,' he had shouted. Finally she was between the huge struts and braces, hidden by the outer doors, comfortably draping her body around the workings like a child in the boughs of a majestic tree. Relaxing in *Oosah's* metal embrace the sounds of the city were finally lost to her. Content, she closed her eyes. 'Hello again, my old friend,' she whispered.

"It's not as bad as it looks," said Roanne, examining the wound. "The shaft's almost straight through, look." As she gently reached out to touch the bloody tip of the arrow protruding from Hulneb's leg, Sol grabbed her wrist and shook his head. She shot him a questioning glance but he simply shook his head almost imperceptibly. Hulneb screamed in agony as she shifted his body, trying to make him more comfortable. "Did you have to do that?" he spat in Kaltesh.

"Get it out, Ro," said Sol calmly. "You'll have to snap the flight off and pull the head through the way it entered.

That may help to close the wound."

Hulneb nodded quickly, sweating and breathing hard as he stared at his leg. "It's numb, should it be numb?"

"You're in shock," said Sol, as another arrow arced over their heads to come to an abrupt halt as the Trophy's skin reached up to stop it. Then another came, followed by a volley of flaming arrows that fell short of them, creating a flickering half-light. Roanne ran over to retrieve one.

The Trophy reacted to the growing onslaught, and three dozen pointed reactions sprouted from its surface. "We'll have to move out of range," shouted Sol. "There's not a bow strong enough to carry an arrow to the top of *Oosah*. We must head for the centre line. Can you walk, Hulneb?" he said, squeezing his arm. The High Celebrant gritted his teeth and nodded, so they helped him to his feet and ran, Roanne taking the lead as the surface of the Trophy created stepping stones to mirror their sandals, leaving the deflected arrows behind them.

They came to an oval protrusion, the width of three houses, the length of seven. Sol lowered Hulneb onto his back against the protrusion and Roanne examined his wound again.

"I'll have to snap the flight off now," she said, passing the flaming arrow to Sol. Without further warning she broke the arrow between her thumbs. Hulneb screamed in agony and swore, his body trembling as Roanne pulled the arrow through his leg. The blood flowed from the lesion and she snatched the flaming arrow from Sol. "Hold his leg down. Put all your weight on it." As he did so, she pushed the flaming arrowhead into the exit wound. Hulneb screamed, arching his back in pain as the wound hissed, producing a pungent smoke that spiralled up into their nostrils. Roanne turned her attention to the entry point and repeated the treatment before the arrowhead had time to cool. She threw the extinguished arrow to one side, then tore off a strip of her sleeve to tightly bind the blackened holes.

"You'll have to rest, Hulneb."

"I... I hadn't made any plans otherwise, to... to be honest!" he stammered, his eyes shut tightly.

Sol retrieved the discarded arrowhead and brought it up to his nose.

"What's wrong?" Roanne asked, wondering why his face had suddenly grown so pale.

He held the broken shaft closer to examine it, twisting it slowly between his fingers and taking care not to touch the metal tip. "It's poisoned – a blend of uncured Farrengrass and Nalean two-cuffed snake venom."

"Tasty," breathed Hulneb. "I've eaten many two-cuffs over the years. I suppose it's only fair one of them will be responsible for my end."

"But there's a cure?" asked Roanne, horrified.

Hulneb nodded, licking his dry lips. "Yes, at the caravanserai. Without it, I'll be dead in a measure." He smiled grimly and closed his eyes before lapsing into unconsciousness.

As the sun fully illuminated the Trophy and the last beacon was extinguished, the Twelve Grand Cardinals' cavalcade came rolling into the Square, cheered by the thousands of onlookers. Flowers were thrown before the feet of the ganapti and children sitting upon their parents' shoulders were afforded a view of the Grand Cardinals graciously waving back to the people.

Analissa heard the cheering and climbed down from *Oosah*'s embrace, watching with interest as the people hurried toward the cavalcade, wondering what had caught their attention. She joined them, jostling past and pushing through to reach the front.

"We'll have to lower him down," said Roanne. "The Deacons will know how to save him." She stared at her brother in desperation. His face muscles had relaxed, cheeks clinging to his bones limply, his eyes set deeper, skin now ash-grey. She touched his damp forehead. It was cold. If it were not for the slight rise and fall of his chest, she would have believed he was already dead.

"We can't," said Sol abruptly.

"But he'll be dead in a measure!"

He held her shoulders and leant over the unconscious High Celebrant. "If we get close enough to the edge to lower him to safety, it will only be a matter of time before we're hit ourselves, and then who would be left to find Opi? Think. If we lower him down, as soon as he is identified there'll be rioting between the Abeonians and Kaltesh – and we need the rope for our descent. No, we have to leave him here. Either way he's dead, Roanne, you must know that." He lifted her head tenderly, speaking quietly. "It's just us now. We must go on. What else is there for us?"

She gazed at her brother and the hopeless position they were in became all too clear. Sol was right, she knew that, however much she wanted him to be wrong.

"He was carrying the rope ladder. We'll need that, Roanne,"

She emptied Hulneb's backsack and passed the contents to Sol, who shared them equally between his own and hers.

Slowly she tore Hulneb's backsack down the seam, opening it out flat. She knelt over her brother and kissed him on the forehead, unable to detect his breath upon her face. Realisation hit her, and she took out her waterskin, sprinkling a few drops onto his dry lips for a reaction that never came. After a moment she took a few sips herself, before passing it to Sol. As she spoke a Kaltesh prayer for the departed, Sol sipped the water, waiting as she gently laid the torn backsack over her brother's face. Sol allowed her a few moments before taking her hand and leading her across the metallic plain.

He pointed. "Around the far side of that structure

there's a grating, perhaps five hundred paces ahead. If we can prise it open it may provide shelter from the sun, and a safe place to rest."

The hexagonal grating levered up easily with Sol's sword, and he lowered himself into a shallow well. There, all manner of symbols ran across the inside surfaces, with two thick metal conduits running along the far wall. He touched them; they were both cold.

"We'll rest here for a while," he said, helping Roanne down into the shade. "Relax against these pipes, they'll help cool you."

She sat in silence, unable to believe her loss. She closed her eyes, unsure if she should shed a tear for her brother. Even after all Rillian had said, part of her still believed he was somehow responsible for her father's death. Sol sat beside her and she rested her head upon his shoulder, the sleepless night and the exertions of the past few measures catching up with her. At last, tears for her dying brother fell from her eyes and she wiped them away before drifting off into sleep.

Her head was level with the back of his neck, and she felt the muscles in her forearms tense as she heaved the rock high above her head. She stood motionless for a moment, remembering what her mother had told her. Concentrate, see the scene, take control, relax. *The rock shaded her eyes from the sun and she noticed how old Mirrimas had become. His long white hair twisted in a horizontal line in the air as the sea winds blew across the delta, revealing a patch on the back of his head where the hair had fallen out. There, the skin was dry and mottled, and she concentrated on that patch, staring hard. As the rock came back over her head she tried to scream to warn him, but could not summon her voice.* Focus. Pause. Look. Mirrimas was kneeling at the water's edge, kneeling to pull something out of the water. She stared down at her feet.

But I'm *standing* behind him, she thought. *Then the rock was brought down swiftly. She heard the crack of bone and a whimpering cry as his body jerked forward and his arms came up.*

Now the spray was warm and red and she licked her lips, dropping the bloodied rock into the water.

She waited, struggling to remain inside the dream, to allow everything to play out, encased in the murderer's mind, until the truth released her.

His grip began to relax, his head tipping backward, the last breath exhaled, rising to the surface of the pool as foamy red and white bubbles.

Her hands remained tight around his throat, fingers waiting for that tell-tale pulse to cease, for she did not trust him, even this close to death. The water began to calm, the blood gathering at the bottom of the pool and she waited, watching the sticky red mess cascade around his face, tumbling in great globs around his cheeks to reveal his staring eyes. The water calmed and finally she was able to shift her focus, to push back into a blur the face of her dead father, revealing the reflection of his murderer.

The murderer didn't smile, as she had expected, didn't possess an expression of twisted insanity or of triumphant achievement. Instead, the face was calm, somehow distant, as if unaware of the events of a few moments before. The murderer's eyes then focused upon the corpse, and Tulteth released his hands from his father's neck, removing them slowly from the water. It was done. No time for sorrow or regret now. They would come later, perhaps. Now, all there was left to do was to entangle his father's body in the nets he was trying to retrieve, and return to his bed. Roanne remembered her father's final words now, hearing them in her brother's memory, words tempered with happiness and love. *"Come to help me with the nets, have you, son?"*

The commotion far below bordered on hysteria – the

news had travelled fast, spreading though the throng like an unstoppable infection.

The Deacon responsible for raising the alarm had no idea his idle comment to his gathered comrades would cause so much unrest as they helped him to his feet, and all the more damaging, change public opinion in a heartbeat. He had seen the defiler several days earlier, as it was he who had helped him in his attempt to save Yan Arramosa's life.

'I saw his face – it was Sol Timmerman!' He had said, with mixed emotions.

They believed him, of course. Sol Timmerman had achieved the impossible. He had survived the Pinnacle of Judgement and was now making his way across the surface of the Trophy, out of sight – to what end was anyone's guess. Bets had been placed, arguments and fights had broken out among the populace concerning the circumstances of this, 'miracle.' *'He has been saved by Tal Salandor! Could what he said at the Necropolis be true?'* whispered some who had only heard his accusations to Zoloth second-hand. *'The man is a terrible threat to everyone and must be stopped!'* shouted others.

Several troops of Deacons were brought into the Square to quell the disorder, and slowly the small outbreaks subsided into muttered curses. The people waited. A veil of oppression fell over the Square, a fear far greater than any Kaltesh threat, as they too were now part of this insecurity and uncertainty. What would be done? What *could* be done?

Aboard his carriage, Zoloth held court.

"And you are absolutely sure you saw Sol Timmerman, Deacon...?"

"Windmarsh. Sef Windmarsh. Yes, Your Holiness. Absolutely certain. My eyesight has grown accustomed to the contrast of daylight and beacon light over seventeen cycles of duty. I'm sure of what I saw."

Zoloth sat, emotionless behind his festival mask.

"Good. Was there anyone else with him?"

"Yes, Your Holiness. One other."

"And this other individual – have you any idea of their identity?"

"Everything happened so fast. It's difficult to tell, but it appeared to be his wife, Your Holiness."

"I see, Sef. And no other accompanied them?"

"Not that I noticed. But I found this," he said, holding out Roanne's pendant. Zoloth took it slowly, holding the bizarre design close to his face.

"It fell from *Oosah,* Your Holiness, as it helped them climb. I theorise it is a magical talisman, and its enchantments assisted them."

Zoloth's eyes darted over to the Deacon as he placed the pendant beneath his robes.

"You *theorise*? Such thoughts do not form any part of your duties, Sef Windmarsh! No, you are mistaken. There is no such thing as magic. The heretics simply used an extension to the Firekeeper's ladder, and hauled it up with them to prevent the Deacons giving chase. *Oosah* has been defiled, and it *did not* assist them. Do I make myself clear?"

"But I saw it, Your Holiness! The Tro–"

Zoloth raised his voice, aware of the stories concerning Sol Timmerman's ascent. "You are wrong. It was simply a trick of the light, coupled with the blow to your head. Understandable considering the circumstances."

"I'm not lying, Your Holiness. I'm speaking the truth."

"I understand. The truth as you perceive it, but not the actuality of the circumstances. Your assignment as a Deacon of *Oosah* has undoubtedly caused a certain amount of monotony for you during your long and faithful service. This 'vision' you said you saw was simply a manifestation of your boredom, your mind wanting something inexplicable to occur to alleviate the tedium." He sat back, pausing to study Sef's reaction. "You will be transferred to more active duties in the Ravine Quarter after the festival."

Zoloth managed a smile behind his mask. "You are relieved of your duties until then. Join your family in the Square and enjoy the festival, Sef Windmarsh," he leant forward, lowering his voice. "You will speak to no one of what you *think* you saw, and will not theorise again. Dismissed."

Zoloth took the stage built for the closing speeches that were always given during the last day of the festival. He knew whatever he said had to be strong, unambiguous. He couldn't allow idle gossip to spread, to grow amid the populace, giving a determined faction undeniable credence to Sol Timmerman's reappearance. He knew speculation would undoubtedly steer the populace to unpredictability, ruining the many preparations he had set in place to bring to fruition Tal Salandor's whispered instructions. Upon seeing the Senior Grand Cardinal standing silently, word quickly spread through the crowd, the people slowly turning from their speculative discussions, waiting for him to speak.

He removed his festival mask and placed it at his feet, raising his hands for silence.

"There is truth in the stories you have heard this day. Sol Timmerman and his wife are alive."

The voices rose in disbelief, and Zoloth was forced to pause. He waited for silence, pacing along

the front of the stage with his hands clasped behind his back as the Deacons at the front of the stage shouted for order. When silence finally fell he turned to the crowd, pointing with a wagging finger at the Trophy looming behind him. "Furthermore, as I speak, Sol Timmerman and his wife are committing the most heinous outrage ever to disgrace the Church and this city." He continued to pace back and forth along the stage, watching his audience's attention fix upon him, pausing, enjoying their silence as they waited for him to continue. "But be told, and be assured, this is *not* the work of the Almighty. Tal Salandor would never condone or support such an act. It is not the work of an enchantment, or some unseen magical malevolence – and be certain of this, good people of Abeona and welcomed Kaltesh guests, it is *not* the influence of his Kaltesh wife." His voice rose with hatred as he stopped pacing. "This is simply the work of a single madman's determined *evil!*"

The conversations grew again, some mumbled to each other as others argued with neighbours over opinions overheard, some shouted for justice from Zoloth, while very few cursed him for bringing this upon their city. "I will not allow everything our forefathers built – Abeonian and Kaltesh alike – to be defiled. I will maintain the peace for every single one of you and your children. You have heard stories of Sol Timmerman's behaviour during the funeral of Yan Arramosa. His disrespect is an insult to us all. His contempt for our way of life threatens everything we hold true in our hearts. He would have this taken from you in a breath! He would celebrate the evil which scoured our land many centuries ago! He worships it, embraces it! He would assist the invaders in destroying us all, should they return!"

One pair of eyes, unimpressed by his remarks, remained fixed upon him, her heart beating fast beneath her ribs. There was no mention of Hulneb, and Rillian became deeply concerned. She had made preparations for the worst. Her warriors mingled in the crowds of Abeonians, disguised, ready to take up arms if the Senior Grand Cardinal decided Hulneb's support of Sol's actions was an act of war. *'One man,'* she thought, as Zoloth continued to rally the crowd. *'That's how it always begins.'*

"This unashamed contravention of our laws and beliefs will be punished! Sol Timmerman will be executed for this crime!" He looked above the crowd, closing his eyes to make the sign of *Oosah* on his chest, before raising his arms as if to embrace a long-lost friend. Smiling, he looked down into the crowd, nodding, making eye contact with as many as he could. He knew now was the perfect time. His gaze then returned upward, and he shouted triumphantly. "Behold!"

Everyone turned and looked up. At the edge of the Square, twenty-four ganapti hauled a gargantuan vehicle slowly forwards. The people parted as its shadow fell across them, shocked into silence at the sight of the sixteen-wheeled tower creaking above. It was a masterpiece of craftsmanship and engineering; its wheels twice the size of the largest Kaltesh caravan, its rectangular tower, protruding from the chassis, taller than any building in the Square. Three white poles extended from each side of the monstrosity, placed at equal intervals up its height, each holding a white banner emblazoned with the crest of a Grand Cardinal. Beneath a dark grey, slated roof at the tower's summit a gangway extended, decorated with ornately carved handrails at either side. From several of the small, shuttered, arched windows set back into the tower a few helmeted faces could be glimpsed. As the vehicle halted outside the Square, Zoloth spoke again.

"Listen to me. I will put an end to Sol Timmerman's transgressions now, and return his wife to her family. I will bring him before you by this day's end." He picked up his mask to hurry from the stage, where a line of Deacons had secured an avenue of linked arms to protect him from the congratulations of the crowd.

Rillian pushed her way to the edge of the chain of Deacons. There she stood as the people shouted around her, fists stabbing the air as Senior Grand Cardinal Oen Zoloth walked leisurely by, nodding, waving and superciliously smiling his appreciation to the fleeting faces around him.

She barked at him in Kaltesh as he came close, and the sound touched his ears, forcing him to stop in his tracks. He turned, eyes studying the crowd, searching for the speaker, recognising the voice. Finally their eyes met, and his expression set. He checked himself and forced his smile once again, mouthing a few words in Kaltesh back to her before covering his face with his mask. She turned away to rejoin the family elders to inform them of what she had seen and heard.

Roanne's consciousness drifted in the twilight between her dream and reality, unable to come to terms with what she had seen. She decided it must have been a mistake – a distortion, the last thoughts of denial circling Hulneb's brain before he died. *Tulteth? No. Impossible. Why? What possible reason could he have had to commit such a violent and terrible crime? To become First Son? Never. To elevate Hulneb to High Celebrant? No – I cannot, will not, believe that. Perhaps it was just a calculated manoeuvre amid many? To eventually challenge Hulneb, to take his position from him a few cycles later?* She remembered their conversation as they looked at each other in the mirror and her heart sank. Had he given her clues, played with her, hinted at his intentions then? She felt movement beside her and was suddenly awake.

"We must move," said Sol, sitting up.

"There's something I must do first," she murmured.

"*Something you must do?*"

"Hulneb. I must see if he is really dead. If he is, then his body must be treated with the respect it deserves."

"Ro, we don't have time for this. We must–"

"You're right, *we* don't. I must do this Sol, on my own. No arguments, please. Wait for me here." And with that she climbed up onto the surface and hurried away to where her brother's body lay.

A single flaming arrow would be enough, she thought. Once she had enticed the Deacons to release arrows at her, she would seize one and set fire to his body, returning his soul to the wind. The Deacon's robes he wore did not matter, they were not flesh, just coverings of coverings. It was his soul that mattered. In the distance she saw his dark, inert shape upon the surface, shimmering in the morning haze. She began to run.

Tulteth stirred in his bed and turned over, disturbed. The dream had woken him again. He tried to ignore it as he had done so many times. *'Guilt? I have nothing to feel guilty about,'* he thought as he dressed. He walked out of the caravan and into the Kaltesh enclosure for communal breakfast, laughing with his friends as the dream tore at him. He held his head and made excuses, leaving his people to their fastidious duties.

The city streets were busy with people heading to the Square of Remembrance. He weaved through them as his mind spat memories at him again, as it had done so many times since the murder. There were little flashes of incident, fragments playing over and over like a repeated play upon a bright, lantern-lit stage. But usually there were only two performers to this one act. Now there was a third, an interloper. He shook the feeling off as it fought to deliver its lines to him, struggled to take the stage in front of the customary players, to upstage them. Again and again its beauty intrigued the young man – the silhouette imprinted in his mind's eye was not one to be ignored. He stopped and thought about it, closing his eyes to concentrate.

He was back at that shallow pool once again. *'How many times must I put myself through this?'* he thought. The water began to calm and the player came forward, encroaching upon his territory. The ripples ceased, the sunlight finding peaceful, gently undulating water to grace with its warmth. She looked back at him from the water, her reflected expression a distorted mixture of horror, sorrow, condemnation and disbelief. Realisation sent blood rushing to colour his cheeks and his legs became weak.

Roanne knew.

His eyes narrowed on the people around him. Some smiled and nodded as they passed, others shot him disapproving looks, wondering why he chose to walk away from the Square. Had Roanne told anyone? Had she informed his mother? Were there warriors now searching for him amid the crowds? For a moment the sun was hidden from view and he turned to see Zoloth's wheeled tower crawling towards the outskirts of the Square. The priests leading the animals began to whip the creatures and they snorted and obeyed. Gradually the vehicle began to turn, taking the wide, main thoroughfare where the Deacons had halted all traffic. Slowly it moved toward the Trophy.

The morning sun was all the more tolerable for the breeze which blew across the surface of *Oosah*, and for that Sol was thankful. He cupped his hands around his eyes, looking for a sign of Roanne. He was hoping he had been wrong about the arrow, that they would both return and Hulneb would chastise him with his humorous bravado, *'I woke up and sucked the poison out,'* or, *'Poison? My diet consists of antidotes to all your city toxins, apart from your foul ale, which has no known remedy.'*

Yes, then they could continue together. He could hope as much as he wanted, but he knew neither scenario was credible and that the arrowhead *had* been poisoned, that paralysis *would* prohibit Hulneb sucking out the pollution in his blood if he awoke, even though Roanne's cauterisation had prevented any such chance of either of them doing so. That Hulneb's diet consisted of what he wanted to eat, and not what he should, even if the Kaltesh had such paranoid precautions concerning the food they ate during their visit to the city. Besides, the aroma of that arrowhead and the tradition of arms for Deacons of *Oosah* confirmed the awful truth. Hulneb was dead. Perhaps he should have warned them, perhaps the Kaltesh did have an antidote and a simple warning would have provided them all with peace of mind. *'No, I'm punishing myself again.'* he thought. He couldn't think of everything, he couldn't blame himself. He had warned them it would be dangerous and he should do this on his own, but that didn't stop the guilt from rising in him. He should have come alone, but then realised if he had, he would not have made it this far, and his body would have replaced the young Deacon's which was now nothing more than breakfast for the sewer rats. He owed his brother-by-union more than he was prepared to admit. Hulneb had given him more than he had ever received from any other man, and for that he was truly sorry, and at the same time thankful the High Celebrant had insisted on coming with him.

A shape appeared in the distance and he climbed out of the well into the heat. It was as he expected.

As he ran to meet her, he realised Roanne's expression was not one of sorrow and loss, but of wide-eyed disbelief. She stopped and waited for him.

"Ro?"

"I'm sure I saw him for a moment," she said, looking up at him, wiping the sweat from her eyes, "It wasn't a mirage."

"A moment?"

She nodded slowly and held out the backsack that had covered his face. "This was where we left him, but Hulneb," she tried to swallow but her mouth was dry, "he's gone."

TWENTY-TWO

ASCENSION

Sol jumped into the air and the skin of the Trophy rose up in a perfectly-mirrored representation of his feet. He dropped the looped rope he held at his waist, letting it fall over the Trophy's protrusion beneath him. Roanne passed him the slack, tying the remaining end around her waist. She lay on her stomach facing him, edging slowly backwards over the curved surface above the entrance Sol and Opi had entered by. They had to move fast now. She agreed with her husband; the Deacons had found their way up onto the surface of *Oosah*, and had carried Hulneb's body back to Zoloth. She worried about her mother, how she would react to her son's death, and what conflict would arise between their people. Sol was right; many more would soon be searching for them.

Beyond his view, hidden by the curve of *Oosah*, lay a narrow ledge barely two paces deep. Sol watched her, holding firmly to the rope and letting it slowly down hand over hand, one knot at a time. The sun had now climbed above the horizon, providing a panoramic view of Abeona, and as he looked down beyond the edge of the Trophy, he noticed in the distance something huge traversing the main thoroughfare running through the heart of the city. Every vehicle in front of this monstrosity moved out of its path, their drivers choosing side roads, others simply turning to head back the way they had come. He blinked, sure his imagination was playing unkind tricks upon him. But no, as it came closer it revealed itself, and recognition dawned on him. He remembered part of the structure at the garrison upon his visit to the Citadel, and its purpose was now obvious to him.

"You'll have to hurry, Roanne!" he shouted, letting out more slack as an arrow fell forty or so paces ahead of him.

He found he was bearing more of her weight now that she was on a steeper gradient; the rope became taut in his hands and he quickly let out more, taking care not to let it slip through his fingers. The arrows came again, and Sol thanked Tal for the wind that hindered the archers from finding their marks, the arrows carried off to be deflected by *Oosah's* skin. He continued lowering Roanne into the entranceway, hurrying now as the tower loomed towards him. At last the rope went slack in his hands, a single tug telling him she was safe and the rope untied from her waist. He untied the loop at his feet, running back across the surface, weaving left and right as the archers gradually became more adept at compensating for the high wind. Once at a safe distance, he tied the rope into a harness around his waist, under his crotch and shoulders, waiting.

Roanne breathed hard, running into the entranceway, dragging her end of the rope behind her. Her husband's instructions were clear, his descriptions and directions as perfect as she had expected. Ahead of her, the seals were still open from his visit several days before. She found the auditorium with its huge rotating sphere and the low handrail enclosing the walkway. She tied the rope around the handrail, making several knots before taking up the slack, pulling with all her might.

Far above her, Sol took a deep breath, feeling the tension in the rope. *'This is the moment. If this doesn't work, then this really will be the end.'* Breathing hard once again he started to run toward the tower, and as the gradient became too much for his legs to keep up with his momentum, he fell onto his back, speeding down the surface of the Trophy toward its periphery.

The archers in the tower lowered their bows and stared in disbelief. This madman would fall to his death, surely? They watched as he rolled onto his stomach and clawed at its surface, trying to repeat the process of his ascent. But the small protuberances that jutted from it were too smooth and fleeting to slow his descent, and as he came rushing towards the edge of the Trophy, he kicked out to take him clear of the entranceway, for at this speed he knew the fall would kill him.

In the crowd below someone shouted. Shielding their eyes they pointed upward. There, the rope dangled in a loop from the entranceway, barely visible, a flaccid, diaphanous thread against the bright morning sky. Then all eyes watched and many mouths screamed as a figure tumbled through the air, arms and legs flailing, falling like a spider connected to its transparent lifeline filament, caught upon the wind.

Zoloth turned as he heard the cries, watching with disgust the heretic's act. Behind his mask hatred creased his face. He waved a Deacon over. "Assemble your best archers and end this stupidity now! Whoever cuts him down earns one thousand tokens and the next festival free of his duties." He turned to Irrianna who stood watching him intensely, as the Deacon began issuing orders to his men.

"Now is the time," smiled Zoloth. "Come with me."

The assembled ten Grand Cardinals waited for Zoloth and Irrianna beside the tower.

"Holy Brethren," he began, "this is a time of uncertainty. For your own protection I would advise you all to return to the safety of the Citadel. I will secure *Oosah* and the Square from this outrage, personally ensuring your safety. Grand Cardinal Irrianna will send word once it is safe for you to return."

One stepped forward and bowed. "We thank you for your consideration, Senior Grand Cardinal Zoloth, and will take your advice." He pointed. "But what of this... this... whatever it is?"

"A precaution. I theorised there was a seventy-nine percent chance *Oosah* would fall foul of defilement during this festival, despite my having dismantled the means of entry." He shielded his eyes as the emotionless mask tilted up to the tower. "It was constructed as a mark of respect to you, my Holy Brothers, at my own personal expense. A far safer and more comfortable way for us to enter *Oosah*."

The Grand Cardinal bowed. "With thanks. May Tal Salandor assist you in your charitable endeavours." He turned and boarded his carriage, the remaining nine following his lead.

As they left the Square, Zoloth's personal Deacons escorted him and his confidant up a wide flight of steps lowered between the rear wheels of the tower, locking and barring the door behind them as they entered.

A broad-shouldered figure, unlike any Tyn had seen before, attired in full armour of intricate

workmanship, waited for Zoloth and bowed with some difficulty. "Your Holiness, everything is prepared. The men are ready," he bellowed.

"Then begin. We will retire to my chambers. Three raps upon my door when we reach our

destination, if you would be so kind, Constable. Dismissed."

The formidable figure bowed once more and turned on his heels with a clatter of armour.

"Come, Irrianna," said Zoloth, walking ahead, but the old man was looking in the direction

of the Constable.

"Irrianna?" said Zoloth, turning.

Tyn looked at him and nodded, following Zoloth as the vehicle began to move off.

The Senior Grand Cardinal's windowless chambers were a surprisingly small affair. Two oak chairs upholstered in brown and white ganapti hide, a low, slate table of white, a door leading to a sanitary room. The low ceiling held broad structural supports running its length, the wooden walls sparsely decorated with bright tapestries to add colour. Three lanterns upon metal tripods elucidated the room with a harsh light, exaggerating the sharp corners of the rough woodwork. Only Zoloth knew the room's origin, and he had drawn up the blueprint for it from memory. It lacked a door to a bedroom, a door to a bright and airy kitchen, double doors out to a veranda with a view of the lake beyond but otherwise this was a replica of the room in which, many cycles ago, he had made his life-changing decision as his daughter sat outside, watching the sun slowly set behind the city wall.

He had returned from yet another festival filled with duties below his station. A festival of obsequious remarks, of stolen glimpses when her eyes were elsewhere, of another denial. He would take no more subtle insults from her, which only they understood; he would no longer plan and scheme to catch half a measure alone with her. He would wait no longer. The place in his heart for her had finally suffocated beneath her refusals, leaving just an ugly, jagged scar upon his memory of those times.

"The final chapter," said Zoloth, walking to his writing desk. He took out a key and unlocked a drawer and reverently pulled it open. Inside lay an ebony box with brass corners. Upon the box a single word illustrated with gold inlay, the five letters of the word entwined with silver ivy, the leaves of the finest jade, veins of ruby filaments. He removed his mask and placed it upon the desk, his hands trembling as he picked up the box.

"Truth," he whispered. He unlocked the box and pulled out three parchment pages, ornately illuminated and bound at the margins by red ribbons threaded through gold eyelets. "These are the final answers, the revelations and directives that will finally bring my lifetime's desire to a close." He smiled, allowing himself an uncharacteristic chuckle. "The pain these three simple pages have caused over the cycles is beyond measure. My daughter's sanity, the Ten Grand Cardinals drugged daily to ensure their compliance, countless others swept aside. Would you like to see the truth, and what all this has been about, *Hathranelzra?*" He wheeled around, holding the pages to his chest.

The old man stood before him, mask in one hand,

dagger held at his side.

"So, after all these cycles, after catching so many glimpses from the corner of my eye and finding evidence of you, left either accidentally or by design, I finally meet the fabled Hathranelzra. I've been aware of your presence for a while now. You have a distinctive odour, my friend." He lowered the parchments. "Poor Irrianna, I theorised there was a ninety-eight percent possibility that you would be there waiting for him. Never mind," he waved his concerns away. "Neither outcome is favoured over the other, as both are acceptable. In a way, I am relieved and somewhat pleased you are here. You have saved me the trouble of finishing Irrianna, and have presented me with the honour of finishing you myself. An opportunity I must admit with all honesty I never expected, and thank you for. Besides, I think it only right you should be afforded a brief opportunity to see the magnificent work of your charge." He held up the illuminations. "After all these cycles of faithful service would you not agree?"

Tyn dropped the mask and shook his head. He took a step forward, holding the dagger out in front of him.

Zoloth grinned, turning to carefully place the illuminations upon the table. When he turned back, he held a thin dagger in each hand, both catching the lantern light dancing along their silvery lengths. "Do you remember these, Hathranelzra? My right hand holds the dagger you used to cut out your tongue, the left, the dagger that stole your hearing." He tapped the blades together, enjoying the pure, identical note they produced without the trace of a harmonic beat. "Perfection, pure and simple. I've polished these fine instruments, oh, almost every day since they were last used." His eyes wandered up and down the length of the blades. "Magnificent Kaltesh workmanship, the only gift from Rillian worth retaining," he whispered.

Tyn signed flamboyantly with one hand as he recognised the daggers, causing Zoloth to raise an eyebrow. "Come now, such foul language, and from a man who has spent the last third of his life free from such profanities. Surely you would like to know the real reason you've spent so long exiled from your family?" He took a step forward, raising his eyebrows and softening his voice. "Would you know this, before you die?" He gave a mocking smile. "Of course you would. For dying without knowing the reason governing your vocation is akin to living a lifetime without one."

Tyn's expression changed. *'I've never questioned,'* he thought, his inner voice with its rich tones remembered from long ago. His occupation had been so very long, without support, acknowledgement or praise from his people. *'Not once have I been able to ask why.'* He lowered the dagger and relaxed a little. It was true. Mirrimas had never given him a complete explanation. *'Follow her unseen, and look after her during her Alonetime,'* he had ordered. It had been as brief and as simple as that. As their supreme personal guard, it was enough for him just to follow the High Celebrant's orders, whatever those orders entailed, whomever they concerned, whatever the situation, however much they contradicted Kaltesh dogma. It was his calling, as it had been his father's and his father's before that. A family tradition of great honour and absolute service to the High Celebrant and his wife, a convention he would never soil. But now? He looked back over all those cycles spent in hiding, moving from job to job, making just enough money to survive, performing his duties to the letter.

He remembered it could have been so very different, but for a simple mistake.

He had shown himself late one night, as Rillian found herself in a scuffle with an armed thief. When her assailant lay dead at his feet and she looked up from the dust to recognise her rescuer, she was furious. Her anger was such that he was sure the dagger she held to defend herself would have finished him then. Instead, she wept as she saw his eyes take in her swollen belly. *'This is my Alonetime!'*

She had screamed at him. *'How dare Mirrimas send you to watch over me. This is unforgivable. If he had just left me alone then I would be dead, along with the guilt I carry in my womb.'*

But he had learnt Rillian was not a woman to be taken on face value. She could use this situation, turn and manipulate her predicament to serve her own needs.

His punishment was straightforward and appropriate. Hathranelzra for invading her solitude, and a new calling, for Rillian knew Mirrimas would never mention Tyn's absence to her, or any elder member of the tribe.

He remembered her words; her voice the last sound he had heard, following the birth.

'I cannot trust her father; I cannot be here for her. Protect my child. I have told him someone will remain here to watch over her, and he is aware of your charge, but he does not know who you are. It is sufficient for him to know you are the finest warrior the Kaltesh have, and will soon be Hathranelzra, your senses heightened, your lack of communication elevating you above the trivial lives of ordinary men.

'You can never return to the Kaltesh, for if you do, Mirrimas will have you killed for exposing his betrayal of my Alonetime, and your family will suffer for your failure to remain anonymous. You don't exist,' she had told him, finally. *'You are a spectre guarding the future for everyone. You hold this world and the lives of thousands of Abeonians and Kaltesh in your hands.'*

Zoloth grinned as Tyn's eyes widened with curiosity. "Good," he murmured, as he began pacing slowly around the cramped room. "So, the wife of the grand and self-righteous Mirrimas, and a priest whose duties are but to escort and protect her during the festivals, fall in love. She lies with him and they conceive a child. She returns to this city for the length of her pregnancy and to give birth, during her Alonetime. The child remains with her father, later exhibiting the unique skills this city has sought since its very first foundation stone was laid. And you were caught up in all this. How dare Rillian even think I would harm my own daughter, and introduce *you* into this whole affair to watch over *me*." Zoloth shook his head and allowed himself a chuckle. "But surely, you must see the irony of the entire situation?"

Tyn adopted a knife-fighting stance: knees bent slightly, arms reaching wide, hands tossing the dagger back and forth.

Zoloth raised the dagger in his right hand. "Obviously you do not. Then allow me a little self-praise when I explain to you how I intended to release myself from your continued harassment. I found I had a willing collaborator in Mirrimas." Tyn shook his head and his body tensed. "Oh yes. You see, I realised once he knew of his wife's transgressions, he would lead an assault on this city, and his people into a massacre. So, I simply waited until I was in a powerful enough position to end his brainless religious rivalry. Unfortunately, he died before he could deliver himself, his family, and the Kaltesh to me." Zoloth laughed and shook his head. "I almost forgot. One more thing, concerning your family's deaths..."

Tyn's eyes darted between the Senior Grand Cardinal's right hand and his mouth.

The lie was all Zoloth needed to put his opponent off guard. The dagger leapt from his left hand. Tyn turned sideways on, the dagger burying itself in the door behind him. The remaining dagger had left Zoloth's right hand as the first passed the Hathranelzra's body, now embedding itself into his left shoulder. His throat issued a strange croaking sound, a cry like a newborn baby's, but with the rasping gasps of an old man, as his stubby tongue lapped uselessly in his gaping mouth. Falling against the door he clutched his shoulder as Zoloth walked forward.

Sol climbed the rope, pushing on the knots with his feet,

towards the ledge above as he swayed back and forth in a wide arc. Arrows sped around him, their flights whistling above the cries from far below. Reaching the lip at last he pulled himself up and over, turning to see the tower rolling towards him, the protruding walkway slightly higher than the entranceway he lay upon. Rolling over, he scrambled toward the auditorium of one hundred seals, locking each seal behind him, calling for Roanne at the top of his voice.

The kick caught Zoloth in the stomach, sending him tripping backwards with awkward little steps into his writing desk. Tyn pulled the dagger from the door, and took several paces back to launch himself through it. The flimsy lock, more for decoration than security, burst at its clasps and hinges, splintering into the seven planks that had briefly made the door whole.

Zoloth took deep breaths. Although winded by the kick, he regained his posture quickly, watching as the Hathranelzra tumbled through the splintering wood to fall in an ungainly heap in the narrow corridor. He picked himself up faster than a man of his age should have been able to, managing somehow to use his momentum to find his feet, giving that bizarre, infantsenile cry again as he pulled the dagger from his shoulder.

The Deacons standing guard on either side of Zoloth's chamber door gaped in shock as they recognised the robes covering the figure. *Grand Cardinal Irrianna?*

But Tyn threw the robes aside now, and his attention was focused on the burly Constable some way off, staring with disbelief at the remains of the door he was supposed to rap upon.

Now the two Deacons were upon him as Zoloth screamed orders from the doorway. A swift kick to the temple sent the first into the second, and Tyn was heading towards the Constable and the stairway beyond, as the Deacons untangled themselves at Zoloth's feet.

TWENTY-THREE

THE DEEPEST LEVELS

Serenity soothed the city streets, and if you listened closely, the wind could just be heard. Its voice, now free of the overwhelming rattle of carts, hurried footsteps and the babble of the inhabitants, was the only sound in the Abeonian suburbs. It sang an ancient tune as it coursed down alleyways, through courtyards and over rooftops. Its melody, an erstwhile requiem for the mountain with which it had once shared the sky, seemed different somehow. It was true its harmonies were ever-altering as the city bore another building or intricate, skeletal stone passageway to confound it, but today there was more to it than that. It was as if the wind had chosen its own circumforaneous path, picking out the ancient stone blocks it had once touched on the exterior of the mountain, so many thousands of cycles ago. Its lament now caressed these blocks in a gentle breeze, when before it had sought to erode them. Now it seemed intent on freeing minute particles from their imprisonment of angled order and returning them to the chaos of nature's whim. If you stood and concentrated, you could just decipher its sweetness of song, swimming through these vacant streets, a reassurance for the vestiges of the mountain. Its many notes coalesced, formed from caressing wood and stone alike, creating whispered chords in a hymn of impending change.

Only a handful of citizens had decided to wait until the morning of the festival before making their pilgrimage to the Square – more for the sake of revelry than reverence. Thus a handful of Deacons patrolled, ensuring any unsavoury characters could not exploit the city's nakedness to loot or defile. Several listened to the wind's lament, some believing they heard voices of the long-since dead, murmured curses levelled at them as they stood watch beneath flickering torches.

Twenty-four junior priestesses walked barefoot from the Citadel, the cue for their departure taken from the return of the ten Grand Cardinals. Their faces were set and emotionless as they stood upon the pinnacle, waiting patiently as the drawbridge lowered. Black leather cups strapped around their heads to blinker them forced their concentration ahead and to their grim future. At the junction beyond the garrison they parted into three equal groups, each group having its own destination, descending into the eternal shadows of the Ravine Quarter below the wind's placation. This mantra was not for them, for they had comfort from a higher power. To the bases of the giant buttresses their feet took them, enjoying the damp, cool flagstones there, the clammy atmosphere hanging in their throats like an indigestible lie. Here was a place of forever-still, save for the shadows cast by torches, of scurrying rodents and the occasional malcontent inhabitant. These turgid structures held no awe for them. Their masterful designs, as intricate as they were ancient, were but part of the landscape on their way to their goals, acceptable landmarks requiring neither respect nor trepidation. A single word spoken from the lead priestess ordered them to halt, a second directed their gaze. In unison they looked up at the magnificent buttresses.

Their true identities had been lost over the millennia, as the overcrowded inhabitants of the Ravine Quarter had built extended accommodations onto them over the cycles. These wood and stone scabs protruded like fungi from the remains of a dead tree, slanted roofs jutting from their sides, protecting a child's room, supported from beneath by iron girders and moss-encrusted scaffolds. In several places, the abutments were joined to one another by teetering annexes, sagging as their zigzagging arched supports struggled with their load. In recent cycles, it had become fashionable for affluent Bohemians to own a second residence at their apex, as only these lofty dwellings became blessed with sufficient daylight to illuminate their pursuits. The buttresses stood silent and motionless now, save for clothes hanging out to dry between balconies, like crucified spirits. Coughing from a few bedridden souls afflicted by the damp air escaped from tiny dwellings, punctuating the coagulating spirals of smoke from bakery ovens, as they interweaved into a murky pall which the wind refused to dissipate. The priestesses watched a visiting neighbour, hurrying along one of the thousands of narrow stone walkways connecting the monstrous supports. Open mouthed, breathless, carrying her bloated tongue ready to burst forth an inundation of overheard tittle-tattle, prouder of these lies than the tatterdemalion child she dragged moaning in her wake. Another word was spoken from the priestess, and they lowered their heads to walk on.

Far below, in the perpetual dark of beginning, they found themselves amid the green coils, their girths three times that of the priestesses' own minarets, meandering toward the distant light, reaching with branches as they struggled to thrust their glorious white petals up into the daylight, along with their esurient, fleshy green leaves for photosynthesis. Their fruit was bountiful, free to the inhabitants there. To these ancient trees the priestesses bowed as they passed beneath them, for it was said Tal Salandor had sown their seeds so very long ago.

They walked on. Their objectives were not considered holy, in need of respect, veneration or protection, so a single Deacon was assigned to patrol each building for the sake of continuity with similar areas of the city. For their employees, they were simply a place of work. For most, their aesthetic shortcomings were outweighed tenfold by their unsophisticated beauty and provided a certain romanticism, a charming reminder, leading back to the ancient and functional. For the priestesses, they held a promise of the beginning of new life.

The Deacon sat in a pool of light with his back to the

wall, reading beneath a lantern. As the eight white-robed priestesses approached him, he stood, placing his book on the ground behind him. The swords were the last objects he expected to appear from beneath their robes. In the back of his mind he imagined they had brought him refreshment, or perhaps news he was being replaced for the day and could enjoy the festivities. Instead, they encircled him, and as he fumbled for his weapon and shouted confused questions they cut his throat, then beheaded him. They had to be certain; there could be no mistakes.

"We're safe for a while," said Sol, breathing hard and wincing from the rope burns which had saved him. Roanne helped him climb out of the entanglement of rope. "All the seals are closed, up to this point," he spluttered.

"Are they locked?"

"Of course, but it's only a matter of time until they reach us. You saw that wheeled tower?"

She nodded.

"We haven't long, Ro. Come on."

Tyn ran at the Constable as he drew his broadsword, thrusting it out in front of him. He knew there was no escape for this intruder. "Hold!" he shouted. But the old man leaped forward, holding his two daggers crossed before him. As the three blades met, they slid against each other with a metal cry. As Tyn expected, the Constable pushed upward, and Tyn brought his knees to his chest, somersaulting over the Constable's head to land behind him. Before the Constable knew what had happened, he felt two feet catch him squarely between his shoulder blades, sending him clattering forward in his clumsy armour to fall against the two advancing Deacons.

The Hathranelzra slashed with the two daggers as he ascended the stairs, the three Deacons waiting there taken by surprise as they stood discussing their orders and polishing their swords. The last thing they expected to see was this madman in their midst. He picked his way through them towards the natural light of a shuttered window on the left-hand wall, his blades severing veins as he ran, his concentration undisrupted by shouted curses and dying calls for assistance or compassion. Following two swift kicks, the shutters splintered into the open, allowing daylight to flood the cramped compartment, picking out the dust particles in the heavy air. Like a snake writhing across sand, the Hathranelzra appeared to glide, and in a single movement he was out of sight as the last wooden splinter hit the floor.

Zoloth stared, breathing hard as the Constable picked himself up with some difficulty and snapped to attention.

"Assemble the men," rasped Zoloth. "Have them join me."

If the Hathranelzra had taken his time, he would have noticed the narrow door set back at the far end of the compartment. Zoloth pulled this door open and stepped into an enclosed box, followed by the Constable. Their weight caused the casket to dip slightly, triggering a bell far above. Slowly the lift carried them up through the tower as the Deacons above pulled on the winch wheel there.

They had expected to see only their Constable as they opened the door. Falling silent, one stepped forward to bow. "Your Holiness, Sol Timmerman has just been seen entering *Oosah*."

"I see. Constable, I require your two best swordsmen beside me, four behind them, followed by six archers. You will come last. The remaining men will wait here, ready until called for. Have the doors opened immediately."

The Constable pointed to his men, issuing orders as Zoloth took up position in front of the heavy doors to his left. He closed his eyes. *'Now it is my time,'* he thought. *'They have nowhere left to run. They are cornered like the wild animals they are.'*

In a dramatic gesture, the Senior Grand Cardinal spread his arms wide, and the doors to the exterior gangway crawled apart. The Trophy dominated the view from the doorway as the walkway swayed almost imperceptibly in the wind. Zoloth stepped into view and the crowd roared. He didn't hear their cheering; his focus was set upon the entranceway. Stopping at the end of the gangway, he waited. The Constable appeared, carrying a flight of four wooden steps. He kneeled down and placed them onto the entranceway, bridging the small drop between the tower's walkway and *Oosah*'s entrance. Zoloth turned to the crowd below. Adrenaline surged though his body, a feeling of omnipotence as he watched the people. A smile creased his face. "Justice!" he shouted, stretching his arms upward, but they could not hear him above their own cheers. "Justice for all of you!" And with that he nodded to the Constable who hurried back to his men.

The armoured figure composed himself, then lifted his head, barking orders, "Follow me and keep to your ranks." They marched forward to stand behind Zoloth, who had pulled out the illuminated pages from beneath his festival robe. Reading the first line in his head, just for memory's sake, for he knew it all by heart, he closed his eyes. He took a step forward, speaking the lines aloud and opening his arms wide. The entrance seal breathed open.

The Hathranelzra stood upon a flagpole jutting from the side of the tower. Above him, another waved a colourful crest through the air, beyond that, the roof. His shoulder bled profusely, soaking his tunic sleeve to the wrist. He hugged the surface of the tower, standing upon one of the narrow straps holding the structure laterally sound. There was only one way left for him. He shuffled around the straps to face *Oosah,* then down onto the tower's gantry to hurry inside, following Zoloth.

The Senior Grand Cardinal came to the first seal and spoke the word. Again, the seal slid open, the auditorium of one hundred seals just a short distance away. He began to walk faster until he came to the three seals at the end of the entrance corridor, his attention fixed upon the centre. *'Behind this seal,'* he thought, *'that's where I'll find Timmerman and his family. Perhaps I'll let them live, to witness the Grand Event and then have them executed, or perhaps I'll have their bodies thrown from the walkway for the people to judge.'*

To Zoloth's surprise the seals slid apart in unison before he had a chance to speak. He stared, blank-faced, bewilderment folding his brow. *'Tal Salandor is with me,'* he decided. He turned to his men. "The Almighty is aware of our presence and is willing to assist our holy cause. The defilers are ahead. Ready yourselves."

The auditorium of one hundred seals was completely silent. The globe turned on its axis, causing the Deacons to stare in awe. They had seen paintings of it, had read descriptions of it, but seeing this gigantic sphere rotating unsupported in mid-air was altogether different. A few broke their ranks and backed away, unseen by the Constable, who was also having great difficulty believing his eyes.

"What is this?" he murmured, lowering his broadsword.

"Search every alcove and once you find them, bring them to me. Constable, attend me."

Regaining his composure, the Constable divided his men into two groups of three swordsmen and three archers, sending each group in opposite directions. They moved off at different speeds, some still staring at the sphere as their comrades hurried ahead, eager to complete this task and return to the natural light outside.

"Your Holiness," said the Constable, forgetting to bow as Zoloth stood before him.

"I want no mistakes now. If you feel you are unable to

conduct your duties with the respect and attention they deserve, then assign a better man."

"I will not disappoint, Your Holiness."

"Then assist your men."

The constable ran off, leaving Zoloth to gaze at the sphere.

They could hear the shouting above them as it echoed down the shaft into the deep levels.

"How many do you think are up there?" asked Roanne.

"Ten, perhaps fifteen. It's hard to tell," said Sol, working on the huge seal set back into an alcove. He struggled to maintain his concentration; among the many wonders were shining jewels set into reflective desks, and paintings, some of which moved on their own to display areas beyond their frameless canvases. The atmosphere, much cooler than outside, caused their breath to billow before them as they spoke.

There were only three seals here. The two at the rear were narrow affairs, situated either side of a row of five paintings. In front of these lay a white desk of shining jewels, inlaid with no discernible order of size or colour to their arrangement. Three bizarre shapes protruded from the floor in front of this desk. They appeared to be chairs of restraint for some poor, disfigured souls, reclined, uncomfortable, their straps of black material finishing in large silver buckles with a red gem set into the centre of each. Roanne shuddered at the sight of these strange objects, and she could only wonder at the torment endured by their occupants, the chairs mutilating their bodies into contorted aberrations.

The Constable returned. "Sol Timmerman is not here, Your Holiness, but we found a Kaltesh rope ladder tied to this handrail around the opposite side of that... that..." He pointed to the sphere, not knowing what to call it. "He must have climbed down."

"So. Timmerman has entered the deep levels." The Senior Grand Cardinal took a step forward and the seal to his right hissed open. He stopped, taken aback by the sudden movement. The hallway beyond the seal was in darkness, and as the air touched his nostrils he detected a stale odour, a smell of decay, of something once alive. He ignored the tiny fragment of fear that pulsed in the back of his mind, fighting it off with reassurances of his calling and continued along the walkway. Each seal opened for him in turn as he approached, his fear replaced by excitement, until he had come full circle and every seal lay open before him. The men stood silent, apprehensive of the dark tunnels encircling them as the Constable barked an order, "Form a perimeter." They readied themselves, gripping their swords tightly as they created a circle around Zoloth.

The Constable bowed. "Your Holiness. The invaders – if they were to attack now my men would not be able to fully protect you." His eyes wandered around the open seals, watching for any sign of movement.

But the Senior Grand Cardinal was intoxicated by the events. *'Recognition from the Almighty! I am blessed. The truth lies beyond one of these seals!'* He gave a gentle smile. "Take solace, Constable," he raised his voice for the Deacons and it echoed around the auditorium. "Tal Salandor protects us. He has shown us our cause is just. This is a message! Sol Timmerman the defiler has not passed through these seals, otherwise only one would have opened." He turned to the Constable. "Show me this Kaltesh ladder. We will return here to explore the wonders Tal Salandor has laid before us after we have Timmerman."

To Sol's surprise the seal began to breathe, slowly at first, causing them to back away. Then, all at once, it parted at the centre, the two halves receding back into their frames. The shouting from the auditorium above had increased, and he knew what this meant. Holding Roanne by the hand to reassure her they ran over the threshold, both rendered speechless by the sight ahead. There, a wide metallic path stretched into the distance. It was perfectly uniform, with tiny illuminations dotted at equal intervals along its edges, throwing light onto its dull, grey, metallic surface.

"What is this place?" asked Roanne, letting go of his hand and slowly turning full-circle, arms stretched wide. "It's beautiful."

Sol looked around in the half-light. In the glow bleeding from the pathway he could make out shapes, leaves, tall stems containing contracted petals, the unmistakable contours of bark. All were strange to him; their odours and shapes unlike any he had ever seen. His eyes found a clump of trees in the distance, their narrow trunks reaching up to leafy branches bearing what appeared to be fruit. High above them, a single dull yellow orb shone. This place appeared to be a garden in the open air, but the temperature was still uncomfortably low. As Sol looked to the far horizon he noticed the otherwise featureless wall opposite held another illuminated seal set into an alcove. He walked forward as Roanne spoke.

"Is this the Garden of Contentment?"

He shook his head and shivered. "Hardly. The Garden of Contentment is limitless, has many terraces, the lowest wild and unordered, a place for our souls to tame before we prove we are worthy to move on to the next." He crouched down and touched the soil. "It's damp. This place has been tended, planned and planted."

"If the soil is still damp..." whispered Roanne.

Sol stood and looked around, rubbing his hands together, removing the soil. "Then it is as we've always feared. *Oosah* is still occupied."

A sound from above caught their attention. They

watched as a huge hexagonal plate, the size of the Timmerman living area, whirred into view high over their heads. Suspended from a track that criss-crossed at right angles, it moved slowly over the expanse of plants and trees. They both stared with curiosity, Roanne gripping her husband's hand tightly. The plate was connected by what appeared to be coiled ropes, and as it halted above the foliage with a click and hiss they took a step backward. At once the plate erupted with a fine rain falling in perfect vertical lines, issuing from thousands of tiny nozzles. The sound filled their ears as the water bounced from branches and ran down leaves to soak into the dark soil. Slowly the dull sphere of light grew a little brighter, making everything around them clearer.

Sol looked at the seal behind them as the plate whirred away. "We must move on, Roanne. If I can break that seal so easily, then I'm sure Zoloth can also."

They hurried forward along the metallic thoroughfare and finally came to a crossroads. Sol turned to the left where the path led to a wall identical to the one straight ahead. They whirled around, seeing the same in the opposite direction. "Which way?" asked Roanne, cupping her hands over her mouth, breathing into them and rubbing them together.

The seal exhaled and Zoloth pointed. "Head Archer," he whispered. The archer stepped forward. He was a young man, tall and confident. "I want him dead." said Zoloth, *"Do I make myself clear?"*

The archer nodded and brought up his bow. There was no wind here to take his arrow off its mark. The conditions were almost perfect, although the target stood a long way off and both the light and temperature could have been higher.

There was no sound to warn him, just the pain following a thud and his hand forced to spasm, his grip on

Roanne lost. The arrow had glanced across his right shoulder, clattering onto the floor ahead. He heard himself scream and saw Roanne turn. "Down!" he shouted through gritted teeth, as he stumbled to the ground holding his wound.

The archer swore under his breath, more for fear of the Senior Grand Cardinal's recriminations than the failed impact of the arrow. He quickly drew another to notch it, but Zoloth was striding forward now in his line of sight, aware victory was just moments away. "Detain him!" he cried, and the Deacons drew their swords, running forward.

Stumbling along the right-hand path, out of sight, Sol quickly ducked between rows of trees, dragging Roanne behind him. They kept running, and when he was satisfied they could not be seen from the path, they crouched down and waited.

Reaching the crossroads Zoloth halted, his Deacons looking along the paths left and right. In the distance they could see tiny rows of lights picking out identical crossroads to that they stood upon, the paths separating trees of entirely different varieties.

"Which way, Your Holiness?" asked the Constable quietly, in awe of the forest surrounding him. The men had lowered their weapons, the tranquillity of the environment easing their concerns. They had broken their ranks, each of them looking around at the expanse of colours.

'Where would he hide?' Zoloth wondered to himself. "Ahead, Constable. We shall take two swordsmen and two archers, the remainder you shall divide equally to explore the left and right paths and their surroundings."

"At once!" As the Constable spoke to his men, Zoloth noticed the plate sliding overhead; again it erupted in a downpour of clear water, a few hundred paces distant.

The sound of rain filled Sol and Roanne's ears as they peered from behind branches, watching the Deacons upon the path. They slowly backed away, creeping deeper into the undergrowth as the cold droplets chilled their skin. Sol stopped, "This is far enough. If we can't see them, they can't see us." Roanne nodded, convinced they were out of sight. "I'll take a look at your wound, but we're out of water." Puddles had formed around them, turning the dark soil into a thick mud and Roanne found several plants with cupped leaves which held some of the rainfall. She caressed one in her hands and carefully sipped. "It's clean," she said, before draining the leaf, then moved onto a second to bathe Sol's arm.

"I've drinking water, if you like?"

They turned, startled by the strangeness standing before them. Sol unsheathed his sword, holding it out in front of him as he took a step in front of Roanne.

The creature continued, "It's just that the water contains plant nutrients, and will upset your stomach if you drink too much of it."

Roanne peered around her husband. It was an odd-looking individual, unlike any she had ever seen. It was dressed entirely in black, its tight-fitting tunic and hose stained with brown mud. Short, black fur covered part of its round head, touched with flecks of grey above its tiny, almost circular ears. What appeared to be lines of age creased its forehead and around its eyes, forming what looked to be a frown. Its large, dark brown eyes stared with concern at the tip of Sol's sword, inches from its neck. It stood a little shorter than Roanne, and as she wiped her mouth with the back of her hand she thought how handsome it must have been in its youth, although as she thought this, she reminded herself its appearance was particularly dissimilar to anything she had ever seen before, but with a strange, undefinable familiarity. She pushed the contradiction aside as she studied it. It held an ornately carved pole of varnished wood at waist height, which ended at the top with a canopy of thin black material, sheltering its head and shoulders from the downpour. Upon its feet were high, black boots with no noticeable straps or fixings. The strangeness took its eyes from the sword and raised its thin eyebrows. "Sol and Roanne Timmerman. At last." Its voice held a croaky authority, neither deep nor high. It sat in the midrange, with a sweet tang as it pronounced the letter r. The mouth finally stretched into a smile, revealing flat, off-white teeth like tiny spades.

"What are you?" whispered Sol, aware the Deacons were just a few hundred paces away. "How do you know our names?"

"Me?" The stranger's expression seemed to flicker between one of disappointment and surprise. It lowered the backsack it carried in its stubby-fingered left hand, and Roanne noticed it was full of red apples. Lifting its head to look at the tip of the sword once more, it spoke again. "I've known about both of you since you were born."

"Answer the question! Who are you?" Sol hissed with impatience, as the rain continued to soak them.

The creature's smile broadened as it placed its free hand upon the wooden pole. At once the rain ceased and the canopy protecting its head and shoulders became limp in equal, segmented folds. The strangeness shook the droplets from the material and the folds tightened upon themselves, sliding into the pole. "I'm very pleased to meet you both," it said, passing the pole to its left hand and placing the tip into the mud by its side. It held out its right hand. "My name's Tal Salandor."

TWENTY-FOUR

THE GARDEN OF DISCONTENTMENT

The Deacons returned, assembling before Zoloth at the crossroads, arriving in twos and threes, muttering to each other about the futility of their search. Some were drenched from the downpour; all were untidy and visibly shaken by what they had found inside the Trophy. They all believed in the truth of the scriptures – there was no doubt about that – but the sheer enormity of scale and the strangeness of the interior had been amplified as they explored. The outside gave them comfort; they could walk away from the Square of Remembrance to return to their loved ones at the end of the day, satisfied they had completed an honourable and loyal day's work. Now they felt trapped in uncertain surroundings, despite the Senior Grand Cardinal's reassurances. *Oosah's* reality was strange indeed.

The Constable could see this on the faces of his men, and part of him understood their fear. But what of the feeling of exploration? Did they not have one shred of inquisitiveness running through their souls? Was it just enough for them to carry out their orders and then return home? He decided the answer was yes.

"Assemble, quickly!" he shouted.

They fell into line, all eyes fixed upon Zoloth, who paced behind the Constable with his arms folded across his chest, muttering to himself. He looked down at his toes jutting from beneath his robes as he walked back and forth as if following an invisible line. He had not expected the cold; nor expected failure. Timmerman and his wife were here – not far from them – of that he was certain.

"Well," began the Constable, looking over his Deacons. "Where are they?" The troop remained silent. Then the tall archer lowered his bow and leant upon it.

"With all due respect, sir, this search is futile. They

could be anywhere. You don't have enough men to find them. It's cold and it's getting dark in here. Perhaps the best idea is to…"

The Constable held up his hand for silence, walking briskly forward, pushing through his men to stand directly in front of the archer. "You're questioning the arrangements of His Holiness? How dare you, Deacon!"

Zoloth walked forward. "Constable, enough, please. Deacon...?" he tilted his head and the Deacon responded.

"Zaf Hentor, Your Holiness. Archer, grade one, Tor district."

"Deacon Hentor," continued Zoloth, looking over his men, "has a valid point. It is decidedly cold, and the light has faded considerably." His eyes met Hentor's, and his mouth slowly transformed into a smile. "I admire candour." He turned and walked back to stand beside the Constable, pausing for a moment before looking across the ranks. "All of you can learn from his example. I think a change of rank is in order for Deacon Hentor, for his honesty, and certainly for slowing the heretic with his arrow. Your sword, if you please, Constable."

The Constable drew his sword and passed it to Zoloth.

"Kneel and bow before me, Deacon."

The Deacons shuffled aside to make space as Zaf Hentor nodded once, removing his helmet to step forward. His hair was sun-bleached with yellow streaks, curling untidily over his ears, and Zoloth realised how young this archer was. He bowed once, before kneeling on one knee in front of the Senior Grand Cardinal.

Zoloth walked slowly forward, raising the sword above his head to bring it down swiftly. The heavy blade cut through Deacon Hentor's skull to his lower jaw, the sheer force of the blow snapping his collarbones and shattering his first and second vertebrae. A red spray cascaded over the Deacons standing either side of him, and Zoloth released the sword as Hentor's arms began writhing about like a grotesque puppet, the dead, nerve-triggered body exhibiting an ugly paroxysm as it fell sideways upon the metallic crossroads. As it lay there kicking, retching, leaking great streams of thick pink and red, a few of the Deacons brought up their last meals, others stepping clear of the expanding mess.

"A demotion," cried Zoloth, stepping over the body into their midst. He turned to look each of them in the eye. "A demotion is a fitting reward for failure." He was furious now, screaming at his troop. "They are but two, *a single man and a Kaltesh woman!*" Tracing a wagging, accusing finger over them he continued. "You are the finest Deacons this city has ever produced. They must be found – it is your holy calling." He lowered his arm and steadied himself, catching his breath. "Rest for a few moments as you contemplate your failures. Look upon your colleague as you do so, and remember, success is rewarded, generously." He looked over them, each avoiding his gaze. "Non-achievement, punished with finality. Then, return to your search, after you have buried that." He turned to look at the Constable who was staring at his dead colleague. "Constable, your sword, I believe?"

He came forward and withdrew his sword with difficulty, wiped it on Hentor's cloak and sheathed it. He had hand-picked the boy from the ranks at the Citadel garrison not too long ago. He had been a talented archer with an uncanny eye and a quick wit. He stared at Zoloth, who looked up at the distant ceiling, watching the dulling yellow globe arc slowly overhead. From the undergrowth, a pair of eyes watched the group as the Deacons sat to rest. The Hathranelzra counted the men before moving slowly off in search of a weapon.

The masses celebrated. This first festival day was traditionally the day of the mummers. Several stages of varying sizes had been erected for the actors to perform their latest interpretations of scripture. Backstage, revisions to a fairly recent libretto were hastily being made. New silhouettes were being cut from paper, sets were being painted, costumes altered. Sol Timmerman's life had become worthy storytelling fare. His latest escapades had both enthralled and horrified the population, and the Senior Grand Cardinal's role in recent events had elevated public opinion of him for better and for worse. The last few days' dramatic events were exceptional material for any playwright to expand upon, and every one of them realised this festival would still be spoken about until and beyond the next.

Rillian stood with the tribe elders, watching as Tulteth approached. She nodded to him and held out her arm. He took it and they walked in silence, Rillian's thoughts dwelling upon Hulneb and Roanne, and the uncertain future for her people they had perhaps contributed to. She regarded her son.

"Tulteth, you heard Zoloth's speech?"

The boy nodded. "I should have gone with them, mother – I could have helped."

She reached down and held the boy's right hand, shaking her head. "It looks as though your brother will not return with Roanne and Sol, even if they both return at all. You know what this means, don't you?"

"I'll be High Celebrant?" said the boy, aware of the answer but wanting to hear the confirmation from his mother.

Rillian closed her eyes. "There are things you must know. Things Mirrimas told me, shortly before he died. I can *help* you. Together, with you as High Celebrant, we can lead the tribe away from all this..." she opened her eyes and looked up to the Trophy then back at him, unsure she could say the word, "this pointless *charade* we've all been caught up in. And, in time, we can take back what is rightfully ours, by force."

The boy's face creased with confusion. "But the Festival *is* our future, Mirrimas always said so – we must maintain peace, surely?"

She shook her head slowly. "No. The Aboenians' beliefs are true, Tulteth. All is as they claim. Your father found proof, and this cannot be revealed, yet."

"But that's not right! I heard father threaten war!" said the boy, without thinking.

Rillian turned, holding him by the shoulders. "When did you hear him say this?" *'Could this be true? Did Mirrimas lie to me, just a few days before his death?'* she wondered to herself.

Tulteth faltered, remembering his Alonetime. He had tracked Mirrimas ascending Mount Goraknath, and, as was the Kaltesh custom, had written an account detailing the events of his Alonetime, to perhaps share with his children upon their return from their own. He liked this idea, to create a collective history from so many differing Alonetime accounts, to be written as one history of the tribe. Yes, this would be his first decree as High Celebrant, his the first entry in the new tribal records.

He remembered the passage he had written:

THE WHITE SHADOW

I followed my father from the desert up into the Goraknath range. The blizzard hid everything until a shape appeared. It was a fur-covered ganapti, clothed with the skin of its own, held down with leather straps and bronze buckles, the fur encrusted with clumps of snow. Upon its back my father rode proudly, black fur around his wide shoulders bristling in the wind. I saw our family's crest fluttering from a pole fixed to the saddle, itself adorned by three dead Gen'hib-Maun. He halted his ganapti as it bellowed, and I thought for a moment I had been seen. I held my breath as I hid beneath the snow in a trench I had dug with my bare hands. He spoke a word which the wind carried away and the ganapti moved off, heading down the pass by the river where the tall trees cast long shadows across the blued snow and the water shone as clear as precious crystal as it coursed over the rocks. My father made camp, and I watched him roast a kill as his ganapti fed. I had come so far, tracked the greatest of the Kaltesh unseen, and now my abilities were equal to his. From this day I knew I could only better him.

While he slept, I walked upstream along the tree line. The following morning I smothered my body with ganapti fat, dressed, then lowered myself into the freezing water. Slowly I made my way back towards his camp before he woke, my body changing the course of the water, altering its voice. The sky was full of colliding clouds. I knew the signs and waited. As the snow fell again I pulled myself slowly from the river, the falling snow burying me as just another white shape at the riverbank. He walked past me, his feet almost touching me as he pulled his nets from the water. He packed several fish in snow and stuffed them in his backsack, then returned to his fire to cook. It was then that my heart sank. He had laid a place for a guest at the other side of the fire.

I thought he had discovered me, that perhaps during my sleep he had tracked me and would soon turn in my direction and shout my name, offering to share his catch with me while he taught me another painful lesson. I was preparing to stand, to reveal myself and apologise, but no. As he lit his pipe, a stranger appeared. My father stood and the visitor dismounted. I was interested now, but more than that, proud he hadn't found me. The stranger was uncomfortable with the cold. He sat close to the fire to warm his hands. He passed my father a letter. My father stood as the man enjoyed his roasted fish.

Suddenly my father screamed, throwing the letter into the fire. The wind carried his words to me. 'I will level Abeona!' he shouted. 'Be prepared, Irrianna! Your city walls will fall, your Citadel will burn and I will have the head of Oen Zoloth upon my standard pole.'

Irrianna left as quickly as he had arrived, obviously fearing for his life. My father called after him. 'Tell Zoloth I will come for him during the next festival. I will reclaim Agasanduku and end this, forever!'

Irrianna disappeared into the snow and my father sat and wept until the fire died. I never knew what was written in that letter, but I did know a war was approaching. A war that would wipe the world clean of our people. We could not stand against the might of Abeona.

I had to know what was written in that letter, so I followed Irrianna for several days. I kept my distance, wondering what to do, how I could find out what was written and who had written it.

We came to a steep, narrow ravine where a new scent found my nostrils to join those of the old man and his ride.

His ganapti halted, aware of the scent also. From the sides of the ravine a pack of snow dogs appeared, starving and determined, their neck frills raised, yellow eyes glowing, forked tongues tasting their prey's scent upon the freezing air. Irrianna's ride reared up as they barked, growled and snarled, throwing the old man to the ground. He lay there screaming in pain as the snow dogs jumped down and ripped the stunned ganapti to pieces. As they fought over their kill, a younger snow dog stalked the old man, fangs bared, head down, advancing slowly, so I hurried forward with my sword drawn, for if he died I would never know the importance of my father's letter. The old man shouted at the beast, struggling to stand, but pain gripped him and he fell unconscious into the snow. The snow dog reared up, jumping at me to strike but I twisted to the side as best I could in the deep snow. The creature nipped my arm, drawing blood. As it prepared to strike again, an arrow found its breast, killing it instantly. The pack turned as it yelped, another arrow finding its mark, then another and another, so very fast. They ran, their long tails sweeping behind them to hide their tracks as Irrianna lay motionless.

"You're safe now, youngster," I heard a voice say.

He was dressed in white, with almost skin-tight hose and jacket, perfectly matching the shade of the snow. His voice was full of authority like my father's, but his accent was not Kaltesh. It was calm, perfectly measured and confident. "Did you hear the crack of bone when Irrianna fell from his mount?" he asked, replacing his dull bow of a silver-coloured metal behind his back. I shook my head, unable to speak, surprised I had not noticed his scent.

"I've followed you for a full day, Tulteth," he told me, producing a backsack and opening it. "You'd best return from wherever you came. Once you've emerged from this ravine, you'll be straying close to Abeonian territory; it lies just five leagues distant."

He examined my arm, cleaning the wound and opening a glass vial containing a clear liquid.

"Drink this," he insisted, as my arm began to throb with pain, my head feeling heavy. "Or the snow dog's poisoned saliva will paralyse you and end your life before this day's end."

I drank the liquid, asked him his name, why he'd followed me, how he knew my name.

"To protect my friend's son," he said, gently resting Irrianna against the carcass of the slain ganapti. I asked if he would tell Mirrimas of our meeting.

He tore Irrianna's hose, revealing a badly bruised and broken leg. "The bone is broken in two places. He'll never walk again without support." he said, taking the standard pole from the saddle and breaking it in two across his knee. He cut the saddle straps with a dagger from his sleeve, strapped the broken standard pole either side of the old man's leg and pulled tightly upon the leather, tying knots.

"To answer your question – one truth life has taught me, long before my escape from the city of fools. If you find yourself beneath a canopy of lies, the light of truth will illuminate you. I will not lie, but will not mention our meeting to Mirrimas." He turned to me, his eyes a

penetrating blue, forceful, set, not to be argued with. "Your account of this meeting is for you to tell as you see fit. But be aware, in time, light illuminates lies, for they are dark and hide in shadows, afraid of exposure." He winked at me with a smile. "The cave I share with your father has many shadows for this day's events to lie hidden."

I asked if he would help me take Irrianna back to Abeona.

"No. There death awaits not only me but my son, and a grandson I've yet to meet. I theorise there's a ninety-eight percent chance of reward awaiting you for an act of charity, helping Irrianna home. Your baggage will no longer be heavy upon departing Abeona, if that's the path you choose." He reached beneath his jacket to produce a strange object of black rock and shining metal, of an intricate design which I'd never before seen, hanging from a silver chain. "Besides, this I must give to your father immediately, to confirm our suspicions. Perhaps I will return to Abeona one day, with your father's support and protection."

"To conquer it together?" I asked. He smiled and stood, replaced the object beneath his jacket then retrieved his arrows from the dead snow dogs. The arrowheads were of the same dull silver as his bow, and I remember thinking how perfectly crafted they were.

"Abeona can only be defeated by intellect, rationality and truth." he answered. The snow began to gently fall again, his clothes bristling like a snow dog's fur as the flakes melted against it. He placed a balaclava over his head and like a ghost amid the falling snow, he became a white shadow, gone as swiftly as he had appeared.

I saw my chance and drew my sword, thrusting and cutting into the dead animals. I set a fire to keep us warm with wood from the old man's saddle bags, then roasted part of the ganapti's flank, untouched by the snow dog's venom. And when the old man woke, we ate. I helped him to his feet and toward Abeona we slowly ventured.

At the approach of our second sunset together, we made camp and I left the old man to collect firewood for the night. Far from camp, where the dead branches lay, three Deacons encircled me with their rides, taunting me, insulting me, one, the senior, climbing down from his saddle to assault me. The others joined him, stripping me of my clothes, tying me to a tree and taking it in turns to hit me once, to see which of them could render me unconscious...

Irrianna's shout stopped them and they turned, bowing, explaining they had followed our tracks from the slain snow dogs, believing I had taken Irrianna prisoner.

Irrianna was furious at their actions and after I explained what had happened, he took the senior Deacon's ride for himself and me, ordering him to strip naked and await his comrades' return. The two remaining Deacons escorted us to Abeona and during that journey, my lies found Irrianna's ears, eager as they were to hear of my heroic acts, killing the snow dogs and tending his injury.

Hidden somewhere in the Goraknath foothills a secret entrance to the Citadel, for Irrianna blindfolded me long before it was reached, lest I learned this secret. With my blindfold removed, I found myself in a seemingly endless, ancient tunnel, with only torches illuminating the way, the drip of water from above and the echoing ganapti's footfalls upon the smooth cobbles finding my ears.

I was fed well in the Citadel and a reward did indeed fill my empty purse as the White Shadow had suggested. I rested for one night, then Irrianna (who could never again walk without the aid of a cane, following his injury) and a squad of Deacons escorted me back into the mountains to continue my Alonetime. We ventured to the tree I was tied to, finding the remains of the Deacon's body, torn and broken, bones scattered and stripped clean. There, Irrianna chose a stout branch, ordering his Deacons to cut it down for him, while he picked one of the Deacon's bones from the snow. "Both for my walking cane," he said with a smile.

I never discovered what was written in that letter, but my time in the Citadel provided me with further, lucrative tasks...

Rillian spoke his name once more. "Tulteth, *tell me what you heard!*" she demanded, gripping his shoulders as tightly as she could.

But he couldn't speak. He was never told what was written in that letter, what proof it held, the details of his mother's lovemaking, her sexual preferences, the real reason for her Alonetime and where it was spent. It was an in-depth character study of Rillian, designed to reduce Mirrimas to a fundamental impulse. An assassin of his entire people, or so the author had intended.

"Tulteth! I saw you!" cried the old woman at last, tears in her eyes. "I finally found the courage and strength. I saw your reflection in the pool as you dreamt. Why Tulteth? *Tell me why you murdered your father?*"

The boy trembled, his eyes wandering around the crowds of revellers, searching for a saviour. Their laughter filled his ears and he closed his eyes, trying to shut them out. Hulneb would understand. Yes, he would support him; his actions and the path he had taken were for the good of the tribe. He wanted to tell his brother and mother everything, how he had helped Irrianna, how he was eventually brought before Zoloth. The Senior Grand Cardinal was a kind and respectful man, and had treated him with equality and respect as they discussed what he had seen at Mirrimas' camp. At the close of their meeting he had offered the boy a future, a role to play in the new order following the inevitable war, for a small favour. He would simply become a messenger – to inform the Senior Grand Cardinal of Kaltesh strategy a few days before their arrival for the festival. Thus empowered, Zoloth promised to end the war swiftly and with as little bloodshed as possible. As he left the Citadel, with a full purse and clear conscience, deep down he knew he could not trust the Abeonian leader. His way was better, just one lie to hide from the light, the blood of just one man on his hands instead of thousands.

Finally he found his voice, and as he heard it he was surprised. It didn't resound with proud authoritative clarity, didn't reduce his mother to the submissive subordinate as his father's sometimes had. It simply wavered in pitch between tears, pathetic and juvenile. He told her of the meeting by the river and Rillian knew exactly what was written in that letter, realising she had almost delivered the Kaltesh to Zoloth. She felt her throat tighten and her heart pound as the events fell into place, as she realised Mirrimas had loved her beyond measure. The boy repeated himself as Rillian held him close.

"Father would have led us all to our deaths. You, me, Hulneb, my friends, Roanne, everyone. I had to stop him, mother. I had to."

Rillian sobbed as she stroked his hair. "War always starts with one man, Tulteth. One man, or one woman."

They followed the entity calling itself Tal Salandor to a clearing. There, a square of dull metal was surrounded on three sides by a low handrail of silver. He waved them forward to stand with him.

"We're being followed," said Sol, stopping. "Men eager to kill us, and perhaps you also." He glanced at Roanne. "If you're *really* Tal Salandor, you would know this, would put a stop to this by declaring your presence to them, and the people outside."

"I'm aware of them. Don't worry, they can't follow us."

"You're expecting us to trust you?" asked Sol, with a little anger.

"I'm expecting nothing. You can either remain here to face whatever transpires, or join me in safety. It's really that simple."

They looked at each other for a brief moment, Roanne nodding. "He's right. You know as well as I, it's only a matter of time before we're found."

They joined the stranger on the dull metal square and as they did, four sides of glass slid up silently from beneath, sealing at their edges with thin silver rods. The square dropped away, taking them beneath the earth through an illuminated shaft.

"There's nothing to fear," it said, noticing their expressions. "This is a simple mode of transport, a little easier on the knees than stairs. Oh, and please excuse my gardening clothes, I had hoped to finish in the arboretum before you arrived. You're a little earlier than I'd have liked. Still, someone will be pleased to see you."

"Opi!" shouted Roanne, holding the stranger's arm. "Our son! Is he alive? Is he okay?"

He smiled up at her. "Don't worry, Roanne. He's almost ready to join you."

Upon hearing Opi's name, Ebe poked his head out from Roanne's backsack, jumped out and scampered over to the stranger. He picked the little creature up, placing him on his shoulder.

"Ebe!" exclaimed Roanne.

"It's okay," said the stranger, passing Ebe an apple from his backsack. "He's fine, aren't you, Ebe?" The little creature chatted back, then bit into the fruit.

Sol was unfazed. "Tal Salandor died tens of thousands of cycles ago," he said, his eyes fixed upon Roanne.

Tal fingered his cane. "Cycles? Oh, by my definition, years. Well, that all depends on how you measure a year, doesn't it, Sol?" He glanced up at the former Cardinal, and his face seemed to adopt an expression of superiority.

"Are you expecting me to believe you are the very same Tal Salandor who led the people to the site of *Oosah* hundreds of generations ago? That's preposterous!"

The stranger grinned. "Preposterous? Well, I didn't

insist they deify me, worship me. Listen, you've believed in my existence your entire life, and after all you've seen – which is not a great deal, I can tell you – you suddenly decide I'm not real, as all three of us stand here talking? Now *that's* preposterous, if you ask me. Where is your misplaced faith now? Has meeting me dissolved it so fast?"

He said nothing.

"Accepted." said Tal Salandor.

The square they stood upon began to slow. As it came to rest, the glass slipped away and the strangeness offered his hand to Roanne. She found herself taking it, glancing at Sol and raising her eyebrows, eagerness to see her son filling her thoughts.

Before them stretched a wide area with a dull white sheen to its walls and ceiling. Opaque shapes sat in rows, their sizes ranging between those of a merchant cart and the largest Kaltesh caravan. Roanne let go of his hand and walked forward to examine the shapes, the stranger watching her closely.

The shapes' material coverings were not unlike the finest silk, but upon closer examination she could not find any trace of a weave, however minute, nor a hem at the edges. "What are these things?" she asked, holding the cool material between her fingers.

"Metal beasts of war," murmured Sol. "The scriptures tell of armies of them ridden by the invaders. They marched across the land killing every living thing in their path." He pulled a covering aside to reveal a long, serpentine neck ending in a huge maw, elongated silver teeth spread wide apart, the jaw of gold. The metal beast sat in silence, six legs tucked beneath it, at rest. It was an apparition, something from a nightmare, an eyeless ghoul of untold evil. Sol imagined these terrible things crawling across the land, feeding with their great jaws. He took a step back and turned quickly to the foreigner. "There. Mechanisms of war. How do you explain them?"

"Oh, they're nothing more than gardening equipment,

actually," replied the stranger lightly, walking to a seal set into the right-hand wall. "I'll change out of these dirty clothes and see if Opi's ready." He turned, biting a thumbnail as the seal breathed open. "Oh, I nearly forgot. Would you like some refreshment? Water, fruit juice, something to eat, perhaps?"

"Water and fruit would be appreciated," said Sol, holding his injured arm.

"Good. Oh, yes, I'll send my helper to tend to that wound for you." The stranger grinned, placed Ebe on the floor and disappeared though the seal which closed behind him with a brief hiss and click.

"This is unbelievable," muttered Sol, anger creasing his face. "He can't be Tal Salandor."

"We're here for Opi, that's all," said Roanne, placing Ebe into her backsack.

Sol nodded, his eyes remaining upon the seal. "I know, but I've several dozen questions for Tal Salandor, or whatever it is, before we leave."

They sat on the floor for some time, then a seal behind them hissed apart. A figure carrying a tray with a bowl of various fruits, a glass jug of clear water and two small goblets hobbled in.

Roanne stared in disbelief as Sol stood and took a few steps forward, unsure of what he saw smiling before him.

The figure placed the tray upon the floor and looked frustrated at their reactions, placing his hands upon his hips. "Well," he sniffed, "at least one of you say you're pleased to see me!"

Roanne ran forward and embraced him. "Hulneb!"

After tears and congratulations the High Celebrant showed them his bandages, as he began his third apple. He continued his story. "And then, after all the poison-induced nightmares, I woke up from my *coma*, I believe it's called, with him, Tal Salandor, or whatever he is, standing over me, telling me I was alright and that I'd be okay to stand in a short while. That's it really, nothing much else to tell." He took another bite.

"I'm so pleased you're alive, Hulneb," said Sol with a broad smile, slapping his shoulder.

"Not as much as I am," he replied, revealing his mouthful.

"Have you seen Opi?" asked Roanne, unsure if she should tell her brother about Tulteth.

"No, just whatever he is and that obscene thing that follows him around from time to time. They argue and it repeats itself a lot."

"What thing?"

"Horrible thing, very tall and ugly. Face like a ganapti's rear end smoking a handful of Farrengrass pipes." He inhaled sharply and whistled between his teeth. "But with skin like that of a shield made for night-fighting," he searched for a better description, forming a shape in the air with both hands. "Like a piece of walking jewellery," he looked at Roanne, "you know, the cheap and dull kind without the jewels, that whores wear."

She shook her head and Sol folded his arms with dissatisfaction, also unable to conjure up an image from the High Celebrant's fanciful description. "So, Hulneb, do you now believe Abeonian dogma, or am I still a myth-maker, bastardising an…"

Hulneb held up a hand for silence. "Enough! You've made your point." He threw the apple core onto the tray and belched. "I'm not sure what to believe, but I'm going to ask whatever he is as many questions as I can think of before we leave, that I guarantee." He passed Sol a curved and elongated something from the fruit bowl. "Here, try this. It's beautiful. Called a brandrana or something."

Sol sniffed it and was about to take a bite as Hulneb snatched it away. "You must remove the skin," he said, demonstrating, "like this."

A seal at the opposite end of the room whispered apart

and a shape stood in the frame.

"Ah, the walking talking jewellery," muttered Hulneb, dropping the half-peeled banana onto the tray.

They turned to see the giant apparition approach. It was bipedal, masculine in outline but at the same time epicene. Its long legs of dull metal led to a narrow, circular waist. Its chest contained four ovals, their tops leading to wide shoulders supporting spindly arms beneath, with six thin fingers at the wrists. But its head was the most disturbing aspect of the figure. It was gaunt, angled, sitting atop a thin neck, its five bright eyes of different sizes protruding from the blank face, the eyes reminding Roanne of her telescope. It had no ears, mouth, nose or hair. Its metal body bore scars, disfiguring scratches in the surface, along with several dents, as if it had been attacked with a sword or spear. In its right hand it carried a case of the same dull material. At first, Sol imagined it was an armoured suit, with a warrior protected inside. Then he realised no one could fit inside such armour; its distorted physiology prohibiting such.

"You are rested and nourished sufficiently. Is that statement correct?" The voice appeared in the air, its timbre delicate, almost feminine, Sol decided, but with a slightly uneven rasp at the edges of each word.

Sol stood. "It is."

The object walked up to him, its neck tipping the head down to regard him with the widest of its elongated eyes.

"You are assigned the primary prefix Sol, secondary designation Cardinal. Is that statement correct?"

"Sol's my name, if that's what you mean."

The eye whirred back and forth a few times.

"You are the paternal progenitor of the juvenile assigned the primary prefix, Opi. Is that statement correct?"

Sol nodded, "I am his father, yes."

"You are injured and require attention. Display your damaged area."

Sol rolled up his sleeve, and the object's arm extended, lowering the case to the floor. The case slowly sprouted legs and elevated itself until it was level with Sol's waist, then split down its centre to reveal a host of curious, polished metal objects and glass vials. The machine cleaned Sol'-s wound with the instruments inside the case then turned to Roanne.

"You are the mate of Sol Timmerman—"

Roanne cut the object off, "Yes, that statement is correct."

The machine passed her a roll of bandages. "Attend your mate. The Captain will be present in five and one half minutes." With that, the case folded back on itself and the object picked it up, its torso rotating towards the seal as it began to walk backward.

"Wait," said Sol. "Who is the Captain? What is his designation?"

The torso rotated again and the object stopped. "Tal Salandor is assigned the secondary designation Captain, of the vessel *Jophiel*."

"And his primary designation?"

"Taliboriyus Evarian Salandor."

"How long is five and one half minutes?"

"The captain will attend you in five minutes. Does that answer your enquiry sufficiently?"

Sol thought for a moment. "It does."

Its eyes whirred, focusing upon him for a few seconds, and Sol was sure he detected a slight nod of its head. Then the seal opened and it was gone.

TWENTY-FIVE

VICTORY FOR THE HOLY CHURCH

The Hathranelzra returned to the crossroads with two stout branches, sharpened into points, their weight balanced with strips of leather from his sandals, the grips formed by a supple climbing plant he had found on the fringes of the Arboretum. They were crude, but as close to Kaltesh hunting spears as he was able to remember. Considering the materials at hand, he decided they would make fine weapons.

The archer's body had been buried beside the path, his bow marking the head of the grave. Tyn watched the Constable distributing his arrows evenly between the remaining five archers, before turning to Zoloth.

"A systematic search is required, Your Holiness. The company are just retreading old ground, which, with all due respect, is understandable, considering they have no landmarks to gauge their positions. We'll sweep the area in a row, at arms' length."

Zoloth looked up at the ceiling. "I have a better idea, Constable. Summon your best archer."

The Constable glanced at the mound of earth beside the path, then bowed, "Your Holiness."

As Tyn watched, the archer released his arrows up into the air, aiming at the rainplate that glided overhead towards a dry section of foliage. The second arrow found its mark, severing the coiled rope, bringing the rainplate to a whirring halt, belching a thin, black liquid from the severed coil.

Zoloth began issuing orders again, and the archer brought out a leather purse containing straw, a rock and flint. In a few moments an arrow was alight. The Deacons collected fallen wood now, hacking at it with their swords and laying it in a line at the edge of the path. Zoloth took the flaming arrow and walked slowly along the line of dry wood, igniting it in several places. The fire caught, drying the few damp trees, billowing black smoke that clung to the ceiling, cutting out what little light they had.

"We wait," said Zoloth, passing the flaming arrow to the Constable. "Have each Deacon light a torch and instruct them to wait on the path at equal distances. When this area is clear, we move on to the next."

But the fire spread quickly though the arboretum, the paths insufficient to halt the lapping flames. Zoloth ordered his troop to retreat to the seal as the billowing smoke descended like storm clouds, catching in their throats. The seal opened for them and they hurried through, back to the compartment of paintings and torture-chairs to wait. The last Deacon stumbled through the alcove with a cry, a crude spear protruding from his back.

"There's a fire in arboretum number four, Seta," said Tal, as the object appeared through a seal. "The irrigation controls are not responding."

Seta stopped by his side, her waist and legs contracting until her head was level with his. "Recommend expulsion of oxyparticles to eliminate further damage to yield."

"Are there any further uninvited guests in that area?"

The machine collected data for a second. "One," she replied. "Not a required organism."

Tal turned to her, taking a deep breath. "How many times must I tell you not to refer to these beings as organisms, or to judge them simply by our requirements? They're intelligent life and deserve respect, just as I give you. How many more are there in total?"

"Twelve. Currently situated in the satellite monitoring station beneath display sphere five, crew section twelve, level twenty."

He eased back into his chair. "You'd better re-route all irrigation panels to put out the blaze, Seta. I'll be along in a while." He stood. "I want to talk to our guests first. I think after all these years they deserve a few explanations, don't you?"

"No," said the machine, her torso rotating as it extended to full height.

"Seta, retrieve the guest in arboretum number four, before you start prepping. Oh, and take a jeep. It'll be quicker. We might be able to save the life of whoever it is."

The machine hesitated, its largest eye receding into its skull. "We have saved too many already. An increased quantity of these organisms aboard *Jophiel* will introduce unpredictable situations with the potential to escalate into a severe risk to you. Your decision has been logged as inappropriate. Your file reference number pertaining to this decision is, B1626855."

"Just do as you're ordered."

"Yes, Captain," she said, and walked away.

Tyn dug a trench near the edge of the path as the flames came closer. The soil was fine, free from stones or grit, and he was sure he could bury himself and sit out the blaze. Then a shape in the distance caught his eye. A magical chariot approached without animals to pull it. Upon it sat a phantom, surely an inhabitant of *Agasanduku*. The vehicle stopped as a gale began sucking at the flames, drawing them toward the far wall.

"My order is to retrieve you," Seta informed him. But the Hathranelzra just stood and stared as the armoured object climbed out of the vehicle. It began to rain, the irrigation panels brought in from the other greenhouses turning the decorticated trees to steaming charcoal.

Tyn backed away, snatching up his spear, holding it back ready to strike as the rain pelted him.

"Can you hear that?" asked the Constable, pressing his ear to the seal. "The water's falling in there again."

Zoloth turned from examining the paintings and walked up to him. The seal separated. "Find them!"

The Deacons were not prepared for the sight that met their eyes as they ran forward; a huge ogre of metal standing amid the smoking ruins of the forest. She turned her torso to face them and they halted.

"A daemon!" shouted one.

"Yes, an invader, in league with a murderer," shouted Zoloth, upon seeing Tyn. "Archers! Bring them down!"

Seta plucked the Hathranelzra from the black mud in less than a second. She held him
around the waist with the long fingers of one hand, spinning her torso around to protect him from the arrows that clattered and splintered against her back as Tyn clubbed her repeatedly with his spear. He struggled to no avail; her grip could not be broken. Her head rotated as she walked away, watching the small creatures stare with bewilderment as she exited the arboretum through a seal.

"Arboretum four locked until report collated by Captain," she said. One of her eyes looked down to Tyn. "Are you damaged?" But the Hathranelzra just stared at her, exhausted.

"If Timmerman is in league with the invaders, then our quest to bring him to justice is futile," said the Constable.

Zoloth breathed hard, cursing under his breath the steady flow of water and his troop's failure. He walked along the path, staring into the remains of the forest. "We've seen but one and forced it to withdraw." He wheeled around. "You're forgetting, scripture tells there was but one left alive following the final battle, mercy for the invaders, to warn others of its kind of our determined strength." He pointed. "That is what we have just seen. It is only one, and will be defeated in close combat. Swords will bring it down. This was achieved before, it can be achieved again, now, today. Belief in the power of the Almighty will give us strength. Follow me. Swordsmen ahead, archers to the rear. We will follow it and kill it."

As Zoloth neared a seal set back from the forest he spoke, and it opened before him.

The stranger calling himself Tal Salandor appeared at the seal. "You're ready?"

They stood.

"Then follow me."

He led them through a network of seals, each compartment holding intricate mechanisms to distract them.

"If we live to a ripe old age we'll still not live long enough to hear explanations for all this," said Hulneb, tilting his head to Sol.

"Perhaps we should ask now," suggested Roanne.

Hulneb nodded. "What is all this?" he asked, raising his voice to the stranger several paces ahead.

"What is all what?" replied Tal, pausing before a seal.

"These things," said Hulneb, pointing toward a desk. "Are these gems your booty, spoils of war perhaps, laid out on display as a reminder of your victories?"

The stranger smiled. "No, I think this is a monitoring station, I forget. Let me see." He walked to a desk and stabbed at a few jewels, followed by a combination of symbols set on raised squares that sprang back as they were depressed. The picture's glass canvas set above the desk immediately burst into life, showing a passageway identical to most of those they had walked through. "Wait, let me try this." He stabbed at another jewel and the picture showed something quite different. There was Seta, surrounded by Zoloth and his Deacons. Tal uttered a foreign word they could not understand as the swords continually battered the tall machine, her torso spinning back and forth to protect an unconscious Tyn. "Seta!" shouted the stranger. "Evade through level seven, route six. I'll lock access behind you."

"Zoloth," muttered Hulneb. "What's he doing here?"

"He's after what you're all after – answers." replied the stranger, moving swiftly to another desk and screen. As they watched, the machine walked away, picking up speed along the corridors. The Deacons followed and Tal altered the display, swiftly flicking between feeds. Finally Seta rounded a corner and came to a junction of three seals, disappearing through the right-hand one before she was seen. The Deacons halted and Zoloth brought up the rear.

The seal behind Hulneb breathed open and Seta appeared. "Report!" ordered Tal.

"Hostile natives, twelve in number. No damage to my systems. Order reference number Y6-2522661783 completed." She held out Tyn. "Basic evaluation follows. Organism is damaged. Mild searing to lung tissue, left shoulder haemorrhaging, mild shock."

"Tend to his wounds immediately."

She walked past them and out through another seal.

"I don't understand how he's managed to reach so far," said Tal, pointing at Zoloth upon the display.

"He's the Senior Grand Cardinal," said Sol, standing beside him. "He's accumulated an incredible amount of knowledge following his elevation, stolen a fair amount also, I would theorise. You should be aware of that, *if* you're Tal Salandor."

"I *am* aware of that," returned the stranger. "But knowledge alone has not enabled him to come this far so quickly. I locked all of the access seals behind Seta, and it's impossible for him to be able to break the security codes so fast." He turned to Sol. "You're skilled – in a way your math is probably better than my own – you were very close to deciphering the code to the arboretum before I instructed Seta to allow you though."

"You *allowed* me?"

He straightened up and motioned toward the screen. "Zoloth would have taken you back into the city. I couldn't allow that. I need you, Sol. I couldn't come to you – one step outside and I'd be a dead man. You had to come to me."

"You're not a man," said Hulneb, standing at Sol's shoulder, "You're... you're a thing," he pointed to the seal ahead. "Like that thing carrying the Hathranelzra."

Tal Salandor smiled up at him. "You're mistaken, Hulneb. I am a man, a human being. You," he looked over all three of them, "all of you *lusus naturae,* on the other hand, are far from human. The Gen'hib-Maun – as you call them – are closer to being human than any of you."

"I've heard enough of this! Where is he?" demanded Sol, stepping forward, drawing his sword for the first time. "Give our son back to us now, whoever, whatever you are!"

Roanne and Hulneb drew their swords, and Tal Salandor took a step backwards.

"Do as he says," warned Hulneb.

The stranger held up his hands. "Relax, all of you. Opi's fine." He tilted his head toward the seal behind him, "He's just a few compartments away. Please, give me a few more moments." He turned back to the display. There, Zoloth's progress was momentarily barred by the seals, then, as he turned to the right, the seal ahead opened. Tal Salandor's face coloured. "It's as if he's following an invisible path leading directly to us! The locking codes are not working!" He spun around, his face contorted in what Roanne decided was panic. "You're going to need those swords for him now, not me," he shouted, pointing behind them. "They're just one compartment away." He stabbed a sequence of symbol squares and headed toward the next seal. "Follow me, quickly!"

They took a couple of paces then turned to the sound behind them. There, just a few feet away, stood Zoloth, bedraggled, his face full of hatred. The archers behind him raised their bows as the group ran toward the open seal, Sol pushing Roanne ahead to follow Hulneb.

The first arrow punctured Sol's right leg, just above the knee. He stumbled, falling into a desk to his right, dropping his sword. As Roanne and Hulneb gained ground across the threshold into the next compartment, the second arrow caught him squarely in the back, splintering a vertebra, glancing from it and entering his left lung. Turning, Roanne screamed, but Hulneb sheathed his sword and held her around the waist with both arms, locking his fingers, pulling her backward as an arrow sped above his head. With difficulty, Sol centred himself toward the seal, but fell to his knees, unable to believe he had come so far, only to be stopped this way. All those cycles of study spent in cold determination and dedication, convinced he would be the one to know the ultimate truth, to unlock *Oosah*'s secrets, to bring enlightenment to his people. Now he realised just one glimpse of his son was all he craved. As the third arrow pierced his throat he knew the questions he had nurtured his entire life were to die along with him without a single answer. He watched as Hulneb dragged Roanne though the seal, dropping her sword, her fingernails tearing at Hulneb's hands, then reaching out to her husband, fingers wide apart, screaming at her brother, kicking back at him with her heels. Hulneb's face became suddenly ashen, streaked with disbelief, and he looked away. Behind them stood Tal Salandor, beyond him, the seal that led to Opi. Finally the seal closed, silencing Roanne's screams as he fell forward and died from the volley of arrows finding his back.

"Sol Timmerman! For crimes against the city of Abeona, for heretical acts towards *Oosah*, attempted murder of His Most Revered and Respected Holiness, the Senior Grand Cardinal, Oen Zoloth, you are sentenced to death," said the Constable, raising his sword.

"Wasted words, Constable," said Zoloth, staring down

at the inert body. "He cannot hear you."

The Constable sheathed his sword. "What of the others?"

Zoloth pushed the body onto its side with his foot, the arrows in its back supporting it. He crouched down, his eyes remaining fixed, staring into the dead eyes of his most successful Cardinal.

"Unimportant. We shall return with more men for them later. For now," he waved his Deacons forward. "Bring him. We shall display my triumph to the people."

Roanne screamed hysterically at the human, "You should have saved him! Could have saved him, if you're who you say you are!" Hulneb held her back as she continued to struggle and Seta came forward to hold her left arm tightly between her fingers. She pushed a needle into Roanne's arm as she continued screaming, fighting her brother. Within seconds she was unconscious in his arms, and he lowered her onto a low bed of black leather before turning, equally enraged. "She's right. Is there *nothing* you could have done, with all this... this... whatever it is?" He pointed to Seta who now tended Tyn's wounds. "With that monstrosity you could have done something! Don't you have any more of them? An army to defend yourself?"

"I wanted to save him as much as you, believe me, Hulneb. I needed him more than you can understand, but there's nothing we could have done. We have no weapons, no army. There's nothing to be done now." He nodded toward Roanne. "Calm her when she wakes, Hulneb." He turned to a monitor and watched Zoloth and his troop leave. "I'll bring her son to her once she's rested. Seta, protect the organisms." With that he turned and walked into the next compartment, leaving Hulneb alone with Seta and Tyn, who was slowly returning to consciousness.

Hulneb signed to Tyn, explaining all that had happened, reassuring him as Seta continued tending to his wounds.

The old man signed back, explaining his confrontation with Zoloth aboard the tower. Hulneb could not believe what the old man was showing him and constantly interrupted, sure he had misunderstood Tyn's signs. Afterwards, he sat alone for a long while, churning over the facts the Hathranelzra had given him, trying to come to terms with his mother's indiscretions. He paced up and down. Why had she betrayed his father, a man who had taken her in and given her more than any Kaltesh could ask for? Why did Mirrimas profane one of their most sacred rites, invading Rillian's Alonetime? He walked back to Tyn and signed once more.

'Sol's dead. I will personally see to Zoloth. I'll not rest until I have his head upon my saddle standard.'

Zoloth's appearance upon the walkway sent a silence across the Square. The crowd could not believe their eyes. He had fulfilled his promise. As he exited the tower and took the stage with his Deacons, they saw the body of Sol Timmerman being carried, a lifeless puppet held upright for all to see. Zoloth muttered a few words to his Constable, ignoring the cries for an explanation from the crowd as they pushed forward for a closer view. The Constable returned a while later with two Deacons carrying a broad pole, sharpened at one end.

Within minutes the body of Sol Timmerman was stripped naked, the Constable throwing his bloodied clothes into the crowd as souvenirs. There his body rested, impaled upon the pole, through his anus to exit from his mouth, the crowd of onlookers both bewildered and shocked by what they saw. Hundreds cheered, others wept and turned away from the horror, while above them, Zoloth stood blessing the crowd.

Rillian saw this. *'Where was Roanne? Was she next? Would Zoloth go that far? Would Hulneb be brought to trial?'* She turned to Tulteth. "Summon everyone remaining at the encampment. I want them all to see this. Hurry!"

Zoloth spoke at last as he stood beside the corpse. "Citizens, guests. Here is the justice I have promised you."

They applauded now, and as the sound died down a single cry was heard. "What of his wife?"

"Yes," shouted others. "Where is his wife?"

"I shall return to *Oosah* and bring her. Tal Salandor will give her to me, and I shall return her to her people. That is my gift to the Kaltesh. No more bloodshed shall mar this festival."

Rillian's heart leapt, and she hurried into the crowd toward Analissa's shared tent.

Tal Salandor sat at his desk, reviewing the events upon a screen. He studied Zoloth intently, leaning forward and rubbing his chin with thumb and forefinger, unable to understand how he had managed to pass through the security seals. Pausing the playback, he skipped back a few frames. There was the answer. As Zoloth bent down to examine Tyn's blood upon the floor, an object had fallen from his robes. He paused the frame and zoomed in, nodding to himself. He began playback as Zoloth picked up the object, absently placing it around his neck. He pressed a jewel set into his desk and sat back.

Seta studied the language of hands with interest.

"Excuse me," she said to Hulneb, and then signed with her metal fingers. "Is that statement correct?"

He nodded. "It is."

Her torso rotated slowly to face Tyn, and she signed again. The old man grinned and signed back to her.

'I have no tongue to speak with, nor ears to hear. This is why I speak with the language of hands.'

She signed back. *'Then we are similar. I have no voice*

of my own, just remembered words, spoken for me from memories within. Like you, my true voice hides inside me, waiting to be heard.' With that, she turned and entered the next compartment as if answering a silent summons.

Tal spun around in his chair as she entered. "Zoloth has part of Kala with him. *Jophiel* recognises her signature isotope, that's how he can come and go as he pleases."

Seta scanned the information on the screen in front of her, and her eyes slowly contracted.

"A serious problem, Captain."

"To say the least. We must retreat."

He stood and walked into the next compartment, holding a small glass plate the size of his hand. Roanne sat up, then huddled into a ball upon the couch, with Hulneb sitting beside her with his arm around her.

"What do you know about this?" Tal asked flatly, thrusting the screen in front of them.

"My pendant," replied Roanne, rubbing her eyes and staring. "It fell from my neck as we climbed *Oosah*."

"This ship is called *Jophiel*," he said with impatience. "How did you come to have this *pendant*?"

"It was a gift from my father, and no, before you ask, I don't know where he found it. What is it?"

"The biggest problem we have." He turned. "We must all leave, right now. Follow me."

"Where are we going?" asked Hulneb, standing.

"As far from the entrance as possible."

The High Celebrant drew his sword. "We'll be going nowhere until we have my nephew."

Tal sighed, unfazed by the High Celebrant's threat, glancing at him over his shoulder. "Kill me and then what? Spend a lifetime working on the seals as you try to find Opi, then a way out? Seta won't help you. You'll starve to death, all of you, Opi included, before you even reach him. And if you do manage to find him *and* your way out of here, what's out there for you? Zoloth and his Deacons?" he took a step forward and pushed Hulneb's sword to the side. "Now put that away and do as I say."

Hulneb glanced at Roanne. She nodded and he sheathed his sword as Seta appeared, carrying a single flower in her right hand. "It is time, Captain."

Beyond four further seals they found themselves in a circular compartment. Placed around the wall were huge alcoves. Roanne noticed similar alcoves set into the shaft stretching high above them.

"Hub twenty-eight," said Tal. "This is where it gets a little difficult for me."

"Difficult?" questioned Hulneb. "How difficult?"

Tal depressed a series of symbol squares set onto a tray protruding beside the seal. A tone sounded before the seal breathed open. Gradually, rows of lights set into the ceiling blinked on, illuminating an enormous area of flat ground. They walked behind Tal as Seta led the way, Tyn bringing up the rear.

The crosses stretched for half a league into the distance and a quarter of a league either side of them, row upon row of tiny white metal markers protruding from the grass, perfectly aligned, all standing at exactly the same height. It was silent here, the lush grass well kept, its tiny shoots standing proud, as if mimicking the crosses standing above them. Hulneb tried to count the markers as Tal walked along the narrow cutting worn by his footsteps.

"What are all these?" asked Roanne.

"Burial markers. To the left, my previous lives," murmured Tal. "To the right, the crew, my family, I believe." He shrugged. "I don't remember their names, didn't know most of them to begin with."

"You bury your dead as the Abeonians do," breathed Hulneb, at last finding a little compassion for the creature that had saved his life.

Roanne stepped in front of Hulneb. "I want to know, Tal, what's so important about my pendant?"

He stopped and turned, angered by her lack of respect, her breaking of the sanctity he had preserved for so long.

He waited for an apology that never came. "Your pendant is part of a being slightly similar to Seta, but also very different in many respects. From what little information I have, after *Jophiel* became stranded here, my father and mother built a machine called Kala. She was sent out to collect mineral samples and conduct experiments to assist in the repair of *Jophiel*. Back then, this planet's atmosphere contained many poisons, the gravity was too severe for our kind to venture outside and the solar radiation fatal. So Kala was conceived using a combination of genetically engineered organic, nanomechanical and plasmonic elements, to overcome these problems." He turned and continued walking in a slow, rhythmic pace, unwilling to explain the intricacies and meanings to Roanne.

"Organic. You mean she was alive?" asked Hulneb, from the rear.

"To a degree, yes. The organic elements forming part of Kala's brain gave her a certain amount of freedom – intuition, judgement – allowing her to make decisions that could not be instilled sufficiently into just a machine. Kala functioned on her own, with little or no assistance from my parents. She came and went as she pleased, working independently. *Jophiel's* core intellect, or brain, if you like, the Mainbrain, is programmed to allow her access at all times."

"Kala could think for herself – is that what you're saying?" asked Roanne.

He took a few more paces and stopped as Seta's torso rotated to pass him the flower she carried. "Thank you, Seta. Yes, Roanne. Kala completed several excursions, then failed to come back home. My mother sent up an orbital observer to–"

"A what?" asked Roanne.

He placed the flower in front of the first cross and mumbled a few words they didn't understand, before turning back to her, having paid his respects. "Do you remember the rotating sphere where you climbed down the rope ladder?" he asked quickly. "The pictures upon that sphere are sent there by an eye positioned high in the sky." They stared blankly back at him. Then as he continued, he became animated, reminding Hulneb of the way Mirrimas would tell his fantastic campfire stories. Tal locked his thumbs together, fanning out his fingers. "Like a bird of prey, remaining completely still in the air, watching. The eye my mother sent into the sky found Kala. She had fallen into a ravine." He thought about what he was telling them, how they stared at him like Opi did when he had told the child a story, realising he needed to simplify his explanations. "Her limbs were smashed. She had tried to pull herself out of the ravine, but she'd died from exhaustion." He turned and walked on, then looked over his shoulder at Roanne after a few paces. "Your father must have found this small component of Kala after all those years, a part which survived the turmoil of this planet's adolescence as it grew to adulthood." His explanation triggered memories he had long since forgotten, of the millions of images he had seen, watching the planet (he had decided, quite unashamedly, to call it *'Salandoria'*) tear itself apart during its development, giving names to the continents that fractured their way into existence, watching them grow and dissipate as the planet's ice caps cooled and warmed, its oceans swell and recede, in cycles. He had measured the seasons, days and years, even going so far as to build a *Salandorian* clock, many thousands of years ago, the timepiece slowly measuring *Salandoria's* eras as his own ship's clock, linked to Earthtime, raced ahead. Now the clock was obsolete, measuring the passage of time of a world altered by the violence of its adolescence, of its settling into the comfort of a stable orbit, its survival of the many mass extinction events that had threatened its life, until it finally found its own diminutive part in the cosmos. He allowed himself a brief smile as he recalled seeing the first signs of life emerge, their evolution accelerating with the assistance of Kala's DNA, until the primitive bipeds appeared. He stopped and turned sharply, his face creased with anger, staring vacantly at Roanne for some time as he pushed the memories aside. "Zoloth now has part of Kala, allowing him full access to *Jophiel*." he said, more for himself as a way of confirmation than communication.

Hulneb hurried ahead a few paces and turned, holding out his hands to stop him. "Why don't you just turn that part of Kala off, like you do with your doorways and your paintings, and stop him?"

Tal Salandor ran his stubby fingers across his head and exhaled. "The component will allow him access only to Kala's point of return, her home, her birthplace, if you like. The area where she performed her experiments, where I studied a lifetime to build Seta." He paused, uncertain he should continue.

Roanne joined her brother, staring into Tal's eyes. "You're terribly concerned about this. Why? What are you not telling us?"

He looked down, clasping his fingers together. "Everything I have is there. It's my home, where I've grown up, where I spent my childhoods. From there I watched everyone die of old age around me. It's a home I've had with Seta for thousands of cycles." He appeared distant as he stared past them to the machine walking ahead, looking out across the field of crosses once more. "I'm all that's left of them, their memories. But even I can't live forever. That's the reason I needed Sol." He stepped forward and took Roanne's hands, causing a shiver to course through her body. "Roanne, I've died an old and lonely man, but Seta gave me life, time and time again, so on and so on over millions of years, reusing my DNA, my ingredients, for want of a better term. She copied me over and over again. The last forty times she completed this procedure, a sickness was found, a disorder, a mutation. I'm basically dying from having cheated death over and over again. Sol would have changed that."

"How?" she asked, her eyes narrowing.

He continued to walk. "Since Opi has been with me, I've come to know him quite well. Would you say he looks like you, or Sol?"

"Well, everyone says he has my eyes and his face is more the shape of Sol's. Why do you ask?"

"These similarities are passed down to him from your coupling, Roanne, through something called genetics. Seta is an expert in these systems. She believes Sol's skill as a Cardinal, all Cardinals in fact, were passed down to them through genetics, that they filtered through, over millions of years, from Kala's dominant core genetic material. Somewhere, hidden in his head, were the answers I needed to open the final seals aboard *Jophiel*. Perhaps, just perhaps, he could have given me the information, the clues, steered me in the right direction I needed to reach the command deck and its systems. Then I could continue on to our destination, whatever – wherever – that was." He glanced over his shoulder then back to them, speaking enthusiastically.

"Sol partly understands, sorry, *understood* the systems aboard this ship. Seta believes his DNA contains remnants from the key personnel whose DNA was included in Kala." He pushed past them and hurried after Seta. "After all, that's where you all come from. Without Kala's accident and the subsequent introduction of her human DNA into this planet's ecological system, none of you would exist."

"Absolute gibberish," said Hulneb, wishing he still had his father's pipe to puff a cloud of smoke to show his disgust.

Tal turned to walk backward, calling after them. "We have to hurry before Zoloth returns. Don't you see, Kala will lead him along this route, to my home, where I left Opi."

"You were going to imprison Sol here to work for you, weren't you?" shouted Roanne. "Holding Opi over his head in case he refused to do as you asked?"

He spun around and walked on, his silence all the reply

she needed.

TWENTY-SIX

THE GRAND EVENT

With the assistance of his Constable, Zoloth hand-picked a squad of Deacons to accompany him, including three of his favourite junior priests, then headed for the tower. At the doorway, he signalled to trumpeters who stood in a line upon the stage, their fanfare heralding the official commencement of festivities. The wind caught their notes, carrying them across the Square, through the streets of Abeona to the grateful ears of the Monitor in his tower. He rang the great bell five times, and this signal swept across the city to the three groups of waiting priestesses. They lifted their heads, removing their hoods to begin their work.

Tal reached the end of the graveyard where a seal led to a circular corridor of glass. High above it hung mechanisms of intricate complexity, and the three guests stared at labyrinthine conduits, cables and pipes connected to great, silent engines suspended from the ceiling on tracks. Far below them the surface was smooth, marked out with geometric shapes and labels, their meanings unclear. Thirty walkways leading from sealed alcoves joined the glass corridor on either side of the gently curved walls. Roanne stopped and pointed. "Those markings, the three symbols, pronounced *Oosah*. They're on the outside of the Trophy also. All Abeonians respect them, using only three letters for their names. What do they mean in your language?"

Tal looked down at the floor. "USA?" he murmured absently. "United Space Administration, perhaps agency, something like that. The group of people who built *Jophiel*, that's all, I believe."

Roanne nodded and tilted her head to the side, none the wiser.

"More gibberish!" exclaimed Hulneb. "Abeonians read backwards! It's ASU, The ancient holy brothers, Alamala and Unamanu, with the snake symbol, esh, between their initials, signifying their family bond; the brothers that built this carcass!" He looked pleadingly between them but they ignored him as Seta stood, reading a screen set above a tray of squares. "Captain, he is almost awake now."

"Excellent. Thank you, Seta." He turned to Roanne. "Shall we?"

He led them along a metal walkway into an expansive compartment where the little boy stirred in a large chair. Roanne began to sob as she neared him, unable to believe her eyes. As she sat next to him he yawned, stretched, and opened his eyes. "Mummy, I fell asleep waiting for dad. I'm sorry. Where is he?"

The little Gen'hib-Maun climbed from Roanne's backsack and sat on the ground, chattering to itself, and Opi looked down. "Ebe!"

Seta passed Tal a glass tablet, and he studied it with a frown.

"You're sure of this," he asked, without looking up.

"I have run the calculations one hundred times. You would like me to check once more. Is that statement correct?"

"No, that won't be necessary." He passed the screen back to Seta, then looked over to Roanne and Opi. "He suffered a minor fall when Seta opened the compartment he was sitting by. He ran, tripped over the railing and fell, breaking his left leg." He ruffled the boy's hair. "He's fine now, the bones have knitted well, just a few superficial bruises here and there. Nothing to worry about."

She ran her fingers through his hair, smoothing it down. "Are you okay? Have they looked after you?"

The little boy nodded. "Seta plays games with me," he looked around. "Mum, where's dad?"

As Roanne's mouth quivered and her tears began to well up again she turned away. Tal picked the boy up. "Your dad's running an errand for me, Opi. We'll all meet up with him later."

Roanne glared as Tal spoke again, maintaining eye contact with her. "Opi, can you and Seta go to your room and bring the toys she has made for you? I think your mother would like to see them, don't you?"

"But I want to–"

"Opi, please?"

Tal passed him to Roanne and she hugged him tightly, before reluctantly letting him go with the machine, Ebe scampering after them. As the doorway sealed behind the trio, she faced the human. "Why did you say that? Why lie to him about Sol?"

"Do you want to see your husband again?"

"Of course, but that's–"

"Then trust me and listen closely, all of you. If you remember, Seta tended Sol's arrow wound. She filed his blood sample away, and checked with him verbally to confirm he was Sol Timmerman. She then checked his DNA with Opi's, to confirm Sol's fatherhood."

"So? What does all this mean?" asked Hulneb, impatiently.

Roanne lowered her head and turned away from them. "You're going to make him again, that's what you're saying. From his blood, like Seta made you, over and over again?"

Tal nodded. "Seta says there's a high percentage it can be done. But Seta and I will need something from you, Roanne. An egg for the incubation process."

She spun around, tears in her eyes. "I'm sick of percentages. You're going to use him, as you'd planned before, aren't you?"

He spoke softly now. "Just for information, nothing more. I can give Opi back his father, you your husband. In return he will have all the information needed to stop

Zoloth, and hopefully reach *Jophiel's* core systems for me."

Hulneb took a deep breath and put his arms around his sister. Tal shot him a look to keep quiet. "It's up to Roanne." He looked back to her. "I'm not going to force you into allowing this."

She was shaken by the prospect, and her voice wavered as she finally spoke. "Will he be the same, the same Sol I've known all this time?"

He nodded. "Identical in appearance. He's a strong individual, he should be fine."

The little boy came running back into the room with Seta hurrying dutifully behind. "Mum, mum! Look at this chariot! Isn't it fantastic?"

She bent down and picked him up. He held a wooden chariot with leather reins harnessing a single wooden ganapti. The animal was jointed with brass pins, and upon the vehicle rode a man carved from wood. He seemed to be shouting with excitement, his left arm held a whip made from twine and his robes flowed behind him as though he was travelling at great speed. His right hand held the shoulder of a young boy who stood on tiptoe, peering over the edge of the chariot. "It's beautiful," she said quietly. She looked down at the human, her face set straight, her mouth tight as though not wanting the words to escape. "You can show this to your father, when he returns from his errand for Tal Salandor."

Hulneb and Tyn played with Opi and his toys, while Seta escorted Roanne into an adjoining compartment. "I'll be as quick as I can, Opi," she said with a reassuring smile. The little boy nodded, engrossed in his games.

"Hulneb, we'll be a short while," said Tal, pointing to a screen. "If you see anyone in this area just press this key, here, and I'll instruct Seta to build a barricade as best she can. I'll be watching as well, but I will be extremely busy."

Hulneb nodded, narrowing his eyes as he looked up from the floor. "Tell me, Tal Salandor, do you have a twin brother?"

He thought for a moment. "You know, I can't remember."

"And where is home?" persisted Hulneb, propping himself up on an elbow.

"I can't remember that either. Still, hopefully in a few measures, all that will change." He walked through the seal and it closed behind him.

Jophiel's passageways widened as Roanne followed Seta, and she found herself in a compartment of low white desks and walls. All manner of curious objects adorned the walls and the pure odour cut into her nostrils, overwhelming, like that of her herb garden.

"Remove your clothing," commanded Seta, while operating a panel of black gems. Roanne did so, reluctantly, wondering why she turned her back on the machine.

Seta's torso spun around as a low hum caused Roanne to take a few steps back. The wall projected a thick glass table with inlaid gold striations running though it. "Lie down," said the machine.

The table was warm to the touch, and as she laid her head back upon it, glass sides grew from the table's edges, another growing from the wall and sealing across the top, encasing her in a glass box. She began to panic and pushed against the sides. "What is this for? What are you doing?"

"Do not alarm yourself. This is the standard procedure. Lie completely still or a sedative will be administered."

But Roanne was screaming now, kicking out at the bottom of the enclosure, slamming her fists into the top and shouting at the machine. Slowly a mist appeared around her head and within seconds she was unconscious, the table sliding back into the wall.

When Tal Salandor appeared a few minutes later, Seta was busy at another panel. She spoke without turning to him, as if deep in concentration. "Complications, Captain."

He could tell by the tone of the sampled words the machine had chosen that the statement was not a question concerning his lateness.

"Why?"

"The organism designated Roanne contains a recently fertilised egg."

"She's pregnant?"

Her head rotated swiftly to face him. "That is what I have just reported. Is that statement incorrect?"

Tal studied several screens in front of the machine.

"The statement is correct," he muttered, staring at a screen showing Roanne's womb. "A recent fertilisation." Looking up to Seta he spoke quickly. "Will this pose a problem?"

"No, although the procedure will take longer than previously reported. This designates complication."

"How much longer, and how complicated?"

"One point four one three hours, maximum extension."

Tal shook his head. "We don't have the luxury of time."

"Removing the complication will result in its termination," Seta's hand moved to a cluster of jewels. "Procedure's estimated time reduced to zero point two eight hours."

"No!" shouted Tal, seizing her hand. "Could the embryo be incubated upon removal, then reintroduced at a later time?"

Her eyes whirred as her hand retracted. "Possibly." She paused, then pressed a combination of gems, changing the overhead display. "Seventy-nine percent chance of the proposed procedure resulting in success."

"Proceed. But, when she wakes up, mention nothing at all to her concerning this. The pregnancy is at such an early stage I doubt if she's aware of her condition." He looked up into the machine's largest eye. "Have this information actively encrypted, highest priority, order identification protocol, Amon and Amonet. You'd better include all medical procedures concerning Opi and Sol too under this title."

Seta turned and walked to the opposite wall. "Order reference number Y6-2522661784 understood and in progress. Encryption protocol status sealed until further instruction from you."

The single storey house, set back from the roadway between two taller, ramshackle houses, appeared blind. Its face held no windows, no beautifications such as carvings or columns either side of the double doors. The gently sloping wooden roof gave the building the character of bullied oppression, as if it was hiding in the shadows created by the buildings on either side, ashamed of its unadorned ugliness. It was an old house, a house for a family from many cycles ago, converted for storage only, it seemed.

The priestesses set about stripping the beheaded Deacon, dumping the naked body into an alley where the shadows and sandrats consumed the sallow corpse. One of the sistren hurriedly changed into his clothes, taking out his key and unlocking the doors to allow them inside. She bowed to them and they returned her respect as she closed and locked the doors behind them to stand guard.

The remaining seven stood in a circle in front of the interior's only feature, a wide stairway spiralling down into a deep stone shaft that was the continuation of the building's exterior walls. They whispered, finalising their plans, ensuring every detail, every action was accounted for and every member of their holy troop knew their responsibilities for the ceremony to follow. They unbuckled their leather blinkers, dropping them to the ground with a clatter, to look up at the wall opposite. There, a collection of giant chains and ropes led up to the ceiling, where a complicated set of pulleys and gears sat motionless in the shadows like roosting metal bats. Upon the walls behind these chains were streaks and smears of rust like guano, the only sound a distant throb of machinery from below.

They hid their swords beneath their robes and took to the stairs, descending the shallow footings with determined caution. Fifty steps later they came to the first landing. Four beacons, somewhat smaller than those placed around the Trophy, illuminated the silence and the stacked supplies. Barrels of ale and wine, bread, smoked meats and fish were piled neatly beneath a beacon, their odours mingling with those of the damp and sweat and the stale, left-over meals from below. As they turned upon the landing to face the next fifty steps, a worker almost ran into them as he hurried home, eager to meet his family and friends in the Square now his shift was at an end. He bowed to them, and as he lifted his head it was cleaved from his shoulders to tumble to the next landing with a diminishing red trail.

The next four landings were traversed without incident, and as they neared their goals, the air became cool and fresh, carrying the flavour of the mountains upon it.

The great cog driving the central shaft turned almost silently before them, the diameter of one hundred Kaltesh caravans, its spokes obscuring the view ahead momentarily as it rotated, its greased teeth interlocking with smaller wheels to its lower right and left hand sides. A larger wheel containing thirty spokes, half-buried by the tunnel floor met it at its base, and another smaller wheel's teeth interlocked with it at the top. These smaller wheels interconnected with hundreds of others, varying in size and speed as they rotated, forming the Grand Complication. The central shaft held cogs and wheels of varying diameters and lengths, diminishing along the tunnel that ran the span of the dam wall, far into the gloomy, lantern-lit distance. Other cogs sat motionless high above the central shaft, positioned on rails, enabling them to be drawn along the shaft and mated with whichever cog or wheel was required. These motionless components were supported by clutch mechanisms, teeth held away from the spinning shaft like jaws eager to close upon a prey. Some solid wheels without spokes held counterbalances of stone strapped with metal, others, giant spheres of rock arranged upon cantilevers of varnished wood. All the wheels were sheathed with precious metals, gold and silver adorned the largest, pinned with bronze studs at equal distances apart. Precious stones were inlaid into the gold along the great cog's spokes, and at the centre sat a giant diamond the size of a cartwheel, its hundreds of thousands of facets creating a stunning display of colours as the cog rotated, refracting light from a dark lantern set above it. All around the Grand Complication the workers swarmed, hanging from metal saddles suspended by chains from the network of rails above, criss-crossing the ceiling, others walking along narrow gantries examining the mechanisms, polishing the metalwork, greasing the grinding teeth as the faceted diamondlight danced across their sweat-soaked bodies.

Directly below the great cog's diamond, elevated high above the floor upon an ornately carved ebony dais, in a chair of solid black marble, sat the Regulator. He watched as the shafts of coloured light refracted, their beams directed onto a flat and featureless wooden board before him. The Regulator's position was a highly sought one, and very few met the exact physical requirements, as his chair was the position's measure. He sat as if it was part of him, his naked body motionless and in complete comfort, as if the marble had been moulded directly from his physique. Watching the patterns of light dance across his reading board, he decided they were not quite correct, and shouted orders to his assistant standing on a gantry several paces away. The figure nodded and turned, issuing orders to the grease-smeared men standing at the wheels and cogs to stand clear.

The priestesses watched with curiosity as a worker made tiny adjustments. This old man took a bronze ring from a hoop on his belt, on which were hung fifty square cups of varying sizes on long curved stems. He found the appropriate cup and scooped what appeared to be silver sand from a trough at his side, slowly levelling the heap with his forefinger. The sand was the purest the priestesses had ever seen, and as the excess fell back into the trough it sparkled in the diamondlight like a trillion falling stars.

The old man covered the cup with the appropriate lid from his belt and hurried along a gantry to a bronze container suspended from black chains. He removed the lid, slowly tipping the platinum sand into the container, ensuring his cup was empty with a single tap from his thumb. He turned and nodded, holding up his hand, "Calibrated!" he shouted.

The dancing light slowed upon the Regulator's board, less urgent now, tranquil and soothing, changing the atmosphere of the subterranean chamber to that following an electrical storm. Following an order from the Regulator's assistant, the workers began to move once more. His voice carried down the passageway, passed on from one worker to the next with clarity and enthusiasm. They took their positions, standing ready, hands on clutch levers, feet on pedals, eyes closed, ears waiting for the command. It came and they moved in unison, their timing as perfect as if they were mechanical themselves. Awaiting cogs were lowered and engaged, mechanisms interlocked, folded together to alter the shadowy shapes in the tunnel for the watching priestesses.

The Regulator allowed himself a smile, another annual calibration completed. Deep below him baffles moved aside, filters engaged, drains flushed, directing the water from the dam to where it was needed most, the Square of Remembrance.

In an identical chamber, following a similar calibration, the refuse water was channelled also, sweeping away the detritus accumulating beneath the Square, pushing it though the tunnels toward the river and the inhabitants of the sea, waiting twenty leagues beyond for their feast. Again, the air in the circulation tunnels was redirected from the city's homes to urge latecomers from their houses, as the cool air drawn from above the river now flowed only from the cooling posts dotted around the Square.

The priestesses removed their robes and set to work. The first worker to fall screamed as the sword severed his right hand at the wrist. He had been foolish, reaching for a large steel spanner to wield against them, and as he clutched his bloody stump the tip of the sword pierced his heart.

All three groups in adjacent tunnels moved fast, ignoring calls for mercy as they slaughtered. No one could be left alive, and before the measure bell tolled they had achieved their task, sweating, gasping for breath, their limbs aching as they stood in triumph.

The Regulator observed them from his elevated throne as they took up their positions at the mechanisms. Their instructor's explanation had been clear, and they found their places fast.

"Don't touch them!" he screamed, leaning from his seat, the shafts of diamondlight streaking across his face.

They engaged gears, altered weights, switching between cogs to increase momentum, forcing the great wheel to quicken. "You can't do this!" screamed the Regulator once again, stepping from his chair, only to find a sword drawn across his throat. As he slumped forward with his head upon his reading board he saw his blood, shining as it reflected the quickening patterns created above. Their colours became clearer somehow, their identities escaping from the kaleidoscopic display as the diamond's speed increased. Now the light was different, it was free. The great wheel began to smoke on its axle, its metal screaming for lubricant. Smaller wheels jumped from their spindle mounts, spitting teeth as if trying to flee. Others embedded themselves into the tunnel walls, some bouncing around, splintering wood, sending dull metal cries to echo along the tunnelway.

Finally the great cog began to die, its spokes throwing off their precious coverings before the hub snapped from the drive shaft, wobbling as it slowed on its spindle, the dancing diamondlight diminishing, until the giant jewel refracted still colours across the smiling faces of the priestesses who stood and watched as Abeona's heart finally stopped.

With identical tasks completed by the two other groups of priestesses in similar locations along the base of the dam, the arteries running from these hearts far beneath the city streets flowed freely with the river's blood, as baffles splintered inside the dam wall. Slowly the water filled the numerous underground passages. Finding the sewage outlet doors closed it rose, flooding with sewage the homes circling the Avoram lake, forcing the water level beneath the Emakurow Bridge to slowly rise. The Fall of Tears spewed black water into the Necropolis of the Holy as mourners paid final respects before hurrying to the Square. Sludge spilled from their ducts, washing away floral tributes, creating a stench around the central island where the sewage gathered. Finally, all stone eyes shattered from the pressure built up behind them, as if in grief, sending their jagged remains to tumble into tombs, statues and mourners alike.

TWENTY-SEVEN

THE SALANDORIAN

"He won't remember his death," reassured Tal. "Those final moments have been removed from his memory. Don't worry, Roanne."

"And your interest in this arrangement?" enquired Hulneb, as she turned away from the image of her husband, suspended before them in a glass sphere of cloudy pink bile.

"We'll know soon," replied Tal, his eyes scanning the information on a screen, a stubby forefinger hovering above a red jewel. "Growth acceleration's complete. Genetic memory maps are ordered, secured and locked." He depressed the jewel. "He'll be awake in a few moments."

As he struggled to capture the fading echoes inside his head, he became vaguely aware that an unfamiliar tone had spoken to him, and as he lost the struggle and his mind and body wandered slowly back towards consciousness, he remembered the words the voice had said. *"Sol Timmerman. For crimes against the city of Abeona, for heretic acts toward Oosah..."* The voice trailed off, and he found himself diminishing into an infinite black void, populated by immeasurable shafts of light. They sped past him in every conceivable direction, as if avoiding him, threatened by his presence. Then they turned in unison, advancing towards him to impact upon his mind. Each brought with it gifts of knowledge, which he accepted with respect and gratitude.

He stood in the void as an arched tunnel appeared, building itself around him from a quantum spin liquid, smooth and seamless, pure white. Behind him, the tunnel infinite. Ahead, a wall of ancient quantum cryptographic algorithms barred the way forward. He shook his head with disappointment, finding the first weak key instantly, with a linear congruential pseudorandom symbol generator. Seams appeared on the wall, creating hexagonal blocks. His generator caused the wall to fall, block by block. A dactylogram glared at him from within the pattern of fallen blocks, unashamedly left within the system by its long-dead author. Sloppy workmanship, he decided. He walked forward, disintegrating every wall thrown up before him in an attempt to prevent his progress, finding potential solutions behind every one, never imagining it would be like this. The unanswered questions that had sat unnourished inside his head like bleached skeletons gradually grew from this sustenance, flesh forming around their bones, enabling them to walk forward and stand at his side. Questions were slowly answered by these long-dead individuals amid their trivialities, a tumultuous tide of voices clamouring for recognition, for respect of their histories. He arranged them, cross-referenced them, pushing the commonplace aside, for he knew from experience the loudest voices demanding to be heard seasoned their half-truths with lies to make them all the more palatable. Encouraging the quiet significant, they came to him gradually, reluctantly, from behind ghostly cupped hands whispering their truths which he cross-referenced, forming a pattern of believability. He knew their names now, and along with them he became aware of possibilities fashioned from shadows of the past...

He emerged from the tunnel, finding himself in a canyon, the sheer walls on either side infinite. Their blocks were mathematical imperfection, and he realised the author to this landscape was different to the last, and of a far, far superior intellect. The author hadn't expected him to come this far, this excavated passage just for him, it seemed. As the quantum wind coursed through the canyon he reached out to touch a block at his side – it was in a neither state, a superposition, existing in non-existence and in-between simultaneously. He smiled as his hand withdrew, recognising the block's three neither states; not, and, xor. He continued through the dusty terrain, leaving footprints in the discarded spoil, the grains of outcome at his feet, the quantum remains from each block's honed birth. Bending down, he scooped up a handful of dust, the key, the Quantum Instruction Language he now called Qil, left by the author. He smiled and nodded, knowing the truth of the past always lay beneath his feet. He threw the dust into the air, retuning it to the now, and as the wind carried it down the canyon, minute particles touched the blocks, establishing their states, removing the neither-in-between to clarify them before him.

He copied a fingerprint and a block dissipated at his feet only to be replaced by another, sliding into place from the rear of the canyon wall. This angered him and he repeated the process, shouting his instructions only to find the blocks replaced one by one as he removed them. He turned, but his companions had abandoned him, as if knowing they could not assist him here, so he quickened his pace, attempting to remove six groups of four adjacent blocks simultaneously. But the blocks simply matched his speed and the walls remained, insurmountable, unassailable. He concentrated, determined to uncover the truth, realising there were two authors to this puzzle now, two artificial minds working against him, responsible for this landscape, dwarfing him, refusing him, imprisoning him.

He threw dust into the air again and again, instantly determining each block's state as viable, as it became replaced by his adversaries, preventing the intelligences from ordering them as super-positioned.

He touched each block, recognising them: granite, sandstone, onyx, basalt, alabaster and marble. A smile touched his lips, his laughter echoing back to him. Perhaps these intelligences had chosen these materials for their common uses – buildings and bridges, walls and ornate edifices – knowing he would recognise them to be impervious to his bare hands. Then again, perhaps he had been given a chance now, as though the intelligences wanted him to prove his superiority. His forefathers were stonemasons, after all...

But here it was impossible to fashion tools, to carve fault lines into the surfaces of these blocks, to drive wooden wedges there, to split them apart with multiple blows from a hammer. He touched a giant granite block, its smooth, quartz-encrusted surface shining back at him, struggling to reflect the determination on his face. At once a memory surged. Information. He knew this block's composition now, knowing every atomic bond the potassium, feldspar, quartz, amphiboles and mica shared in a permanent, covalent handshake of electrons. He altered the negative charge of the electrons contained in the potassium to positive, causing the granite to crumble before him. He touched a block of alabaster, changing the charge of the electrons in the calcium. The blocks crumbled, the walls now uneven, zero-state rubble at his feet, eroded by his interference and the quantum winds.

Staring into an unsettled sky of jagged clouds, they gradually softened and dissipated. Two groups of symbols surrounded him, one of four, the other of seven. Gigantic, uniform, hanging there, encircling him like a cage, barring the way to the file they protected beyond themselves. Eleven in total, each unique, each surrounded by a protective membrane, shimmering like silver to both hide the true shapes hidden beneath and distort his reflection as he stared at their beauty. Now free of the canyon walls, the quantum winds carried the Qil dust into the void. He watched it spiral and curl, reaching out. A reward for his achievements, he decided, as he allowed himself a congratulatory smile. Was each symbol a puzzle in itself? Were they entire words, or keys to eleven differing realms or dimensions? Perhaps each unlocked a separate historical epoch – an almost endlessly detailed encyclopedic chronicle for him to sift through to find an answer. Or a story of an individual's entire life, and once he found its minute interaction with the symbol life next to it, it contributed to build that reality, until each of the ten interactions, correctly identified as significant, coalesced, unmasking the identity of truth the symbols protected? This seemed to be a remnant of a past instruction, a memory fragment from another, searching for an answer. But how would he unlock the first life, how would he recognise one solitary interaction as pertinent, thus unlocking the next symbol life? Although the computations came easily for him, this enigma was almost impossible to solve – twelve meaningful social interactions on average per day, a memory told him, over the average of twenty-eight thousand days for the average life. A one in three hundred and thirty six thousand chance to be correct for one life. Ten total interactions between the symbols giving him three million three hundred and sixty thousand correct choices to be made. That, only if the interactions were sequential. However, if all the lives interacted with each other... he ignored the possibility.

Or were they clues, deceptions, the ultimate truths he yearned for? They were too far distant to touch, for him to establish their states, so he simply watched as the Qil finally embraced them. Their membranes decayed to reveal the true shapes there, each more complex than he could imagine, extraordinary and without comparison to each other, until they revealed there were only six different characters. Something nagged at his mind, tenuous, subtle, distracting, growing.

One by one he translated them, cutting through their deceptive veneers, stripping them of their camouflage. Ultimately, they exposed themselves as simple letters.

They read: ***Blue Bullets***.

Now it was simply the task of discovering what lay within, but at once the sky filled with red as the void vanished, and there he saw his son. His eyes stared back at him, afraid, invaded, pleading for assistance beneath a mask made from many probing tendrils, removing and providing information, he somehow knew. His cheeks were caressed by clouds, and his forehead carried the outline of a figure, its face obscured by a bright light. And above, a multitude of stars – far more than Sol had ever seen on a clear summer evening sky.

As he reached out to touch his son's face, he awoke.

A light flickered above him, stinging his eyes. As he blinked and tried to shield them, he felt the restraints tugging at his wrists, the warmth surrounding him and the sweetness of the liquid within him.

"Sol?"

The voice was different from the angry words spoken in his head moments ago. Fragile, uncertain, nervousness colouring the monosyllable it had verbalised. *'Yes, that is your name,'* he heard a voice say.

"Parthenogenesis complete. Illumination intensity appears excessive for comfortable retinal reception," something said. "Reducing to point seven." The clipped words sounded counterfeit as the light slowly diminished.

"Give him time." A different accent now, strong, forced from a foreign tongue, undoubtedly, but somehow all too familiar. It had a flavour of nervousness too, but with something else, the sharp edge of anticipation, perhaps? Was this a voice he had heard from a half-forgotten dream? He tried to recapture it, to reference it, but could not.

He felt something warm on his body, his skin pulled outward as invasive objects retracted from it. As his nerve endings fired with the pain instructions, he became aware of the discomfort. Something was coiled around his penis, another something in his anus. A growing warmth surrounded him, enabling him to flex his muscles slightly in his foetal position.

"His nose looks bigger." The voice contained a humorous edge, waiting for a response that never came.

"Well, it does to me," it said, as if responding to a silent objection.

"There," said the fragile voice, a little more confident now, its vagueness evaporating as it continued with the sentence, "look, he's moving his fingers."

He slowly opened his eyes to an opaque film, his body immersed in a viscous liquid.

Tal depressed the red jewel and the liquid fell away beneath him, sucked from the receptacle he was curled up in to disappear into an opening between his feet. He began to choke, coughing up the fluid from his lungs and stomach. The voices sounded simultaneously in panic, louder, confused now, only to be placated by another: a forgery, he decided.

"Stage two complete, Captain. Applying final stage protocols, removing restraints."

A burst of nanotricity caused his chest to spasm, and at once he began to breathe unassisted for the first time. A silence followed as he coughed up the last of the pinkness, itself coloured by streaks of blood and sticky dark clots. He wiped them away with trembling fingers, the pain in his chest subsiding as he took a breath, and after some time, he spoke.

"Where is he?"

Thirty reactions were shocked by that timbre. He heard their voices all reject his as their own, thirty shafts of speeding light jostling for control inside his head as he creased his face, closing his eyes tightly. They calmed, slowed into hovering glowing points, and as his brain displayed its supremacy to these guest personalities they all acquiesced, except one. He ignored her, and she reluctantly joined the others.

The sphere surrounding him opened in eight segments like the petals of a flower, and he raised his head to the lights above.

"Keep still, Sol," said Tal. "Seta will dissolve your corneal protectors. Keep your head back and keep looking up. That's it, eyes open."

The machine depressed a jewel, "Procedure initiated." A small, circular plate slid over his head, issuing a cleansing solution as it clicked into position. He blinked rapidly as the hot shower ran down his cheeks to wash away the incubating gel. The machine depressed a second jewel, the invasive tubes connected to his anus and penis uncoupling, receding into the floor. Gradually his eyes began to focus as the deluge ceased and the steam cleared, bringing the blurred shapes standing before him into sharp relief. He stood up slowly, wiping the tears from his eyes. "Where is he?" he murmured, holding his head in his hands. "The Master of Clouds?" He looked down at Roanne, her eyes studying him closely, hands held over her mouth. Gradually she pulled them away, revealing her expression. It reminded him of the first time they had met, a mountain of silent questions shone in those eyes, an uncertain inquisitiveness. An attraction? He smiled back at her confidently. "Opi?"

Hulneb nodded slowly, almost imperceptibly, allowing himself a broad grin as his friend stood before him. He realised how he had misjudged his brother-by-union, and how much he had missed his company in such a short period of time. The Abeonian had finally proved himself, through his actions, to be worthy of his sister's affections, and his respect.

Roanne stepped forward to embrace him as her tears welled up, the numbness he had felt now transformed into aches covering his body at every joint, firing back to his brain as he in turn slowly bent down to hold her, placing his arms around her thin shoulders, resting his cheek next to hers. "What happened?" he whispered, kissing her lightly on the forehead. "I was talking with Tal, the next moment there was darkness all around me. It was so absolute."

Tal nodded to Seta, who passed Sol some folded clothes. He took them with some embarrassment, realising he was naked, hastily pulling them on. They were similar to Tal's, except their colour was a light blue, matching his eye colour perfectly.

"You blacked out," said Roanne, as Tal lowered the semi-sphere to floor level. "The arrow that grazed your arm contained a poison, much like the one I pulled from Hulneb's leg." She turned to Tal, who walked from his desk to support her deception.

"Seta had no problem neutralizing it. It was a drug designed to render you unconscious, so the small amount that entered your system took effect much later. Sorry about the tubes, but we had to make sure all liquids and solids were drained from you. We didn't want you to have another blackout from residual poison, of which there is none, I should reassure you."

He wasn't listening. "Where's Opi?" he persisted, looking at Roanne as he dressed.

"He's in the next compartment. You remember how Hulneb looked, after he was hit by an arrow? I didn't want him to see you like that." She glanced at Tal with a half-smile. "I've told him you've been on an errand for Tal, if he asks."

Sol Timmerman took a deep breath and stretched, swallowing hard, tilting his head from side to side, shaking his limbs rapidly for a moment, as if to remove a light summer rain. "Seta," he said with a thickness to his voice Roanne had never heard before, "accept primary overrule command, priority one. Password A-a, definition, Mesopotamian sun goddess."

The machine's eyes retracted in unison, then protruded to their full extent with a sharp click. She straightened, her arms falling to her sides as her torso rotated to bring her to a stance much like a Deacon standing at attention, her eyes finally retracting and extending separately in a rhythmic sequence. "Primary overrule command accepted, Captain," she said, as her eyes became still. "Awaiting order reference number A1."

As he stepped from the semi-sphere he spoke again. "Security protocols follow, A-a to Zurvan, latter definition, Persian god of temporal time and fate. Override all compartmental locks from Kala's umbilical route." He glanced at Tal with a grin. "Zurvan, quite fitting really, don't you think, Tally?" He sat on the floor and pulled on his shoes.

"You can't do that!" said Tal, stepping in front of him. "*I'm* Captain of *Jophiel*."

"I'm sorry," said Sol, standing to face the human. He brushed down his trousers then looked around him, refusing to make eye contact. "Your services have been noted and will be rewarded, your grievances given the proper attention, when I have the time. For now, as your father used to tell you when you were a child, '*Tally, my boy, as you grow older you'll find time is something which we have very little left of.*' And you, Taliboriyus," he patted him on the shoulders once with both hands, "are very, very, very old." He pushed past the human, leaving him agape, entering the next compartment, followed by Roanne, Hulneb and Tyn. Tal followed, taking a few rapid steps to catch up with them, wondering if the slight lilt to Sol's voice had in fact been an exact representation of his father's tone.

The little boy looked up from playing with his chariot. "Dad!" He ran over and Sol knelt down to him for an embrace. "I'm so sorry I'm late, Opi, but I've been so busy. It won't happen again, I promise." He squeezed the little boy tightly and closed his eyes, his right hand cupping the back of his head as he kissed him on the cheek.

"Can we go home now?" asked Opi, looking up as Roanne joined them.

"Soon, perhaps," said Sol, holding the lad by the shoulders. "First of all there are a few things I must do." He pulled away and held his son's hands, staring at him with that mock seriousness he was so used to. "Will you promise to stay with your mother and tell her about all the adventures you've had here, until I return?"

He nodded but looked disappointed. "You will come back soon, dad, won't you?"

Sol smiled. "I'll be back before you know it." He stood and turned. "Everyone, please listen closely. This is what we're going to do."

TWENTY-EIGHT

DESTINATIONS

The Trophy seemed to shiver from bow to stern as a narrow strip of bright white energy slowly rippled across its nanosurface. A handful of praying individuals saw the object shimmer and pointed, gasps of disbelief sweeping over the crowd. Power was restored to its subsidiary systems after five and a half million years. *Jophiel* was awake.

Zoloth heard the shouts from below and halted upon the stage, turning to see what the crowd was pointing at. The undulation coursed across the surface, a raised, blue-white light now, passing by the entranceway with a low hum. He shielded his eyes from the sun as the streak continued. *'What is this?'* he thought to himself, uncertainty colouring his cheeks. *'Is this another sign from the Almighty?'* He had no other explanation.

"This is the sign I have awaited!" he cried. "A portent heralding the ultimate triumph!"

"No, Hulneb. Tal's right," said Sol, irritably. "I can't override the signal *Jophiel* picks up from Roanne's pendant, and that's the end of it. It's not a signal, as such, more of a signature, like a wax seal used on an envelope to identify the sender." He stabbed at a few jewels, then folded his arms, leaning back against the desk.

"Well," began Hulneb, "we can't defeat all Zoloth's Deacons. What shall we do?"

Sol gave a smirk. "Seta, please examine Hulneb's sword." He nodded with raised eyebrows to the High Celebrant, who reluctantly obliged by passing the heavy blade to the machine.

"A compositional analysis please, Seta, linked to

Jophiel's Mainbrain."

"Order A2 logged and processing, Captain," she replied.

Tal stepped in front of Sol. "What are you doing?"

Sol placed a hand on Tal's arm and spoke quietly. "Taliboriyus, you've achieved remarkable things here. You're a credit to your parents and their work. Now, let me finish this as you intended me to."

"Compositional analysis complete, Captain. Report to follow–"

"Report unnecessary," said Sol, cutting off the machine, his eyes remaining upon Tal. "Can you duplicate this weapon?"

"Yes, Captain."

"Do so, scaled specifically for yourself to wield. Maximise blade strength, durability and efficiency." He turned his head momentarily to her. "Come to think of it, you had better construct two."

"No!" shouted Tal, slamming his clenched fist down onto the desk beside Sol. "Seta will *not* harm a human being! It goes against her primary programming."

Sol's eyes narrowed on him. "Seta, organism designated with the prefix, Hulneb. Is he human?"

"No," said the machine, "organism composition from genetic markers establish–"

"Report unnecessary. Binary replies only from now on unless otherwise instructed. Interface with *Jophiel's* Mainbrain. Are the organisms that recently visited crew section twelve, display sphere five, arboretum four, human?"

"No."

Tal turned away to take a seat as Sol continued. "You said it yourself, Tal. We're not human. Seta, escort Roanne, Opi, Hulneb and Tyn to machine shop three." He began typing on a tray of symbols. "I'm relaying instructions for you to the central *i*con there. Please comply with them."

He wheeled around to face Roanne. "I need to talk with

Tal in private. Please follow Seta. We'll meet back here when she has completed her tasks. Do exactly as she says and everything will be fine."

"Wait!" said Hulneb, taking him by the arm to lead him a few paces away from the group, turning his back to them.

"Seta, wait," barked Sol.

Hulneb spoke quietly into his ear. "We don't have to fight, we could escape. I have brethren in the deep desert, food, water, animals. Leave this all behind, Sol. You've been given a second chance with your family, come with us and don't throw it all away and be used by Tal."

Sol put his hands on his hips, staring hard into Hulneb's pleading eyes. "I owe him a life debt, my friend. You know that."

"But if he can copy you, how do you know he's not done all this before – with a previous Sol Timmerman, Cardinal, whatever. Or even a Kaltesh theologian. We did have them many hundreds of cycles ago, believe it or not. I believe what he's looking for can't be found. You can't trust – I don't trust him!"

The ideas circulated in Sol's head. Perhaps Hulneb was right – perhaps all this had happened before, perhaps an individual had found themselves in an identical situation to the one he now found himself in. He remembered waking up in his prayer tower, just a few days ago, then again, less than a measure ago. How long would the human wait for his answers, and what steps had he taken previously, attempting to unearth them? Had he gone to such lengths to copy the entire population of Abeona, to rebuild and repopulate after a natural calamity, or a slaughter at the hands of a Kaltesh tribe, centuries ago? The idea seemed as plausible as it was perverse.

"Hulneb, I need to know as much as Tal. We'll get through this. I theorise we have a..."

"Don't throw everything away for someone else's desires, Sol."

"I'm sorry my friend, I must see this through. Seta,

resume."

As the machine headed for the seal with Hulneb and Tyn following, Roanne came over to him with Opi holding her hand. "Are you sure you know what you're doing?"

He nodded. "More than ever. I'm doing everything I can to protect us. This will all soon be over." He kissed her on the forehead and winked at his son, and as they left and the seal closed behind them he joined Tal Salandor, sitting on the floor in front of him as the human slumped into a chair.

"What are the routes, seal ciphers and security defence system override codes to the command deck, Sol?"

"I haven't remembered anything concerning those yet. It's coming back to me in little unconnected segments that I can't, at this time, order or make any sense of on their own." He rubbed his temples with his forefingers and closed his eyes. "I can feel them in my head, crew members, trying to surface and make my voice their own. I know so much now, thanks to you, but it may take longer than you've anticipated." His hands found his trouser pockets and he thrust them inside instinctively. "A-a to Zurvan has unlocked compartmental seals leading off Kala's umbilical route, but as for the central shaft's code leading to the forward quarter, and from there the command deck," he shrugged, "for now, your guess is just as good as mine. Active quantum cryptography's not the easiest nut to crack. As soon as there's time I'll enter all the data manually to an Information Console for your perusal."

For a moment, Tal decided he appeared quite human. His mannerisms had altered slightly and his overall air was one of relaxed confidence. He pushed the conflicting thought aside. "I don't have time to spend staring at an *i*con, I need–"

"Then perhaps you should have asked for Ana Zoloth's assistance, when Seta met her, rather than mine?"

Tal shook his head. "That was an accident, nothing more. Seta was custodian of *Jophiel* while I was between lives. She found herself opening a seal in the auditorium of one hundred, as you call it, to find Ana standing there taking notes. They spoke for a while. She's a very gifted individual, and was remarkably calm, considering their meeting. Seta quickly showed her a connecting compartment, an arboretum, and gave her the code to an insignificant seal to encourage her work."

Sol nodded. "So you didn't ask for her help?"

Tal sighed. "Oh, I might have done, had I been alive, but that wasn't the time, as I said. There were others not too far behind her," he chuckled, "you being one of them." Leaning forward he clasped his hands together, his expression suddenly changing. "*Why* did you take command from me?" he demanded, narrowing his eyes upon his re-creation.

"I'm more qualified than you are now, you've seen to that. I know you don't have very long to live. Your cathodic protection, or CTP, has failed at base level. You have a rather aggressive and inoperable nanocancer, so my taking command was the only rational choice."

Tal rotated the chair away from him as he spoke. "Seta can give me life again, then I'll–"

Sol stood, seizing the armrests of Tal's chair, pulling it around to face him. Suddenly the great Tal Salandor took on the appearance of a trapped animal, manoeuvred into a corner, fearful and unpredictable. "You'll do what?" demanded Sol, comfortable with his anabiosis at last. "Wait another forty or so of your years to hear Seta inform you your Charge Transfer Protection has failed, and that yet again you have oxidative damage to your base guanine? You can't combat the natural order at that level, even with DNA-based nanostructures. Your nanocancer has gone too far, it's now a part of you that's indistinguishable from your original self, that even this technology cannot separate or destroy without killing you in the process. Besides, what would a further copy give you, another six months, another short lifetime of compacted memories? Then what? The same news for you aged thirty, twenty, until your head is so full of jumbled memories you'll go insane trying to remember how to comb your hair?"

Tal shuffled uncomfortably in his seat, staring up with anger, an emotion he had not felt for another living being for as many lifetimes as he could remember.

"I have to ask you – were you responsible for Yan Arramosa's murder – and Opi's subsequent abduction?"

Tal shook his head rapidly. "Neither. It was Opi's own inquisitiveness that caused him to fall in your absence. Seta retrieved him. Then later I saw an opportunity, knowing you'd pour all your efforts into finding him, perhaps, in the process, pulling to the surface the information I need."

Sol relaxed a little, finding sympathy for the human, whilst at the same time unable to shake off a feeling of pity for him.

"I know how much you wanted to complete your calling single-handedly, Taliboriyus, and I understand and respect your dedication, but it can't be done, not now. It's time to take a step back and ask yourself whether it's enough for you for *Jophiel* to complete her journey, or if you just want the glory of being alive to witness and be part of the occasion, when she finally does?"

The human spoke quietly. "It's not about plaudits, Sol."

"Then tell me! What is it all about?" asked Sol, slapping his palms down hard on the chair's armrests.

Tal sat forward, shouting in Sol's face. "Reaching the end! Discovering her destination, what her true purpose is! Why my parents were heading there, where they came from. This is all that concerns me! Surely you can empathise with that?"

Sol turned his back on the human. "Truth. So it's the destination, not the journey." He thought for a moment, giving him time to come to terms with all Tal had revealed. He held out his right arm and pulled back his sleeve. At last he spoke, quietly now, with a calm authority he had not exhibited for a very long time. "You missed a very important detail in your haste to deceive me." He shot Tal a smile of smug superiority, his voice mocking in a slow rhythm. "My wedding bangle's missing. Not only that, I'm aware of what you've done to me. I know you've *tinkered,* for want of a better term, with my DNA. *Jophiel's* Mainbrain wasn't designed to defend itself against my combined and enhanced intellect. You're forgetting, I was once a Cardinal." He pulled down his sleeve and paused for a moment. "You used Ebe to speak to me during my sleep, to plant ideas and messages to aid my work – the *Hathranelzra* message, for example, so I'd realise Tyn's importance once I found out his Kaltesh identity, so I'd then discover and release Ana, so she could assist me in unlocking further seals for you."

The human looked down, nodding slowly. "I had no choice, Sol. Time's against me, as you said. Using Ebe wasn't the most successful method of communication, I'll admit." He looked up with a little embarrassment as he continued. "Ana's 'medication' in the asylum prohibited her from fully understanding the majority of the messages I sent via the little creature, speaking to her from the cavity of her cell wall. It was then Seta's idea to send the Gen'hib-Maun out to you, to befriend Opi. He has been my eyes and ears outside *Jophiel*. After Seta performed a complicated implant into Ebe's brain, it was almost as if I could walk Abeona's streets and alleyways myself."

Sol shook his head. "I may have been your second choice to assist you, but my subconscious spent a great deal of time reading the data in *Jophiel's* recent memory cache-tunnel before I was reborn. In fact, it was that easy, she practically invited me in. However, there were three files I could not enter. The first two, Amon and Amonet, I theorise she only allowed me to read the data she wanted me to know, but underestimated my appetite as much as my ability. She thought I'd be so caught up with absorbing the information that I'd awaken before I reached the three locked strands. Would you care to tell me what they contain?"

Tal gave a half-smile and broke Sol's penetrating stare. "You know half the contents of one of the strands, so I'll tell you its remainder. Yes, I intended to keep your death and subsequent rebirth from you, as I couldn't predict what impact that fact would have had on your sanity – I couldn't have you running around like an idiot trying to convince everyone you've been resurrected by some magical power. But, you've proved this concern is unwarranted, so I'll go so far as to tell you your DNA has a modification which I should have spliced into my very first copy. I've removed your ageing gene, Sol. You'll remain the age you are now, forever. You won't suffer from CTP failure as I have." He folded his arms and eased back into the chair. "In addition, Seta now has a non-removable command line to protect you, as well as myself. She'll be your guardian now. Furthermore, as you've already chosen your vocation, *Captain*, you're now *Jophiel*'s guardian in return, and will see she completes the journey she was designed for." His face remained emotionless. "You have all the information you need in your head, it'll just take time to unlock and understand it all. The other storage strand?" He shook his head and chuckled, self-assured, reflecting Sol's earlier smugness. "Well, that's up to you to discover and all in good time." He lifted his head defiantly. "A little recreation for you, in the tradition of your past life's vocation, Cardinal Timmerman."

Sol leapt at the human, grasping his throat and locking his fingers together around the back of his neck. He lifted him slowly from his seat as Tal held onto his forearms. "What is hidden in the *Blue Bullets* file? The primary encryption level's saturated with layers of protection."

Tal clawed at Sol's grip, "I don't know *what* you're talking about! I've *never* heard that phrase before!" he croaked. "Seta and the Mainbrain write and share essential files for maintaining *Jophiel* – you probably wandered down the wrong path in your obsession for the truth! It's likely nothing more than an automated air-purifying protocol."

Sol's grip tightened. "I don't believe you. What is a bullet?"

"I've told you, I don't know! Ask Seta!" He relaxed his grip on Sol's forearms. "Go on!" he grunted, refusing to resist. "Go on, do it. Don't you think I've wanted to finally die? So many, many lifetimes, years upon years stuck here with all these unanswered questions? Do you realise how many times I've ended my own life, sometimes as soon as Seta rebirthed me? I'll invite my inevitable final death with open arms!"

Sol dropped him back to his seat and pointed to the seal. "What if I simply choose to walk out of here, leaving you alone with your obsessions?"

The human coughed and massaged his throat. "An Abeonian such as you, with all of what you've seen so far?" He managed a mocking smile, curling the left side of his mouth. "You said it yourself, you're still as much a Theorist as you were before, eager for the truth of *Jophiel's* purpose, her destination as well as her origin, *your* origin. You won't walk away that easily after my death."

Sol's thoughts tumbled through his head. He listened to the voices and their advice. There was no denying it. It was true there were still secrets to be known; the human had planned everything perfectly, and he was right, of course. There would be no difference for him if he survived his confrontation with the Senior Grand Cardinal. His normal life would return with the sense of purpose it had always had, and with just the knowledge he had now the quality of life for all Abeonians and Kaltesh would be improved immeasurably. If Zoloth could be defeated, then the 'new order' he spoke of could no doubt rise, with Hulneb's assistance, as Kaltesh dogma had been disproved, up to a point. He smiled to himself, wondering if the High Celebrant still expected to find a hollow shell at the very heart of *Jophiel*, with the remains of Kaltesh twin brothers waiting to be discovered there. He stood and fingered several jewels, remembering his promise to Roanne to leave Abeona. Compromises would have to be made. Finally, after a long pause, he spoke. "Tal, I'll not let you die. You have given me life, admittedly, for your own reasons as much as for my sake and my family's, but, I promise you now you will see *Jophiel's* destination. I'll store your memories, find a way to relocate them into an organism similar to that you now are. I will strive for this, to the best of my ability, and give you back your life, your six months, a month before we arrive at *Jophiel's* destination." He watched the human's face change. It was as though a veil of depression had lifted from him. His thin-lipped mouth began to move, but no sound came. His eyes filled up with tears and he quickly wiped them away.

"You would do this? I have your word?"

Sol nodded. "My word. I'll not have Opi see me as a failure, as I saw my father, dead before reaching his goal, unable to maintain his honour."

"Thank you, Sol Timmerman – or *Captain*, I should I say." Tal breathed deeply as he lowered his head. "You can tell me about your father, later, when less pressing circumstances demand our attention."

"Agreed," said Sol, keying a jewel, wondering if they had met. "Now, best we keep an eye on the outside, and the progress of our mutual friend Zoloth."

A small sphere appeared in the centre of the room and Sol made a few adjustments. The image flattened out, a rectangular picture now encompassing the entire city. "That's better," Sol muttered. "Now," his fingers danced across the desk, the image before them concentrating on the Square and the thousands of revellers surrounding *Jophiel*. He increased the magnification. "There doesn't seem to be a strong Deacon presence outside. Perhaps Zoloth only intends to employ the forces he has with him." Again he altered the picture, scrolling across the city towards the Holy Citadel and the garrison building. It was deserted. Then a fluctuation upon the screen caught his attention. He studied the narrow columns of numbers running down the left hand side of the image.

Tal sat forward in his seat. "That's strange," he muttered.

Sol glanced to him. "0.75 degree angle variance, is that what you mean?"

Tal nodded as Sol turned back to the image focused upon the dam, bringing the resolution up to its maximum. As they watched, a section of three ancient blocks spewed into the air to fall onto the little dwellings nestling at the base of the dam wall. A deluge followed, miniscule in comparison to the scale of the dam, but a torrent forceful enough to eradicate the buildings before it. The Grand Event had begun.

This infant river coursed through the streets and alleyways of the Ravine Quarter, eradicating everything before it. Where the wind had softened the edges of the buildings over countless centuries, the water now disintegrated them, their remains jagged projectiles carried amid and pushed ahead of the outburst to shatter everything in their path.

The priestess dressed in the Deacon's uniform heard the deafening sound a league distant, and walked from the double doors she was protecting to stare at the buttresses straddling high above. To her left one began to shake, the dust and detritus falling in clouds, walkways splintering from their fragile mounts, annexes bowed, falling vertically, disintegrating into matchwood and rubble with still half a league to fall. The buttress to its right copied the motion of its neighbour, as its connection to the wall fractured. It fell in a complete section, its component blocks moving away from each other slowly during the long descent. The dwellings built upon it and jutting out from the buttress's crest tipped the delicate balance, momentum carrying the homes into the abyss as it cracked at its base like a child's toppling skittle. People fell now, the angle of their homes flinging them from shuttered windows, affording them a vista they would never share with others. Their bodies danced amid the dust clouds, unseen from below, catching brief glimpses of the horror around them as the buttress fell into the sunlight.

High in the Goraknath range, the stranger Tulteth called *The White Shadow* heard the sharp crack and subsequent rumbling as the dam burst, echoing all around him as he waited for Mirrimas. It was an unnatural, disturbing, angry sound. He hurried from his tent to the treeline at the cliff edge, affording himself a wide view of Abeona far below. He had spent many occasions throughout differing seasons observing the city of his birth from this vantage point, studying the inhabitants through his duoscope, hoping their magnification would perhaps one day afford him a glimpse of his son. He hastily pulled the alien device he and Mirrimas had discovered from his backsack. Staring through their view-plate in disbelief, the horrific destruction unfolding far below caused his hands to shake. A single tear fell into the snow. He was too late to wipe it away, too concentrated on the scenes of unstoppable devastation the device presented to him. He let the duoscope fall to his chest, hanging by its strap, pushed back momentarily by the fabric of his tunic. His tear, with just a miniscule amount of salt, eroded the fine, dusty snow, burrowing a perfect shaft before dissipating, dying amid the dilution of an overwhelming environment. He looked down, having felt the tear leave his skin, wiping its trail from his cheek, and there he noticed this tiny imperfection in the snow between his feet, realising his fellow Abeonians were now also as miniscule as his dead tear, vulnerable, naked and at the mercy of their ancestors' ancient theological prison. He turned away, realising he was helpless once more, again too late to save those he loved so very much.

In the Square of Remembrance water poured from cooling posts and children gathered around them to play barefoot, running into the spouts, jumping in the puddles, laughing and shouting together. Their parents all agreed, *'Another gift from Zoloth,'* as the sunlight caught particles of water deflected from the children's hands like silver shards of splintering glass.

Zoloth watched a thousand tiny rainbows fill the Square around the cooling posts as the Ravine Quarter drowned, many leagues distant. The signal had arrived at last.

"Constable. It is time. We enter *Oosah* once more to finish this." He marched toward the tower as the people thanked him for the refreshing water. Nodding to them he hurried into the chassis, leaving the children's laughter behind him.

Sol stared in disbelief as the most ancient part of Abeona was consumed by the advancing waves. He flicked the display back and forth, watching the Pinnacle of Judgement crumble into the boneyard as the water lapped around its stubby base like rabid dogs encircling their prey perched in a tree. The water gradually rose as it reached the opposite wall some seventy leagues distant. He remembered the tireless labour of the city's workers, and how Zoloth had told him he was ensuring the walls were safe to be dismantled. Now that lie became clear. The walls had been reinforced to hold the water, ensuring Abeona would drown inside the walls constructed to protect it.

The ten Grand Cardinals gathered upon the dining room balcony, watching their city die. The river had already flooded the Citadel's basements, forcing the few priests still in residence up from their quarters to raise the alarm. Foundations began to soak up the water, turning them into nothing more than damp sand. Now the front of the Citadel collapsed in a deafening crash, its face shearing off and tumbling into the onslaught, leaving its interior network of passageways and accommodations exposed to the sun, obscene, like viscera open from a quartered corpse. These intricate networks crumbled one by one, as if politely waiting their turn. Whole rows of stairways with priests still scrambling up them, adjoining rooms containing the Citadel's staff collapsing upon one another to allow others to fill the ugly void they had created. Now there was nothing more than a slope of tumbling rubble leading into the rising waters, with fragments of gold, silver, collected treasures, works of art of untold beauty and other precious belongings glinting in the sunshine for recognition amid the dust and spray.

The wind gratefully carried this reverberation to the Square of Remembrance, and there, on the fringes of the crowd, a few heads turned. There was nothing to see, so they turned back to enjoy the water cooling the soles of their feet.

Sol was pacing now as Tal took control of the satellite's eye, awestruck by the scenes transmitted to *Jophiel* from geosynchronous orbit. "There's nothing we can do, Sol," he said quietly, his voice touched with sadness. "Within an hour the entire city will be levelled." He watched as the dam wall between the two fallen buttresses burst, wishing a great hand would appear from the sky to hold the water back. He brought another rectangle into view. "Zoloth and his Deacons have just boarded. There's not much time."

Sol glanced at Abeona's higher being sitting in his little chair. Old, weak, pathetic, unable to halt the demise of the city built to worship him and his vessel. He forced his eyes back to the rectangle. The river behind the dam became choppy, the agitated little waves impatient to join the others ahead of them, surging into Abeona like freed prisoners eager for retribution. Fishing piers were pulled from their moorings to course over the waterfall chasm in a slow and silent fall, turning end over end to vanish beneath the mist. He watched Zoloth marching purposefully forward.

"There's always something that can be done," said Sol, refusing to believe all was lost for his people and his city. "Stop the feeds, Tal."

The rectangles vanished and Sol crouched down to him. "Tell me, the cargo lifters comprising levels zero through twelve. Are they still operational?"

"Cargo lifters? I don't know. I suppose so, I–"

Behind them the seal breathed open and in came Seta and the others. She carried a huge broadsword in each hand, the blades as wide as Sol's chest, their lengths twice that of Hulneb's height. She had replaced her outer casing, which now shimmered with myriad colours, and Sol noticed they were all dressed in identical garments, carrying balaclavas of the same material as Seta now wore. The substance fitted without a visible seam from toe to fingertips, the padding outlined with exaggerated muscles, giving Hulneb a slightly inflated, comical appearance. Hulneb noticed Sol's amusement. "I suppose this was your idea, was it?" he growled in his deepest tone, dropping his balaclava onto a desk. "What's all this for anyway? It's a little early for a victory carnival, isn't it?"

"Pass me your broadsword," said Sol. He obliged and Sol swung it in a wide arc against Hulneb's chest. The garment leaped out at the blade in a perfect mirrored copy, halting the otherwise fatal attack. Sol passed the sword back as Hulneb watched his garment recede.

"Your armour's constructed from a similar material to that of *Jophiel's* hull, although considerably thinner. It should protect you from swords and arrows alike when you face Zoloth and his Deacons."

"And what will you be doing?" asked Roanne.

He recalled the display feeds and explained the situation.

"My mother!" exclaimed Roanne.

"And the tribe," added Hulneb.

"Tal and I are going outside. We'll do what we can. Seta, intercept hostile organisms in arboretum four and protect organisms prefixed Roanne, Hulneb and Tyn, priority order A3. Transferring obedience protocol to organism prefixed Roanne, until cancelled by myself. Re-route all Mainbrain systems to..." he glanced at a panel above his head, "aircar, recess twelve, berth twenty-one." He looked at his son and held out his hands, "Opi, pick up Ebe. You're coming with me. Everyone," he glanced at each of them in turn, "when all this is over, we'll meet back here." Opi and Roanne walked over to him and he held her hands as he continued. "Stay safe. Seta will do as you say from now on. Choose your words carefully." He looked over to Hulneb and Tyn.

"I'll look after her," said Hulneb, picking up his balaclava and placing it over his head.

Roanne kissed her husband. "Don't forget your promise. When this is over we're leaving this city, or what's left of it. All three of us."

He held her face tenderly with both hands. "Don't worry," he said, smiling. "I remember."

TWENTY-NINE

DEPARTURES

The shining alloy aircar, just wider than a two-man velocipede, was a dream come true for father and son alike. Under more pleasant circumstances, Sol would have taken the little craft along the banks of the river Breede, tracing its meandering flow up to the Goraknath range and beyond. Tal, on the other hand, felt sick climbing into the vehicle.

"There's hardly enough room for all of us," he complained, standing up. "I'd better stay behind and coordinate things from here."

"No," said Sol, adjusting Opi's harness. "I need the people to see you." He reached up and pulled Tal back into his seat. "Stay in the front with me."

Tal turned. "But the atmosphere out there will kill me if you lower the canopy."

Sol depressed a series of jewels and a tray appeared at his right, and a curved staff directly in front of him. He seized the staff with both hands, fingered a few jewels set into the tray and turned to his reluctant passenger. "Now we both know *that's* a lie. Your past incarnations have ventured outside many a time, otherwise we wouldn't be aware of you, would we?" He read information from a screen, depressed a jewel and the canopy slid over them from behind to form a perfectly clear half-teardrop above them.

"That was one mistake I'll never forget! Chased back into *Jophiel* by grunting savages throwing sticks and stones at me."

Sol's hands swept across the control surface as the craft began to hum a low note. "I know of another – one occasion when you went outside to retrieve your previous self, who chose not to be buried with your others when he died. The origin of Kaltesh beliefs?"

"Possibly," sighed Tal. "That was the last time Seta copied me in advance of my death, so I could pass on information to my successor. Strange and uncomfortable conversations, all of them – although playing chess was enjoyable."

Sol buckled his harness and turned to the human with a grin. "How time changes truth to legends. Hold on tightly, both of you."

Above them came the sound of servos whining. Opi stared through the canopy to the ceiling as it parted, revealing the blue sky touched with wispy white clouds. Then the aircar lurched into the air with a sharp jolt, to hover just a few feet from the floor.

"Sorry," said Sol, frowning at the readouts before him as he rapidly depressed jewels. "This may take a minute or so. Bear with me."

"Are you sure you're capable of controlling this thing," asked Tal, gripping his knees.

"It's been a very long time, so someone's memory tells me," replied Sol. "Ah, this one." He depressed a jewel and the craft responded by rising slowly into the open air, free of *Jophiel's* embrace, and as the sun caught the little object it shone like a daylight star above its parent vessel. Slowly they rose higher than any Abeonian had ever ventured, to look down upon the city sprawl.

"Dad, this is fantastic!" cried Opi, looking at the ground. He turned. "Can you make it go faster?"

"All in good time, son," said Sol. "Tal, look. The river Breede has breached the dam completely." He pointed, and raised his voice above the melodic hum of the craft's displacement generator. "We don't have much time." He brought the aircar's bow around to face west, toward the former site of the Holy Citadel, and as they watched, the wall of water advanced through the city, eroding forever the majestic towers, toppling them in their dozens just as a farmer harvests his crop with a single sweep of his scythe.

Sol brought the aircar closer to the ground to hang

motionless in the air, low enough for the crowd to see its occupants. The people shouted, pointing at the craft as it halted.

Depressing a jewel, he unbuckled his harness as the canopy slid back. He stood. "People of Abeona, Kaltesh guests! Listen to me! You have been betrayed!" he shouted, pointing north. "The dam wall is no more. Abeona drowns as I speak!"

They all fell silent, mummers jumped from their stages to gawp at the figure shouting from this low silver and blue cloud, musicians dropped their instruments, food was left to burn upon spits and in pots as the throng turned their attention skyward, gathering beneath the little craft.

"It's Sol Timmerman!" someone said, and their words travelled faster than the approaching tide.

"Listen!" shouted Sol, holding up his hands for silence. "Tal Salandor comes before you now," he unbuckled the human's harness and pulled him to his feet with one hand, causing the aircar to wobble along its central axis. The crowd gasped at the sight of this strange creature, some turning to run back to their homes, a horror such as this and a ghost floating in the air too much for them to behold.

"You're dead! Zoloth saw to your heretical acts!" someone shouted, pointing toward the stage.

"Yes! A demon! Creatures of evil!" cried another voice in the distance.

"No! Don't you see?" someone called. "He's returned from the Pinnacle of Judgement! His words were true! Zoloth lied to us!"

"Listen to me! Abeona is doomed!" shouted Sol. Sitting back into his seat he relayed a series of instructions to *Jophiel's* Mainbrain. A deep roar filled the air beneath the enormous vessel as seven perfectly flat sections of its underside dropped slowly to the ground, unsupported. He stood once more and pointed, bringing the aircar in a low arc to face its mother vessel. "We can save you all, but you must listen to me and hurry to the platforms." He knew it was a lie, that even the immense capacity of *Jophiel*'s cargo holds could not accommodate the entire population of the city.

But now stones flew through the air as fear gripped the crowd, and he turned to watch as small pockets of revellers made their way to the cargo platforms, gazing in amazement at the wonders high up inside the vessel's hull. Now the angry mob began perching upon each others' shoulders, standing upon stalls and carts to improve their range, trying to bring this apparition to the ground. Sol sat back down and closed the canopy, forcing the aircar high above the crowd. He looked to his left; the flood was just ten, perhaps twelve leagues away, the wall of water sweeping toward the Square the entire width of the city. It had engulfed the Archbishops' residences along the eastern bank of the river Faro, and was making its way steadily up the incline toward Gal Bapsi Park and the priests' finishing colleges. Now arrows creased the air around the aircar as a troop of Deacons had decided to take it upon themselves to rid their city of this stupidity, while others drew their swords to prevent the revellers from climbing aboard the cargo platforms and defiling *Oosah*.

"You've done all you can, Sol," said Tal, placing a hand on his shoulder. "We'd be better off caring for those who care for us."

The metallic creature stood motionless amid the ruined forest, its giant swords shining in the half-light, reflecting the faces of the trio crouching behind it.

Hulneb's expression was set and determined. He would settle for nothing less than Zoloth's head, and had promised himself he would never again clean his blade after it had served that purpose. He would ask Seta to construct him a new sword, and mount this bloodied blade upon the wall of his caravan, if he ever resided in one again.

Roanne's thoughts were far removed from the moment, dwelling on Sol's (the *real* Sol, she had decided) death. She couldn't remove the image of his last expression from her mind's eye; he knew it was the end for him, the look of utter bewilderment and pain. Every time she blinked he was there, staring back at her, a mountain of silent apologies shining in his eyes.

This new Sol, this copy, was different somehow, and as she caught her reflection in Seta's blade she understood. He was a reflection of the man she had married, an imperfect distortion. Opi had his father, which for her was the most important aspect of her agreeing to the human's proposal. As for the husband she knew returning to her, that remained to be seen. She clutched the bow Tyn had retrieved from the grave of the archer, and a handful of crude arrows the three of them had hastily prepared, unsure of her future with Sol Timmerman, or whoever he actually was.

Tyn sharpened his spears. Seta had tried to stop him from collecting more, but Roanne had told her to leave him alone. Now they each carried a fairly crude Kaltesh hunting spear at their sides. The Hathranelzra ignored his reflection, his eyes fixed upon the seal in the far distance.

"This is all quite amusing, really," said Hulneb, turning to them. "For thousands of cycles the Abeonians and Kaltesh have feared war. Now, we find ourselves participants in a small battle to protect everything we hold dear, *inside* whatever this is, of all places!"

Tyn signed without looking at him, then gripped his spear with both hands.

"I know it's called *Jophiel*," said Hulneb, "but that still doesn't explain what it's for."

"They're here," said Roanne.

The Deacons wore metal armour, clattering as they marched, echoing through the arboretum in a cacophony of discordant rhythm and tone, their open faceplates revealing grim determination.

Zoloth stood at the fore, his eyes fixed upon Seta.

"The demon has returned!" he cried. "Aim for its eyes and blind it!"

The front row of ten Deacons simultaneously dropped to their knees, swords held before them. Behind these, ten archers lined up, notching their arrows. The Constable gave the order and the flurry was released.

Seta stepped forward into the onslaught, bringing the huge broadsword in her right hand up to protect her eyes.

"Seta!" shouted Roanne. "The archers are the greatest threat. Attack them first!"

Responding instantly, she brought the blade in her left hand from around her back in a bizarre dislocated movement as her wrist and elbow rotated.

Zoloth ordered his men forward. "The Kaltesh. Swordsmen, kill them!"

Ten more swordsmen appeared from behind the archers and joined the ten in front, screaming as they ran with some difficulty through the shallow black mud of the arboretum.

Bringing her broadsword around in a wide arc, Seta brought the second blade protecting her eyes up, then down though the stillness to meet the first attacker. The Deacon was highly trained, and he noticed with some relief the attack whistling through the air toward his right shoulder was a standard manoeuvre, the angle easily deflected to the ground to provide him with the advantage of an upward thrust. He did not, however, account for the sheer power of the attack, his sword shattering a moment before Seta's blade sliced through him from shoulder to shoulder, to halt embedded halfway though the Deacon he stood beside. Her blow from the opposite side effected similar carnage, and as she raised her arms and twisted her blades to remove the dangling corpses, Hulneb and Tyn ran forward, launching their spears, Hulneb screaming an ancient Kaltesh battle chant above the cries of the dying. Their crude weapons were effective, killing one Deacon and knocking a second from his feet.

Stumbling backward with dread, the archers retreated as Seta turned her torso toward them, eyes measuring distance, feet crushing spent arrows, swords raised above her head as she advanced.

Zoloth ran, aware Hulneb's eyes were fixed firmly upon him.

As the archers notched their arrows once more, Roanne let off her first, missing Zoloth by a considerable distance. Hulneb changed his grip and Tyn copied, holding the heavy spear horizontally before him as Hulneb launched himself at the archers, sweeping his spear across them, realising only a moment stood between his attack and their arrows' release. The spear caught the lower halves of four bows, their arrows spending harmlessly into the damp, black earth. Picking himself up, he pulled out his broadsword, smashing an unguarded nose with the pommel, kicking an armoured chest with his foot, finding a gap between breastplate and armpit with the tip. As it cleaved an arm at the elbow, he dropped the heavy weapon to retrieve two short-swords from the ground.

Now the remaining swordsmen encircled Seta as her scythe-like movements killed another two of their comrades. The sounds of deflected impacts, like those heard in the metal craftsman's quarter, filled the arboretum, iron upon unknown alloy as Seta's body bristled in defence of her intricate mechanical organs. Her blades rotated again, severing one, two, three, seven heads in a deft circular assault of devastating strength and speed. Then as she steadied herself an arrow found its mark, her largest eye shattering from the impact, the arrowhead embedded in the cylindrical socket.

Tyn's spear had the opposite effect to Hulneb's upon his row of archers, their arrows arcing through the air as his spear impacted above the archers' grips. Stepping back as they fumbled for their swords, he continued his attack, releasing a dagger into an eye, wincing from the wound in his shoulder.

Zoloth stood with his Constable, watching Seta curiously. "We cannot defend ourselves against such a horror," said the Constable. "We need its commander." He pointed, "There!"

Roanne shouted orders again, having taken cover behind a blackened tree stump. "Seta! Join Hulneb and Tyn! Protect them!" The machine surged forward, cleaving as she went, leaving a trail of mutilated bodies as Hulneb brandished the short-swords against three archers. Realising they were no match for his skill and determination, they glanced between him and their weapons as they walked backwards, fumbling to notch their arrows as he advanced, his blades shimmering as they twisted in unison through the air before him. Distracted by the metallic beast striding forward, they dropped their bows and pulled out their swords, readying themselves for close combat. One delay was all Hulneb needed and now he faced two advancing on him. Noticing Seta from the corner of his eye, the High Celebrant ducked back, tumbling head over heels beneath her as the Deacons ran forward, their determination to end Hulneb's life their undoing. They ran onto Seta's blades and she casually removed the skewered bodies with her free hands as the remaining archers released another volley. Arrows rattled against her cranium once more, finding her second largest eye, forcing her to stop in mid-swing. As Hulneb watched from the mud behind her, the momentum of her heavy blades caused her to stumble as she overcompensated with her counterbalance stabiliser. The machine faltered, taking ungainly steps as she attempted to right herself, but it was no use and she came crashing down upon three archers, ramming their bodies into the earth.

A cry echoed across the battlefield as the machine lay prone. "Slaughter it!" screamed the Constable, running forward with his broadsword held above his head. His troops regrouped, running to him as she tried to stand, battering the back of her head with their swords as Hulneb and Tyn retreated to Roanne.

"We can't help her!" said Hulneb breathlessly, wiping the sweat from his eyes. "What can we do, Roanne?" But her attention was now on Zoloth as he procured two shortswords from the ground and began to advance on them. He turned for a moment to his troops who now swarmed over the fallen machine. "Constable!"

The armoured figure spun round, panting from his exertions, striding over to join Zoloth as he removed his festival mask. His face was set with hatred and Hulneb signed to Tyn, who simply nodded back his agreement.

"Now this is going to be a pleasure," said Hulneb, taking deep breaths. Then, as he watched his adversary, his expression changed. Zoloth walked confidently forward, brandishing the swords expertly, performing thrusts and parries with both weapons against invisible opponents in a display of considerable skill.

Roanne glanced down, knowing she had spent all her arrows, but wanting to check all the same. "We fight on," she said grimly, drawing her sword, standing clear of the tree stump.

"Hurry! All of you!" shouted Sol. But the revellers below continued to scream abuse and hurl projectiles at him. He sat and fingered the canopy closed again, looking toward the approaching water. It would be upon them imminently, the leading wave voraciously consuming everything before it. Like an escaped wild animal imprisoned for an eternity, its white claws shattering buildings and monuments, unrelenting, ravening, leaving chaos in its wake. The bell from the Monitor's tower now rang out over and over again in quick succession as he watched the approaching onslaught.

"Surely that was not a measure?" some questioned, confused by its first toll. As the notes repeated, some turned to the direction of the tower several leagues distant, just in time to see it removed from the skyline, along with the smaller towers surrounding it. Screaming, they pointed, alerting many more to the Grand Event. Landmarks that had once given contours to the sky had vanished; comforting points of reference that had stood for generations were no more.

Sol turned the aircar towards *Jophiel*, accelerating the craft beneath the hull and up into her largest cargo hold, trying to shut out the imagined scenes in his head as the wave front invaded the distant edges of the Square.

Beneath *Jophiel*, hundreds of people scrambled to the rising platforms as they saw the approaching water. Others just stared, unable to believe their eyes as the waves thundered towards them, consuming the network of makeshift wooden alleyways, flinging the fragile stalls and carts into the air, some whole, splintering others upon impact. Animals and people were hurled along with the debris, no more now than drowning flotsam amid the breakers. Some clung to the steps of Zoloth's tower, pounding upon the barred doors, screaming for entry. They too were swept aside as the tower was carried into the side of *Jophiel*, its gangway snapping in two as the vessel deflected the tower back into the rising water.

Fighting broke out beneath her hull as the platforms slowly cleared the tide, brutality and hatred burned in the eyes of the people struggling to save themselves, kicking, punching and pulling neighbours and friends away from the platforms to fall back into the waves. Hands reached down for outstretched hands, pulling loved ones aboard, struggling and pushing children upward, climbing upon each other, scrambling frantically over bodies. Hands parted, families separated forever. Slowly the cries of the drowning diminished as they were swiftly carried away by the torrent, and as the platforms sealed themselves, all that could be heard were the mixed vocalisations of grief and disbelief.

The water continued on toward the primary colleges and Archbishop's longhouse, the publication tower and wealthy residences behind Ellendale Crescent. It coursed on, flattening estates, overwhelming the many Kaltesh who ran back to their encampment, further on until it engulfed the caravanserai itself, where work continued rebuilding homes. Beyond this, out into the farms and fields of livestock and crops, the affluent lake houses and cottages of the eastern district, until it found the wall. There its advance ceased, the waves folding back upon themselves in defeat, trapped, the water rising gradually against its imprisonment, contained by the enhancements Zoloth's workers had made to the wall.

The aircar hovered above the crowds and Sol opened the canopy. He stood, staring, his eyes damp, his throat dry, and as he searched for a few comforting words for them, he heard a voice some way off, shouting his name.

"There," said Tal, pointing to a figure in the distance, frantically waving.

Sol sat, moving the vehicle closer. "It's Rillian, Roanne's mother." The crowds backed away as the aircar landed. "Tal! Help me get her aboard."

"Tulteth! Where's my son? Where is he?" she pleaded as Tal helped her onto a rear seat.

"We'll find him," said Sol, keying the controls, "but later. If he's aboard, he'll be safe."

As the canopy slid closed, a pair of hands thumped against the plastic.

He turned to see Ana staring at him, and the canopy slid open.

"Leaving without me?" she asked breathlessly.

"How did you escape the asylum? I would have come for you, if there had been time," he said as she joined Rillian on the back seat.

"I doubt that. I have a great deal to tell you, Sol – but that must wait."

He ignored her remark, assuming it concerned her

meeting with Tal Salandor. Then one of his voices questioned how the two women came to be so close together. He ignored the puzzle, concentrating on the situation at hand. "Undoubtedly, and yes, it must."

Slowly the aircar ascended. "Mainbrain, open floatways from cargo bay one to arboretum four," barked Sol, "quickest route, maximum speed, aircar set to automatic." He depressed a jewel and turned to Rillian staring wide-eyed at her surroundings. "Listen, both of you," he said urgently. "There's much I have to tell you, and very little time to tell it."

THIRTY

SOOL NALESH

He thought it would be easy for him; he was used to the water, after all, and his father had taught him to swim just a few months after he had learnt to walk. He remembered being held in those cold little pools down at the Tethes ocean, staring at the sky as his father and mother watched him splashing about. Then, when he was older, his father had pointed to a rocky projection where the white waves creased around its base.

"There, and then return," his father had said, diving into the water. He had watched nervously as he swam toward the rock. It seemed so far away, the tiny crests of water catching the sunlight of early morning, marking the distance. He saw his father touch the rock and turn, heading back to him with powerful movements, ploughing into the water with his strong arms, kicking out with his legs as his head remained beneath the water for nine strokes.

It seemed so very long ago.

Now, he was carried along with the currents beneath the surface. They pulled at his body as they weaved between the subaqueous streets and alleyways of Abeona. Like the wind before them they coursed angrily amid the mass, as if searching for something, before their paths were merged and they lost their identity to the whole as it carried them onwards. Momentarily, he was afforded a glimpse of the sky and the chance of a single breath as a current released him, his ears filled with screaming voices, then bubbling pressure as he was dragged beneath the surface as another undertow seized him. At once the violence ceased, its grip lost, permitting him to swim toward the light, up through the murky silt of the city, past sinking bodies with expressions agape, between the rubble and ruin of civilization.

Air and stillness, a welcome silence coupled with the warmth of the sun upon his face as the cold gripped his muscles. He swam around the macerated bodies and floating detritus, all sense of direction lost, until he found the remains of a caravan's deck and pulled himself up onto it.

Wiping his stinging eyes, he stared at the carnage. Not a single tower remained standing in Abeona. The city walls now embraced the water, when for centuries they had embraced the buildings, transforming the city into nothing more than a gigantic pool of devastation beneath the intumescence of a counterfeit tide. Here and there, the stubby remains of a few buildings could be seen protruding from it, adding scale to the destruction. Upon these ugly prominences he noticed figures, some sitting, others standing, pulling others from the waves. Far behind this was the Trophy, its legs elevating its hull clear of the rising water.

The vehicle sped along the floatway corridor, the bands of illumination circling the wall briefly highlighting the disbelief upon the faces of the two passengers as they listened to the Salandorian's story.

Sol sat on the back seat with them, having sealed the compartment from the ears of his son. The little boy sat at the controls, pretending he was in command of the craft as Tal sat alongside him, ensuring he kept his hands away from the inviting jewels.

His passengers listened in silence, Rillian's expression one of utter disbelief.

"You're telling us you're a *new* Sol Timmerman, the... the Sol I knew is now *dead*?"

Ana held her mother's shoulders as he nodded, her mouth set curved slightly upward at the right-hand side, a telltale indication of envy Sol remembered so well. With some effort she spoke. "So, you now know all there is to know, all the secrets laid bare before you?"

He shook his head as their eyes met. "Not half of it, Ana, but far more than I knew before."

At once they were clear of the corridor, speeding high above the ruined forest. Sol depressed a jewel and the canopy slid back. Tal moved the little boy closer to him to make room, as Sol spoke. "Mainbrain, resume manual control of aircar."

He steered the craft over the battle as Zoloth's Deacons continued to pound Seta's head, her protective covering mirroring every blow. Now they stopped and turned as the vehicle hummed some way off. "Hold on tight, everyone," said Sol, placing an arm around Opi. He brought the aircar into a steep, curving descent, causing the Deacons to dive onto their stomachs to avoid a collision.

Roanne watched the craft banking from the corner of her eye, sidestepping the Constable's heavy blade, her slight frame and nimbleness her only defensive advantage against her adversary.

Tyn fought by her side as best he could, the pain had returned to his shoulder now Seta's painkillers had worn off, and the Constable saw this upon his face.

The High Celebrant clashed swords with the Senior Grand Cardinal again and again, his concentration betraying his lack of confidence as the aircar set down. Zoloth had broken Hulneb's defences twice; only the shimmering skin of his armour had saved his life. Now the old man had altered his attack, aware a blow to the face was the only way to achieve victory.

"Opi, stay here. Mainbrain, lock aircar controls," ordered Sol, as the canopy receded and they climbed out. Once the canopy was sealed again, the little boy pushed his palms against the surface to watch the battle, wide-eyed.

"Seta!" shouted Sol. "Priority order A4. Transfer obedience protocol to Captain. Position your arms directly behind your back, bend elbows forty-five degrees and rotate your wrists, maximum torque and speed."

The machine obeyed immediately, sending several Deacons to the ground. As they stood, the spinning blades killed all but two standing over her, the others backing away at the sight of their comrades' blood gushing into the earth.

Sol ran towards Roanne as the giant machine dropped her blades, picking herself up from the red soil. Retrieving her weapons, she despatched the two remaining Deacons with a single blow, her torso turning immediately to advance on the battle.

Zoloth's attacks finally found a weakness in Hulneb's defence, the tip of his blade slicing through his right cheek, cutting him to the bone. Hulneb stumbled back, dropping a sword and holding the seeping wound.

"Enough!" cried Sol, running forward, "Seta! Defend Hulneb, Roanne and Tyn!"

As Zoloth's blade extended towards Hulneb's face, a block met it as a shadow fell over him. He staggered back, his Constable joining him as Seta stood before them.

Zoloth looked toward Sol and dropped his swords with incomprehension. *"I saw you die!"* he spluttered. Then his eyes fell on his daughter and her mother. "You should all be dead!" he screamed. "*Oosah* is mine!"

Analissa Zoloth let go of her mother's hand and stepped forward, and for a moment her eyes met Roanne's. She ignored the look of curious jealousy as she stood beside Sol, as Roanne stood at his opposite side, the others gathering behind them.

"There's nothing here for you, father," said Ana quietly. "Nothing for Sol, or anyone."

"She's right," said Sol. "Listen to her. This vessel belongs to Tal Salandor. There are no confirmations here to support our fictional creed, no easy path to a Garden of Contentment, nothing but what you see and bring with you."

"This is heresy!" screamed the Senior Grand Cardinal.

He swept his hand before them, fingers curled in a bizarre pattern as if performing a rite of exorcism. The gesture completed, he pointed at Sol. "You are a creation of evil, yet you do not know it. Tal Salandor for us died *centuries* ago, promising that one day we would understand all that comprises *Oosah*, that it would be ours to command, to defend ourselves against a second arrival of evil!" He looked up at Seta as her remaining eyes fixed upon him. "That holy day, that promise, is now!"

The human walked in front of Sol to face the Senior Grand Cardinal. "Actually, I'm very much alive." He walked forward, snatching Roanne's pendant from Zoloth's neck, brushing it clean. "This belongs to me, and I believe," he said pointing, "the coat you're wearing also."

Zoloth could not believe his eyes, as he was reminded of the paintings that had hung in his private accommodation in the Holy Citadel. The individual that stood before him did indeed resemble a younger Tal Salandor, although his features were somewhat contorted.

"No!" he spat, "You are a deviation, your words–"

"You'll be judged for your crimes by the Abeonian and Kaltesh survivors," insisted Sol, as Tal walked back to join the group.

"*Them*? Judge *me*?" Zoloth could not help but smile. "All of you are beneath me. I'll rebuild this city, and my name will replace that of Tal Salandor. Everyone will recognise my worth, as much as *Oosah* recognises my superiority – my right above anyone here. You'll not judge me," he raised his hand and pointed at Rillian, "as *she* did."

Ana took a step forward. "It's over, father, you must know that. What Sol told you is the ultimate truth. The truth which you have sought for so long." She turned to face Rillian. "And you, mother? I'm so *very* happy to disappoint you." She glanced at Tyn. "The Hathranelzra is an honourable man. He told me many cycles ago of your plan to nurture hatred in my heart toward the Abeonians, to encourage me to strive for a Grand Cardinalship and replace my father, to destroy Abeona from inside, in your name, and for your obsessive Kaltesh retribution."

Rillian ambled forward, defiant, her eyes burning with the hatred she had harboured for so very long. "It could have been so very easy. You've wasted such a wonderful opportunity." She spat into the earth before Ana. "You are *nothing* to me. You have betrayed me, for what?"

Hulneb couldn't believe what he was hearing, but Rillian held an outstretched hand as he approached, stopping him as Ana spoke."My father was an honourable man," she said, glancing to Zoloth, "faking my death, protecting me from a biased trial, so I could live and work for both of us," she looked at Sol. "Work for the enlightenment of the Abeonians and Kaltesh alike, as declared in my oath as a Cardinal. And where were you, mother?"

Rillian shook her head, noticing Roanne had bowed hers. "Waiting, praying, hoping everything would turn out as it should."

Zoloth lunged forward and seized Rillian by the arm, pulling her body to his. "Oh, it seems it almost has." Swiftly a dagger appeared from beneath his belt. Holding the tip to her stomach, his left arm locked at the elbow around her throat, he commanded, "Enough! You will leave now, all of you, including that daemon." His voice regained its melodic composure. "I am chosen! *Oosah* is mine, and when the waters recede, my priests and I will rebuild this city and the Preferred will repopulate in *my* name."

"Zoloth, let her go. Listen to me," pleaded Sol, hands open wide, taking a step closer. "This vessel, *Jophiel*, allowed you inside because of the pendant you were wearing, that's all. It's similar to a key, let me–"

But Zoloth backed away, dragging Rillian with him. "Constable, a sword, if you please."

The Constable crouched down, prising a blade from the dirt, placing the hilt in Zoloth's free hand. He raised his broadsword in defiance, pointing it toward Sol.

"You will leave now!" screamed Zoloth.

Tyn glanced at Rillian, his sworn duty to protect her as fresh as ever in his mind, and as she caught his gaze she understood. An almost imperceptible smile touched her lips as she breathed, "Thank you."

The Hathranelzra released his dagger for the final time, the blade embedding itself into the Constable's left eye. As he dropped forward to his knees to die, Tyn was in the air, only to find Zoloth stepping in front of his lover from long ago, his dagger held out before him. The Hathranelzra's attack halted by the blade, he fell backward onto the earth, clutching the pommel where it projected from his throat. Zoloth's grip lost, Rillian broke free as Zoloth turned and ran. Tyn's chest rose and fell rapidly, choking blood as Rillian knelt by his side. "Your duty has ended, Tyn Narrat of the Kaltesh, last of the Hathranelzra. I will speak and they will hear your name." He managed to sign one last time before he died.

"What did he say?" whispered Sol to Hulneb, as the old woman closed the Hathranelzra's eyes, but the High Celebrant ignored him, snatching the broadsword from the Constable's dead hands and heading after Zoloth.

"Hulneb!" shouted Sol, "Leave him, there's nothing for him out there, he can do no more harm."

But Hulneb strode on, and as Sol began to follow, Roanne placed a hand on his shoulder.

"Leave him be." He turned and was about to reply when the ground moved beneath them, causing them all to stumble.

"What was that?" shouted Tal, looking around.

"The water outside has risen high enough to support *Jophiel.* She's afloat. Mainbrain, satpic please."

A rectangle appeared before Sol and the others gathered behind him as he spoke again. "Pan left...stop. Times forty-eight hundred magnification."

There, they saw the southern wall had been breached,

the ruins of the city pouring out into the refuse-filled river beyond, bloating beyond its banks. *Jophiel* pitched again, and they felt a steady motion.

"Mainbrain, retract landing stages. Seal and flush compartment wells," said Sol. He turned to his companions as he headed over to the aircar for Opi. "There's nothing I can do. We're at the mercy of the water."

Zoloth climbed up the rope ladder tied to the handrail in the auditorium of one hundred seals. His mind raced. Where would he go, what could he possibly do now? If he could wait for the water to recede, then he could find enough followers to join him. He'd send for the Preferred, hiding in the desert, and together they would lead a second assault upon *Oosah*. Yes, he imagined it. He would wait, there was time.

"Zoloth!" cried Hulneb, as the Senior Grand Cardinal cleared the handrail. "Our fight is not over!"

As he looked down, he could see the High Celebrant, climbing rapidly toward him upon the swaying rope ladder. He raised his swords to strike, but *Jophiel* lurched again, sending him to the floor. Hulneb's face appeared at the balustrade and the Senior Grand Cardinal swung his sword, Hulneb ducking, springing back up, launching himself over the low railing to roll across the floor, sword held straight above his head. He stood facing his opponent, catching his breath, wiping blood from his wound.

"It's just between us now," he said, and Zoloth was surprised by the calmness of the High Celebrant's voice.

"I am a far better swordsman than you," declared the Senior Grand Cardinal with a wide grin. He pointed with his sword and began to pace in a circle, edging toward the corridor and the exit beyond. "Your wound proves such. I would suggest you acquiesce, lest my next strike end your miserable life." He rotated his sword before him and quickened his pace.

"Better swordsman perhaps," grunted Hulneb, "but fighter?" As Zoloth lunged, the big man blocked with the broadsword and kicked out, his foot finding Zoloth's side. He tumbled backward, righting himself, twisting his body so his back was now to the exit. He paced slowly backwards, glancing over his shoulder momentarily as Hulneb advanced, matching him step for step. The Senior Grand Cardinal winced, and Hulneb was at last aware he had hurt him.

"Do you realise now what you have casually cast aside, Hulneb?"

"Your offer did not include the murder of every Abeonian and Kaltesh soul."

"I knew you would not have the stomach for such an ambitious event. But, I will admit, for a few moments I considered offering you a share of the magnificent kingdom I will bring forth."

Hulneb brought his sword around from behind his back and over his head, Zoloth easily deflecting the blow into the corridor wall. He spun around, but Hulneb saw the move coming, jumping back as Zoloth's blade narrowly missed his nose.

"I've had enough of this," said Hulneb, holding his sword by his side. "These garments, they deflect every blow to the body and limbs, but limit movement." He pulled off his balaclava. "Are you confident enough to fight without this unnatural defence?"

Zoloth removed his coat and dropped it to the floor, Hulneb opening his tunic and easing his arms from the sleeves. As he dropped the garment, *Jophiel* rocked violently, sending both men to the floor. Impacts could be heard reverberating around them as beneath the waterline, the hull encountered the ruins of Abeona as it was carried toward the breach in the southern city wall.

Tulteth clung to the floor of the caravan as it began to

pick up speed, looking to his right as *Jophiel* moved alongside him, its shadow falling across his makeshift raft. He turned. Ahead, poking from the water, were the remains of a tower where three men stood, calling and waving for him to jump and swim to them. But, as he stood the deck rocked beneath his feet, the current having increased considerably now, carrying his raft beyond the reach of the tower. Estimating the distance and the strength of the tide he kicked off his sandals, stepping back three paces, taking one last look at the tower before taking a running dive into the water. He swam a good distance beneath the surface, then as his head cleared the water, he struck out as best he could against the current threatening to drag him away from his objective. He kept his head down for six strokes, then raised it for air, gauging his progress. Another six, and another, the cries from the men becoming louder, cheering him on. At last his hands found the damp stones and he pulled himself up onto the broken edifice, panting, smiling up at the three men as one of them held out a hand to assist his climb. But now their attention was elsewhere, staring agape behind him, and as he raised his hand to be pulled clear they dived into the water as a shadow fell across their island ruin. He turned as *Jophiel's* hull sent out a fist of metal into the remains of the tower, and Tulteth dived beneath the surface. Here, conflicting undertow tides and eddies pulled his body between the ruins in a bizarre, uncontrollable tumble. He watched helplessly, unable to alter his path. At once, he found it strange to be taken though the streets above the rooftops, over parks and bridges as he fought against his body's demands for air. He found himself below floating bodies, above the Square of Remembrance, and as he watched, a whirlpool pulled him toward a narrow hole at the centre of the Square. He closed his eyes, convinced here he would meet his end. Then, silence. His face cleared the surface and he opened his eyes, gulping mouthfuls of air as his chest pounded. As he looked around, a manufactured shoreline beckoned him from the flickering torches illuminating this subterranean cavern. He pulled himself clear of the water to lie on his back, breathing hard. At last he sat up, staring at the circular island some way off where two sarcophagi lay, their surfaces and markings almost identical to those upon *Oosah*. He nodded. "The Holy Brothers."

Further on, *Jophiel* demolished the remains of the Monitor's tower and its surrounding measuring towers, causing the vessel to list steeply to starboard. Water surged into the main entranceway as it dipped briefly beneath the surface, drenching the two combatants in the corridor.

The vessel continued on, reaching the breached wall, her bow impacting into its remains, sending hundreds of blocks showering down upon it from both sides of the wound, every one either deflected into the air or reduced to rubble in a cloud of dust by the vessel's skin. Her stern swept around to impact the wall on the opposite side, wedging itself in the gaping abyss as the water continued to swell around its hull.

Both Hulneb and Zoloth tumbled toward the exit, unable to slow their motion as *Jophiel* shook violently. Hulneb clawed at the walls as he lost his grip on his broadsword and it slid through the exit into the spray. They found themselves clinging to opposite sides of the entranceway alcove, water showering them, the clamour of the deluge filling their ears, the drop below them a league. As they both stared, remnants of the city fell before them, the residues of homes, animals, trees, and people. It was a horrific sight, and Hulneb closed his eyes tightly, turning away.

"Glorious!" shouted Zoloth, above the clamour of the water as he watched, wide-eyed, "Tal Salandor's Grand Event. Together our cleansing is glorious!"

"The main entranceway," said Tal. "It must be sealed. If water finds its way in, the connecting systems could be damaged beyond repair."

Sol nodded, shouting orders to the Mainbrain.

The water continued surging around the vessel, pounding against the blocks wedging it in place. A crack appeared behind the torrent and slowly the vessel broke free, angling into the spray.

Hulneb opened his eyes as his hands felt the movement of the seal. He looked to the opposite side but Zoloth was no longer there. Had he heard a scream moments before? As the seal began to close he pulled himself through, climbing inside as the exterior hatchway sealed.

Jophiel fell into the river, her skin easing the impact. She sped on, coursing down the waterway, her curved underside assisting the water's angry surge as it carried the vessel toward the Tethes ocean.

There she finally rested, buoyant upon the open water, subject to the whims of the ocean tides as the remains of Abeona were spewed from the coast before and behind her, as if the land itself was aware of the misplaced veneration the Abeonians and Kaltesh had given her for so many thousands of years, and was relieved to finally be free of her intervention into its environment.

Sol stood. "Mainbrain, report via Seta." He angled the screen ahead and studied it for a few moments as the others climbed to their feet.

"We're safe?" asked Ana.

Roanne glanced at her, and then back to the seal, her thoughts with Hulneb.

"Safe," said Sol, as Roanne stood beside him.

"Three thousand five hundred and five organisms survive aboard *Jophiel*," said Seta. "Minimal damage to operational systems. Three thousand four hundred and ninety seven organisms in cargo areas one though seven. Individual damage assessments to follow: One: Subject male…"

Sol noticed a shape from the corner of his eye, turning to see a drenched Hulneb strolling casually toward them.

The big man's face was set expressionless as he approached, diluted blood streaking his neck and left shoulder.

Sol quickly reached into the earth, retrieving a broadsword, flinging the heavy weapon at the High Celebrant's chest. "*Ticandra-esh-roo-neth!*" shouted Sol. The sword rotated in the air, Hulneb catching the grip with both hands, pivoting instinctively to his left to carry the blade swiftly through its trajectory behind him, neatly severing the Senior Grand Cardinal's head as he rose to strike. Hulneb watched breathlessly as the headless body remained motionless, upright for a few moments before toppling to its knees to fall forward into the mud. He turned, his heart pounding, his eyes wide. "How?"

"Seta reported there were eight survivors, excluding those in the cargo holds. Meaning one other, Zoloth, was still alive. I could tell from your expression you hadn't killed him, and knew he would not rest until he had killed you."

The dead were buried in a corner of the ruined arboretum and, much later, several survivors stood upon *Jophiel's* exterior, watching the daylight fade behind elongated streaks of soft, orange-tinted white clouds. Below this sat the coastline, a thin sliver of diminishing colour, sandwiched between the dark blue of the sky and azure sea. The air was fresh here, cooling and odourless, save for a hint of salt. Sol took a deep breath as he turned, his eyes falling upon the slender horizon ahead, as *Jophiel* was drawn toward it by the tide.

"So, what are you going to do now?" asked Hulneb, sitting beside Sol with his legs crossed, puffing on a borrowed pipe.

"I have work for Tal, the Abeonian and Kaltesh survivors will need food and water, and I promised Opi a trip in the aircar early tomorrow morning. Apart from that..." he shrugged and looked down at his friend. "Yourself?"

Hulneb sighed, his eyes narrowing before taking a deep inhale, speaking through the smoke. "Well, I still believe the Holy Brothers will be found on the...the *command deck*, is it? And I have a half-sister to accommodate, however uncomfortable Roanne and I feel with *that* situation." He looked up, folding his arms. "Sol, I was thinking, with all the trees in the arboretums, and what with Seta clearing space to house the survivors," he took the pipe from his mouth and motioned over his shoulder with the stem, "we could perhaps build a boat, several even, travel back to the land and search for other survivors. Tulteth's strong, he may still be alive. Shouldn't we search for them?"

Sol's eyes returned to the horizon as he rubbed his vacant right wrist slowly with his left hand. "We will, one day." Other vague justifications that were not his tumbled through his head before his thoughts returned to recent events. "Hulneb, I was wondering. What did Tyn sign to you, before he died?"

He shook his head slowly, "I've been waiting for you to ask that, which thankfully leads to something else I must tell you."

"Well?"

"My *Sool Nalesh*."

"And that means what, exactly?"

He felt Roanne's fingers interlock with his and squeeze gently. He glanced at her, then back to the big man, realising from their expressions there was something both of them knew, and had hidden from him.

The High Celebrant stood, reaching into his robes to produce a crumpled envelope, the flap fluttering in the breeze with the broken, red wax seal of Arramosa upon it. He held it out to Sol.

"What's this?"

"Your *Ticandra Sool Nalesh*," said Hulneb, glancing at

his sister before puffing on his pipe, "a choice no man should face. I found it in your friend's classroom. Spent almost the entire morning searching for a clue to help us find the young lad. This letter was very well hidden, and rightly so, considering the contents."

The sun dipped beneath the streak of cloud as Sol took the envelope.

"Enjoy the evening, all three of you," said Hulneb, patting Sol on the shoulder before heading inside.

Roanne watched him leave, taking a deep breath before turning to her husband. "*Sool Nalesh*. When you find two teammates without weapons, who do you defend with yours? If one cries, *Sool Nalesh*, it roughly translates to, *'protect my family'*. A noble sacrifice. But, if neither speak, then *Sool Nalesh*–"

"Then the decision rests solely on the player with the weapon, as to which of the two is more important, the other condemned to die." Sol nodded slowly as the breeze rose, the envelope flapping for his attention with urgency, as if to encourage him to read what lay within, he decided. He calmed it, holding the flap down with his thumb. "Shhh," he whispered, tracing slowly over the broken seal of Yan Arramosa, remembering Tal had wanted to speak to him further, concerning his father.

"*Sool Nalesh*," he repeated as the sunlight found his face, his thumb and fingers relaxing, allowing the wind to carry away the truth he now realised into the sea.

Roanne turned from watching the distant shoreline, her thoughts with her father and brothers. Yes, they should return, and she would insist on visiting the shoreline where her father was murdered. She pushed the thought aside, saving it for another occasion as her eyes met her son's, perched upon his father's shoulders. "Time for bed, Opi," she said, taking hold of the boy's hand. "You have a busy day tomorrow." She looked at Sol, noticing something different in his eyes as he faced her. A mountain of silent questions shone amid their pale blue, inquisitiveness and attraction. But she was unsure whether these feelings were for Analissa Zoloth, conversing somewhere far below with Tal, for *Jophiel,* or for herself. Time would tell, she thought, as Sol lowered Opi down. She placed an arm around her husband's waist as a chill swept across the vessel, and as they walked back inside, Roanne was content with the fact that her husband had finally kept his promise to her.

~ To be continued ~

Printed in Great Britain
by Amazon